# Praise for Mercedes Lackey and James Mallory

"Fans of high fantasy will surely enjoy this."
—*SFRevu* on *The Phoenix Unchained*

"The book strikes the right balance between the struggles of a young girl thought to be the 'Child of the Prophecy' and the epic mythology that leads her to embrace a queen's destiny with Joan of Arc fervor."
—*RT Book Reviews* on *Crown of Vengeance*

"Spectacular. A fascinating and complex world."
—*BookLoons* on *The Phoenix Transformed*
(a *New York Times* bestseller)

"As entertaining as the first trilogy. Engaging characters and a tighter plot than many fantasy epics make this a must-have."—*VOYA* on *The Phoenix Unchained*

"[A] captivating world [is] conjured by veteran Lackey and classical scholar Mallory in this high fantasy. The narrative speeds to the end, leaving the reader satisfied and wanting to know more."
—*Publishers Weekly* on *The Outstretched Shadow*

"Lackey and Mallory combine their talents for storytelling and world crafting into a panoramic effort. Filled with magic, dragons, elves, and other mythical creatures, this title belongs in most fantasy collections."
—*Library Journal* on *To Light a Candle*
(a *USA Today* bestseller)

# BLADE
## OF
# EMPIRE

### BOOK TWO
## of The Dragon Prophecy

## MERCEDES LACKEY
## and JAMES MALLORY

**TOR®**
**fantasy**

A TOM DOHERTY ASSOCIATES BOOK
NEW YORK

This is a work of fiction. All of the characters, organizations, and events portrayed in this novel are either products of the authors' imaginations or are used fictitiously.

BLADE OF EMPIRE

A Tor Book
Published by Tom Doherty Associates
175 Fifth Avenue
New York, NY 10010

www.tor-forge.com

Tor® is a registered trademark of Macmillan Publishing Group, LLC.

ISBN 978-0-7653-6398-5

Our books may be purchased in bulk for promotional, educational, or business use. Please contact your local bookseller or the Macmillan Corporate and Premium Sales Department at 1-800-221-7945, extension 5442, or by email at MacmillanSpecialMarkets@macmillan.com.

First Edition: October 2017
First Mass Market Edition: September 2018

Printed in the United States of America

0  9  8  7  6  5  4  3  2  1

# CONTENTS

# BLADE
## OF
# EMPIRE

# DARKNESS VISIBLE

**B**efore Time itself came to be, *He Who Is* had been: changeless, eternal, perfect. And all was Darkness, and *He Who Is* ruled over all there was.

Then came the Light, dancing through the perfection of the Dark, separating it into Dark and not-Dark. Making it a finite, a bounded thing. Where there had been silence, and Void, and infinity, there came music, and not-Void, and Time . . .

A world.

*He Who Is* lashed out against this debasement, and the Light realized *He Who Is* meant to take from it the beautiful world of shape and form and time and boundary it had created. Light could not destroy the Darkness without destroying itself, but it could bring life to flourish where destruction had walked.

And to this life, it gave weapons. The new life was as changeable as *He Who Is* was changeless. Light Itself coursed through its veins, and Light fell in love with silver life. Light left the high vault of heaven and scattered itself across the land, and silver life traveled to the places of the Light to rejoice in it.

But *He Who Is* vowed He would win in the end. This time, He bound His war into time, to let His tools learn from the enemy He would ultimately destroy. To all the things of the Light, *He Who Is* held up a dark mirror.

For the Bright World, a World Without Sun. For life and love, death and pain. For trust, treachery. For kindness, power.

For skill . . . magic.

For Life . . . The Endarkened.

The Endarkened swept forth from Obsidian Mountain and glutted themselves upon blood and pain. The land around Obsidian Mountain became a wasteland where nothing lived, and each night they ranged farther.

And it was still not enough.

The children of *He Who Is* were bound by the laws of time and matter, and in that realm even *His* vast power could not create a sorcery that did not require payment. The power of the Endarkened came from the pain and fear of their victims and from the anguish and despair of their victims' deaths. Each spell they cast was paid for in the blood and suffering of slaves.

The first Elflings the Endarkened took cried out to Aradhwain the Mare, and wept for the vast openness of the Goldengrass. Time passed in the Bright World, and the Elfling victims cried out to the Sword-Giver and the Bride of Battles, to Amretheon and Pelashia, to the Starry Hunt.

None of their Bright World Powers saved them.

Then one day, a captive struck back with the Light itself. Once, the Elflings had possessed no magic. Now they did. In the changeable world of form and time, the Light had hidden the only weapon which could slay the eternal, beautiful children of *He Who Is*. Only the arrogance of the Light had disclosed its secret, for had it not shared that secret with the Elvenkind, the Endarkened would have remained ignorant of it . . .

Until too late.

The King of the Endarkened threw himself into preparations for the coming war as never before.

If Virulan had been stupid, he would have been long dead. Virulan was not stupid, and so he was not dead, but remaining king in the World Without Sun was a thing that took work.

He'd been preparing for the Red Harvest for nearly as long as he had been promising it to his subjects. As their numbers grew, so did the numbers of those he bred in his nurseries in the Cold North to be their allies. He was not foolish enough to imagine denying his fellow Endarkened the opportunity to slaughter every living thing in the world. But the Life he meant to scour from the world in the name of *He Who Is* was vast and intricate, and his subjects impatient. They would slaughter Elvenkind and Centaurs and everything that had a heartbeat with glee, of course—but all Life, Silver and Red and Green, must die. His beasts were not impatient, nor were they ever bored. They were only hungry.

And best of all, when everything else was gone, his brethren could destroy them as well. A final treat, before they returned to blessed nothingness and the Void. That reunion was nothing so ordinary as death. If it had been, the Endarkened would have ended their own lives long ago. Death was ugly and terrifying. It held the hint of an eternal *living*, an eternal awareness, even— dreadfully—transmutation and rebirth. The threat that lay behind death for every Endarkened was the horrifying possibility of discovering themselves somehow housed within Brightworlder flesh, their surviving atomie of self screaming in endless torment in a Life-prison.

No. Reunion with *He Who Is* was eternal darkness, eternal joy, eternal—perfect—utter—nothingness.

But such joy must be earned, by completing the task *He* had set them.

And so he summoned the remainder of the Twelve to the Heart of Darkness.

In the vast sweep of time that stretched from their creation to this moment, the Heart of Darkness had . . . changed. First, a throne and a crown for its King. Then, walls and floor and arching vault ornamented with representations of the infinite complexity and beauty of pain. There was even light, for what use was there in creating a cathedral of agony and terror if its most perfect sacraments could not see the stages of their apotheosis? But today there were no Brightworlders to tease and enlighten, and so the Heart of Darkness held only the absolute lightlessness of its first creation. The Endarkened had no need of light.

"You have summoned us, great King Virulan," Uralesse said obsequiously. "We are eager to hear your words."

Uralesse was a problem. Virulan knew that. His foremost rival, the only other Endarkened who remained as *He Who Is* had made them—and thus, Virulan's greatest rival. Uralesse hoped to sow dissention among Virulan's subjects, all of whom chafed at the restraint their King had placed upon them.

"As you know, my dearest comrades, the time of the Red Harvest is not yet upon us," Virulan began. A faint rustling of wings greeted those words, for though none of his people dared to defy him—not openly, at least—they were emboldened by their own numbers. "And I know you grow restive at the thought of so many lives unclaimed."

Bold or not, none of the Created dared to speak. Virulan allowed the silence to stretch before he spoke again.

"And yet, know that I, your King, feel that impatience as my own. I will not deviate from my plan, for it is a glorious one, but it has come to me that there is one place in the Bright World where we may hunt the Elflings with no chance of discovery—one infestation we may cleanse without giving warning to the others before the glorious day of the Red Harvest." The rustling of wings grew louder, and now it was a sound of anticipation, not discontent. "Because of the great love I bear for you, my first comrades in this great task *He Who Is* gave to us, I give this place to you alone." He gestured expansively, giving them permission to speak, and the Heart of Darkness filled with the susurrant noise of praise and exclamations.

"To us?" Shurzul's cry rose above the rest. "Now? My King—never had I hoped to even witness such generosity, let alone partake of it!"

"This is only the beginning of the wonders of the Red Harvest," Virulan said. "My darlings, this day I give to you the place called Hallorad, the most far-flung of the Elfling domains. Soon, I shall give you . . . all of them."

The Heart of Darkness rang with Endarkened cries of joy.

## CHAPTER ONE

# SNOW MOON TO ICE MOON: THE END OF ALL THINGS

*One cannot pledge fealty to the wind.*

—*Elven Proverb*

From Rade Moon to Storm Moon, Winter High Queen was the true ruler of the Grand Windsward. Only the Flower Forests, locked in their eternal Springtide, were exempt from snow and cold, and Elvenkind did not enter the Flower Forests.

*It is a great mystery,* Gonceivis Haldil mused once again, *that we draw our ultimate power from a place we dare not go.*

In the West, Lightborn might enter the Flower Forests whenever they chose—save, perhaps, on the Western Shore, and there it was merely dangerous. Only in the Grand Windsward was it impossible, for in the Grand Windsward, the Beastlings ruled. The Beastlings had been the enemy of Elvenkind since before Amretheon had reigned. They were monstrous and cruel, a terrible parody of Elvenkind in shape and manner. Centaurs—Minotaurs—Gryphons—there was no end to their horror, the shapes they came in . . . or their bestial sorcery.

Gryphons had weather magic at their command; Aesalions could control the hearts of their prey; Bearwards were masters of sickness and plague. The Minotaurs slaughtered Elvenkind's herds and flocks, and Centaurs razed their villages. Sorcery could only be fought with Light, and so in the Grand Windsward, the Lightborn went regularly into battle. Mosirinde's Covenant demanded that the Lightborn draw their power from the Flower Forests alone, and by Mosirinde's Covenant, Elvenkind was bound to a dreadful bargain, for the Flower Forests were home to a thousand races of Beastling: fairy and sprite, dryad and Faun, nymph and gnome and pixie. To keep the Covenant, the Lightborn must hold sacrosanct the strongholds of their enemy, for those strongholds were the only source of their protection from that same enemy.

*At least Winter brings us some respite from the eternal battle,* Gonceivis thought. In Snow Moon, Haldil—first among the Houses of the Grand Windsward—opened its doors in revelry and celebration to any of the Hundred Houses who wished to enter. If the sennight of the Midwinter Festival was named a time of tacit truce throughout the Fortunate Lands, here in the Grand Windsward the Midwinter Truce was more than empty words.

Gonceivis Haldil looked down the length of his Great Hall. Its ceiling was low, the better to defend them from the incursions of fairies and pixies. It had no windows, for even an arrow slit could provide entrance to a Faun. It was so vast that there was not one Storysinger performing before the High Table, but rather half a dozen performers scattered among the revelers. The talk and laughter echoing from the banner-hung stone hushed the sounds as easily as a spell of silence might. Gonceivis had little interest in songs, and as War Prince he could see Lightborn Magery any time he chose. The entertainer chosen for the High Table was a Lightless illusionist: one who used deft trickery to make a pretense of Magery. He watched, diverted, as she turned one disk into two, then a dozen, then juggled them deftly. They glowed in the Silverlight set upon the walls and ceiling, flashing brightly before they returned to her hands. When they vanished, she replaced them with lengths of shining gilt ribbon that continuously swirled through the air. The fire trenches that crossed the floor were golden with coals, and one of the ribbons, swooping too close, burst into flame. For a moment Gonceivis thought this was an error, and made a note to have the steward who had chosen her flogged, but then all the ribbons burst into flame to become lanterns, then batons, and at last a single white bird. The illusionist flung the dove toward the ceiling; it flew along the line of war banners that hung upon the walls, their bright heraldry cooled by the Silverlight's soft radiance. The banners belled softly in the rising waves of heat, and at last the bird vanished behind one of them.

The Lightless illusionist swept him a low bow, and Gonceivis tossed her his empty cup in reward of her skill. She caught it with another low bow, then ran toward one of the staircases that entered the hall at its four corners.

"Thank the Light that's over," Ladyholder Belviel said. "My father had no patience with such trickery."

"Your father did not rule in Haldil," Gonceivis told her. He chewed thoughtfully upon a salted fig as his cupbearer brought him a new cup and filled it with wine. It was not the plain and lightweight sort he'd tossed to the performer, its worth only in the gold of which it was made: this was a massive thing, carved and jeweled, and capable of holding six gills of wine.

"Nor did my father lead his House into ruinous rebellion," Belviel responded, choosing a morsel of cheese from the tray before her.

"As I recall, you did not find it objectionable when we began," Gonceivis said.

"I was fond of Demi-Prince Malbeth," his wife replied placidly. "A pity he did not survive."

"A pity we did not know that had we but waited half a century we could have had the victory without the war," Gonceivis snapped.

A Wheelturn ago last Harvest, Oronviel fell to the last child of Farcarinon. At Midwinter, Vieliessar sent messages inviting the Windsward to rise up as her allies. The Windsward had declined Vieliessar's gracious invitation—still smarting from its inglorious defeat fifty Wheelturns before—but it had watched with interest. It was Serenthon Farcarinon's madness reborn, but the daughter outstripped the father. She struck the shackles of Mosirinde's Covenant from the Magery of the Lightborn. She armed the Landbonds and offered full pardon to any outlaw who would pledge to her. In War Season, half the Houses of the West fell to her in a handful of moonturns, and the rest, plunged into madness, formed a Grand Alliance, following her over the Mystrals. The Windsward Houses promptly proclaimed their independence from the West for the second time in a scant half-century. Vieliessar sent demands of fealty and the Grand Alliance sent demands for aid. Haldil and the rest of the Windsward Houses ignored them both.

No one expected the war to continue beyond moonturn.

Mirwathel, Haldil's Chief Storysinger, stepped forward to begin *The Courtship of Amretheon and Pelashia*. Gonceivis did his best to conceal a wince; it was a very long song. It was also the signal for all who had left childhood behind in the past year to gather before the High Table, and for the Lightborn to come to await them, for this was the sixth night of Midwinter, and on this night, everywhere across the whole of the Fortunate Lands, the Lightborn would Call the Light. Each Lightborn had a servant by their side; each servant held a basket filled with sweets and ribbons. Silver ribbons for those who would go to the Sanctuary in the spring, gold for those who would not.

*If anyone goes anywhere in the spring,* Gonceivis thought, for this had been a Wheelturn of wonders.

Kaelindiel Bethros raised his cup in a mocking toast. He was seated at Gonceivis's tuathal side, the place of greatest honor. "So we are once more in rebellion, Lord Gonceivis. Only . . . against whom, this time?"

"I see no rebellion here," Gonceivis answered evenly. "Haldil is held in clientage by Caerthalien, as Bethros is by Aramenthiali. If they are no more, well, one cannot pledge fealty to the wind."

"But now—so they say—we are to have a High King. The Child of the Prophecy, perhaps, as Haldil once foretold—though, perhaps, prematurely," Kaelindiel answered.

"Then I wonder why you did not declare for Oronviel when Lord Vieliessar first sent to you," Gonceivis said tartly.

"Had I done so, I would be now as her princes are," Kaelindiel said. "Mourning so many dead no Tablet of Memory could contain them all."

The first of the children reached the waiting Lightborn. A brief touch, hand upon head, and it was done. Gold ribbons only, as was only to be expected: the nobles and the offspring of the Lords Komen were first, and Light was rarely found there.

"Yet her cause endures," Gonceivis said.

"Are your spies less able than mine?" Kaelindiel asked archly. "She flees. The Alliance follows."

"And Thurion Lightbrother tells us she will win, and we must pledge," Gonceivis answered. This was old news to them both: Thurion Lightbrother had come seeking alliance for his master moonturns ago—and many had listened. Kerethant, Penenjil, Enerchelimier, Artholor . . . nearly a taille of Windsward Houses had declared for Lord Vieliessar before Thurion Lightbrother headed Westward again. *Let them go,* Gonceivis told himself. *Let them all go. Let Kerethant and*

*Artholor strip themselves of defenders. Let Enerchelim-*
*ier follow a dream.*

"Perhaps Penenjil's Silver Swords will grant her victory," Kaelindiel said. "It is an omen, you must agree. The Silver Swords have not left Penenjil since the fall of the High King."

"The *last* High King," Gonceivis corrected. "If she is to have her way."

"Let her be High King, or Astromancer, or the Mother of Dragons," Kaelindiel answered dismissively. "I care not, so long as she does it elsewhere. Perhaps she and the Twelve will devour one another and leave us in peace. And if she calls those Windsward Houses which have declared for her to her battlefield, well . . . a domain is not merely its grand array. There will be Land-bonds and Craftworkers in plenty seeking protection."

"Peace is what you and I most desire, of course," Gonceivis answered. He smiled as the first silver ribbon of the night was placed in a child's hands.

*If Vieliessar Oronviel can become High King, so may Gonceivis Haldil,* he thought to himself. *A Kingdom is land, and wealth—and armies. It is not an empty throne. Or a handless sword.*

❧❧

Snow Moon became Ice Moon, and the news from the West was a muddle of conflicting information. Useless demands for aid came from the High Houses. Other words, private and clandestine, came from the Lightborn: Farspeech was the only thing that could reach across the Feinolon Peaks before Spring Thaw, and the Lightborn—now, as always—spoke among themselves. Every House of the Grand Windsward had sent children to the Sanctuary, and every child of the Windsward—given, as so many were, in tithe to the Great Houses of the West—hungered for news from home. Thus, Gonceivis had spies in the Grand Alliance and spies in the "High King's" army, for in exchange for the promise to pass word to their Lightless kin—a promise Gonceivis saw scrupulously kept—the Lightborn spoke of where they were and what they did. Once their words had been of weather and harvest, of minor triumphs, of such things as anyone might know. Since Thunder Moon, it had been of the daily life of an army upon the march, and the word had always been the same.

The High King fled. The Grand Alliance followed.

As the two armies drained the Flower Forests of the Uradabhur, the news became the merest trickle, for Farspeech needed Light. In Frost Moon it became a torrent once more, as the Lightborn—first of one array, then of both—found a new and seemingly inexhaustible wellspring to draw from. But the news did not change. The High King ran like a stag in winter. The Alliance followed, dogged as a pack of hounds.

"And what am I to think of it?" Gonceivis demanded of Othrochel Lightbrother. "This 'news' you bring me is no more than the mutterings of Lightborn! Even Caerthalien has stopped its eternal prating that Haldil do the impossible!"

The day was clear, and so Gonceivis had called a council in his solar. It was not a particularly private council, for the solar was one of the most pleasant rooms in the Great Keep, and anyone permitted to be here by birth or office had come. Of that perhaps two dozen souls, nearly half were gathered around the table which dominated the center of the chamber.

"It is the only news there is," Aenthior Swordmaster pointed out. She fingered her necklace of Gryphon talons. "As you well know, Lord Gonceivis."

"Don't tell me what I know," he answered irritably. "Tell me what I do *not* know."

"The outcome of the battle yet to be fought?" Ranruth Warlord asked. "All we know is that it will come."

"My . . . colleagues . . . in both arrays say this," Othrochel Lightbrother said. He was a Lightborn of middle years, and he'd been Gonceivis's closest advisor for more than half his life. "The High King's Lightborn say she leads them to Celephriandullias-Tildorangelor—"

"A myth," Ladyholder Belviel said.

"—to claim Amretheon's city and the Unicorn Throne in actuality," Othrochel finished, unperturbed. "I find it interesting that the Lightborn of the Grand Alliance do not speak of a destination. Save, of course, wherever the High King's army stops."

"*Do* stop calling her that," Ranruth Warlord urged. "Or I shall feel the need to leap to my destrier's back and ride to lay down my sword at her feet at once."

Aenthior snorted rudely. "We have to call her something. If not that, what? Oronviel? Farcarinon? Lightsister? She styles herself High King, and holds the fealty of forty of the Hundred Houses. Although, of course, not Haldil." The Swordmaster bowed slightly in Gonceivis's direction.

"She has been promising to fight since last Flower Moon at least," Gonceivis said. "But when?"

"Soon," Ranruth said. "She's running out of room. Already she is hundreds of leagues south of the southern bounds. She'll be underwater soon if she keeps on as she is."

"There's nothing there," Heir-Prince Paramarth said. He peered down at the surface of the table. It was covered by a single sheet of velum containing a map that had taken decades to make. Its northwestern edge ended with the Medhartha Range. The southern boundary was towers and forests. And where Vieliessar now was . . . blankness.

"Othrochel?" Gonceivis asked.

The Chief Lightborn came forward with a fragile sheet of parchment scraped almost to transparency. He set it carefully over a portion of the southern edge of the map. It was covered with marks in silverpoint. A few in ink. And a long line, straight as the flight of a fleeing dove, in charcoal.

"There is indeed something there, my lords," Othrochel said. "There is a Flower Forest so vast that the Lightborn of sixty houses cannot drain it. They call it Star-Bright Forest, and it is believed to lie to the west of the, ah, the Rebel Vieliessar's route, which lies through the forest her Lightborn have named Janubaghir. She and the Alliance are now upon the plain Ifjalasairaet, which is bordered upon the south by cliffs and upon the north by forests. This map is necessarily both incomplete and inaccurate, but it provides some notion of their present location. And of the size of the area across which they travel."

The party stared at the map in silence.

"But what is she going to *do*?" Gonceivis asked again.

No one had any answer for him.

⊰⊱

Hallorad was far to the east of the other Windsward Houses; a mere sennight's journey west of the perilous shores of Greythunder Glairyrill. And Hallorad stood, as she had always stood, alone.

In season, Hallorad sent her Lightborn to the Sanctuary of the Star. She paid her tribute in the wealth of the Windsward: fur and feather, horn and bone, for her people grew barely enough grain to feed themselves. There were no vast farmholdings or manor houses in Hallorad: Hallorad's Great Keep was the only building anywhere upon the lands it claimed. Generations of Lightborn had worked to expand its underground chambers, until ten times as much living space lay below the ground as above. There were a hundred entrances into Hallorad's underworld, each entrance surrounded by a few dozen hectares of cropland.

Hallorad survived in a world filled with monsters by quickness and cleverness.

⊰⊱

"Three Candidates, a mad Astromancer, and a High King," Paramarth Hallorad said. "What am I to do?"

Far to the east of Haldil, War Prince Paramarth and his advisors were gathered in the solar at the top of Hallorad Great Keep. The slanting rays of late-afternoon winter sunlight streamed through the slit-windows, its illumination almost enough to make the Silverlight lanterns unnecessary.

"The High King is there and we are here," Ladyholder Ingwinde said. "She is the least of our problems."

"Except for the fact she wishes me to go halfway across the world and swear fealty to her," Paramarth said.

"Swear to Haldil instead," Swordmaster Anande said. "Gonceivis is closer."

"If I swear to Haldil," Paramarth Hallorad said reasonably, "I still have to go west to do it." He sighed. "I have less objection to Vieliessar than to Gonceivis. I object to having to go and tell her so."

"The Windsward Houses pledged to her have done that and more than that," Anande pointed out. "They have gone west with everything they own. Meanwhile, Antanaduk and Rutharban have pledged to Haldil, so that alliance has ten Houses now."

"So Gonceivis is King at last. How nice for him," Ladyholder Ingwinde said.

"Over all save Hallorad," Paramarth said again. "In that, he and Vieliessar High King are equal. So far."

"Let us ignore Haldil until it comes, then surrender," Warlord Arturkiel said. His counsel wasn't cowardice as much as it was practicality: Hallorad could shelter her people, but not her herds.

"He won't come," Swordmaster Anande said. "He'll bluster and send messengers. But he won't come. He knows his army would be nothing more than a grand feast for the Gryphons and Aesalions. He'd probably rather try to break a Hippogriff to saddle."

Most of those in the chamber joined her in laughter. Arahir Lightsister did not.

"But come! You have been silent, Lightsister. And much of this concerns you. What window upon the future do you have for our ears?" Paramarth asked.

Arahir was Chief Lightborn of Hallorad. At Rosemoss Farm, in the years of her Postulancy, she had seen what the people of the West called windows—great holes in their walls large enough to ride a fully armored destrier through. She had kept her opinions to herself: westerners were all mad, living in peace and safety and calling themselves constantly imperiled. She sighed at Paramarth's question, one she had been hoping to evade. "The Candidates are of no matter. We can apprentice them here—"

"As if they were Craftworkers?" Ladyholder Ingwinde exclaimed. "What an odd notion!"

"—but all know the reason Vieliessar fought," Arahir said, finishing her thought.

"Amretheon's Prophecy." It was not an inclination to scholarship that brought Paramarth's quick answer. The Grand Windsward—though not Hallorad—had fought the High Houses only half a century before on the pretext that the time of the Prophecy had come. "Lightsister, she did not win in the field because anyone believed her."

*The commonfolk believed her,* Arahir answered silently. *But they were desperate.* "I do not say the Prophecy brought her victory, my lord," she answered carefully. "But I say she fought to become High King because she believed the time of the Prophecy is upon us."

"You knew her when you were at the Sanctuary, did you not?" Paramarth asked curiously.

"When she was Sanctuary servant, not Lightborn," Arahir said. "Even then she had a clever mind and a great thirst for knowledge. But we have spoken of her many times since Hamphuliadiel sent warning she left the Sanctuary, my lord. This is old news."

"She wasn't High King when she left the Sanctuary," Paramarth pointed out. "Nor was Hamphuliadiel mad."

"Haldil has ever nurtured goblin fruit," Swordmaster Anande said. "It is well to remember the Astromancer's lineage: he claims descent from Kaelindiel Bethros through Einartha, Lady Ringwil's sister and squire."

Centuries before, Haldil had taken Bethros by treachery, forcing a ruinous ransom that had brought Bethros to its knees. Kaelindiel had blamed Einartha and exiled her, not knowing it was Ringwil who was the traitor. Ringwil had begged to be able to follow her sister into exile for love of her—but when they sought sanctuary in Bethros, Ringwil was garlanded with honors and wealth . . . and Einartha ended her days as slave and scullion, even though they were sisters, for it had been Ringwil who betrayed Bethros, not Einartha.

Paramarth threw his hands up in a mocking gesture of despair. "My Anande! You make my head ache with this tale—am I to imagine a long and terrible plot on the part of the Astromancer against Bethros? Or Haldil? Or both?"

"If that were so, he would be the High King's ally, my lord, rather than her enemy," Anande said. "I think he is as maddened with ambition as . . . another we knew."

"Ivrulion of Caerthalien," Arahir said quietly. "You need not fear to speak the name in my hearing, Anande. He broke the Covenant, and too many paid the price of that arrogance. Hamphuliadiel's madness is a different thing. He does not seek to rule as War Prince, but as Astromancer. And in other days, that would be the threat I counseled you against."

"But not now," Paramarth said shrewdly.

"No," Arahir said. "Not now."

⁂

When Paramarth had determined to his satisfaction that Hallorad would be best served by delay on all fronts, Arahir returned to her own chambers. As befit the Chief Lightborn, they were located high enough in the castel to permit actual windows. Arahir wasn't sure whether she liked the windows or not: her parents had been herdsfolk, and the sky meant nothing but danger. Now she walked to the nearest one, folded back its shutters, and peered out.

"What news from the deliberations of the great and mighty?"

Arahir startled as Monthir entered the room. Like her, he had been sent to the Sanctuary. Unlike her, he'd served only his Service year.

"None, I suppose," she said. "Or what was to be expected: Lord Paramarth will say 'yes' and 'no' to the High King and 'yes' and 'no' to Haldil. And we shall train our Candidates here."

"And yet you do not caper in glee," Monthir said. "Nor, I think, did you counsel our prince as completely as one might hope."

"How can I?" Arahir said wearily, turning away from the window. "He would say—*all* of them would say—it is the echoes of Ivrulion Oathbreaker's darkness that disturbs my visions."

Arahir's Keystone Gift was Prophecy. It was untrustworthy at best, utterly unreliable at worst: most of her time at the Sanctuary had been spent learning to ignore her Gift rather than to summon it. What use was a Foretelling when it could not be deciphered until after it had come true?

"But you think not," Monthir said, moving to the tea-brazier and preparing tea.

"I think not," Arahir agreed. "But I do not know what to make of it, so how can I counsel Paramarth? The Windsward becomes an ocean of blood—it sounds like something out of *The Song of Amretheon*. And just as useful."

"Ah, well," Monthir said. "Let us hope this ocean does not come as high as the windows, then. It would take forever to get the stain out of the linens."

Arahir laughed dutifully and drank her tea when it was ready. She gave no more thought to her vision.

❧⊱⊰❧

That night Arahir stayed late in the Great Hall, hoping to tire herself enough to sleep without dreams. She had barely returned to her chambers and begun preparing for bed when . . .

One moment she was unknotting the sash of her robe. The next, she was kneeling on the stone floor beside her bed. Bile rose in her throat and she gagged, trying to understand what had felled her when there had been no blow to strike her down.

She forced herself to her feet, staggering as she ran for the door. It opened nearly in her face. "Arahir! What—?" Alpion Lightbrother clutched at her arm, his face stark and grey with the same nauseated horror she felt. She shook him off, running for the stairs that led to the watchtower roof. Three doors set at intervals blocked the staircase. Frantically, she flung them all open, lurching drunkenly up the stairs and onto the roof of Hallorad Great Keep.

All was silent. The night air was sharp and cold, but it brought her no relief. The two Lightborn on guard—Iandal and Kerligan—knelt on the stone, moaning, struck down as she had been. The two guardsmen leaned over them, their voices low and worried.

"Alarm, attack, sound warning," Arahir gasped, her voice little more than a whisper. She never knew, afterward, if they'd heard. But by then she knew it wouldn't have done any good anyway.

"You've come to meet me. How nice."

As if it were some Lightless illusion, a figure appeared on the battlement. It was winged, but it was no kind of Beastling Arahir had ever seen. It was tall and beautiful, with a body lushly, unmistakably, female. Its skin was bright scarlet; it wore tall boots and a wide jeweled belt, and nothing else at all. Its great ribbed wings were spread against the wind, and its barbed tail writhed. The alien stranger smiled a predator's smile. Its mouth was filled with long white teeth.

Iandal Lightbrother clawed himself to his feet. The guardsmen advanced with their pikes lowered. Arahir felt a prickling over her skin: Iandal was summoning Storm. She gathered her own magic and struck: Fire. Simple and deadly.

It had no effect.

She summoned Send, to cast the winged monster from the roof, but Send had no more effect than Fire had.

"Do not play with them yet, Shurzul!" a second winged creature cried laughingly as it landed on the roof beside the first. "There will be time later!"

Then the guardsmen in front of her were gone and Arahir felt a warm splash of wetness on her skin. It took her a moment to realize it was blood. One of the winged ones bounded past Arahir to rip the door to the castel off its hinges as if it were paper. Kerligan Lightbrother screamed, throwing himself at it. And then he—and it—were gone.

"Run," Shurzul said, gazing at Arahir with glowing pupilless yellow eyes. "Run."

And Arahir did.

## CHAPTER TWO

# ICE MOON: THE END OF THE HUNDRED HOUSES

*If you were not at the Battle of the Shieldwall Plain, you could never afterward make anyone understand what it was like. It had begun as the grand alliance of the Hundred Houses against the High King and ended as a battle of the living against the dead.*

—Thurion Pathfinder, *A History of the High King's War*

She lay where she had fallen, in the jagged desolation of frozen mud, conscious only by a supreme act of will. But even that will could not give Vieliessar Farcarinon the use of her limbs. She breathed in Darkness with each breath, heard the chittering laughter of ghosts, felt her very flesh liquefy and rot. *Illusion*, she told herself desperately, but she could not force herself to believe it. Against the burning horizon, she could see the shambling forms of the unquiet dead.

Here, today, the last breaths of the High King would measure out the end of the Hundred Houses. Begun in Amretheon's death and madness, ended in her death and Ivrulion Lightbrother's madness.

She saw Gunedwaen walk past her, toward the spreading column of desolation. Her voice was a harsh caw in her throat as she tried to call him back. He walked onward, his slow and measured steps those of a man walking to his execution.

She could not breathe.

With a grim determination she forced herself to lift

her head, to set her palms against the befouled earth, to force herself upright. *I will die here,* she thought, and could feel nothing. Not relief. Not regret. Only a horror she prayed would end with death.

Then suddenly it was as if all the light Ivrulion's spell had stolen from the field was returned in one star-bright flash. The ground trembled as ten thousand *mazhnune* bodies fell to the earth, and the sudden absence of the Banespell was its own blazing agony. Vieliessar lurched to her knees, and fell, and struggled upright again, and at last grabbed a discarded spear and used it to gain her feet.

The Magestorm clouds were gone. The sky above was clear and star-flecked. The smoke of burning that had hung in a low pall above the battlefield began to skirl and rise. A strengthening breeze began to bring motion to the tattered garments of the fallen. Vieliessar stood motionless, staring upward, until the faintest of the stars faded with the approach of dawn. Then she began to stumble slowly forward.

It was as if the sun had never risen before, as if this sunrise were something wholly unique in the whole history of the world, never before seen. She did not realize how silent the battlefield had been until a sound ended the silence: a low single note from a war-horn, sustained to the end of the musician's breath.

She walked on.

There was no living thing around her, only the forms of the twice-dead. The bodies, grey with the slowly settling dust, lay pale, bloodless, mutilated, where they had fallen at the moment of Ivrulion's death, and no raven flew down to begin its feast. Even the pavilions in the distance seemed to have lost their brightness.

She reached the place where the spell had centered. Here the ground was not churned and frozen, but smooth as a frozen lake. Its color was the soft grey of the dust that covered the bodies. Her feet sank into it as she walked. It eddied up; a powder so fine it was nearly weightless, coiling like cool smoke around her legs. She smelled the stench of rot and burning, honest and almost wholesome in the wake of what had come before.

At the spell's center lay Ivrulion and Gunedwaen, embracing in death. Ivrulion's body had already begun to liquefy; Gunedwaen's corpse was not yet stiff. Vieliessar knelt beside them and gently pried Gunedwaen free of Ivrulion's eyeless corpse. There were dark trails of blood upon his skin. Burns upon his hands and face. Lesser wounds, taken earlier in the fighting, covered with hasty, makeshift bandages. She pulled off her helm and drew him into her arms, as if he were some wounded knight she might yet Heal, some sufferer come to the Sanctuary of the Star for aid. But Gunedwaen was beyond aid.

Her friend, her teacher, her guide. The last noble lord of House Farcarinon. Dead. She wanted to weep for him, but she had no tears. Her grief was too vast, too aching, for such a petty display. Gunedwaen had loved Vieliessar Farcarinon, not Vieliessar High King—loved her deeply and always, without believing in the Prophecy, or her cause, or even the hope of victory. All he'd done in her service, he had done for love of her.

She bent over him, and her hair, unraveling from the makeshift knot she'd tied it into the morning of the battle, fell down around her face.

"See?" she whispered. "It is long enough now for a proper komen's braid. You always said it would give you joy, the day you could braid my hair for battle as you once did my father Serenthon's . . ."

That day would never come now, and she would give no one else that honor as long as she lived. She kissed his forehead. Then she took the dagger from his hand and began to cut her hair.

⊱⊰

Vieliessar High King sat on a chair beneath a canopy erected over a carpet laid on frozen blood-soaked earth so that the War Princes of the defeated Grand Alliance might ride across the battlefield to swear fealty.

"You must do this now," Rithdeliel said to her unyieldingly. "You must give them a thing they can understand, so that they can honorably give their folk to your care."

"Honor," Vieliessar answered bleakly. "What was there of honor upon this battlefield?"

"Yours," he answered simply. "And it comes at a heavy cost."

It was a necessary business conducted in a charnel house, for the battlefield would not be cleared in a sennight or even a moonturn. Among some of the High Houses, the Throne had passed through a dozen hands in the course of the battle: War Prince, and Heir, and Line Direct, all slain. Cadet branches—elder sisters, elder brothers—who had never looked to rule had become the heirs of the High Houses. The knight heralds did their best to discover who still lived and who held the fealty of all below them within their gift.

Even as Vieliessar took pledges from the surviving War Princes—sometimes taking the fealty of the same House a dozen times before all could be certain its rightful War Prince had pledged—she ordered scouts to search Janubaghir for survivors and deserters. The Alliance encampment was slowly dwindling as new-sworn lords ordered pavilions struck, wagons loaded. By late afternoon, only one cluster of pavilions remained.

Caerthalien's.

Vieliessar sent War Prince Annobeunna Keindostibaent to them, for Annobeunna was one of the few

War Princes who had not taken the field—leaving that glory to her children, so that there might be someone of sufficient rank to give orders behind the lines—and though recently an enemy, hers was a face Caerthalien might know. Aradreleg Lightsister and a taille of komen who were yet fit to ride—though there were few enough who were still hale and whole in the battle's aftermath—accompanied her. Within a candlemark, they returned—not with any member of Caerthalien's Line Direct, but with a knight of Caerthalien. The komen they escorted was neither armed nor armored, and knelt at Vieliessar's feet the moment she could, bowing her head.

"There is no one of Caerthalien who can swear, Lord Prince," Helecanth said simply. "I am come to tell you this, and beg your mercy for her people."

"No one?" Vieliessar asked. "Bolecthindial . . . ?" She would not speak of Runacarendalur. But if she lived, so must he.

"Dead," Helecanth said. "Three of his sons died in the West. His daughters died today. Lord Mordrogen's line, Lord Baradhrath, Lady Nimphant—their children—all are dead. Only one of noble Caerthalien lineage remains within our encampment," Lady Helecanth added, and for a moment Vieliessar's heart beat fast. "But Lady Glorthiachiel has said to me she will not give you Caerthalien."

Vieliessar looked down to meet Helecanth's eyes. Even weary as she was, True Speech brought her the Lady Helecanth's thought as clearly as if she had spoken aloud: *Nor is it hers to give, while Runacarendalur Caerthalien lives. But for love of him, no other shall have of me the words he spoke: he rides to outlawry rather than bend his knee to his destined Bondmate.*

The knowledge was joy and sorrow, bitter and sharp.

"If she will not swear to me," Vieliessar answered evenly, "then she must become my prisoner. And if she is the last of the Line Direct, as you say, I claim Caerthalien and all it holds by right of conquest."

"Let it be so, Lord Vieliessar," Helecanth said, preparing to rise.

"But I will have your oath of fealty from your own lips," Vieliessar said, stopping her. "Swear to me you hold me your liege and your King."

She'd expected resistance, but Helecanth only smiled. "This I shall swear without reservation," she answered. "Caerthalien is fallen this day in battle, and she has no prince save yourself."

⊰⊱

The afternoon sunlight flickered through the trees as he rode, but Runacar—Runacarendalur Caerthalien, War Prince of Caerthalien for less than a sunturn—did not see. The land he rode over was as unknown as his future. He had gone forth from the encampment with nothing more than his clothes, and his sword, and his dead brother's horse. He stopped at midday to drink from an ice-rimed stream, but he had no food, nor any means of getting any.

He wasn't hungry anyway.

He spared only enough attention to keep Nielriel moving westward at a steady walk, giving thanks to Sword and Star that the mare was fresh and rested. His body ached with the strain of a day and a night upon the battlefield. His spirit ached with its ending.

She'd won. Vieliessar had won.

He thought of a skinny girl, all dark eyes and elbows, nothing more than another of the countless fosterlings who sheltered beneath Caerthalien's roof. Varuthir had been her name then, for no one but Lord Bolecthindial and Ladyholder Glorthiachiel had known her true parentage. When she was twelve she'd been returned to the Sanctuary of the Star to live out her days, as Celelioniel

Astromancer had decreed when she had set Peace-bond upon Farcarinon's infant War Prince. The Peace-bond had permitted her to grow up. Its end had kept the Hundred Houses from turning on one another, for she had still held Farcarinon, and to claim Varuthir, to claim *Vieliessar,* would be to claim her lands. The Peace of the Sanctuary had been her defense.

She'd been supposed to stay there.

She hadn't.

She'd taken Oronviel by challenge and then armed for war—and Caerthalien had answered. He remembered catching sight of her upon the battlefield, of seeing her raise her hands to lock her helm into place with a practiced warrior's gesture. He'd thought it was all for show, then—a play, and Vieliessar the puppet, her strings pulled by Thoromarth, Rithdeliel, Gunedwaen . . . all masters of war.

But she'd been no one's puppet. She'd proven it on that Oronviel battlefield. And afterward, in all the battles that followed, she had snatched the meat of victory from the cookfires of defeat time and again, and with each victory Runacar's dread had grown. The High King's War had shown all the War Princes how fragile their world was in the moment Vieliessar shattered it. Runacar had consoled himself with the knowledge he would not see the world she had worked to summon—and she wouldn't, either, for with the end of his life would come hers.

They were Bondmates.

He had known it from the moment his *hradan* had come to him with that battlefield sight of her, and ever since he had longed for the moment when death would claim him and Vieliessar both. No one, even the Lightborn, knew anything of the Soulbond. It could not be predicted. It could not be broken. Bondmate met destined Bondmate and . . . it was done: a binding so absolute that one heart would not continue to beat when the other was stilled. He had kept that secret too long, thinking first that she would be easily defeated, and next that to reveal it would be thought by the rest of the Alliance to be a trick on Caerthalien's part to take the Unicorn Throne for itself. Always, he had clung to the knowledge that even if she won, he could snatch that victory from her with the stroke of a blade.

And then his brother Ivrulion—Ivrulion Oathbreaker, Ivrulion Banebringer, Ivrulion the Mad—had discovered Runacar's secret, and denied him even that. But now Ivrulion was dead, and the *geasa* that forced Runacar to live was broken. From that moment he had been free to do as he chose.

*She won. And yet you live.* He shook his head wearily.

Vieliessar had destroyed chivalry and nobility and grace upon the battlefield. She had profaned the Way of the Sword and the very art of war. She had destroyed the Hundred Houses. But Runacar could not bear to be the architect of their ultimate destruction. He had seen her gain the victory, seen Caerthalien humbled in the dust, the power of the Hundred Houses broken forever. In that moment, he could have ended her life—but he'd seen the Uradabhur dissolve into chaos and banditry during the Winter War as their two armies swept through it. Someone must restore order, and she was all that was left.

But he could not bear to bend his neck and give her Caerthalien.

Could all this have ended differently if Vieliessar had been raised with the knowledge of who and what she was? If his parents had bound her to Caerthalien with chains of love and service, brought her to agree that her domain should be divided among Farcarinon's destroyers? She might have become a komen of his own meisne—even his bride. A prince without obligation or treaty, a prince whose lands could have enriched Caerthalien, a prince whose bloodline would have strengthened Caerthalien's own claims to the Unicorn Throne—both War Prince and Ladyholder would have considered it an excellent match.

But instead they had done what they had done. And now the world lay shattered at Vieliessar's feet, and Runacar did not wish to see how its destroyer chose to rebuild it.

⊰⧖⊱

That night Runacar slept huddled in his stormcloak in a drift of leaves, too exhausted for the labor of coaxing a fire. He woke in the morning, stiff with cold and light-headed with hunger. He saddled Nielriel and rode on. There was nothing else to do.

The next day he reached the Ghostwood.

It had been a Flower Forest whose power the Lightborn had claimed was as infinite as Great Sea Ocean was vast, but it had not been vaster than the hunger of Ivrulion's last spell. As if some great blade had scribed a boundary between Here and There, the forest Runacar rode through went from the deep sleep of winter to the barrenness of death. The ground was bare even of leaves, for everything living had been turned to dust. Only the trunks of the great trees remained, and among them the uluskukad no longer glowed. Even the air smelled . . . empty.

*I would have gladly surrendered my birthright to you, my brother, to have never seen this sight.*

Runacar looked back the way he'd come. Nielriel's tracks were plainly visible in the patches of snow they had crossed, and in the aftermath of any great battle its Generals sent out search parties looking for those who had fled or been borne wounded from the field. He must ride on, or risk capture. If he continued across the Ghostwood, Nielriel would quickly starve. South was unknown territory.

*North it is, then.*

He walked Nielriel to the edge of the Ghostwood, then turned her head northward.

❈

On the second day of his flight, as he rode north along the boundary of the Ghostwood, Runacar saw a cluster of huts about half a league into the leafless lifeless forest. While he knew it was not impossible for him to be gazing upon the remains of some small steading—for Landbonds fled their masters, disgraced or unransomed komen fled the field, servants and Craftworkers fled their villages—there were no Elves here, uncounted leagues south of the edge of the Uradabhur. That meant it was some squalid Beastling camp. Runacar had often led Caerthalien's komen into Unclaimed Lands in the West to burn them out.

He hoped the creatures had fled in fear when the Flower Forest had died, for he did not have the stamina for an extended fight, nor was Nielriel a destrier. But if he did not mean to lie down here and die, he must take what they had. Beastlings or no, a settlement meant shelter. Tools. Food. He turned Nielriel's head toward the Ghostwood and urged her to cross its border.

❈

The leaf litter crunched brittlely and white puffs of dust rose up from beneath the mare's hooves as she walked, and after a moment, Runacar dismounted to investigate, since he did not wish Nielriel to take injury from this unnatural footing.

At first, the ground seemed as if it was covered with ash, or sand. Then he looked closer and saw it was covered with tiny skeletons. But these were not the skeletons of mice, of rabbits, and birds. They crumbled in his fingers as he sifted them from the leaves. The fragile bones fell apart in his hands. Only the skulls remained intact. Hundreds of skulls, some as small as his thumbnail. Tiny skulls that looked Elvenborn.

*Ivrulion drew all the life from this forest . . .*

He recoiled in a shudder of distaste and as he got to his feet, he looked, for the first time, at the trees through which he'd been riding. Each trunk was distorted and split, and in each fissure was a skeleton made of wood, its jaws open in a soundless scream, posed as if it were attempting to drag itself free of the tree. For a moment Runacar thought he stood amidst grotesque carvings, then he realized what he was seeing.

*Dryads.*

He looked around. Tree after tree was the same. Skulls. Clawing fingers.

He'd had thought Ivrulion's raising of the *mazhnune* to be atrocity enough to bring shame to his House and his Line until the stars grew cold. But if he'd thought of what Ivrulion had done to gain the power for that raising, he'd only thought of it as the death of a forest. The birds and beasts would have fled, just as they would from fire, and some would starve, but they would not have been harmed. Only now he knew differently. Nothing had fled. Ivrulion had killed Janglanipaikharain and everything within its bounds.

Nothing he might find here was worth remaining in this charnel house another instant. Runacar mounted Nielriel and turned her head back toward the living forest.

On the third day after the Battle of the Shieldwall Plain, a Challenge Circle was drawn in the earth of Ifjalasairaet. On one side of it stood the High King's pavilion, its scarlet walls a bright mockery of the winter-grey plain. On the other side stood Caerthalien's viridian pavilion, still flying the banner of its War Prince.

Within its walls were all that remained of Caerthalien: Lady-Abeyant Glorthiachiel of Caerthalien, Demi-Princess Rondaniel, who was Ivrulion's daughter and hence barred from the succession, and a handful of servants.

No one doubted the outcome of today's circle.

"I still say you do her too much honor," Rithdeliel said. "The Hundred Houses acknowledge you as High King over them all—or they will by Midsummer."

"It is Ice Moon," Vieliessar answered absently. "Thunder Moon is five moonturns away." Bragail laced Vieliessar's aketon snugly into place. The elaborate green-lacquered armor that would be donned over it stood waiting on its arming form. Her surcoat, with its gleaming silver unicorn—the High King's device—was neatly folded upon the table that held her sword, her dagger, and her spurs.

"Yes, yes, I know the calendar as well as you do," Rithdeliel said. "And as soon as the Lightborn stop cowering in the forest and are willing to make themselves useful, you will send to the Uradabhur and the Arzhana and their War Princes will come to pledge to you."

"Perhaps," Vieliessar said, standing carefully still as her arming page lowered the heavy chain shirt over her head and began to lace her armor into place over it. "The Uradabhur was unsettled by our passage. It may take some time to restore order."

"Which is why," Rithdeliel said in nicely-judged exasperation, "you should be planning how you will do that. And leave this execution to me."

"She has asked to die at my hand," Vieliessar pointed out mildly.

"And is she the Queen of the Starry Hunt?" Rithdeliel demanded. "War Princes have Champions for a reason. Old Thoromarth, may he ride forever, was perfectly willing for me to handle little things like this."

"I was once one of those 'little things,'" Vieliessar pointed out with a small grave smile.

"And it was the liveliest Harvest Court Oronviel had ever seen—as well as the last," Rithdeliel said.

"Do you think I mean to end all that we are?" Vieliessar answered. "We will hold Harvest Court this year, just as we always have."

"What I think is that you are refusing to take my point," Rithdeliel answered in frustration.

"If I have not taken it in the last three days, why do you think I will take it now?" Vieliessar answered simply. "Lady Glorthiachiel will not swear fealty to me. She has asked to die at my hand."

"She doesn't deserve to!" Rithdeliel finally burst out.

"Ah," Vieliessar said. "At last we come to it. But I spent my first twelve years of life as a child of Caerthalien, as all know. Should I not honor the house that sheltered me?"

"And killed your father!" Rithdeliel snarled. "And erased your House!"

"And yet I stand here before you having erased all Houses," Vieliessar said. "And I will do more." She held her arms out from her sides as Bragail fitted her sword-belt into place over her surcoat. Vieliessar reached out to pick up her helm, tucking it under her arm. "Come. It is time."

⊰⊱

The crowd parted for her as she walked from her pavilion. Even at noon, the day was cold, and Vieliessar could see her breath upon the air. Rithdeliel and Bragail followed her until they reached the front ranks of the spectators, then Rithdeliel and Vieliessar walked on alone. When they reached the edge of the circle, she stopped just outside. Rithdeliel raised his warhorn to his lips and blew a call familiar to everyone here:

*A Challenge. A Challenge. Come and fight. Come and fight.*

He lowered his horn and stepped back among the witnesses.

For a long moment it seemed there would be no answer, then the ranks of spectators opposite Vieliessar began to draw aside. Down that corridor walked Lady Glorthiachiel. Alone.

Every noble child of the Hundred Houses trained in war, and Lady Glorthiachiel had won her sword and spurs in honest battle. For a Challenge Circle she would have worn armor, but this was an execution. Lady Glorthiachiel bore a sword as tradition demanded, but wore only ordinary garments. Over her tunic and trousers, she wore a surcoat in Caerthalien green, with the three gold stars of its badge upon the front, and a hastily-added silver Vilya blossom—symbol of the head of the Line Direct—at her left shoulder. Her face was an expressionless mask.

She stopped just outside the Circle, as Vieliessar had.

"Wait," Vieliessar said, not moving from where she stood. "This need not be. Lady Glorthiachiel, if you will pledge to me and keep my law, I will gladly pardon you. This I swear upon my name."

"You have no name," Glorthiachiel answered, her voice pitched to carry. Her black eyes held unflinching hatred. "Farcarinon is erased. You have slain my husband, my children, all my kin. Let the Silver Hooves determine Caerthalien's fate." *I should have smothered you in your cradle.* True Speech brought Vieliessar the words Glorthiachiel did not say.

Glorthiachiel stepped forward, over the boundary. "Will you join me?" she asked coldly. "Or do I name you coward?"

Vieliessar locked her helm into place and stepped forward.

❧❦

Armored, she was in no danger. She hoped to make this a quick and merciful kill: in the Great Hall of Caerthalien, where she'd been raised, she'd seen Challenge Circle executions take a full candlemark, as Lengiathion Warlord cut his victim to pieces in slow degrees. She meant to show her audience that the High King did not intend to follow that tradition. Not vengeance in the name of power. Not cruelty for the sake of sport. *Justice.*

Ladyholder-Abeyant Glorthiachiel was making that difficult.

She met Vieliessar's first stroke blade to blade. Strike, block, disengage, attack. Vieliessar caught the return blow upon her forearm shield, but she felt the force behind it. Glorthiachiel sprang backward before Vieliessar's response could touch her. The two combatants began to circle, warily.

*Does she seek the Silver Hooves' favor by this display?*

Let Glorthiachiel step outside the circle and her life was forfeit—ignominious execution instead of honorable death. Let her remain within, and weariness would eventually render her too slow to defend herself—a lesson Vieliessar had learned at Gunedwaen's hands long before she had held her first true sword.

*I will not make this death into sport!*

She knew that was what the spectators expected. The execution of a defeated enemy was the time for a display of power. It was how it had always been.

It would not be so any longer.

It took only a heartbeat for Vieliessar to change her tactics. Instead of waiting, watching for an opening, as she would have against an armored challenger, as training and instinct demanded, she flung herself into her attack. She forced Glorthiachiel back toward the edge of the circle, giving her no chance to maneuver. It was a move that would spell death on the field, where survival demanded care, caution, the husbanding of one's resources. Glorthiachiel fought back savagely, but a part of her attention must always be on the boundary, lest she step over it.

The moment of inattention came.

Vieliessar struck. An upward blow that severed Glorthiachiel's sword arm. Then a downward blow that severed her neck.

The body fell. Vieliessar stepped back over the edge of the circle.

The entire battle had taken less than an eighth of a candlemark.

A sigh went up from the waiting spectators. Relief? Disappointment? True Speech could give no single answer in the presence of so many thoughts.

She shook her bloody sword as clean as she could.

"Let this body be laid with the others," Vieliessar said. "Lady-Abeyant Glorthiachiel of Caerthalien rides now with the Starry Hunt."

## CHAPTER THREE

# ICE MOON TO STORM MOON: THE KINGDOM OF THE WEST

> *In Bethros, they sing songs of Princess Ringwil's stainless honor, but it was Ringwil who betrayed Bethros, and by this pretense sought sanctuary in Haldil thereafter. There is no Song of Einartha, who called Ringwil to the Challenge Circle when she discovered the truth, and whom Ringwil spared to toil as a kitchen-servant until the end of her days.*
>
> *— A History of the Hundred Houses*

How am I ever to have peace?" Hamphuliadiel bellowed.

His outcry was muffled as much by the rich carpets and tapestries that lined the chamber as by the layers of Wards and Shields that underlay them. The minor Lightborn might be satisfied with their stark Meditation Chambers. The Astromancer required . . . more. No longer did Hamphuliadiel possess merely a sleeping room and an Audience Chamber, but a proper and fitting private dining chamber, a personal study and library, and a private receiving chamber. This last was the mirror of his public Audience Chamber, and many of the fine ornaments and furnishings had been moved from the one to the other. The windowless chamber was now the most secure location in all the Fortunate Lands. No spell could breach it, and the use of physical force against the Sanctuary of the Star was unthinkable.

It was here that he received Momioniarch's latest—unwelcome—report.

"My lord Astromancer, I cannot tell you what I do not know," Momioniarch said patiently.

"How is it you do not know?" Hamphuliadiel demanded. "Have those you have taught grown too proud to listen when you Call?"

"One of my students gave her life to Farspeak me that news," Momioniarch said softly. "More news must wait."

"Yet you are sure of this?" he demanded. "She has won?"

"She has won, my lord Astromancer. Vieliessar Lightsister is now Vieliessar High King."

Hamphuliadiel turned away, struggling to keep himself from screaming aloud. It would not do for even Momioniarch to see him less than master of himself.

*How is it that I have all that I want and yet Vieliessar's victory turns it to ash?*

Hamphuliadiel's heart had lifted with hope when at last Momioniarch Lightsister had brought the news that the battle he so eagerly awaited was to begin with the next day's dawn. Surely the Starry Hunt would favor the virtuous, and Vieliessar would be defeated. But incredibly, Vieliessar had won. The time of the Hundred Houses was at an end.

"To ruin and darkness with the so-called High King!" Hamphuliadiel growled. "The Sanctuary of the Star will stand against her madness, no matter how surges the tide of her followers! It was I who was summoned to greatness, not she—and soon enough she will know this! She will beg me for forgiveness and lay down her sword at my feet to gain it!"

M omioniarch remained prudently silent as Hamphuliadiel paced and muttered, knowing he had forgotten she was here. *My lord Hamphuliadiel has no way of bringing such a thing to pass, and well he knows it. But nothing was ever gained by speaking hard words to the ears of princes. Neither force nor reason will bring Vieliessar Farcarinon suppliant to Hamphuliadiel.*

Vieliessar, too, had been Momioniarch's student once. Momioniarch remembered her well: stubborn, difficult, secretive, and far too proud. As if she had known herself to be High King even when she was scrubbing pots in the kitchens. Momioniarch Lightsister could see no possible compromise between Vieliessar and Hamphuliadiel, for each of them made of the Lightborn game-pieces in a vast and living game of xaique.

It was a game Momioniarch had gladly played since that Midwinter Court in Haldil so long ago, when she had been Called by the Light. There had been four of them that year: her, Hamphuliadiel, Galathornthadan, and Sunalanthaid. She'd been a Craftworker's daughter. Galathorn and Sunalan had been Landbond. But the kitchen boy who was their fourth was the greatson of the War Prince of Bethros. He had told her that secret long before he shared it with the others, and Momioniarch had prized it. Born in slavery and orphaned early, he had never forgotten his mother's dying words. *Avenge me,* Einartha had said. *Avenge my shame.* How better to do that than to take for himself the rulership he should have had by right of blood?

*Swear yourselves to me, and you shall be princes.*

And they had, following Hamphuliadiel's long sight without question. He told them they would all take the Green Robe, and it had come to pass. He told them he would see to it that they did not live out their years as the slaves of Caerthalien, and that, too, had come to pass.

*He saw, long before Vieliessar did, that it is the Light-born who hold the true keys to power.*

Everything the Hundred Houses had ever achieved

was built upon the power of the Lightborn and what they could do. War was what the Hundred Houses knew and loved. It made them easy to control, to manipulate—if one sought *true* power. Lightborn Magery had been what made it possible for the War Princes and the Lords Komen to battle eternally without being subject to the devastating cost of war. Mosirinde Peacemaker and Arilcarion War-Maker had leashed that Magery: Mosirinde's Covenant and *The Way of the Sword* were the jesses upon the ankles of every Lightborn, saying how—and when—Lightborn power could be used.

But lift the twin yokes of Mosirinde Peacemaker and Arilcarion War-Maker from the necks of the Lightborn, as Vieliessar had done so casually, and the Lightborn became more powerful than any War Prince. In the end, Lightless fear would destroy the Lightborn.

At least, it would destroy the High King's vassal Lightborn.

But Hamphuliadiel meant to train all who came within his power to give their first loyalty to the Sanctuary of the Star. Let the War Princes make them handmaids to their sport once more—and let them know it was Hamphuliadiel Astromancer's gift . . . a gift that could be withdrawn whenever he chose.

*Only let Vieliessar play at Kingship in the east until it is too late for her to undo what she has done. She has no gifts to compare to what the Sanctuary can offer her noble lords.*

*She will not bow. But neither will she reign. Not so long as we.*

❧❧

I have faith that day will come, my lord Astromancer," Momioniarch murmured.

At the sound of her voice, Hamphuliadiel startled, for in his dismay at the disastrous news she brought, he had forgotten her presence. No matter. She had witnessed nothing to his discredit.

"Send for my servant," he said. "I will walk upon the grounds. And say nothing to anyone of what you have said to me."

※

His servant came quickly, bringing not only Hamphuliadiel's opulent fur cloak, but also his fur-lined boots. The Bearward pelt was thick and silky, and Magery had altered its hue to Lightborn green, so that no one might mistake Hamphuliadiel Astromancer for a mere komen. His boots rang upon the marble floors as he made his way to the antechamber; in the absence of new Candidates, the Sanctuary of the Star was emptier now than it had been since its first stones were laid by Mosirinde Peacemaker in the long ago. Nearly all the Lightborn who had lived and taught here had been summoned away by their War Princes last Sword Moon, and the hospital's Teaching Chambers stood empty of Healers. If not for the fact that Hamphuliadiel had held back everyone who had dared the Shrine since last Woods Moon, he would be able to number the Lightborn within these walls upon the fingers of his two hands.

*But they are mine, as all who come after them will be mine,* Hamphuliadiel thought with grim satisfaction. *Where else would they go? The Hundred Houses are erased, and there are no tailles of komen to take them to the so-called High King, even if they wished to seek her out.*

When he reached the antechamber, he stood for a moment in the center of its silver compass rose. Behind him lay the bronze doors of the Shrine. Hamphuliadiel hesitated. He knew he must be ready for whatever came next, now that the world had gone mad. He could make a propitiatory sacrifice, even ask a Foretelling. He could not believe the Starry Hunt would favor Vieliessar, but Their ways were mysterious and Their favor perilous.

He decided to wait.

The servant who stood ready to unbar the doors bowed low in humility as Hamphuliadiel walked out into the morning. The wind was sharp and snow crusted the ground. Hamphuliadiel went down the wide stone path that led to the outer gates. They opened at a touch.

To his right lay Rosemoss Farm. The sound of axes striking wood was a faint regular sound. Bellion Farmholder was clearing more land for planting, as Hamphuliadiel had directed. Many hectares had been cleared already. More must be, if the Sanctuary was to feed itself—as it must now that there were no War Princes to send the tribute caravans. Fortunately Hamphuliadiel had already begun to do what was needed to make certain the Lightborn could survive without those gifts and tithes. He debated a moment, then turned left.

Here was the work of his moonturns of labor. Duty had called him to remain as Astromancer in defiance of all custom. A lesser man would have broken beneath the weight of that call, but Hamphuliadiel had been ready. The Light Itself had forged Hamphuliadiel in its fires to stand against Vieliessar's madness when it came. If Candidates did not come now to the Sanctuary, Farmfolk and Craftworkers eager for safety and security did. Soon the Sanctuary would rule over more chattels than even Caerthalien at the height of her power could boast. His new village would outshine all Vieliessar's conquests.

Areve—named for the nearby Flower Forest—was less than a Wheelturn old. It was still primarily a thing of tents, scavenged pavilions, and crude huts, but Hamphuliadiel had laid out its design himself and summoned up the wells with his own hand when its border stones were set, and someday it would be magnificent—a vaster domain than any the High Houses had ever claimed; larger and wealthier than Bethros or Haldil or even Caerthalien itself. Someday even that which had once been Farcarinon would belong to the Sanctuary and its Astromancer, and he would be the greatest power in the land.

But if, in a sense, Vieliessar was responsible for the existence of Areve, it was the Hundred Houses that had given Areve its wealth. Vieliessar had fled across the Mystrals amid a mob of Farmfolk and laborers. When the High House Alliance had followed, they had wisely left such folk behind, expecting to return to their domains within a few sennights at most. But by Hearth Moon the army was far away, the Dragon's Gate was sealed, and the Alliance's great army had taken with it all that it needed to feed itself. The people of the West had fled to the only source of safety and rulership they could imagine.

The Sanctuary of the Star.

His Lightborn had wanted to send them back to their homes, but Hamphuliadiel was wiser than they. Moonturns before, when the High Houses had declared alliance, he had ordered Master Bellion to begin clearing more land for spring planting. When refugees began to arrive at the Sanctuary, Hamphuliadiel announced that all who wished to seek the protection of the Sanctuary of the Star were welcome—not in the Sanctuary itself, of course, but in the new village that would soon hold thousands.

There were already a few small houses in the Craftworkers' quarter, and a curl of smoke rose up from the chimney of the forge. Someday Areve would have cottages and workshops and Craftworker halls—even a hospital for Lightless Healing. But barns and granaries were far more important than houses, and so the labor of the refugees and the timber cut in Rosemoss Forest went first to that. Graciously, Hamphuliadiel had even allotted land within the village walls to the Landbonds who had come to him, but that quarter held little more than holes scratched in the earth and a few flimsy lean-tos.

*If they want to be warmer than this next winter, they will labor more quickly. It is said that Vieliessar erected a Battle City at Oronviel in less than two moonturns. My people can do no less.*

Hamphuliadiel walked along the high road of the village to come, admiring the one he saw in his mind. There were only a few folk within its bounds at this time of day. Most of them were clearing land for plowing or tending livestock, and the most trustworthy were gathering the bounty of Arevethmonion herself. Those who remained looked on in wonder as he passed. At least they were capable of the respect and deference the Light deserved, if they were capable of little more. He wrinkled his nose in distaste at the piles of garbage and litter, the sheer untidy *mess* of the village. There were few senior Lightborn to spare for the task of governing, and the Postulants were utterly untrustworthy; a few years before, they had been chattel and laborers themselves. They had no notion of what was needed to make the usefulness and living wealth of a village increase.

Despite the disappointment, Hamphuliadiel forced himself to be optimistic. When the news of Vieliessar's triumph reached the west, those who now sheltered within the castels and manor houses would seek out the stability and safety Hamphuliadiel could offer. Prudent folk: Castellans, Farmholders, the better sort of servant. Their skills could lighten the crushing burden of charity Hamphuliadiel felt it his duty to extend. Who knew what great things the springtide might bring for . . . Areve?

*No*, he told himself. *I need no Foretelling of the Silver*

*Hooves to show me my course. Let Vieliessar destroy
the Hundred Houses. All they once were, all they may
once again be, shall be born anew. Here. In Areve.*

He turned his steps back toward the Sanctuary with
a lighter heart.

❧❦❧

The reports of the Battle of the Shieldwall Plain
that came to the Windsward were incomplete and
unbelievable. The High Houses broken. Caerthalien
erased. Forbidden magic used on the battlefield. A fortress raised in a day and destroyed in an instant by its
own defenders. Thousands—tens of thousands—of komen slaughtered. The news was so enormous, so shocking, that Lightborn all across the Windsward pooled all
they knew.

The most unbelievable thing of all was the one thing
everyone agreed upon.

Celephriandullias-Tildorangelor was no myth. Vieliessar High King had done what she had said she would
do: she had found the Unicorn Throne and set herself
upon it.

Vieliessar Farcarinon was High King.

"If she is High King, then she is Child of the Prophecy," Gonceivis said doggedly. "And what of that?"

This gathering was held in a far more private chamber
than the one the moonturn before. In Storm Moon,
Gonceivis had expected eventually to hear of Vieliessar's defeat, or that both armies had been destroyed, or
simply that Vieliessar had fled to some secret stronghold. Now that she had won, Gonceivis had no intention of surrendering Haldil, but Haldil's rebellion had
begun on the same pretext as Vieliessar's war. If Amretheon's Prophecy were more than a convenient rallying point for those who wished to throw off the
oppressive yoke of the High Houses of the Western
Reach, Gonceivis must know. For that reason, he'd

summoned both his Loremaster and his Chief Story-singer to this very private meeting of his ruling court.

"Of course, you are speaking of the Great Darkness that will extinguish all life," Darothel Loremaster said. His reply was a sulfurous glare from his master. "That, of course, depends on the Prophecy being true in every particular."

"It's a *prophecy*," Gonceivis said in exasperation. He gazed toward the tiny slit window. Six sennights to the start of Flower Moon, and soon after that, the passes would open. And who—or what—would come from the West? "How can just *part* of a prophecy be true?"

"*The Song of Amretheon*—" Mirwathel Storysinger began.

"Oh, by all means, let us have a song," Ladyholder Belviel said. "Perhaps it will tell us what course we should follow."

Mirwathel was too wise to take her up on her suggestion. "I only mean to say, my lord, my lady, that *The Song of Amretheon* is very, very long. It is not really a song at all. It is more . . . a library of songs."

"So some of it isn't true?" Lord Ranruth asked in hopeful tones.

"None of it is true," Ladyholder Belviel said flatly. Othrochel Lightbrother looked pained.

"If I may, Lord Gonceivis," Aenthior Swordmaster said, "the Prophecy may well be true in every detail. But not . . . explicit."

"A code?" Gonceivis said, grasping for something he understood.

Aenthior smiled. "A code. Precisely. And a very old one, to which we have lost the key. But consider. We will grant that it gave a precise time for the birth of the Child of Prophecy—a time at which many children were born, including the late and much mourned Demi-Prince Malbeth. Celelioniel Astromancer knew both Lord Vieliessar's birth hour and her lineage, and just as clearly knew this Child of Prophecy must belong to one of the Lines Direct. Lord Vieliessar is Lightborn, and so had ample time to study the Prophecy and shape her ambitions to it."

"Is. It. *True?*" Gonceivis demanded.

"Does it matter, my lord father?" Heir-Prince Paramarth asked. "What if it is? Darkness—monsters—rivers of blood—How is any of that different from the battles we of the Windsward fight every Wheelturn? If the Prophecy is true in every detail, let the High King fight this fabulous peril with her great array. If it is not true, let her rule her vast Kingdom in the west. It cannot matter to us."

Ladyholder Belviel wandered over to the xaique board beneath the narrow window and began rearranging the pieces, naming them as she did.

"The twenty Houses of the Windsward—Artholor, Calwas, Enerchelimier, Kerethant, Penenjil, Morgelian, Yoncividiant—for her. That's seven. Antanaduk, Cazagamba, Narazan, Rutharban—say neither yes nor no. Four. Hallorad maintains its eternal neutrality, of course. Leaving . . ."

"Andhirra, Jirvaleg, Parvochost, Ethrandeb, Dontreis, Helenneis, and Bethros. I can count, Madame. Seven and Haldil," Gonceivis said.

"To lead them," Ladyholder Belviel answered. "And to convince Antanaduk, Cazagamba, Narazan, and Rutharban that the lion at one's walls is a more urgent matter than a wolf in the forest."

"Penenjil is already on the march, and Enerchelimier surely follows as swift as she may," Ranruth said. "But I have never heard tell of the whole of a domain going to war. Their people will seek protection."

"And they will find it here," Gonceivis announced grandly. "Haldil is known by all to be a kind master, generous and strong."

"Just as you say, my lord," Aenthior said. She glanced

toward Othrochel. "The summer will bring joyous celebration, when for the first time in many centuries, all the Lightborn Haldil has sent to the Sanctuary of the Star may return to her freely."

Silence fell.

"You really are an idiot," Prince Paramarth said flatly. "Do you think *anybody* is going to the Sanctuary of the Star this spring?"

⊰⊱

When word of the High King's victory came, Prince Leopheine Amrolion reckoned the sunturns and moonturns until aid could reach the Western Shore, and then resolved that he must seek aid from a closer source. And so his daughter had set out from Amrolion in Storm Moon with a full embassy of both rangers and komen to make Amrolion's petition to the Sanctuary of the Star. The embassy had gone armed and armored for war, but many of its members had been lost to Beastling attacks in Delfierarathadan Flower Forest before it had even reached Cirandeiron's western border.

In Cirandeiron, instead of welcome, Ciadorre and her people found a ghostlands, and even Ulvearth's Green Robe could not gain the party guest-rights at the Great Keep. By the time they had been a moonturn on the road, they had been reduced to four, traveling only with Ciadorre's arming page and Ulvearth's body servant.

But at last they had reached the Sanctuary of the Star.

"How long are we to wait?" Princess Ciadorre asked. This was her first visit to the Sanctuary of the Star, but Ulvearth had said much during their travels of what she expected to find here—and more, when they arrived, on what she found changed. The Guesthouse should be filled with travelers and bustling servants, even in Flower Moon. The Sanctuary should be filled with petitioners to the Shrine and invalids coming to be Healed. And both were nearly deserted.

"Until we are sent for," her companion answered mildly. "Do not ask me to number the candlemarks of our wait, my lady. The ways of the Sanctuary have changed much since Inderundiel Astromancer's day." Ulvearth Lightsister folded her arms and stood as if she never intended to move again.

"I *am* a princess of Amrolion's Line Direct, you know," Ciadorre said, her gentle smile making it clear this was a jest shared between friends. She frowned at the closed door of the Astromancer's Audience Chamber. "If Hamphuliadiel Astromancer was called to more pressing duties, I do not see why you and I could not have waited in the Guesthouse until he was free to receive our embassy. At least there are places to sit there. And a fire."

"You have grown proud since we left home, if you expect a seat and a fire wherever you go," Ulvearth answered gently.

Ciadorre made a wry face and resumed her pacing. Four steps up. Four steps back. The tiny antechamber outside the Astromancer's Audience Chamber held nothing to welcome either eye or body. *Perhaps Ulvearth is right and I have grown proud,* Ciadorre thought. *But I am no hedge-knight come to beg a midwife for his lady! And my need is urgent!* "We have traveled as homeless as the hare in spring since the doors of my father's keep closed behind us, and—" Ciadorre broke off as the doors opened.

"The Astromancer will receive you now," the Lightbrother said.

"It is good to see you once more, Orchalianiel," Ulvearth said mildly. "I hope I find you well?"

The Lightbrother ducked his head and did not reply.

Ciadorre forced herself not to react as they entered. The chamber was as long as the hall in a Great Keep, though narrow. The effect was to focus the eye upon the ornate ivory chair at the far end—if one could take one's attention away from the clutter of cabinets and tables and statuary that lined its walls. The floor was visible only in narrow bands between carpets of price, and the walls were hung with so many tapestries that they overlapped one upon the other like blankets on washing day. *So the Astromancer holds court in a storage room,* Ciadorre thought scornfully. Even as she framed the thought, she knew it was untrue. The Astromancer brooded over his treasures as a Gryphon over her nest. This display was meant to impress.

The grand chair Hamphuliadiel sat in was one that Ciadorre recognized as coming from Amrolion, for its twin stood at the high table in her father's great hall. Some long-ago prince must have felt a great need to curry favor with the Sanctuary. Ciadorre could hardly imagine how they'd gotten the enormous thing through Delfierarathadan, let alone across the Angarussa. When she reached its foot, Ciadorre had to look up to meet the Astromancer's eyes, and suppressed another pang of irritation. *He enthrones himself as if he would be High King himself!*

"Hamphuliadiel Astromancer," she said. "Amrolion and Daroldan send their greetings."

"Do they?" Hamphuliadiel said. "Do they also send their customary tithes, Princess Ciadorre? Or have you come to bring their excuses?"

"Amrolion might send excuses—did send them—by Ulvearth Lightsister alone," Ciadorre answered tartly. "I have come to speak of a different matter."

"Speak, then."

Ulvearth touched her arm before Ciadorre could tell Hamphuliadiel she was no hedge-komen to be ordered about. "I will come to the point at once," Ciadorre said, "The Western Shore is at war. The Beastlings press us harder than they have in centuries. Our folk cannot tend their fields nor graze their beasts. Our fisherfolk dare not set their nets for fear of what they will draw up in them. Already my father and War Prince Damulothir speak of Amroldan abandoning her lands to join her people with Daroldan's. Without aid, such a thing must surely be. And so I am come to beg for the Sanctuary's help."

In the silence that followed her speech, Ciadorre was acutely conscious of the wrongness of all of this. It was true that the Sanctuary of the Star was a thing of importance in the land, and the position of Astromancer was one of great power. But the look in Hamphuliadiel's eye was that of a komen who would turn upon an enemy, not that of the Astromancer upon a supplicant.

"What help could the Sanctuary of the Star render to House Amrolion?" Hamphuliadiel said at last.

"If you were to send your Lightborn to fight beside ours, Astromancer, it would help a great deal," Ciadorre said. "Vieliessar High King—"

"Ah, the great High King," Hamphuliadiel said with a cold smile. "She for whom the very Landbonds rise up and fight. You are her vassals?"

"Both Daroldan and Amrolion pledged to her last Thunder Moon. We made no secret of it," Ciadorre answered, puzzled. "Daroldan and Amrolion were never held in clientage by any of the High Houses, so we broke no oaths in doing so. But the High King is far from here, and—"

"And now you have found that her vast power is not so vast that she can protect you," Hamphuliadiel interrupted her once more. "No doubt more important matters occupy her time. Very well. The Sanctuary will aid you. At a price, of course."

Ciadorre risked a quick glance at her companion, but could read nothing in Ulvearth Lightsister's face. *Am I expected to bargain as if the Lightborn are some Free Company?* "You will not find us ungenerous in our gratitude," she said cautiously.

"Gratitude!" Hamphuliadiel said sharply. "I am

awash in gratitude already. This is my word to Amrolion and Daroldan both: renounce your false oaths
to Vieliessar Farcarinon. Pledge fealty to the Sanctuary
of the Star. And you will receive your aid."

Ciadorre stared at him in stunned silence.

"This is a most generous offer, Astromancer," Ulvearth
Lightsister said smoothly. "You must allow us to return
to Amrolion to present it to Prince Leopheine as quickly
as we may."

"Sunalanthaid?" Hamphuliadiel said.

There was movement to the side of the Astromancer's
great chair. Ciadorre realized with a pang of disquiet
that the Lightbrother had been standing there all
along—she simply had not noticed him.

"Such an offer will be rejected, Lord Astromancer,"
Sunalanthaid answered simply. "The Lady Ciadorre
thinks you arrogant and mad. Ulvearth Lightsister is
merely afraid."

"How dare you open my mind with Magery?" Ciadorre gasped in outrage. "Lightborn, you overstep yourself!"

"By your own High King's word, the time of lord and
komen is past," Hamphuliadiel said. "Do you deny
what my Sunalanthaid has told me?"

"No," Ciadorre said slowly. "I do not."

Ulvearth reached out a hand to silence her, and Ciadorre shrugged it off angrily. "It is true. More than that,
you are a fool, Astromancer. If the Western Shore falls
to the Beastlings, they will be at the walls of your fine
new town before you can bring in your harvest. And
will you then—"

"*Be silent!*" Hamphuliadiel cried.

Ciadorre drew breath to speak and found she could
not. For the first time since she'd reached Sanctuary
lands, she was afraid. Hamphuliadiel Astromancer
meant to play the War Prince. She had delivered herself
into the hands of an enemy.

"Look to your High King for aid," Hamphuliadiel said softly. "You will not receive it here. And now you may leave us."

Against her will, Ciadorre found herself turning away and walking back down the long stretch of carpet. The Lightbrother who had opened the door before opened it again. Ulvearth Lightsister was not beside her, but no matter what she did, Ciadorre could not stop or even look behind her. It was not until she reached the entry hall of the cold and untended Guesthouse that her body was her own again, and she nearly sobbed aloud with relief. The only mercy in any of this was that there was no one to witness her shame. The only folk she had seen aside from the Astromancer and his . . . courtiers . . . were the laborers and herdsmen.

"Lady Ciadorre?" Nindir asked. She was Ulvearth's personal servant.

"Get Alras," Ciadorre said. "Tell her to go to the stables and have our horses made ready at once. We are leaving."

"Now, my lady?" Nindir asked, astonished. "It is the middle of the day." It was no time to begin a journey of any length, particularly in these days, but Ciadorre was now deeply reluctant to spend a candlemark more than she must in Hamphuliadiel Astromancer's new domain.

"We go now," Ciadorre said. "Pack our things while I wait."

It was a greater effort than she'd imagined to turn her steps toward the stairs that led to her guest chamber. There, she sank down on a bench. The fire was nearly cold.

*I must arm,* she told herself dully, gazing at her armor where it lay awaiting her. *We must ride. I will not face what comes without my sword.*

⚔

S he had barely managed to don her aketon and begun to lace it when Alras returned. The young arming page stepped forward and took the laces from her
hands.

"I have been to the stables," Alras said. "Radanding
Stablemaster says it is the Astromancer's word that our
horses are to be taken as part of Amrolion's sanctuary
tithe."

*Four riding palfreys, two pack horses and* . . . "He
cannot mean to take Cariel as well!" Ciadorre said.
"She is a warhorse, not a palfrey!"

Alras looked at the floor and did not answer.

Ciadorre took a deep breath. She had raised Cariel
from foalhood and the destrier was dear to her. *I must
imagine her slain by outlaws,* she told herself firmly. *I
dare not tarry in hopes of reclaiming her.* "Come and
help me out of this again," she said, forcing a smile for
Alras's benefit. "I cannot walk the whole way home in
my armor. Then we will go through our packs and see
what we can bring with us, for we must go afoot."

"Is the Lightsister to accompany us?" Alras asked
quietly.

"We will hope so," Ciadorre answered bleakly.

U lvearth Lightsister had not returned by the time
Ciadorre was ready to depart. Ciadorre hesitated,
then bade Nindir remain and await her mistress.

"It is possible that even now she persuades the Astromancer to send aid to the Western Shore," Ciadorre
said, feigning a confidence she did not feel. "And she
would miss you, were I to steal you away." At least
the Sanctuary would not be strange to Nindir—like
nearly all the personal servants of the Lightborn, Nindir had been Called to the Light and done her Service
Year at the Sanctuary of the Star before she had been
sent back to Amrolion.

"But surely you cannot mean to set out on foot, my lady?" Nindir said in disbelief.

"How else, when the Astromancer claims my destrier and Alras's palfrey?" Ciadorre said. "Perhaps I may find another mount upon my journey." Unlikely though that was: Farcarinon had been a wasteland since before Ciadorre was born, Ullilion, which lay to its west, had been desolated by last summer's fighting, and Cirandeiron—as all three of them well knew—would give no haven.

"Perhaps," Nindir said doubtfully. "Lady, I pray you, let me go with you. Surely Ulvearth Lightsister will follow as soon as she may. If she can," Nindir added, in a low voice not meant for Ciadorre to hear.

Ciadorre hesitated. Nindir was Ulvearth's servant, but she was also Ciadorre's responsibility. She thought of the ragged figures toiling in the fields she had seen as she approached the Sanctuary. Such labor might well be Nindir's lot if she remained.

And in her heart, Ciadorre knew Ulvearth was not coming back.

"So be it, then," she said. "Now come. I wish to be far from the lands Hamphuliadiel claims before the sun sets."

⊰⊱

W hat shall become of us?" Alras asked.

They had been three candlemarks upon the road, circling wide around Areve itself before finally striking the Sanctuary Road once more, and had stopped for a rest. Ciadorre wished with a longing sharp and bitter that she'd had the wit to leave the servants and supplies at last night's camp—or even send Ulvearth to the Sanctuary by herself to petition the Astromancer. But who could have known how demented he had become?

*No sword is keen enough to slay the past*, she reminded herself, and turned her mind to Alras's words. She knew his question was not of his own fate, or hers, or Nindir's.

"Why, we shall return to Amrolion to give the Astromancer's word to War Prince Leopheine, and await the High King's return," she said staunchly. "What is true beyond all things is that Lord Vieliessar will not fail to ride to our aid as soon as she can. Perhaps even now her great meisne passes through the Dragon's Gate to reclaim the whole of the West. And once the Beastlings are driven off, be certain that the Astromancer's come-uppance will not ride far behind," she added with grim glee.

"Of course she will come," Alras said. Ciadorre knew from his tone that he was doing his best to convince himself, and was not succeeding.

"She will come," Ciadorre repeated. "We are her vassals, and she is pledged to us, as we to her. Is that not so, Nindir?"

Nindir smiled a little wistfully. "Indeed it is so, my lady. The High King has come to free both lord and Landbond, and never has she said a thing she has not done."

"And so we have naught to fear," Ciadorre answered. "Come. We have rested long enough. We shall go on until we find some happy spot to make our beds—and then I will hunt our dinner."

The three travelers rose to their feet and walked on. In another sennight, they were deep within what had once been Farcarinon lands.

None of them lived to cross into Ullilion.

## CHAPTER FOUR

# STORM MOON:
# THE GOOD OF THE LAND

*The world itself must bow to the will of the Lightborn.
If we choose, we can drain the life from every leaf and
flower, take the beasts of the fields, the birds of the air,
the fishes of Great Sea Ocean itself. For the good of the
Land Itself, we pledge we will never draw so much
Power from the land that it sickens and dies, nor will we
draw power from the shedding of blood, nor from death,
nor from any breathing thing.*
— Mosirinde Astromancer, *The Covenant of the Light*

Even though Ivaloriel Telthorelandor—one of the
few Alliance War Princes to have survived the
day—could recount every word of the bargain
Ivrulion Lightbrother had struck with the War Princes
of the Alliance, that was only the shape, not the content. The source of the madness that had made Ivrulion
break the Covenant had trickled from the events like
water from a broken jug, leaving behind a mystery.

And more than a mystery.

Any Lightborn not protected by the boundary stones
of Celephriandullias-Tildorangelor had been touched
by Ivrulion's Banespell, and many did not survive. The
loss of so many of their brethren bound them together,
as did the shame that one of their own should do such a
terrible thing. But the thing that set the Lightborn
apart from the Lightless now was more than shame and
loss: it was fear.

The fear the Lightless now felt upon seeing their green robes.

⋊⋉

Thurion Lightbrother walked from the dim warmth of the Healing Tents into the bright chill of the day. The work was light, with Tildorangelor Flower Forest's inexhaustible bounty to draw upon. It only went on so long because they were so few.

And the injured were so many.

*So many and so few,* he thought sadly. *Seventy Houses and all their arrays fought barely three Sunturns ago. Without the Lightless Healers to keep them alive, half of the injured would have died before Healers could ever have come to their aid. I would give praise to the Light we do not have more injured to tend, except for the reason: the* mazhnune *slaughtered the wounded upon the field to increase their numbers.*

His steps took him along a familiar path, from the Healing Tents to the encampment deep within Tildorangelor the Lightborn had made for themselves. At first the Lightborn had only sought a place to tend their own injured. The longer a Lightborn had been exposed to the Banespell, the worse its effects. More than half the High King's Lightborn had been on the field and now a third of the Warhunt was dead. The Alliance Lightborn had been without sanctuary of any kind. One in four of them had died.

*A third of a half of this. A quarter of that. Distinctions which mean nothing, for we are all subjects of the High King now, if we are subjects of anyone at all.*

"Master Thurion!" A familiar voice hailed him. "Our world turned upside down, and you unchanged: Where is your cloak?"

Thurion blinked, drawn from his reverie, and regarded Denerarth as if he had never seen him before. The Lightborn were children of Landbonds and farmers, and used to hard work; they had no need of servants. And yet, there were a few Lightless who found the bonds of honest love more enduring than the sudden lure of freedom. He'd commended Denerarth into Vieliessar's care when he went as her envoy to the Grand Windsward. From all Thurion had heard since he returned, Denerarth was lucky to be alive.

"I have told you a thousand times and more," Thurion said mildly. "I am not your master. And my name is Thurion." He could not repress a smile as he said it, for the argument was an old one between them.

"And, not-Master Thurion, once again you have left your cloak in the Healing Tents," Denerarth said. "And are like to freeze before you reach your own hearth."

"It is warm here in the Flower Forest," Thurion protested. "And I am always so hot in the Healing Tents."

"Come and have tea," Denerarth said, gesturing toward their pavilion. "And I shall go and fetch your cloak. In my own good time, of course, as I am not a servant. Servants have masters, even now."

Thurion smiled, as he was meant to. "Lord Vieliessar has changed so much already. Don't you think she will change that as well?" he asked.

"Oh, aye, very likely. When the great lords learn how to brew their own tea and cook a griddle cake. I am certain of it," Denerarth said with ponderous irony. He lifted the flap of the pavilion to usher Thurion forward.

Though the pavilion was as large as Vieliessar's own, Thurion would not have kept a lord's great state even if he could. A dozen other Lightborn lived here with him, and as he entered, he saw that most of them were gathered here around the table in the outer room. Aradreleg, raised up as Chief Lightborn when Vieliessar took Oronviel. Iardalaith of Daroldan, born a prince, leader of the Warhunt Mages. Harwing Lightbrother, foremost of Gunedwaen's spies, still bitterly mourning his lover's death. Dinias Lightbrother of the Warhunt, whose Keystone Gift was Transmutation. Isilla Lightsister, whose Keystone Gift was Overshadowing. Rondithiel Lightbrother, who had been first teacher to all of them, expert in Mosirinde's Covenant, who had left the Sanctuary of the Star to join Vieliessar, by his presence in the Warhunt assuring all Lightborn everywhere that the Covenant—the *true* Covenant—would be kept.

Each of them, all of them, close to Vieliessar, who had been Vieliessar Lightsister before she became Vieliessar High King.

"I thought you'd be with her," Thurion said to Aradreleg, seating himself. Dinias poured a cup of tea and passed it to him without waiting for him to ask.

"I have seen enough death," Aradreleg answered, her eyes dark and haunted. "She gave no order that I must go."

*Lady-Abeyant Glorthiachiel's execution was today.* He'd forgotten. *Should I have been there?* But no. The work of the Healing Tents was more important, and something there were few enough to do.

"I think she would've been just as happy if no one was there," Iardalaith said wearily. "Why couldn't the damned woman swear fealty and shut up?"

"You speak of the Hawk of Caerthalien and ask that?" Isilla replied mockingly. "Meditate upon your words and learn wisdom, young one."

"Hatred is as intoxicating a passion as love," Rondithiel said. "I think she could not bear to set it aside."

"I'm glad she's dead," Harwing said flatly. "It was her son Ivrulion—he who must ever style himself Light-Prince lest we forget his rank—who brought us all to this day. Adder and son of adders. We should erase the whole of his blood."

There was a murmur of agreement.

"Huthiel is dead," Thurion said. "Slain by his own

father. Bethamioth died on the field. Only Rondaniel is left, and she is outside the succession because her father was Lightborn. She and all Glorthiachiel's household will be asked to swear, now. If she does, she will live." He knew his words were in some sense, a lie: if Vieliessar lived, so did Heir-Prince Runacar. *No,* he thought. *He is Runacarendalur Caerthalien now. Even if Caerthalien is gone.*

"Our High King is generous," Harwing said bitterly.

"Kings and princes have to be," Iardalaith said gently. "Do you think she did not love Gunedwaen as deeply as you?"

"I think if she had, he would still be alive," Harwing snarled. He pushed himself to his feet and strode from the tent.

"But he isn't and she is," Isilla said into the silence that followed. "And we must all ask: What now?"

"Better we ask a different question," Rondithiel said. "One to which we may be able to deduce an answer."

"What question?" Aradreleg asked in a dull voice.

"What next?" Rondithiel answered.

❖

Ice Moon became Storm Moon.

The last of the dead were washed and anointed and ceremoniously placed upon the field called Ishtilaikh in the only funerary rite that could accommodate so many thousands of dead. The bodies lay side by side for leagues, each stripped of arms and armor, of blazons of rank and emblem of House. Landbond lay beside War Prince, outlaw beside komen. There they would remain until the soil had called them back into itself.

In an ordinary war, a summer war such as the Hundred Houses had fought for thousands of years, the honoring of the dead would be the conclusion of the war, but for Vieliessar High King it was only a beginning. She could not summon the War Princes to swear their fealty to her if she could not promise them safe passage, though the six houses of the Arzhana had found a simple and elegant solution to that need. The War Princes of Sigoric, Adovech, Mallereuf, Gucerich, and Rodiachar had all pledged themselves to House Thadan as her true vassals, and now Shanenilya Thadan rode west with all her court to lay their submission at the High King's feet. But to gain more than endless promises and delay from the surviving Houses of the Uradabhur, Vieliessar must bring peace, for the war she had fought against the Hundred Houses had left the land between the Mystrals and the Bazhrahils starving and leaderless.

The aftermath of that campaign had also been a grim lesson in what would happen if she simply abolished the traditional governance her people had come to expect, yet Vieliessar could not retain the structures against which she had fought for so long—nor would they serve her when she had so many souls to govern. Becoming High King was not the end of her task, but the beginning, and her need was as urgent as it had been since the day she left the Sanctuary for the last time. If she did not have an army—a unified army—to lead against the forces of the Darkness when it came, they would all die.

Each night she sat with her great map, marking off the lands she hoped to hold. In her war and her victory she could now claim more than half of the thirty houses of the Uradabhur, but there were nearly as many she could not. As word of her victory reached them, pleas for aid returned. The refugees of the war-torn domains had fled north seeking aid—and what was not given freely, they tried to take. To each Vieliessar returned the same answer: *Cast down your boundary stones, pledge fealty to me, and I will send you aid.*

But refugees fled also along the track two armies had forged. By the time they reached Celephriandullias-

Tildorangelor, they were injured, sick, starving—and wild with abandonment. Once again Vieliessar must set aside her plans of forging her people into an army—or even a single people—to deal with this new disaster. Somehow, she must find a way to keep the promises she had made to those who had followed her when her cause seemed madness. They'd done so as much out of despair as of hope, for the War Princes had ruled with arrogant cruelty. She must do better. All who came must be fed, clothed, housed—and convinced to live peaceably in Celenthodiel. That was the hardest, for among many of the refugees and the dispossessed the idea had taken root that the coming of the High King meant an endless holiday.

Her first priority was to find a way to rule over her War Princes. She must give them as little cause as possible to unite against her, yet she could not leave them as they were. Her solution was to adapt a common practice among the Craftworkers, and to make of her Lords Komen a new guild: the Guild of the Lords of War. The former War Princes still held positions of rank above those they had once ruled, but now they held them as Guildmasters, and all of them were, by her decree, equal among themselves. Like any guild, the Lords of War had the right to meet in council, choose two of their number to speak for them, and present that council's opinions to the High King.

As Rithdeliel Warlord had predicted, the Princes' Council was still arguing over who would lead it when Vieliessar called her first War Council, which was a very different thing than the Princes' Council of the Lords of War.

For one thing, she actually intended to listen to the advice of her War Council.

※

Telthorelandor, Cirandeiron, Aramenthiali, Nantir-woriel, and Vondaimieriel," Rithdeliel said in disgust, having come to escort her to the first meeting of her War Council and taking this last chance to share his views on those she had chosen to advise her. "The three surviving houses of the Old Alliance, and two of the greatest equivocators among the Twelve. A pretty selection."

"There is no Twelve," Vieliessar said simply. "There is only one."

Rithdeliel waved that aside. "You burden your War Council with those who have lately been your enemies."

"I do not," Vieliessar protested mildly. "There is Annobeunna—"

"Keindostibaent is a Less House of the Uradabhur."

"Iardalaith, Nadalforo, Thurion, Aradreleg, Master Kemmiaret, Caradan, Tunonil—" She ticked the names off on her fingers, while thinking privately no group so large would ever reach consensus. *Just as well they need not. They are a council. I am king.*

"Lightborn and mercenaries and the Commander of the Silver Swords. And Tunonil is *Landbond*."

"I fight wars with infantry and archers. Should I ignore the counsel of their captains? Iardalaith is by birth a prince of Daroldan, so you can hardly object to *him*. Rithdeliel, I have never made any secret of what I would do if I won. I have won. Now I am doing it."

"Yes," Rithdeliel said. "And you would not have won without such vows. I only say you must expect little of this council. It will be too busy fighting with itself to listen."

"Then I shall cover my ears and spend a pleasant morning without anyone asking my opinion on any matter!" Vieliessar said lightly. "Come, old friend. Let us go forth to see if we may marry high and low to our advantage."

✦✦✦

Every thread of the War Pavilion's golden fabric was woven with spells: of silence, of durability, of protection from heat and cold. But most of all, it was bespelled against the use of Magery within it. It was little loss for Vieliessar to surrender the ability to hear the thoughts of her council; far greater was the advantage she gained by showing her War Council it was safe from spellcraft, for if they had learned to use the Lightborn as weapons of war, they had also learned to fear them.

She and Rithdeliel were the last to enter. Though she was dressed plainly, Vieliessar did not disparage her rank: she wore the Vilya-blossoms that should have adorned her hair-combs—had she not cut her hair as a death-offering to Gunedwaen—on a coronet instead. The elvensilver gleamed in the dim light.

No one was seated yet, of course—they could not do so until she arrived. She stopped Rithdeliel before he announced her presence: Gatriadde Mangiralas was speaking and she wished to take the temper of the council before it realized she was here.

"The pasturage here is good," Gatriadde said, "and we have been fortunate. Much of the Mangiralas bloodstock remains intact. There are many young horses ready for training. With the help of the Lightborn, we may bring the mares into season, and in a year or two, by the favor of the Silver Hooves, we may replace all our losses."

Vieliessar was aware of Ivaloriel's attention upon her. She thought, not for the first time, that waging the victory was going to be more difficult than waging the war had been. Even now, she found herself looking for those who would never be here again. Thoromarth. Gunedwaen. So many others. Comrades. Friends.

"So Mangiralas is to be Horsemaster to the High

King," Lord Sedreret sneered. "And clean the stables, too, no doubt."

Gatriadde regarded him mildly. "And of what use will Aramenthiali be?" he asked blandly. "I am eager to hear."

"I am certain Lord Sedreret will wish to lead his meisne in the field," Vieliessar said, stepping forward. There was a flurry as they all turned to face her. She seated herself, and indicated they should do likewise.

The moment they were all seated, Sedreret spoke. "We're going to war?" he demanded eagerly. "Against who? The Windsward, of course! Haldil was ever ready to declare itself lord of all. I can—"

"I send my army north, not east," Vieliessar said quietly.

"Nantirworiel Pass isn't open yet anyway," Methothiel Nantirworiel said, with a sneer in Sedreret's direction.

"To ride to war at all is, perhaps, somewhat hasty," Lord Ivaloriel suggested. "We are barely a fortnight delivered of a victory that is the culmination of moonturns of siege, battle, march. In four moonturns it will be Sword Moon once more. Perhaps then."

"The Uradabhur cannot wait," Vieliessar said. "Nor can the spring planting."

"Planting!" Girelrian Cirandeiron cried. "Are we Farmholders now?"

"Do you want to eat this winter?" Nadalforo asked silkily. "I do. And that means getting the seed into the ground."

"But surely, Lord Vieliessar, there are enough Farmfolk here to feed us," Lord Cirandeiron protested.

"The whole of my people are not here," Vieliessar answered. "Nor do I renounce claim to any of my lands, old or new."

"It's still *winter*!" Sedreret exclaimed, as if he were the only one aware of that fact.

"Seasons change," Tunonil said softly. That he spoke at all among these nobles and princes was a tiny miracle—for Tunonil was Landbond—and Vieliessar cherished it. Nadalforo snorted in agreement, and Isilla Lightsister smirked. The War Princes pretended Tunonil had not spoken. Already Vieliessar could see that her council divided itself between War Princes and those who had been mercenaries, outlaws, Landbond ... Lightborn.

Vieliessar let them bicker for a while, more to learn what they were thinking because she thought any plan might arise. Ivaloriel Telthorelandor was quiet, as she'd expected. Finfemeras Vondaimieriel was loudly confrontational—well, Vondaimieriel had little to lose or gain here, and probably relished the chance to tweak the noses of its former allies and masters. Sedreret Aramenthiali found something to protest in every word spoken. Iardalaith and Thurion said nothing at all.

At last Vieliessar had heard all she wished to.

"My lords, my commanders, my advisors," she said, with a small nod including her Lightborn and commonfolk in the salutation. "You mistake me. I do not wish to hear your thoughts on whether or not I should secure the Uradabhur and make provision for the springtide planting. I have determined that it shall be done. I would hear how you propose to do it."

She expected Iardalaith to speak now, for the Warhunt had functioned as her scouts through the whole of her war, and the first thing any campaign required was information. The Lightborn were the obvious choice to send as envoys to the unpledged War Princes, and yet Iardalaith said nothing—nor did any of the other Lightborn present.

"We must send scouting parties first." It was Lord Ivaloriel who finally stated the obvious. "Komen, of course. A taille or two. With servants, the parties can be kept to fifty at most."

"You'll send one or two of your new Lawspeakers with each, of course," Rithdeliel said.

To bridge the chasm in leadership created by the amalgamation of all the domains into one, Vieliessar had created a new guild. The Lawspeakers' only purpose was to go among the people and remind them of the High King's new decrees: that Landbond were not property, that the Lords Komen had no right of justice that transgressed her law, that the War Princes were subject to her will—and that she would tolerate neither theft nor violence among her folk.

"Yes," Vieliessar agreed. "A taille of knights and a taille of infantry to each party. Tomorrow we shall set a timetable and begin to prepare our campaign," she said. "My Windsward Houses will come to me as soon as the passes open, and their presence will help to restore order. Lord Methothiel, can you say when the Nantirworiel Pass will open?"

"It will be another moonturn at least, Lord Vieliessar," he said. "And you would be well advised to scout it in force; Foxhaven Free Company holds lands there, as you know, nor did it choose to take the field when I came west. It is possible their commander has grown overbold in my absence."

"Captain Voldionas is an old acquaintance of mine," Nadalforo said, smiling wolfishly. She had no need to remind anyone here she had once been captain of a Free Company. "If he holds the pass, I am certain I can make him see reason."

"Let it be so," Vieliessar said. She stood, signaling the end of the council. Servants began furling the walls, turning the pavilion into a canopy: Vieliessar had no intention of permitting a permanent stronghold against Magery to stand in the very center of her encampment.

With her escort behind her—she thought longingly of the long-ago days at the Sanctuary of the Star, when she had answered to no one but the Mistress of Servants—Vieliessar walked back to her own pavilion.

Waging the peace would be very much like waging a war. She knew that already. And for war, she must have Lightborn.

⊰⊱

It was a few candlemarks past sunfall when Vieliessar slipped unnoticed from her pavilion and walked toward the Flower Forest. She wore a long hooded cloak; to make herself appear as one of the many servants who tended the Lords Komen was an illusion that required no Magery, for the lords paid no attention to the commonborn. It was a weakness she intended to turn to her advantage for as long as she could.

*And what then?* she asked herself, and had no answer. To be High King did not mean she was safe against treachery: the peace of victory would last precisely as long as her War Princes refrained from rebellion. Some were loyal to her in their hearts. Some were loyal to the Way of the Sword. Some—like Aramenthiali—were loyal only to themselves, for this was the Game of War the Hundred Houses had played since before Celephriandullias-Tildorangelor had fallen.

Vieliessar played a different game, and in it the War Princes were but one force upon the board. The Lightborn were another, and she meant to know whether they were her allies . . . or not.

⊰⊱

Tildorangelor's living magic enfolded her as she walked down the path which led to the place the Lightborn had made for themselves. The forest glowed with Silverlight, but only enough to banish total darkness. At the edge of the first clearing she stopped, and an instant later, a youth stepped into view. Without the Light, she would not have known he was there at all, for instead of dun cloth or garb of Lightborn green, his tunic and leggings were painted in a dappled pattern of greens and browns. He wore a cloak, but not for warmth: it was a thing of strips and tatters, meant to conceal his shape and to fool the eye even further.

"Mistress," he said quietly. "I think you have lost your way."

Vieliessar pushed her hood back. The youth was not Lightborn, for if he were, he would have sensed the Light within her. A puzzle, and one she hoped Iardalaith might be willing to solve. "I have not," she said. "I come to speak with . . . with my friends. If they will welcome me."

He recognized her then, and his eyes widened. But she had not named herself, so he did not, either. "Come, if you will," he said.

She did not know precisely what she expected to see, but it was not what she found. She saw no servants and no masters. The Lightborn themselves tended to the humble tasks of washing dishes, bringing water, even preparing bread for the ovens. The few grand pavilions clearly had communal uses. There was a fire at the center of the clearing. Hearthfire—homefire—as much as cookfire. A few Lightborn sat around it.

"These here will direct you to your friend," the boy said, gesturing.

"May I know to whom I should give thanks for that?" Vieliessar asked gently. She had no need to ask, for True Speech had brought her his name—Leron— and his thoughts. But she wished to claim what she knew, and even to ask his name directly would be a demand: he knew who she was.

"To no one," Leron said simply, returning up the path as quietly and softly as he'd come.

Vieliessar stepped into the clearing and stopped just outside the radius of the fire's heat. There were about a dozen Lightborn present. They were none she knew, so they must be among the few survivors of the Alliance Lightborn. Ivrulion's Banespell had taken a heavy toll upon their numbers. Suddenly, the thought of coming boldly and demanding Iardalaith, or Aradreleg, or Isilla, or even Thurion seemed as wrong as imposing her will on the Flower Forest itself. She waited silently, thinking again of her years in the Sanctuary of the Star.

"We can see you, you know," one of the women said.

"And so I am seen," Vieliessar agreed mildly. "I come in hopes of having speech with friends."

"Don't you have enough of those back at your fine pavilion?" a boy asked. The bitterness in his voice was surprising, and Vieliessar sensed the others at the fire catch their breaths.

"My truest friends in life lie dead," she answered, with an honesty that shocked even her. "Unless I can claim friends here."

"Sit," the Lightbrother sitting beside the boy said, indicating an empty seat. "There is tea," he added.

"Tea is welcome," Vieliessar answered, accepting a cup. It was not, to her surprise, the usual Forest Hearth blend, but something surprising and complex. A tea-blend worthy of the Sanctuary itself. "Very welcome," she added, drinking more deeply.

A few moments later, Thurion and Iardalaith arrived—summoned, Vieliessar was certain, by young Leron. They looked more puzzled than anything else, as if neither could believe the message until they saw her.

"My—" Iardalaith began, but Vieliessar held up a hand to silence him.

"I come as a friend to speak with friends," she said. "Let my name be Varuthir beneath the trees, and let all use it freely."

"I remember Varuthir well, and fondly," Thurion said with a soft smile. "What would Varuthir have of us?"

"Nothing you would not freely give," she answered.

"And who has ever cared for that?" the boy who had spoken before asked. "Lightborn are the pawns and the tools of the High Houses."

"Miras—" Iardalaith began.

"No!" Miras said. "I say it is true and will always be true."

"True once," Vieliessar said. "But now you are free. The High King has said it."

"So now we are the tools of the High King instead," Miras said harshly.

The look the others turned on Vieliessar was half horror, half speculation, and Vieliessar knew she was to be judged by her words. "No," Vieliessar said. "The Lightborn are free. But I have heard many songs of freedom from the Landbond these past sunturns, and as many complaints of it from the komen, so I say this: freedom does not mean you will be given food and shelter and warm clothing for the asking. Nor does it mean you can steal what you wish. Freedom means justice for all. And work for all."

"And peace?" Thurion asked quietly.

"I hope for that as well, my dear friend, but the road to that seems as long as it ever did," she said with a sigh.

"But there's hope now," Iardalaith said. "Miras, you are still an idiot," he added.

"I don't see the Lords Komen plowing," Miras muttered.

Vieliessar laughed. "I don't see you plowing, either, Miras Lightbrother," she said. "There will be work enough for the Lords Komen in a moonturn or two. The war has been a needful thing. This I will not deny—nor should you, who reap the sweet fruits of the victory. But it has left much damage in its wake, and that must be repaired."

"How can you repair anything with a sword?" another Lightborn asked. "We have seen what comes of trying," he added sadly.

"And for that I grieve," Vieliessar answered. "For the Lightborn have suffered most of all in this. Partly at Ivrulion's hand. Partly at the hands of the War Princes. Partly at mine."

"No!" Iardalaith's answer was quick. "You saved us."

"And swore an end to lord and to Landbond," Thurion said, as if she needed reminding. "Though I do not see how it is to be accomplished."

"To end the Landbond takes only a decree," Vieliessar said. "To end the habit of treating people as if they are of less worth than a sheep or a dog will take longer. And I hope many of the once-Landbond will become Farmfolk, or indeed we shall all starve," she finished with a smile. "It is as I have said."

She could sense the crowd that had gathered in the shadows beyond the fire. All of them come to hear her. And many of them come to see her for the first time.

"As Varuthir has said, or as Vieliessar has said?" Miras asked cagily.

"Both," Vieliessar answered. "If Varuthir may speak, then Vieliessar's pledge is redeemed."

There was quiet and appreciative laughter at that, for the Lightborn valued wit and a clever turn of phrase. "But you have come seeking your friends," a Lightbrother said. "And morning comes early, even in winter. We should leave you to your talk."

Vieliessar glanced up at Iardalaith. "I will speak here before all, if you choose."

"Yes," Iardalaith said with a sigh, lowering himself to the ground beside her at last. As if that were some signal, Thurion sat as well. "We would all hear your words. And I confess, to speak here will save me the trouble of repeating them a hundred times for every ear," he added, looking around at the others.

"Then that is well, and I will begin. But first I will wonder: Why it is the Lightborn live apart? It cannot be that they have cause for fear."

"We don't fear," Isilla Lightsister said, stepping into the circle of firelight. "They do. The—The *Lightless*. They have seen what Ivrulion Oathbreaker did. And they think we will do with them as we please."

Mosirinde's Covenant was the instrument that had kept the Lightborn from engaging in war until Vieliessar had come. But it was not the true Covenant that had done that, only the vast web of custom that had grown up around it. The Covenant itself only limited and prescribed the sources from which a Lightborn might draw power. The War Princes' interpretation of it had added a thousand other proscriptions, all meant to keep the Lightborn in servitude.

"They think the Lightborn will use their power as the komen use their swords," Vieliessar said, nodding. "It is true that it can be done, for what can heal can also harm. Nor are any of the Lightless safe from Overshadowing," she added, and Isilla bowed her head in acknowledgment of her own Keystone Gift. "But I say—the High King says—it is not to be," Vieliessar added. "The Lightborn will use their Light to defend themselves, as the komen might use their battle-skill. But no other, and no more. And the Covenant remains unbroken, now and forever."

Silence greeted her words.

"They look at us and see Ivrulion," Isilla repeated at last. "And so do we," she added sorrowfully. This time there was a murmur of agreement from the gathered spectators, soft and sad.

"For that I have no remedy," Vieliessar answered quietly. "And for that I grieve."

There was silence again for a few moments. The fire hissed and popped, throwing out bright sparks. As the night darkened, the Silverlight became brighter, until it was a thousand tiny moons hung among the trees.

"That you ask if we are well is a comfort," Iardalaith said at last. "That you come to remind us we are free is good as well. If we are free . . . We have only shame for our enemy, not fear. But you came for more than this."

"I did," Vieliessar agreed. "The High King sends scouts to bring peace to the Uradabhur. It would be good if Lightborn rode with them." Even now she spoke no words that could be construed as orders, for the High King's lightest whim, she knew, held the force of law to those beneath her.

At that Iardalaith laughed, sounding startled. "To heat their water and gentle their horses?" he asked.

"To heal their wounds," Vieliessar corrected. "To go as envoys who will not be struck down—"

("We hope," Isilla muttered.)

"—and to go secretly before my komen, bringing word and warning, so there will be as little fighting as possible," Vieliessar finished. "The komen may heat their own water over a brazier, if they cannot find a servant who will willingly tend them."

"What Iardalaith is too proud to say," Isilla said into the lengthening silence that followed, "is that we can do few of those things the Lords Komen are accustomed to ask of their Lightborn, even were we ordered at swordspoint, save perhaps act as envoy. The Flower Forests of the Uradabhur are drained. They have no more to give."

This was something Vieliessar had not considered, though she knew better than most the cost of the disastrous flight through the Uradabhur. The High King's War had been a war of spells as much as of steel, and the Flower Forests had suffered. Only Tildorangelor remained a wellspring of power, safe behind its enchanted boundary stones.

"There is a way," Thurion said. "The Flower Forests of the southern Uradabhur are drained, it is true. But we went only as far east as Niothramangh, and while it is true that most of the Domains of the Uradabhur lie in a line, all do not. The eastern and northern domains will still have Light to draw upon. If their boundary stones are removed, it will be available to any of us."

The boundary stones that marked the borders of each domain were bespelled to prevent just such a thing from happening, for otherwise a battle in War Season would drain the Light from domains hundreds of leagues distant.

"I can only order it done in such lands where the High King's orders will be obeyed," Vieliessar pointed out. "It is a good thought, but how is it to be done?"

"By Lightborn," Isilla Lightsister said. "A touch will Dispell them, and no Lightless will know. There are Lightborn still in those domains. They will do it, I think—if we can promise we will leave them enough Light for their needs."

"I will hope we need none at all," Vieliessar answered honestly. "Certainly not to Heal a battlefield of wounded. But if it were done, it would be useful."

"'If' it were done," Miras said. "Is the High King not to order it done?"

"How should that be," Vieliessar answered, "when the Lightborn who must perform this task serve Houses which have not yet sworn fealty? The High King may ask. Just as she can ask for Lightborn to travel with the scouting parties that must go. But I will not order."

"And yet, all here have sworn fealty to the High King," Iardalaith said.

"True enough," Vieliessar said. "But I know as well as any of you that the Light is more than a sword and a shield. It is our breath, our heartbeat. I will permit neither bodies nor spirits to be enslaved. Landbond and Lightborn are free."

"And the great lords will have to heat their own bathwater," Miras said mockingly. No one rebuked him.

"I will see if there are any who are willing, and bring their names to the High King as soon as I may," Iardalaith said. He got to his feet and held out his hand to her. Vieliessar took it, and as she stood, Thurion did also. "And now, permit me to conduct you to your pavilion—though I am certain it will be many candle-marks before you sleep."

It was a graceful dismissal, and Vieliessar accepted it. She folded her cloak more firmly about her as Iardalaith summoned a wisp of Silverlight to guide them, and the three of them left the Lightborn encampment.

"There is a matter you did not wish to speak of be-fore the others," Vieliessar observed, when they had gone about half the distance. "Will you speak of it now, to Varuthir?"

Even now Iardalaith hesitated a moment before he spoke. "You know that Daroldan and Amrolion are domains of close kinship, for between them they hold the Western Shore against the Beastlings. I Farspeak Bel-frimrond Lightbrother at my cousin's court as often as I may."

"As would I, did I have distant kin," Vieliessar an-swered, wondering why Iardalaith—born a prince of Daroldan—was speaking of things they both already knew.

"The Beastlings seem to know the Domains of the Western Shore cannot call upon the Houses of the West for aid," Iardalaith said, sounding troubled. "In fact, I am not certain there is a taille of komen left any-where in the West just now, and if there were, they would be our enemies until they had received word of their liege-lords. But Amrolion and Daroldan must have aid, and it has never been a contravention of the Covenant to use Magery against the Beastlings. Leo-pheine Amrolion sent Princess Ciadorre to ask for help in the only place from which they might obtain it."

"The Sanctuary of the Star," Thurion said.

"Ulvearth Lightsister rode with her," Iardalaith said. "Ulvearth Farspoke Handiniel Lightbrother of Amrolion a sennight ago to say that they would reach the Sanctuary the next day. But there has been no word since."

*Nor will there be tribute caravans this Wheelturn, bringing tithes and Candidates to the Sanctuary of the Star. At least they have Rosemoss Farm to feed those who remain there,* Vieliessar thought.

"Even if the Astromancer delayed receiving them, Ulvearth should have sent to say so," Vieliessar said, understanding now why he was so troubled. "I know of no Warding that can block Farspeech."

"Nor do I," Iardalaith said grimly. "Whether Ciadorre succeeded, or failed, or was simply delayed, Ulvearth should have sent word to Amrolion, and Daroldan would have heard it soon after."

"If she could," Vieliessar said. Warding could not block Farspeech, but at the very least, Farspeech required time and quiet. "Let me think," she said. It was an admission of vulnerability, but she trusted Iardalaith and Thurion as she trusted no one else, even Rithdeliel.

They waited in silence, as still as the trees of the forest. Vieliessar felt herself once more visualizing what must be done as if this were a xaique-board in midgame. History taught that to hold the West, one must hold the Western Shore. She could not retake the West if she had to fight the Beastlings to do it. Nor did she dare leave Hamphuliadiel to his own devices. The Vilya had fruited several seasons before, signaling the change of Astromancers, yet Hamphuliadiel had bespelled the Vilya in the Sanctuary garden so it would not fruit and used that as a pretext to retain his power. He was her implacable enemy, and there was no custom to make the Astromancer swear fealty to a High King—indeed, during their reigns, the Astromancers' fealty even to their own Houses was in abeyance. So long as he was Astromancer, Hamphuliadiel owed no fealty to

Less House Haldil. Or to her. Or to anyone or anything but his own ambitions. And she was no longer certain what those were.

"We must know why," she said at last, opening her eyes. "We must know not merely Ciadorre's fate, but what Hamphuliadiel has done—or not done. And I must keep my promise to those who have sworn fealty to me."

"You can't get an army through the Dragon's Gate in Rain Moon," Iardalaith said. "Not this year. The winter was hard. And . . . I would not wish to be the one who had to order my army into the field a few sennights after the battle they have just fought," he added reluctantly.

"Nor shall I," Vieliessar said, the plan growing in her mind even as she spoke. "But the Southern Pass Road will be clear by the time you reach it, I think. Thurion?"

"It is far to the south of the Dragon's Gate," Thurion said. "Yes. I think so. Caerthalien would send messengers east this early, and they must have gotten through somehow. And the tribute caravans had to cross into the West by Rain Moon to reach the Sanctuary by Flower. As you know," he said with a small smile, for Vieliessar had spent decades longer at the Sanctuary than any other Postulant.

"Then there is a way to reach the Shore," she said decisively. "Iardalaith, you must send such Lightborn as you think best into the West. Bring aid to the Western Shore, and find what you can about Hamphuliadiel's plans. I ask only that you yourself remain here, for I shall need your counsel in the days ahead. But I leave this campaign in your hands."

"It will be another sennight before we can strike the Healing Tents," Thurion said. He turned to Iardalaith. "Send them after that."

"As if I could send them tomorrow even if I chose!" Iardalaith said, relief plain in his voice. "But in a fortnight . . . that can be done." He met Vieliessar's gaze. "I would send two great-tailles of Lightborn. If you intend to move into the Uradabhur at the same time . . . it will not leave many here in Celenthodiel."

Two great-tailles was nearly three hundred people. And the Lightborn injured in the Banespell still required tending. It would leave few indeed for other services.

"To heat bathwater and find lost gloves?" Vieliessar asked lightly. "That time is past. My princes will discover my rule to be harsh, I fear—Lightborn will no longer be ornaments of rank and power."

*An easy promise to make,* Vieliessar reflected. *A harder one to keep.*

⚜

I suppose I am to tell my steward that he is to leave the wine to spoil and the bread to rot?" Sedreret Aramenthiali asked.

The day after she returned from her visit to the Lightborn, Vieliessar gathered her War Council together again, this time to address the matter of the Lightborn. There were many who still resided in the households of their masters, as they always had. And they all, Lord and Lightborn, must be reminded that the Lightborn were now free.

"If you like," Vieliessar answered. "I do not see why it should. The Lightborn wish to eat as much as anyone. They will set those necessary spells as they always have. And you will reward their labor, just as you always have."

"And if another should grant them a richer reward?" Ivaloriel Telthorelandor asked. "A Great Keep cannot be maintained without Magery."

"So it cannot," Vieliessar said. "But you do not ask your Craftworkers to labor without recompense. Nor your Farmfolk. Nor even your castel servants. I say only that you will treat the Lightborn in your service as you treat your vassals."

"As much as if they were great princes—and you have seen to that, with this plan to send half of them away!" Sedreret said. "If my servants do not please me, I can have them flogged. If my komen refuse my orders, I can have them executed. I cannot do either of these things to my Lightborn."

"You can't do it to your servants, now, either," Caradan Master Archer pointed out helpfully. "Not without a Lawgiver's word. Nor can you keep them if they wish to leave."

Only Vieliessar's presence kept Lord Sedreret in his seat. Caradan had spoken only truth: Vieliessar had promised law and justice for all, and it was a promise she intended to keep.

"What an interesting future you plan for us," Sedreret said at last. "My lord *king*."

"Perhaps you will wish to ask Nadalforo for her advice?" Rithdeliel said sweetly. "Somehow she manages to keep order among her people without executions."

"Because we'd kick them out of Stonehorse-as-was if they broke the rules," Nadalforo said cheerfully. "And that meant they'd starve, if they couldn't find another Free Company to take them in. And if they were useless enough, they couldn't. It's simple enough, Lord Sedreret. You pay people, and you take care of them."

Lord Ivaloriel waved a languid hand. "Fascinating as it is to discover that the Lightborn are now to model themselves upon a mercenary company, it begs the question: How are we to do without them?"

"You don't," Annobeunna Keindostibaent said. "You just use them wisely. We are not all High House lords here at this table. Some of us know what it is to have our Lightborn taken from us along with our grain and our cattle." She favored the others with a cold smile. "One survives."

The meeting eventually returned to its purpose—planning the pacification of the Uradabhur—and Vieliessar made sure her words were carried to all in the Princes' Council as well.

*Lightborn are not chattel.*

## CHAPTER FIVE

# RAIN MOON: THE ROAD PAVED WITH SWORDS

*The alfaljodthi were not the first folk of the land, nor shall they be the last. Yet when they came, the same ambition burned in their hearts as had burned there since the stars fell to earth: to be the only folk.*

*— Chronicle of the Nine Races*

Leutric was King-Emperor. From the land beyond the Peaks of Leunechemar to Great Sea Ocean, from Eternal Snow to Eternal Sand, all the folk of the Nine Races agreed: Leutric was King of the Minotaurs, Emperor of all the Otherfolk and of the Brightfolk as well. All had agreed that Leutric should lead them and bring peace to the land and the end of all war.

The trouble was, he couldn't. Not while the Children of Stars had more kings than Leutric had wives and made war as easily as they made more of their accursed kind. It had taken centuries for the Otherfolk to understand that even Pelashia's sacrifice couldn't gain them peace, not while the Children of Stars lived. But now, the war-hunger of the Elves had turned upon their own kind as never before. Now there was a chance.

*The Children of Stars have returned to the city of their shame. We will bind them to the stones of Celephriandullias until the stars they worship grow cold and dark. And, at last, there will be an ending.*

✤

Y ou're brooding again, old bull," Melisha said.
Leutric looked up as Melisha entered the chamber. The living trees reflected the light of the unicorn's coat as if she walked in her own beam of moonlight. Delfierarathadan belonged, as it always had, to the Otherfolk. It did not matter that it was bounded on either side by Elven Lands. The Nine Races had taught the Children of Stars this Flower Forest was entered only at their peril.

He sighed deeply. "I have reason to brood," he said shortly.

"And I thought this war was going so well," Melisha answered. She stopped at the far edge of Leutric's living throne room, for she could approach no nearer: there were certain of the Nine Races that both possessed—and could lose—the elusive quality of purity, and the unicorns, the living embodiment of purity, found the proximity of those that had lost that purity distasteful. It was, Melisha always assured him, nothing personal.

"As you said yourself, the best war is one the enemy doesn't know he's fighting. It looks like that's changed," the Minotaur answered.

"No," Melisha said, taking a cautious step closer, "I don't think so."

"Thousands are dead and *you don't think so*?" Leutric rose to his feet with a growl. His sweeping ivory horns brushed the living canopy overhead, and he lashed his tail in anger.

"I don't deny they're dead," Melisha said, standing her ground.

"I hope not," Leutric snarled. "Spellmother Frause spiritwalked to see. The whole of the Southern Flower Forest is dust—along with every creature in it who could not flee."

Many of the Nine Races—Bearwards, Centaurs, Gryphons; those creatures whose bodies were flesh and fur and feather—could roam as they chose. Others—fairies, pixies, many of the Dryads—were bound to the places they were born.

"I am sorry," Melisha said, bowing her head so that her long spiral horn was parallel to the ground. "It is a terrible thing to lose so many of the Brightfolk. But I, too, have my sources. I say it was not as you believe."

"Then give me your wise counsel, windrunner. Tell me it didn't happen at all. Let us laugh together at my foolishness."

Leutric flung himself into his seat again. Though it creaked alarmingly, it was living wood, shaped and tended as it grew. It held.

"Don't sulk," Melisha said with a sigh. "Not with so many dead. Yes, against all the teachings of Mosirinde Truefriend, the Children of Stars drained the Flower Forest to dust. But not because of us. I don't think they even knew we were there."

"Cold comfort so far," Leutric said darkly.

"True," Melisha agreed. "But it was drained when they fought the great battle they have been galloping toward for even longer than they know, because to win it, one of their Lightborn used the Forbidden Magery. His side lost, you'll be pleased to know."

"Better if both sides lost," Leutric muttered. "Then they'd all be dead."

"And the Darkness would come for us at first instead of at last," Melisha said. "I've told you before: this plan of yours isn't going to work."

"So you keep saying," Leutric said. "And I say I am King-Emperor. War for them is hope for us. The only hope we have. We will drive them east until we drive them into the Sea of Storms and drown them there. It's what our ancestors should have done."

Melisha's sides heaved with the force of her exasperated sigh. "And when the Darkness flies forth on the Red Harvest?"

"They won't," Leutric said uneasily.

"Oh, yes they will, old bull," Melisha said sharply. "Count on it. How many of the herd have vanished just in your lifetime?"

"The Darkness hunts," Leutric admitted. "It has always hunted. So what? Hunting is not Harvesting. I might as well go into battle against winter or storm as against the Darkness."

"They do more than hunt, you great idiot," Melisha said, stamping her hoof soundlessly against the thick moss that covered the floor of the living chamber. "They *breed*. Their numbers increase."

"So their numbers increase," Leutric said wearily. "I can't do anything about that, either. But I can do something about the Elves. And I will."

"Just as you say," Melisha said long-sufferingly. "And doubtless the Darkness will thank you for doing so much of its work for it—and for denying us our only hope of survival."

"You speak yet again of the Bones of the Earth," Leutric said. "And I tell you this: I shall not give up that secret until the last of the Children of Stars is dead."

"At which point there will be little use in giving it up at all," Melisha answered. "There's clearly no use trying to talk to you. Call me when you come to your senses."

With a bound, the unicorn was away.

❧

D o what you can," Vieliessar said to Lawspeaker Commander Gollor, upon hearing the latest tales of drunkenness, fighting, and theft among the refugees she had barely begun to govern.

If she held open court every day to hear the complaints her people had of her and of each other, Vieliessar would have no time to do anything else, but to hear the words of her Lawspeakers was crucial, for the High King's justice could not be meted out fairly if she did not know what was happening. While her War Princes kept her peace and ruled over the komen, and her Lightborn ruled themselves, the refugees that flooded Celephriandullias-Tildorangelor were not bound to answer to any of her lords and Lightborn: she must rule them directly through her Lawspeakers. Most of the new guild had come from the survivors of her army, and though their numbers grew daily, they were still too few to keep the peace—and at the same time, too many for Vieliessar to take the report of each one directly. Fortunately, the Lawspeakers had organized themselves into tailles: each taille's captain collected the reports of their people, and every grand-taille had a commander who did little more than collect the reports from the others and bring them to her. Each sunturn, before she and her private council began the work of the day, she heard from one of them, but the system was unwieldy and becoming more so with each passing sennight.

*Soon I shall have to ask them to choose a grand commander to take the reports of the commanders so I may hear them in a timely fashion, and then I shall be lost, for words that must pass through so many throats to reach me will retain little of meaning or sense.*

"My lord king," Gollor said unhappily, bowing her head. "I know not what that might be. We cannot immure them, as you know, for there is no place. We cannot fine them, for they have nothing. Beating . . ." she shrugged. "What Landbond does not know what it is to be beaten? It means nothing." Gollor had been born Landbond. She knew what she was talking about.

*And to let them do as they will serves no one, for if I cannot assure the safety of my folk in my own lands, how can I expect them to believe I can give them a land at peace?*

This was not a new problem. She thought for a moment before she spoke.

"If they will not work and will not keep the peace, take them through the Fireheart Pass and set them upon Ifjalasairaet," Vieliessar said. "I will set guards in the pass so they may not return. Those who will not keep my law shall have none of the sweets of it."

"I will see that this is spoken to all, my lord," Gollor said, looking more cheerful. She bowed again, more deeply, and walked from the pavilion.

"They'll only sneak back in," Rithdeliel said, from the corner where he sat nearest the brazier. "Or turn to banditry."

"At least we can hang bandits," Atholfol said. As he spoke, he rubbed his arm in an absent gesture—partly to reassure himself of its presence, Vieliessar knew, for the Healing that had restored his severed limb had left him abed for more than a fortnight.

"If they can find anything outside Celenthodiel to steal within a hundred—no, a *thousand*—leagues, I shall be much astonished," Vieliessar answered. "My lords, I never said I meant to simply turn the world upside down so that those who once worked could spend their days in idleness. Come to that, even the great lords work."

"So we do," Rithdeliel agreed. "But we also enjoy the privileges that go with being great lords. When was the last time you spent a day hunting? You work harder than a castellan's least-favorite clerk."

The simile made Vieliessar smile. "I hate to disappoint you, my lord Warlord, but I never learned a taste for hunting. Where is the sport in it, if a spell can bring the quarry to the spear?"

"You know," Atholfol said meditatively, "you were a

lot more cheerful when you were only prince of Oronviel and likely to be dead before the seasons changed."

"The higher up the mountain you go, the more you
can see," Thurion said, not looking up from his scroll.
"I am certain my lord High King much preferred being
in the forest."

Vieliessar shot him an irritated look.

"It's true," Thurion said blandly. "You always told me
peace was harder than war. And we both know that unlearning habits is harder still."

"You're an exception, of course?" Nadalforo teased.

"I'm a Sanctuary Mage who was born Landbond,"
Thurion answered simply. "I know as much about
learning and unlearning as you do, Nadalforo."

Nadalforo smiled brightly, acknowledging the hit.
She had been a mercenary commander, and then a
bandit leader, before pledging fealty to Vieliessar. But
before either of those things, she'd been a Farmholder's daughter.

"Your noble Warlord is right, though," Nadalforo
said, nodding in Rithdeliel's direction. "You sit in this
pavilion from sunrise to sunfall and beyond, and when
you leave it, it's only to work somewhere else. Why not
do something fun for a change? If your *king-domain*
collapses about you in the next few candlemarks, at
least you'll know it needs work."

Behind her left shoulder, Vieliessar heard a sound that
might have been a smothered laugh, but was certainly
well disguised as a throat-clearing. She did not need to
look to see that the face of the armored woman would
be impassive. Helecanth's always was.

She was not certain what whim of madness had possessed her to name Lady Helecanth of Caerthalien the
chief of her personal guard. Caerthalien was erased, and
there were other and easier ways of showing favor to
its surviving Lords Komen. She refused to admit the
possibility she'd done it because Helecanth had been

ordered—by Runacarendalur Caerthalien himself—to remain and serve the new High King when the Alliance had lost.

*Certainly that is no good reason,* she told herself sternly. *It is merely that Helecanth is good at her job. And to show favor to the relicts of Caerthalien costs me nothing.*

"Fun," Vieliessar repeated darkly. "Very well, my lords, advisors, councillors—and captains," she said, to include Helecanth. "What *fun* shall I beguile these hours of nonexistent leisure with?"

"That's an easy riddle," Helecanth said, before anyone else could speak. "Go up and explore the keep upon the rock, as you have been meaning to for a moonturn. If Thurion Lightbrother and I can't protect you there, you were probably cursed to die anyway."

⊰⊱

In the end, they all went: Atholfol, Rithdeliel, Nadalforo, Thurion, Helecanth, and Vieliessar.

At the center of the overgrown gardens and clogged fountains of the Grand Plaza which now held Vieliessar's combined armies, there was a great spire of stone. A staircase wound around this spire, and—were one to borrow the eyes of a falcon—one could see that the top of the spire was flat, larger than ten Great Keeps, and covered with trees and buildings. Vieliessar had been promising herself the chance to go and see since the moment she first drank from the Unicorn Fountain.

And now she was. But not alone. *I fear it is my* hradan *never to do anything alone again.*

The staircase that led to the top of the spire seemed a delicate thing from a distance. It was only when one approached that one saw that it was as wide as the whole frontage of Caerthalien castel. She could not imagine how her ancestors had accomplished such a great work, and said so.

"It could be done," Thurion said thoughtfully, inspecting the staircase. "With all of Tildorangelor to draw upon, one might shape rock in this wise. The Alliance did much the same to the Dragon's Gate when it rode after us."

"And drained nearly all the Flower Forests of the West to sleeping," Helecanth said unexpectedly. Vieliessar glanced at her, and Helecanth shrugged minutely. She made no secret of her former loyalties, but rarely spoke of what she had seen and heard among the leaders of the Grand Alliance. "Aramenthiali's mother had the notion—and she'd know, of course—and the Twelve agreed on it. So outriders took down the boundary stones of the domains as we crossed them. Cirandeiron's still stand, but no others along our line of march."

"That will save me the trouble of removing them myself," Vieliessar said simply.

⊰⊱

It was a candlemark and a little more of walking before the six of them stood at the top of a staircase facing an immense open space laid with worked stone like the Great Hall of a War Prince's castel, but open to wind and sky. At the far end of it was an open archway set into a stone wall, carved and pierced as if it were a wooden latticework in some fine lady's chamber. The same upstart vines that had found purchase on the rough surface of the spire were wound over and around the stone, setting new leaves with the coming of spring. Such a wall couldn't be for defense, and Vieliessar could see no sign there had ever been any barrier closing off that archway.

"These folk had no enemies," Helecanth said flatly, coming to stand once again at Vieliessar's shoulder.

*She is right.* For the first time in many moonturns, Vieliessar thought of the Ghostlords, the folk of Amretheon's court whose lives she had relived in dreams as the Prophecy taught her all she must know to become Amretheon's successor. The ancient dreams that had taught Vieliessar the words for "city" and "infantry" had never showed her this; she didn't have true names for any of the things she saw. She walked to the edge of the low wall that bounded the open space and peered over the edge.

"If you mean to throw yourself over the edge, I could have saved myself the trouble of following you here and be safe and warm in Ivrithir Keep," Atholfol said.

"And taxed to annihilation by the High Houses," Vieliessar answered lightly. She looked to her right; below her she could see the top of the curtain wall, the plain beyond, and the forest beyond that. And beyond the dark green of the winter forest, a sea of grey stretched into the distance: the Flower Forest Ivrulion had killed.

"Perhaps the city was sworn to peace, as the Sanctuary is," Thurion said slowly. He walked past them to stand in the center of the vast open space.

She shivered and turned away from the sight of the Ghostwood. "Let us go on," she said, and walked through the archway.

❧

Even in its death and disarray, the city was beautiful. Anything made of wood had rotted away to dust, but the walls that endured were covered with the twining canes of climbing roses and thick hardy branches of ancient ivy. The utter strangeness of it reduced all of them to silence—and, perhaps, to fear.

"We should turn back," Rithdeliel said roughly. "You've seen it now."

"No," Vieliessar answered. "Not yet. There's something . . ." *There is something I must learn from this place. It is why I have come.* She reached out to place her hand, palm flat, against the nearest wall.

"Thurion," she said. "Come here."

He joined her, frowning in puzzlement, and placed his hand beside hers.

"It cannot be . . ." he whispered.

"What?" Atholfol's question was sharp with tension.

Thurion lifted his hand away and turned. "All things crafted by the Light retain an echo of their making, even if the Light has gone. But there is no Magery here. There never was. If their spells of Preservation had failed, with Tildorangelor to call upon I could wake them again, even after so long. But there is nothing."

"No magic?" The impossibility of it was clear in Rithdeliel's voice.

"There never was," Vieliessar answered.

"You cannot build a Great Keep without Magery," Atholfol said flatly.

"And yet this Keep is here," Helecanth said, her voice schooled to evenness.

"And it will be here tomorrow, and a thousand to-morrows hence," Rithdeliel said sharply. "My lord. It is time for us to return."

Vieliessar opened her mouth to protest, then saw Thurion looking at her apprehensively. He nodded fractionally. "We have stayed too long already," he said in a low voice.

She glanced around, seeing the same disquiet on the face of each of her companions. Reluctantly, she turned back the way they had come. Now Nadalforo led them, her strides so long she was nearly running.

*It is this place,* Vieliessar thought as she followed. *It speaks to all of us, and the tale it tells does not make good hearing.* To see this place—even in the disorder of its long-dead bones—was defeat, was loss, was bereavement so great that she could spend her whole life trying and not reckon up its true extent. Amretheon's royal city was a thing the greatest War Prince couldn't conceive of, nor all the Lightborn joined together build.

It was the place her people had come from, symbol of the power they had once had. *And now we crouch in little stone boxes and plot to kill one another and even I couldn't see how pitiable we have become!*

Vieliessar dragged in a deep breath, shocked to find it catching on a sob. What could Darkness do to them that could compare to what they had done to themselves? What did she battle to save her people *for*, when she couldn't imagine them becoming the builders of a city like this even if a hundred thousand lifetimes should pass? *Iardalaith was right,* she thought wearily. *And Gunedwaen, and Thoromarth, and Rithdeliel, and every one of my commanders whom I didn't consult but who would have said the same: seeking out Amretheon's city was madness.*

They reached the Plaza again.

"We should pause here and rest before we begin our descent," Helecanth said collectedly. She held out a waterskin. "Drink, my lord."

Numbly, Vieliessar took the waterskin. Its contents were sharp and bitter; the water had been mixed with tea and vinegar to keep it from going bad.

"I say we burn it," Atholfol said roughly. "Burn the whole place to ash and cinder. Use Lightborn if you will. Komen with torches if you will not."

"No," Vieliessar said steadily. "This was Amretheon's city once. It is mine now." *Because Amretheon chose you. He looked at the future and crafted his Prophecy and you stood before his living face and he said he chose you.* If she despaired here, if she *gave up* . . . Even the memory of her people's ancient glory would be lost forever.

She was weary of fighting. Sick of battle. And her war hadn't even truly begun.

"You cannot mean to *live* here?" Rithdeliel's voice was a mixture of astonishment and despair.

"No," Vieliessar answered sadly. "We . . . We are not

Amretheon's people. Nor will we ever be. That time is ended. But we may learn from what has gone before."

"Then send Loremasters and Storysingers," Rithde- liel said, slinging his waterskin over his shoulder once more. "For I shall never come back here."

"In that one thing, my lord Warlord, we are agreed," Nadalforo said. "And may the Hunt take me swordless do I ever again say that Vieliessar High King should leave her scrolls and her maps!" She turned and began walking toward the steps, her back straight.

"And you, Thurion?" Vieliessar asked. "What do you say?"

"I say now as I have said before," he answered softly. "The road you walk is paved with swords. But where you go, I will follow."

⚜

Shatub crouched at the top of one of the crumbling buildings, his great crimson wings folded tightly about him. The two Elfling Mages had not sensed his presence, and the others were nothing more than blind meat. He lashed his long barbed tail in frustration. *So close!* He growled deep in his throat. Virulan delayed without reason! The time of the Red Harvest had come, when the Endarkened were to fly forth to purify the Bright World once and for all. It had been *promised.* . . .

He bared his long ivory fangs in defiance, even though there was no one to see. Many things had been promised. Beautiful death, beautiful pain, reunion with *He Who Is*.

*But for us as well?*

Shatub was Born. He had come forth from the body of Shurzul, growing inside her as Life grew in the bodies of the Brightworlders. The shame of it was with him in every breath he took. Born. Begotten of a body's meat. Would *He Who Is* embrace such foulness with His black sterile love?

*Only if such love is earned.*

The only coin to buy such love was blood. Blood, pain, death. And still Virulan delayed.

Shatub spread his wings. Virulan was King. The penalty for disobedience was agony and obliteration. He dared not.

*Not yet.*

He sprang into the sky. A moment later he was gone.

⊰⊱

Once, the power of the Deep Earth had been all the Endarkened needed to sustain themselves. Then, the World Without Sun had been pure and perfect. But that was before King Virulan had cast the spell that had changed the Endarkened so utterly. Now the World Without Sun crawled with life. With *food.* Glowing fields of fungus, nests of pale worms and tunneling insects, lightless lakes of eyeless swimming things. The greatest delicacies of all were kept here in these pens: captives stolen from the World Above, destined to live out their brief, agonizing lives as workers and toys before—inevitably—they made their way to the banquet tables.

The slaves had an even more sacred purpose than nourishing the Endarkened's physical forms, though the creatures didn't appreciate it. All magic in the World of Form came at a price. The Endarkened drew their power from death, from blood, and from pain. The Brightworlders were here to provide all three.

Two Endarkened stood upon the walls of the slave pens, watching over the work of their inferior kin; the Lesser Endarkened. When their numbers had increased to the point that magic could no longer take care of their every need, King Virulan had created the slave race to perform all the menial tasks the Endarkened scorned. Unlike those whose image *He Who Is* had shaped, the Lesser Endarkened were not all of one form. Their bodies might be covered with scales or spines or fur; their feet might be clawed or pawed or hoofed; they might have wings and tails and horns . . . or not. The only characteristic they all shared was a dimwitted and absolute loyalty to their Endarkened masters.

"He says to us our great day comes." Shurzul's tone did not—quite—veer to open mockery.

"Do you doubt the King's word?" Gholak swirled the whip at her side in lazy punctuation to her question. In immediate response, the Lesser Endarkened scurried forward, their hunched scaled bodies rasping over one another with the sound of a horde of insects. The inhabitants of the slave pens cringed away with moans and whimpers of fear. Blind in the darkness that was not dark to their captors, they had only their hearing to rely upon.

"No, fools!" Gholak cried, her whip raining blows on gleaming scaled forms and soft Bright World bodies indiscriminately. "I said feed them—not feed *on* them!"

With despondent chittering, the Lesser Endarkened hurried to obey.

"Now," Gholak said, turning back to Shurzul. "You were saying?"

"Nothing," Shurzul muttered, lifting her ribbed scarlet wings high and furling them tightly around her body. "I said nothing."

"But I heard you," Gholak answered, lightly mocking. "I heard you speak of King Virulan's great word." Her barbed tail lashed with barely concealed glee. Torment was sweet, and the Endarkened did not care who suffered it.

"You heard the King's word as well as I," Shurzul said sullenly, allowing her wings to droop. "King Virulan says the day is at hand when we may fly forth openly to make an end to the Brightworlders. He promises such an orgy of blood and pain as we have never known. We shall go forth from Obsidian Mountain to kill and feed until there is nothing left."

"Yes. He has said all this. You and I stood together to hear him." Now Gholak was puzzled, a sensation she did not care for. She sprang lightly to the pen below and snatched up the first creature to come to her hand. The Faun squealed in terror and pain as her talons pierced its tender flesh, bleating out its death agony as she slowly crushed it. When it was dead, she ripped it open and sucked the hot, tender organs from its body before flinging the gutted body aside and returning to the top of the wall. She licked the blood from her claws as the Lesser Endarkened scurried to retrieve the corpse, disjoint its limbs, and add its shredded body to the food they were distributing.

"You might have shared," Shurzul pouted.

"Why should I, when you come to annoy me with riddles?" Gholak answered.

"Hardly a riddle," Shurzul answered. "A question. When we have slain them all . . . what then?"

"Why, then we shall have accomplished the task for which *He Who Is* created us," Gholak said. "And we will stand before Him once more."

"Will we?" Shurzul asked. She gestured, the sweep of her hand taking in the whole of her lush and terrible body. "How many children have you borne, Gholak?"

Gholak frowned. "Why, how should I know? Bad enough I must carry them. What are the Lesser Endarkened for, if not to perform such menial tasks as raising them?"

"You have created life," Shurzul pointed out. "King Virulan has created life in you."

Gholak took a step backward, her fangs bared as she hissed. "Tainted bitch! How dare you?"

"I?" Shurzul laughed outright now. "Was it I who

twisted my form, or yours, from the purity of what *He Who Is* fashioned? Was it I who chose to turn the Twelve into festering cauldrons of creation?"

"Eleven, not twelve. Eleven is not all. It is true that the King's great spell was to fall upon all the Dark Guard equally, but Lord Uralesse escaped through trickery," Gholak added admiringly, for treachery was as prized as power among the Endarkened.

"And the Created and Changed are now ten, not eleven, for Rugashag displeased him," Shurzul said, mocking Gholak's pedantic tone.

"Her dying was long and exquisite," Gholak said happily. "At the end . . . she begged as the Brightworlders beg."

For a moment Shurzul smiled, contemplating that memory. It had proved Virulan was meant to rule them, for his art was great. Then she sobered again. "But the Endarkened are not ten," she said. "Nor are we twelve. We are many. Not formed by *He Who Is* out of the Eternal Void. *Born.* Those we have . . . *created* . . . have created others in turn, and their creations have created more, and—"

"*Stop!*" Gholak barked.

She turned away, motioning for Shurzul to follow her. They walked along the top of the walls until they reached the edge of the pens. Here the rock beneath their feet was solid, the rock above their head only crudely shaped. When the Lesser Endarkened had made this chamber, they had left room to expand it at need. Once Gholak had gloried in that thought as proof the power of the Endarkened would continue to increase. Now, for the first time, it made her uneasy.

"What is this you are saying?" she asked Shurzul, and now her voice was low, too soft for the Lesser Ones to hear.

"I say the killing will be glorious," Shurzul said. "But that the Red Harvest will have an end, as all Bright

World things end. And when we have slain the Lesser
Ones as well, and the Born, only the Created will remain. What then?"

"War," Gholak breathed rapturously. "Glorious war."

"And it, too, will end," Shurzul said mercilessly, "And
what then? What of the victors? What of *us*?"

At last Gholak's eyes widened with comprehension.
She looked down, running her powerful clawed hands
over the jutting breasts, the narrow waist, the swelling
hips Virulan's sorcery had given her. "*He Who Is . . .*"
she breathed.

"Will take us back," Shurzul said quickly. "Will purify us of Bright World taint and make us, once more,
One with the Void. His power is infinite. He can do all
things. But who will ask this boon of Him?"

Gholak's lips writhed back from her teeth. Her long
ivory fangs gleamed in the faint phosphorescence of the
fungus. Virulan would not ask—this much she knew.
Virulan needed no purification. Nor did Uralesse. They
alone of all the Created were as they had been first
formed. Uralesse and Virulan would bathe in the blood
of all Life, destroy all the Lesser Endarkened, destroy
all the Born, and, when their task was done, would become One with the Void once more. Their reward—
and theirs alone, for both Gholak and Shurzul knew
neither of them would ask a boon of *He Who Is*.

The Created-and-Changed would die with the Born.

Unless . . .

"I am loyal to our King," Gholak said quickly. "He
who sits upon the Throne of Night. He who wears the
Crown of Pain." Even to her own ears, her words
sounded hollow.

"As am I," Shurzul answered instantly. "Never would
I court Rugashag's fate. Never would I displease King
Virulan—nor Uralesse, who is first among the Twelve-
that-Were, the Unchanged. And so, when the day of
glory King Virulan has promised comes to us, surely

both of them must be in the vanguard? First to slay. First to kill."

*Or to be slain,* Gholak thought in the most secret part of her mind. She knew the Endarkened could die. Rugashag had only been the first. As the Endarkened had grown more numerous, so had the plots to take the throne and the crown. All had been foiled. The traitors had died. Should Virulan die also, it must seem—*be!*— wholly an accident. A destruction in battle. It could not be arranged quickly.

But it must take place.

The Changed—the *Born*—must make certain that this war went on for a long, long time.

⊰⊱

Elsewhere in the World Without Sun, the King of the Endarkened and Uralesse, his most treacherous vassal, walked in the Garden of Tears.

The air was vibrant with the power of despair, for the Garden of Tears was filled with delicate, unbreakable cages of vitrified spiderwebs. Each cage held a Bright World captive, his or her sanity utterly destroyed by moonturn after moonturn of merciless, expert torture. All that was left to these shattered prisoners was the ability to feel terror and pain. The first, by now, was an eternal companion. The second . . . well, that was up to them. The strands that formed their cages were sharper than the sharpest razor. The victims could neither sit nor lie down; to rest against the sides of their prisons was to be flayed by degrees. Determination and will could have gained them a speedy death, but their wills, along with their minds, were long destroyed. All that was left for them was to recoil, again and again, from the bright agony of the razor sharp strands, to scream and moan in agony. And to weep.

Virulan paused to inhale deeply, relishing the scent of blood and rot. The exhibits in his garden must be refreshed every few days, for fever, exhaustion, and blood loss took their inevitable toll on the Bright-worlders very quickly. But while they suffered, it was glorious.

His garden had a purpose beyond beauty, however, for Virulan had not remained King of the Endarkened by being either weak or trusting. Every one of his sub-jects plotted and schemed to place themselves upon the Throne of Night, as was only right and proper. Virulan cherished their ambition and greed, even as he did every-thing he could to render it fruitless.

Uralesse was . . . a problem. The cleverest of the Dark Guard. Second in power only to Virulan himself, and far too useful to cast aside lightly. And so Virulan showed Uralesse every sign of favor, such as the invita-tion he had tendered upon his Rising for Uralesse to share the pleasure of his garden. In the heady atmo-sphere of the Garden of Tears, one who was unused to its rich bounty could easily become drunk upon that bounty, rendering them . . . overconfident. Perhaps Ura-lesse, intoxicated by Virulan's flowers of mourning, would make a mistake.

"Why do we not go forth at once?" Uralesse asked his King. "You have said the time is upon us. Yet we delay."

"Do you believe we delay?" Virulan asked mildly.

"We. . . . We're still here," Uralesse answered dazedly. His yellow eyes glowed with euphoria. "I mean . . . my King, you said the hour was at hand . . ." Uralesse took a deep breath, clearly attempting to master the sweet blandishment of the agony that filled the air. "I merely beg the indulgence of your wisdom."

Virulan hid his disappointment. There would be no interesting transgressions this Rising, it seemed.

"Why, my dear brother, you must never hesitate to confide your innermost thoughts to me. We have spent unimaginable Bright World years . . . waiting.

Concealing ourselves. Concealing our very existence from the Brightworlders until the moment is ripe. Why not fly forth at once to slake our appetites, eh?"

"There is a good reason, my King," Uralesse answered humbly. "But I do not know it. Only you know it."

"Just so," Virulan said. "And so I ask you: Would it not be an exquisite thing to fall upon the vast tribe of Elflings as they all gathered together? Think of the carnage! Think of the terror of those we allowed to flee the killing ground—and what sport we could have in hunting them down one by one. Think of the glory beneath the Bright World sun of nothing but butchered meat as far as the eye can see. . . ."

"Beautiful, my lord King," Uralesse breathed in ecstasy. "It would truly be . . . the greatest work of art you have yet revealed to us."

"And so it shall be," Virulan said kindly. He paused before one of the cages to prod its occupant with a long talon. The creature screamed in shock, flinging itself forward and backward against the latticework until its skin was a tracery of fresh cuts and welling blood. The Brightworlders could not see anything, of course. The Garden of Tears was lightless, imperceptible save by the senses of the Endarkened. Virulan's touch would have seemed to come from nowhere.

He turned to Uralesse. "Even now they gather together," Virulan said. "And so . . . we await the moment . . . of *perfection*."

## CHAPTER SIX

# RAIN MOON:
# THE MYSTERY OF CHAINS

*A commander is often faced with two bad choices and
no good ones. One gains the victory by concealing that
truth from the enemy.*

— Arilcarion War-Maker, *Of the Sword Road*

I t was Rain Moon. The patter of raindrops was loud
on the fabric of the pavilion, and the warmth of the
stove was welcome. Though the fabric of the scarlet War Pavilion was bespelled to silence, its front was
open to the air so that messengers could easily come
and go, and the sounds of building—even in weather
such as this—could be heard clearly.

As she had vowed, Vieliessar had sent Loremasters
and Storysingers to Amretheon's dead city, but she had
sent stoneworkers and artisans as well, for if she was
to build a city of her own, the best source of materials
was the ruin above. Both the treasures of the ancient
High King's city—those which had survived the passage
of millennia—and its building stones descended that
enormous staircase in an unceasing stream. Here below,
the foundations of a Great Keep and a *city* to replace the
encampment of tents had already been laid. With the
nigh-inexhaustible Light of Celenthodiel Flower Forest, and the quarried stone from Amretheon's city,
Vieliessar High King would be able keep her vow to
have them all beneath roofs before Midwinter came.

In the War Pavilion set beside the fountain in the courtyard that would become the heart of the *city* she envisioned, Vieliessar read the endless dispatches and reports that would let her keep, rule, and expand her domain. The sheer clerkishness of rulership weighed heavily upon her spirit. A War Prince might hold court once a moonturn, and for a full sennight at Harvest and Midwinter, but the High King held court once each sennight and even that was not enough to grant audiences to all those who needed to see her—let alone to grant audiences to those who merely *wanted* to see her.

*If the War Princes truly knew what it was to be High King, they would have left off vying for the Unicorn Throne long since!*

From dawn to midday each sunturn Vieliessar took the reports of her chief counselors and those of her officials with whom she must meet daily, like the commander of the Lawspeakers, while her personal guard (handpicked by Helecanth) kept all others from approaching her and interrupting this vital yet tedious work. Despite all such care and planning, she could not sequester herself from everyone, for that road led to a disaster of another sort than that which would be summoned by failing to rule. Thus, the pavilion which took the place of a Great Hall was well inhabited, if not crowded, while she carried on the business of her king-domain, for her War Counselors had the right, by that appointment, to seek her out at her private court whenever they chose.

Whether—and how—they chose to exercise that right told her as much about their intentions as if she used True Speech to dip into their minds. Both Ivaloriel and Methothiel found many reasons to be present as she read dispatches, took reports, and read transcriptions of Farspeech or spellbird messages—Telthorelandor said he had lived so long that he was eager to see a thing he had not seen; Nantirworiel said he saw no reason to drink his own wine and sit beside his own brazier when he could make use of hers. Aramenthiali and Cirandeiron still held themselves apart, neither attending her privy court nor making excuses for their absence. It took no Foretelling to know there would be trouble from both War Princes eventually, but what lord had ever ruled without rebellion among their vassals?

*I wish I might be the first.*

"Haldil once again declares itself High King," Rithdeliel said into the silence, brandishing a transcription she had not yet had time to read. "Tell me you're surprised."

"I am not," Vieliessar said calmly. "Aradreleg, what of Hallorad?"

"Othrochel Lightbrother of Haldil has sent a spellbird . . ." Aradreleg said reluctantly.

"*Haldil?*" Vieliessar asked in surprise.

"Perhaps Gonceivis Haldil wishes *us* to surrender," Atholfol said.

"It is not a word sent in Lord Gonceivis's name," Aradreleg hedged.

"It came to my hand," Thurion said bluntly. "I was guested at Haldil, as all here know, and I made certain Othrochel could send to me, were matters at Haldil to . . . change."

"They are unlikely to have changed since this morning," Rithdeliel said, waving the scroll in his hand.

"Nor have they," Thurion said calmly. "And so I left the matter in Aradreleg's hands."

"Left me to play Festival goat," Aradreleg muttered, then, louder: "It touches upon the matter of Haldil, Lord Vieliessar," Aradreleg said. "Yet it is hardly a boon within your power to grant."

"Even if it were not Haldil asking," Altholfol said.

"But what does Othrochel Lightbrother *want?*" Vieliessar said, holding firmly to her temper.

"He asks if any of the High King's Lightborn possess

the gift of Prophecy," Aradreleg said. "That he may learn why Hallorad has fallen silent."

There was a silence in the pavilion as all the members of the council contemplated the outlandish request. *Or perhaps he asks merely to discover what Gifts my Lightborn have, for never did a prince or his vassal lords say one thing without meaning three others,* Vieliessar thought.

"Wouldn't a prophecy tell what was going to happen and not what had?" Nadalforo asked.

"Yes—and no," Vieliessar answered gently. "But I am not sure . . ."

"How shall it matter, when no one now here in Celenthodiel has Prophecy as their Keystone Gift," Aradreleg said, frowning. "It is rare, as you know, my lord. Arahir Lightsister possesses it. I know of no other." And Arahir Lightsister was Chief Lightborn of Hallorad.

"Thurion, you know Arahir well enough to Farspeak her," Vieliessar said.

Thurion sighed slightly. "I do. She has not been willing to answer for some time. Hallorad's position is . . . difficult, as you know."

"With Gonceivis closer to them than we are, and even so, not close at all," Vieliessar agreed. "Thurion, do you know why Haldil is so anxious?"

Thurion hesitated. "Othrochel did not wish to give me more information than he must—for as you well know, Haldil is in rebellion against you—but he is worried. Yet I know not why he would ask after a gift of Prophecy to discover Hallorad's condition when some Lightborn of the Windsward Houses might Overshadow a bird of the air . . ."

"And if they did so, they might have Seen Hallorad through its eyes," Vieliessar said, for the benefit of those present who were not Lightborn. "But only if there is someone in the Windsward who has it as their Keystone

Gift, and they are very skilled." Overshadow was a spell widely feared: it could take away its victim's will, forcing them to move and speak and act at the will of the caster. Those skilled in that spell could even see and hear what their subject experienced—but to hold the mind of a beast hundreds of leagues distant was far different from doing it to one of the Lightless.

"So what Othrochel Lightbrother asks of us, his master may already know," Ivaloriel Telthorelandor said.

"If Gonceivis already knows what happened to Hallorad, why is he asking you?" Rithdeliel demanded.

"Perhaps he does not," Vieliessar said. "Or perhaps he seeks confirmation." She got to her feet and crossed the pavilion to the ever-present map table. With the aid of the map-floor in Amretheon's palace, her maps of the east were more detailed than they had ever been. Hallorad was a tiny speck on the banks of Greythunder Glairyrill. There was nothing nearby to account for its sudden silence. *Unless the Beastlings have risen up there, as they have in the West* . . . "Or perhaps he seeks to unsettle me, so that I will leave him and the Windsward alone."

"If he thinks he can unsettle you, he doesn't know you," Atholfol said flatly.

"Even the other Windsward houses have heard nothing from Hallorad since the end of Midwinter Festival," Aradreleg said with a sigh. "It may be that Hallorad wishes to hold itself apart from political entanglement until the matter has been decided by others, but there is no way for us to know. None of us can Farspeak Hallorad directly, for none of the Lightborn who remain with you know any of Hallorad's people. It is hard to Farspeak someone you do not know."

"Hard," Vieliessar knew, meant "all but impossible." Farspeech relied on both Light and personal knowledge: Lightborn could only Farspeak easily with other

Lightborn they knew. "If they cannot be Farspoken, then send a spellbird to Hallorad's Chief Lightborn, saying I would have Paramarth Hallorad come to pledge fealty to me," she answered.

"It shall be done, my lord," Aradreleg said.

"And to Haldil?" Rithdeliel asked.

"Aradreleg, I would have you see if there is anyone here—aside from Thurion—who can Farspeak Othrochel Lightbrother or any other of Haldil. If not, he, too, shall receive a spellbird; bid him to say to War Prince Gonceivis he may rule what he withholds from me until next War Season. Say that after that, I shall come and take it. But do not say these things yet," Vieliessar added. "Let my loyal vassals cross the Feinolons first."

"Haldil will grow bold, shown such forbearance," Rithdeliel pointed out.

"Then Haldil will grow bold," Vieliessar said. She tapped the map of the Uradabhur on the table before her. The borders had been erased between those domains whose fealty she held, but that did not mean those lands were yet at peace. "I cannot be everywhere," she said in frustration. "I will not move east until the Uradabhur and the West are both secure."

"You won't achieve that by this War Season, or even the next," Master Kemmiaret of the Silver Swords said. He nodded toward the map whose edge protruded from beneath the one showing the Uradabhur. "The West may well be in the same state as the Uradabhur. And it has had longer to fall into disarray."

"Because all its War Princes and their meisnes are here—except of course, for War Prince Hamphuliadiel Astromancer—and most of their chattels are not," War Prince Annobeunna said.

Vieliessar made a face, though there was as much truth as mockery in that naming. "Aradreleg—" she began.

"From the West, nothing," Aradreleg answered instantly. "Only the Western Shore answers when we call."

*And that should not be,* Vieliessar knew. *Momioni-arch Lightsister still serves at the Sanctuary of the Star. She has taught nearly as many Lightborn as Rondithiel has. All the Lightborn know her. If she hears when we call—and she must—why does she not answer?*

"Then we must await word from the Lightborn Iardalaith has sent," Vieliessar said. "Rondithiel says another moonturn will see him at the Southern Pass. And as he must cross the West to relieve Amrolion and Daroldan, at least I will have fresh news of it."

"My lord King, I know you tire of hearing these words of me," Ivaloriel said, "but I must say them again: my counsel is that you leave Celenthodiel. The Fireheart Pass can be held with a great-taille at most. In the Uradabhur you would be better placed to move west when the time comes. And the Uradabhur itself could be pacified more quickly if you were there in person."

"Your words are wise, Lord Ivaloriel, and I will never tire of hearing wisdom," Vieliessar answered promptly. "But I ask you this: What moonturn is it now?"

"Rain Moon, of course," Ivaloriel answered.

"And when do the Farmfolk plant their first crops?" she asked.

"As early as Storm Moon, if the weather softens early." It was Nadalforo who answered this time. "It is milder here in the Vale of Celenthodiel than it is to the north; the Farmfolk who have come to us have been clearing land and planting for sennights already."

"And if they are here, they are not in the Uradabhur," Ivaloriel said, but Vieliessar knew he did not fully understand even yet.

"They will hardly return to the Uradabhur until we have set it at peace," she said. "But even were I to accomplish that in this instant, my lord, they would find there no seed grain to plant."

"Not in the south, at any rate," Rithdeliel answered. "What we didn't take, brigands will have. And brigands won't have saved it for planting."

"There won't be a crop this year," Nadalforo said. "Not in most of the Uradabhur. In the northern foothills—perhaps."

"Nor can the Windsward supply the lack," Thurion said, "for your loyal houses ride Westward. And west of the Mystrals . . . there is silence."

"Do not look to Nantirworiel to replenish your granaries," Methothiel said. "Our fields and orchards are few. *Were* few. I know not what is there now, but I took tithe in grain for good reason." Nantirworiel's wealth had been in gems, precious metals, and furs; it had been one of the few domains to regularly import food.

"As you say, Lord Methothiel. And one cannot eat gems, or gold, or elvensilver, which speaks to my point. Ten domains out of thirty *may*," Vieliessar said, gesturing at her map, "and only *may* be able to plant and harvest this year. In the West, I know not. We did burn most of it," she added with an air of faint apology. "My lords, I must hold Celenthodiel—and farm it. If I do not, as many will starve in the winter to come as have died already."

"It is a new sort of war you wage," Ivaloriel said quietly.

"Oh, we fought across farmland often enough," Rithdeliel said. "But never across all of it at once."

*And if the outcome of your sport meant hunger and want for the least of your people, you never knew it in your Great Keeps.* It was unfair of her, Vieliessar supposed, to think so harshly of Rithdeliel. A Warlord could not choose whether to fight, only how to fight. He had served Caerthalien, Farcarinon, Oronviel, and Farcarinon again as a loyal vassal, but he had never known the folk sent into outlawry or starvation by his summer wars as she did. To the lords and princes, they were invisible. Obstacles on a battle map at most.

"And now we all learn what the Farmholders and the Landbonds have always known," Vieliessar said. "All we have and all we are rests upon the back of the plowman at seed-time."

Ivaloriel shrugged in acceptance. "Then here we remain," he said. "But I tell you this: I do not look forward to another winter spent in a tent."

"No more do I," Vieliessar said. "But it is many sennights until winter comes again. Before it does, perhaps I will have a better answer for you."

"Perhaps you will know how matters stand west of the Mystrals," Ivaloriel answered. And that was no answer at all.

⧓

Soon enough the rest of her council departed to their own work, for no matter what the degree one had been born to, there were more tasks here in the Vale of Celenthodiel than there were hands to accomplish them. Of course, Helecanth's place was always at her side, but when Thurion lingered behind the other councillors, Vieliessar knew what was to come. She did not give him the chance to begin his argument.

"I am not wasting time and resources on an Enthroning," Vieliessar said flatly.

"Don't then," Helecanth said agreeably.

"You must," Thurion said, nearly in the same breath.

Vieliessar bit back her irritated response with an effort. Helecanth did not often add her voice to the discussions that went on in her presence, though Vieliessar had said many times that she would welcome her counsel. If Helecanth spoke out now, no matter how frivolously, it was a warning to Vieliessar that she must give serious attention to what was about to be said.

"I am already High King," she said needlessly.

"In name," Thurion said. "And by right of vassalage over sixty of the Hundred Houses. Sixty is not all."

"I can count," Vieliessar grumbled. "And the rest will come as soon as it is safe for them to travel."

"Save of course for the nine Houses of the Windsward Kingdom, so called," Helecanth commented.

"*Gonceivis* is having an Enthroning," Thurion said in exasperation.

"And I suppose if Gonceivis flung himself from the highest tower of Haldil, I should do the same," Vieliessar said under her breath. She got to her feet and stepped away from the map table, presenting her back to both of them.

"If you wished to rule the Windsward, perhaps," Helecanth said from behind her. "Many are still unsettled by your new ways—"

"That's putting it mildly," Thurion muttered.

"—and wonder if you mean to hold what you have taken, and build a world for their children and great-children to live in," Helecanth finished implacably.

*You mean, they want me to marry.* Vieliessar did not speak the words aloud. It was only to be expected. She had won her throne by force of arms, not force of argument. Most of the nobles hadn't read *The Song of Amretheon.* Those who had did not necessarily believe in the Prophecy. *And even those who do believe in the Prophecy do not understand it,* Vieliessar thought forlornly. *Including me.*

She turned back. Thurion and Helecanth were regarding her with identical expressions of determined concern.

"Say what you will say," she said quietly.

"Show them what they wish to see. What they expect to see. And then you can do with the princes and the Lords Komen as you wish," Helecanth said. "An En-

throning, the foundation of the High King's House . . .
What you intend does not matter, for they will make
their own stories from what they see. Show them a
prophetess with a sword instead of an enthroned King,
and I say this: it does not take Lightborn Magery to
foresee a realm in flames and ashes before the next
snows."

"It will make things easier, my lord King," Thurion
said gently.

"It is a waste of time and resources I could put to better use!" Vieliessar cried in exasperation. She walked
back to the map table and seated herself again. "I am
not making the right choices," she added quietly. "I
must discover what they are."

These were words she would not dare to say even
among the trusted members of her Council. But Thurion was her friend. And Helecanth . . .

She trusted Helecanth, whose loyalty to her was as
unswerving as had been her loyalty to Runacarendalur.
And if, as Vieliessar suspected, Helecanth's heart still belonged to her former liege, then she was Vieliessar's
twice over, for Vieliessar held Runacarendalur's life in
her unwilling hands.

"You will not discover the nature of the Darkness
upon a battlefield," Thurion said. "Nor discover how
to fight it."

"I know," Vieliessar said wearily. "Bring peace to the
Uradabhur and the Arzhana this Wheelturn. Cross the
Mystrals next spring and see if there is anything left in
the West to salvage—and hope Rondithiel and the
Lightborn with him can hold the Western Shore until I
can reach it. Were there a thousand candlemarks in each
sunturn there would not be time enough for me to do
all that I must do. And none of it matters if I am not
ready to face my true enemy."

"Rondithiel should reach Amrolion by Sword Moon.

And then you will have fresh news of the West," Thurion said.

"What I should like is fresh news of the Sanctuary," Vieliessar said tartly. "But you shall have what all have asked, for I know you have both nagged me at Rithdeliel's urging. There shall be an Enthroning of the High King at Harvest Court."

She glanced at the object that stood in the far corner of the pavilion. It had been brought here from Amretheon's palace so that all who came to see the High King would see also the object for which ten thousand years of war had been fought.

The Unicorn Throne.

It was as stark and simple as a building block meant for the wall of a Great Keep: a cube of some unknown white stone, its backrest the width and depth of the seat. The stone's surface had the faint roughness of the skin of a ripe peach, and even in shadow it sparkled like fresh-fallen snow in the moonlight, though Thurion said no Light had been used in its making. It would be uncomfortable to sit on, Vieliessar had thought the first time she saw it, for the seat was so deep one couldn't rest one's back while sitting. Perhaps it had once had cushions; it was impossible to know now.

There was only one thing that redeemed it from its austere ugliness, and proved that it was indeed the object in whose name such oceans of blood had been shed. Where the armrests of a Presence Chair would have been, the throne's unknown maker had carved two unicorns, one on each side. Vieliessar had once seen a unicorn in the Flower Forest in Tunimbronor; these images were not only lifelike, they were life-size. The delicate cloven hooves gleamed with bright metal, and just as with the fountain outside, the long, spiraling horn was carved of a different stone. Not crystal, as the horns of the unicorns in the Unicorn Fountain were, but opal, for the two horns gleamed with iridescent rainbows.

*Surely those who made this must have seen unicorns. I would almost think these statues could draw breath and take flight . . .*

But if they did, they would find flight difficult.

"I have wondered since the first time I saw it," Thurion said quietly. "Why they are in chains."

## CHAPTER SEVEN

# RAIN MOON TO FLOWER MOON: THE EYES OF THE FOREST

*In the beginning we welcomed them, for we did not
have the wit to know what our ancestors across the
Sea of Storms had known when they first looked upon
the Children of Stars, nor did we know their fate. The
Children of Stars came to us as exiles and suppliants,
and so we thought they had no power to harm.*

— *Chronicle of the Nine Races*

Until two moonturns ago, Runacar had never
known what it was to be alone. From the first
moment he drew breath there were always people around him. Even if he'd somehow found himself
alone in Caerthalien without servants or komen, there
were still people nearby. But now he'd ridden sennight
after sennight through emptiness, and when he reached
Jaeglenhend—he knew where he was by the sight of
the Dragon's Gate high in the Mystrals—War Prince
Nilkaran's domain was as deserted as all the rest. The
desolation was disturbing in a way he had no words
for. Jaeglenhend was a ghostlands.

Not for the first time, Runacar wondered what madness had possessed the Hundred Houses all to strip their
domains to follow Vieliessar into the east. He remembered all the arguments—she must be stopped before
she could claim the Domains of the Uradabhur, the Arzhana, the Windsward—but they no longer seemed

compelling. It was as if he had awakened from a long fever to find himself clear-headed at last.

*The forty Houses of the West were the oldest and richest domains in all the world. And now they are nothing. This we needed no help to compass. This we did to ourselves.*

Even the border towers were deserted. There were no people here *anywhere.*

And yet . . .

He was being followed. Or at least he thought he was, though no matter what he did, he could not discover the source of the invisible watchers he'd sensed ever since he'd left the northern bounds of the Ghostwood behind him. Brigands would have made camps, and left some sign of their presence, but he'd seen nothing—no matter how many clever traps he laid, no matter how he circled and back trailed. He'd begun to hope, rather desperately, that it was Beastlings.

*Rather monsters of blood and bone than that I am followed by Ivrulion's vengeful spirit. Rather that, than that I am so disordered in my wits that I cannot tell a stone from an enemy.*

But if he were a Beastling's prey, Runacar could not imagine why—or even *how.* Gryphons and Hippogriffs and Aesalions filled the skies above the Grand Windsward. Selkies haunted secluded streams and lakes, fishtailed Nisse were the terror of Great Sea Ocean. But Bearwards, Centaurs, and similar forest-dwellers had been swept from the Uradabhur long ago. *Though not from the forests beyond,* he thought uneasily, remembering the skeletons he'd seen in Janglanipaikharain.

It was with a deep sense of unease that Runacar approached the tower in the Tamabeth Hills. It was set there to watch over the Dragon's Gate and all who passed through it, and he thought—he *hoped*—that War Prince Nilkaran had stripped it of its defenders early enough that they had left their provisions behind, thinking to return. And that the bands of brigands who had overrun the lands to the east might have so far overlooked something this far from the fighting.

He was right.

The sortie gate was locked and barred, but the main door of the tower—from which he learned its name was Wintereyes—was not. Runacar led Nielriel through the door, and when he barred it behind him, something inside him relaxed for the first time since he had ridden from the battlefield. No matter what followed him, he was safe here.

The ground floor of Wintereyes—like all Border Towers everywhere—was stabling for the defenders' horses. It smelled of grain and leather and old horse dung. Two tailles of empty stalls awaited occupants, and the inner gates to the sortie passage were drawn neatly shut; the defenders had left their tower in good order, clearly expecting to return in candlemarks or sunturns. Though the chamber was windowless, the lamps in the wall niches—cylinders of crystal that glowed with eternal Silverlight—were still there, and there was quite enough illumination for Runacar to see clearly. Water still ran through the trough in the center of the stables, courtesy of Lightborn Magery, and he scooped up a few handfuls for himself before leading Nielriel to drink and then into the first clean stall he found. Now he was free to look around to see what had been left behind.

A wooden compartment was built along one wall, a combination tack and feed room. The tack had gone with the horses, but a few blankets, some Lightless remedies, and a few sets of grooming tools in their baskets remained. The feed bin was still half full, and beside it, safe and dry, were a couple of bales of hay. He made up his mind then and there to stay until all of it was gone—Nielriel should have the chance to regain the flesh that the moonturns of hard traveling had stripped

from her. And if there were no other supplies here, the
feed would do as well for him as for her, especially if
he could find some way to cook it.

After so long fasting, he dared not let Nielriel gorge
herself on rich feeding, but he took a flake of good
grass hay and a basket of grooming tools back to the
stall where she waited. The mare ate hungrily while he
brushed her until she was smooth and shining again—
and the floor of her stall was covered with thick tufts of
winter coat. When he was done grooming Nielriel,
Runacar brought her a second bucket of rich food and a
flake of hay, then took one of the lamps from its niche on
the wall and went up the stairs.

The chamber above the stables was the barracks for
the garrison, which he passed through after determin-
ing that it, too, was untenanted. The floor above held
the larder for the garrison, and here again was proof
that Wintereyes's occupants had expected to return, for
here in abundance were salt, wine, oil, fruit, provisions
of every kind. Some were preserved by Lightless craft,
some had been stored in chests and barrels upon which
(he knew from experience) preservation spells had been
cast. And as well as food, the chamber held spears,
bows, axes . . . every sort of weapon Runacar might
need to supplement the sword and dagger he carried.
Stunned by his good fortune, he sat down at once to
feast upon cheese and apples and one of the flat square
campaign loaves that was still as fresh as the day it had
been baked and packed for transport. He could not remember a more savory banquet, not even at Caerthalien's High Table, and gorged himself until he could eat
no more. Here was food enough to see him across the
Mystrals and back to Caerthalien High Keep, if he could
only figure a way of transporting it. Perhaps he could
contrive some sort of saddlebags from what was here;
there would be time to think about that in a sunturn or
two.

When he had made his meal, he filled his pockets with more apples, slipped another loaf inside his tunic, picked up a jug of wine, and ascended to the top floor of the tower. Here was the commander's chamber with its tightly-shuttered windows. It held a curtained bed, a brazier, a desk, and a chair. The desk was still covered with scrolls and tally sheets. He saw the seal of Jaeglenhend on one scroll-case; Caerthalien's upon another. *Both gone. Both erased.*

In the corner of the commander's chamber was the storage for the silver-and-crystal signal mirrors and the ladder for the trapdoor to the roof. Runacar set the ladder, ascending cautiously, and opened the trap. On the roof stood an unlit brazier, charged with oil-soaked wood and covered against the weather. It was as if the garrison had left sunturns ago, not moonturns. Everything stood ready for use. All the tower lacked was defenders. Tight-drawn with unexamined emotion, Runacar paced the circumference of the tower, looking out over its low wall.

East: the low hills and the silent land beyond. No trace of smoke in the sky to say that here stood a farmstead or there a manor house. South: the forest through which he had come. Pale green with new leaves, dark green with stands of greenneedles, the Ghostwood far beyond sight. West: the Mystrals and the Dragon's Gate. A thick sheet of ice spilled from the entrance and cascaded down the mountainside all the way to the foothills: the widened pass would have filled with snow that melted and re-froze and packed down over the winter.

*The Pass will take at least another moonturn to clear,* he thought. *Longer than ever before. We should have thought of that before we asked our Lightborn to make us such a broad smooth way. But we did not think of it. Between us, Vieliessar's army and mine have broken the world* . . . It was an uncomfortable thought, and he quickly banished it. *Vieliessar started this war. We only did what she forced us to.*

He went back down inside the tower.

⊰⊱

H ello," an unfamiliar voice said.

Runacar was shocked instantly awake. The bed curtains blocked his view of the room. He grabbed for his sword, only to find it wasn't there.

"I'm not stupid, you know," the voice said.

Runacar sat up, yanking the curtains back and looking around. A figure stepped out of the shadows. He— it!—was shorter than Runacar, but twice as wide. The high domed skull and the whole of its body was covered with thick red-gold fur. It held his sword in large thick-fingered black-clawed hands.

*I was wrong,* he thought dazedly. *There are Bearwards in the Uradabhur* . . .

"You're the first of the Children of Stars I've ever seen," the Bearward admitted, wrinkling its blunt muzzle in an expression Runacar could not decipher, "but I know about your kind. Always killing and hurting. Of course I took your sword."

"I should expect such cowardice from a Beastling," Runacar snarled. *Fool, to think yourself safe even here!* Now he would die. An unarmed knight was no match for a Bearward. He looked around for a weapon. There was nothing within reach but the cup and wine-jug he'd taken with him to bed.

"I'm not a coward," the Bearward said reasonably. "If I'd left you the sword, you'd hit me with it. And then I'd yell, and Radafa can't come down, but he'd tell Audalo and Vorlof, and they'd come up here, and . . ." the Bearward wrinkled its muzzle again. Its teeth were very sharp.

Runacar could make no sense of the outlandish names, but they told him the beast was not alone. "Then kill me," he said sullenly.

"We don't want to kill you," the Bearward said patiently. "We want to talk to you. That's why we've been following you."

"Beasts don't talk," Runacar said, with an increasing sense of the surreal. Beastlings did, of course, but after all, that was why Elves killed them. He reached out for the cup at his bedside, and then the jug beside it.

"They do if—"

Runacar flung the jug. It was still half-full, and very heavy. Without waiting to see whether it hit, he flung himself out of bed, caught up the small table at the bedside, and attacked. It was useless, but at least he'd die fighting.

The brawl went much as he expected it to, except for one thing: when he shook himself back to his senses, he was neither dead nor dying. He dragged himself painfully from beneath the desk the Bearward had flung him against.

"What did you do that for?" the Bearward demanded, stepping back and brushing at its fur. It didn't even sound angry.

"Elves. I told you—all they know how to do is fight," a new voice said.

The speaker stood in the doorway—a Centaur; a hideous melding of misshapen horse and misshapen Elf. It stood taller than the Bearward, though not by much. Its horse-limbs were stocky and heavy boned, and its face was flat and wide; the fur tunic it wore blurred the place where its ill-assorted body joined. *I would not ride an animal with such lines,* Runacar thought giddily. Behind it on the stairs—but still towering over the Centaur—stood a creature Runacar had never seen in the flesh, though he recognized it instantly. Minotaur. Its shoulders were so wide they brushed the sides of the staircase, and its neck was as big around as Runacar's entire torso. Its hide was black as a bull's was black, but just as the Bearward's face was not quite that of a bear, the Minotaur's face was blunter than that of the animal it so nearly resembled. If it had stood within the chamber itself, the massive horns that jutted from its brow would have brushed the ceiling. It wore leather armor, and it was carrying a sword.

"Are you all right, Keloit?" it asked. Its voice was a deep rumble.

"I'm fine!" Keloit must be the Bearward; it was he who spoke. "It just startled me."

"It's a 'he.'" The Centaur spoke with assurance. "A male. So, Elf. Fighting doesn't work. What are you going to try next?"

*I don't know.* The realization was enough to make the room revolve slightly around him. He was frightened and faintly sick and he ached where he'd been smashed into the wall, but most of all . . .

*I am tired.*

Tired of running, of fighting, of trying to counsel those who would not listen, of seeing all his plans and ideas and hopes dissolve into ash. Of living in a world where Vieliessar also lived, of knowing he must preserve her life to preserve his people. He righted a stool that lay on the floor beside him, and sat down upon it to retrieve his clothes.

"I am going to get dressed. Then I am going to see to my horse. Assuming you haven't eaten her," Runacar said wearily.

⊰⊱

Half a candlemark later, Runacar led Nielriel out into the sunlight and then slipped off her halter. He left the heavy door to the tower open wide, and he'd tipped the feed-bin to spill out on the floor. Until he'd seen the fourth member of the Beastlings' hunting party, he'd hoped these things might give Nielriel a chance to survive—then he looked up, and saw the Gryphon—Radafa—peering down from its perch. At least now he knew who had opened the tower from above.

*Gryphons eat horses. She'll probably be dead by noon.*

The Gryphon (Runacar remembered how eagerly their feathers had been sought as ornaments by the Elves) was a colorful sight. Its chest, underwings, and throat feathers were an intense blue, while its crest and the back of its wings were a golden bronze. Where feathers turned to fur, it was white on the belly and tawny above. Soaring over the Grand Windsward, it would be nearly invisible both to prey and to other predators.

The wind shifted, and Nielriel's head came up, nostrils flaring. Whatever scent she caught must not be the Gryphon's; she tested the wind for a few minutes then ambled a few feet away and began to graze.

Runacar walked back inside.

"What now?" he asked the other three.

The Centaur—Vorlof—and the Minotaur—Audalo—had preceded him down to the stable floor. Keloit had remained above, saying unhappily that Elven horses didn't like him.

"Now you talk," Audalo rumbled.

"You could tell us your name," Keloit said, hurrying down the stairs. "You know ours."

"Because you told him, little magpie," Vorlof said in long-suffering tones. "It isn't as if he asked."

"If I waited for people to ask me questions I'd never get a chance to tell them things!" Keloit said reasonably. "And I bet he'll tell you more things if you know his name."

If Runacar merely closed his eyes, he could imagine they were people. The thought unsettled him. He looked back at Keloit, who somehow seemed much younger than either the Centaur or the Minotaur. Keloit's ears folded and lowered, and Runacar was abruptly reminded of a hunting hound he'd once had. It would turn its ears just so when it was attempting to pretend it hadn't done what it just had. Once it had wandered away and found a henhouse . . .

"My name is—" he stopped. Who was he? Lord Runacarendalur? Heir-Prince Runacarendalur of Caerthalien? Runacarendalur Caerthalien, War Prince of Caerthalien? No. He was no longer any of those things. "Runacar," he said at last. "My name is Runacar."

"Short name for an elf with a sword and fine boots," Audalo said. He looked up at the ceiling as if its presence was a personal affront. "Come outside. If we talk in here, we'll just have to say it all again for Radafa."

Audalo bent nearly double as he squeezed carefully through the door. Vorlof followed. Runacar looked from Keloit to the open door and shrugged. If he slammed the door and bolted it, he'd be in here with a Bearward. Not much choice.

He walked out into the sunlight.

"You came from the southeast," Vorlof said, when they were all standing outside. As soon as Keloit had come outside, Nielriel had broken off her grazing to canter further away. Now she stood watching them, her ears flickering back and forth. She didn't know what she smelled, but she knew she didn't like it.

"Yes," Runacar said.

"Your people have been going east all winter," Vorlof said. "Everyone is."

"Not in the Goldengrass." The new voice was a high harsh whisper, surprisingly loud. The Gryphon had spoken. "In the Goldengrass, the Elves come west. They cross the mountains, the High Desert, more mountains. Always west."

The Grand Windsward, the Feinolons, the Arzhana,

the Bazhrahils—Runacar matched familiar names to unfamiliar descriptions.

"The South is ours. Now you come there and kill us," Audalo said.

"No!" The denial was automatic, even though Runacar couldn't imagine what use it was. "We only want to kill each other." He laughed bitterly; certainly either army would happily have slaughtered Beastlings as well, if they'd seen any. "Wanted. Until the High King won."

"Amretheon the Betrayer has been dead a long time," Vorlof said, switching his tail in irritation. "Lie less insultingly, Elf."

*The Betrayer?*

*I must be going mad to expect sense from a Beastling. Perhaps if I tell them what they want to know they'll go away.*

*And perhaps this is a dream from which I will awaken to discover I am High King.*

"Amretheon Aradruiniel was High King long ago," Runacar said slowly. "There is a new one."

"A new High King?" Radafa demanded, his voice a whispering scream. "The Children of Stars have a new High King?"

The news seemed to upset Vorlof and Audalo, too. Keloit just looked . . . well, if Keloit had been an Elf, Runacar would have said the Bearward looked puzzled.

"Would you like to go and pledge fealty to her?" Runacar asked waspishly. "She'll probably take it." *Light knows she's taking fealty from outlaws and Landbonds already.*

Audalo and Vorlof moved away, apparently to argue. Keloit came toward Runacar.

"Do you know her name?" he asked.

"Vieliessar," Runacar answered, not even trying to keep the anger from his voice. "Vieliessar Farcarinon. Child of the Prophecy."

"Oh," Keloit said quietly. "That's bad."

"Why?" Runacar asked, despite himself.

"Oh, er, um, well . . . prophecies. Prophecies are generally bad things. My mother always says so." Keloit wasn't a very good liar. Even Runacar could tell that.

"So now the High King makes war on us?" Vorlof and Audalo had returned.

"I doubt it," Runacar answered shortly.

"*Don't lie! She's already begun! Thousands are dead!*" The Minotaur rushed forward threateningly and Runacar recoiled despite himself. The stone of the tower was hard and cold against his back.

"We want to know what she did to the Flower Forest," Vorlof said.

*The Ghostwood.* Runacar thought of dead trees, grey dust, strange tiny skeletons glittering like crystal. The thing Ivrulion had made. For a moment he thought of saying: *Yes, yes, this was the High King's work, she believes Amretheon's Prophecy means her to be the instrument of your destruction and this is her first step . . .*

It would be so easy. Vieliessar needed time to consolidate all she'd won; deny it to her and her *king-domain* would shatter like crystal dropped upon stone.

"No," he said. "It wasn't her. It was my brother."

He closed his eyes and waited for death. Again, it did not come.

"Why?" Keloit asked forlornly.

*Because he was rotted through with madness and ambition. Because he was supposed to become War Prince of Caerthalien and became Lightborn instead. Because something went wrong, long before he, or I, or even Vieliessar Farcarinon were born.*

"He took its power to cast a spell," Runacar finally said.

"He took more than that," Vorlof said harshly. "He took lives. Mosirinde Truefriend promised us: never all. Never enough to kill."

Trying to make sense of this gabble of twisted half-familiar names was like being back in school again, and Runacar wished they'd just kill him, or leave, or do whatever they meant to do. "Mosirinde Peacemaker made the Covenant for the Lightborn. Ivrulion broke it."

"For himself—or for all?" Radafa demanded, as if that were important.

"I don't know," Runacar said, eyes still closed. "I don't care. Ask the High King."

More silence. More shuffling. Vorlof and Audalo must have gone away to argue again. His eyes flew open when he felt a touch upon his arm. Keloit was right in front of him. Even if he wanted to flinch away, there was nowhere to go.

"If everybody's going to join the High King, why are you going the other way?"

He'd always thought Bearwards must stink the way bears did, of musk and blood and animal. All he could smell was warm clean fur. He stared into Keloit's eyes for an uncomprehending moment. They were brown like an animal's, but no true animal's eyes had ever held such an expression of worry and curiosity mixed.

"I don't like her," Runacar said simply.

"*I am not going back to Leutric and telling him I don't know because I forgot to ask!*" Audalo's bellow was loud enough to make Runacar wince and Radafa added his own piercing scream of objection to the noise. That, as much as anything else, told Runacar how deserted Jaeglenhend was. Keloit retreated from Runacar's side hastily.

Vorlof trotted back to where Runacar stood. "All right," he said, as if some decision had been reached. "You're coming with us."

"Do I have a choice?" Runacar asked. The Centaur smiled coldly.

Runacar shrugged in surrender. The very concept

should revolt him to the roots of his being, but it didn't. He was no one, and there was nowhere else for him to go.

❈

He'd been allowed to pack everything he wanted to take with him (except weapons, of course). He'd only been limited by what Nielriel could carry, and since the others would be on foot (or, in the case of the Gryphon, on the wing), he'd chosen to use her as a packhorse (for which he apologized to her sincerely, to the apparent amusement of the Beastlings). They'd followed the Southern Pass Road at a punishing pace, and each night, after he fed, brushed, and hobbled Nielriel, he fell gladly into his bedroll to sleep. He hadn't tried to escape. He was too tired, and besides, the Gryphon would have caught him easily.

Radafa hunted for them as well as for itself—Runacar had been surprised to find that all of them but the Gryphon ate cooked food—but though the scent of the meat made his mouth water, the thought of eating something a Beastling had touched nauseated him. When his bread and cheese ran out, he'd been willing to heat water over their communal fire, but tea and porridge were a poor substitute for meat. His pride survived another day or two, and then he joined his captors at their fire and ate what they did.

Just before they reached the Southern Pass, something spooked Nielriel in the night, and she bolted. Keloit had wanted to chase after her immediately. Vorlof said no. Audalo said that there were predators in the woods (something Runacar doubted), and Radafa (as always) wasn't there to comment (Runacar supposed he must sleep in a tree). None of them got much sleep for the remainder of the night, and in the morning, Radafa found Nielriel and led the others to her.

⊰⊱

Nielriel's body lay in the clearing, utterly despoiled. Runacar knelt beside her, placing a hand on her cheek. Birds had already pecked out her eyes, and her gaping jaws were tongueless. *You deserved better than this,* he thought sorrowfully.

"And you will lay this death at my door," the Gryphon said, in its harsh toneless whisper. Runacar could not guess what Radafa might be thinking, for neither the Gryphon's face nor voice was particularly expressive. Runacar remembered his Master of Hawks saying one must never think of birds of prey as being Elven— they had no compassion, no love, and no loyalty. He wondered how different Gryphons were, if at all.

"I'd like to," he said evenly. "But I can't." He got to his feet.

"Why not?" Keloit asked, clearly wanting to know.

"Look at her wounds, and the ground around her," Runacar said. Keloit obligingly did, but seemed to see nothing that would answer its question. Runacar sighed.

"See these claw marks here? And the bite mark here? They're from what killed her: it severed her spine. I don't know how a Gryphon kills, but its strike must be something like a hawk's."

"I'm right here, you know," Radafa said, and Runacar glanced up in startlement.

"Yes," he said, feeling oddly awkward. "So. She was killed the way a cat kills—ice tiger, snow lion, something large—a lynx or even a leopard would be too small to kill a horse in this way."

"But don't you want to blame Radafa anyway?" Keloit asked. "I mean—" he stopped.

"He means your kind blame us for everything from a bad harvest to plague," Vorlof said with sour amusement.

"All I know is what I see here," Runacar said evenly.

⊰⊱

V orlof and Audalo distributed Nielriel's packs between them, and the party went on. From the westward side of the Southern Pass, they continued south,
and finally turned west. This far south of Mangiralas
the landscape was unfamiliar to Runacar—hills and
canyons, parched and unforgiving, but wildly lush near
streams and rivers. It was in the forest near one such
river that they reached their destination—a longhouse
that stood alone in a wide clearing. Only Keloit had
followed him inside—he wasn't sure whether it was as
guard or companion.

At first, at least in Runacar's mind, Keloit had been
a sort of talking dog, endlessly curious and even trying
to please him. Audalo and Vorlof treated him with
suspicion—and in Vorlof's case, outright hatred—and
it was easier for him to go on thinking of them as enemies. Monsters. But not Keloit, and Runacar wasn't
sure how he felt about that. Or when he'd begun treating Keloit as what he seemed so much like: someone's
well-loved child on the verge of adulthood. After his
capture, his feelings had veered from dejected indifference to his fate to numb horror at his companions and
back again, over and over, until . . .

The Beastlings had stopped seeming any stranger to
him than Lightborn. Or Landbonds. He wasn't sure
how to live with that.

*At least I shan't have to live with it for long.*

It was a fortnight since he'd been captured at the Jaeglenhend Tower. When they left him at the longhouse,
no one said good-bye.

⊰⊱

R unacar glanced around the interior of the longhouse. There were several doors along the long
walls, but aside from the gigantic presence chair that

occupied the whole of the back wall, there was nothing here that seemed designed for sitting upon, though the tables and cabinets all indicated this was a place where someone lived—and lived well, for the woodwork was beautiful. The ceiling beams, the lintel over the door, the furniture, all was beautifully carved. The hearth at the opposite end of the chamber was faced with glazed ornamental tiles. It might have been the great room of a wealthy manor house.

Except in all the ways it so clearly was not.

He wondered what the Beastlings used such a structure for. In his imagination (when he'd thought about them at all), they'd lived like any other beasts: naked in the forest, eating raw meat. It hadn't been so strong an image as to survive his journey with Beastlings who cooked over a fire and ate with knives from plates and bowls just as Elves did, but this . . .

Talking animals did not make things like this. *If Vieliessar High King had known the Beastlings were capable of this, I'm sure she would have demanded they swear to her . . .*

If she could have found them in the first place.

"Everything's going to be all right," Keloit said. He was pacing the floor like—Runacar could not stop himself from making the comparison—a bear in a cage. "I'm sure it's going to be all right. Mama says King Leutric is a good person. He won't just kill you. Even if you are one of the Children of Stars."

"Thank you. I think." Runacar wasn't sure whether Keloit believed what he was saying, or was just trying to reassure him, but at least now he knew why he was here: the Beastlings had a King and he was to be given an audience. "You know, you'd be a lot more convincing if you'd stop pacing."

"I'm not pacing. Am I pacing? If I'm pacing, it's not because I'm nervous, you know." Keloit dropped to all fours and curled around himself. In that position, the

Bearward looked very much like a large ball of red-gold fur.

"Of course not."

Keloit got up and began to pace again. "He's very busy, you know," he said. "That's why you have to wait."

"Keloit, I was born and raised in a Great House," Runacar said gently. "I understand how these things are done."

The Bearward looked toward him, ears swiveling and flattening. By now, Runacar knew Keloit well enough to interpret his expressions. No matter what he said, the young Bearward was very nervous indeed.

"I am sure this so-called King of yours will do as he thinks best." *King Leutric, who and whatever he is, who holds me prisoner and has no reason to love me.*

The door opened. King Leutric entered at the vanguard of his court. Leutric was a Minotaur, his skin—or hide—as black as Audalo's. Behind him came three other Minotaurs including Audalo, half a dozen Centaurs armed and armored—Vorlof was among them—a Bearward shamaness, and a few creatures Runacar could not put name to. Runacar flinched a little at the sight of the shamaness; he didn't like magic just to begin with, and Beastling sorcery was even worse. Not all of them wore clothes—the Bearwards seemed to favor nothing more than belts and vests—but all of them were groomed and ornamented in an intentional and deliberate fashion.

"Uh-oh," Keloit said quietly. "Mama's with him."

Runacar had thought Audalo was gigantic. King Leutric towered over him by more than a head. His horns were painted and gilded, and his tunic and trousers were of a rich cut velvet. The tunic left his arms bare, and he wore prize-rings, beautifully carved and chased, on his upper and lower arms. The hair about his eyes and his mouth was grey with age.

*He is an old man,* Runacar thought wonderingly.

Runacar stood quietly as Leutric seated himself upon his massive throne and his courtiers moved to their places around him, resolving to take whatever came with as much dignity as they left him.

"This is the prisoner," Vorlof said, stepping forward and putting a hand upon his dagger.

Runacar bowed ironically. "Runacarendalur Caerthalien, once War Prince of Caerthalien," he said. He'd never felt less princely. But he would die under his true name.

"Approach," Leutric said.

Runacar started forward. Keloit walked beside him, until the shamaness gestured impatiently. Keloit gave Runacar one of his odd bared-teeth smiles, and hurried to his mother's side. Runacar walked the rest of the distance alone.

"They told me your name was Runacar," Leutric said. His voice was a low rumble, giving the impression of deliberation when he spoke.

"That is what I told them," Runacar answered.

"Which is it? Runacar or Runacarendalur Caerthalien?" Leutric asked. "We know of Caerthalien," he added.

"Then perhaps it will please you to know it is gone," Runacar answered. "If it wasn't, I would be War Prince Runacarendalur Caerthalien. Now I am merely Runacar." His truncated name, without rank or House, still felt unfinished in his thoughts; a constant low-level irritation like a hole in one's boot sole, but one he must live with now.

"Then, Merely Runacar, tell us what you know of how so many of my people came to die."

*He means the Ghostwood. And he knows already what the others told him. But Audalo thinks he might want to know more than that. It's why I'm alive.*

"Forgive me, King Leutric, if I include in my account things you already know," Runacar began. It was hard to believe, standing here, giving a Beastling the same courtesy he would have given his own father, that any of this was really happening. Perhaps it wasn't. Perhaps it was a might-have-been dream. Perhaps he was already dead.

"Speak," the Minotaur said.

"As you know, our Lightborn draw their power from the Flower Forests. Mosirinde's Covenant—" something he only knew so much about because of endless lectures from Ivrulion "—requires them to take power only from that source, and not to kill the Flower Forest by taking too much."

"Close enough," the Bearward shamaness said. Runacar noted she'd put herself between him and Keloit. *Am I such a threat, even now?*

"The Hundred Houses fight among themselves— *fought* among themselves—to determine which of them, of us, would become High King and rule over all." He went on, telling the tale he knew, beginning with Varuthir the Peacebond child, going on to Vieliessar Lightsister, Vieliessar Oronviel, Vieliessar High King, of the battles he'd been there for and the ones whose outcomes he'd only guessed at, through the whole of the West, through the Mystrals, across the Uradabhur, and far beyond. He omitted nothing.

The court listened in absolute silence. And at last he came to the final battle.

"My—" Suddenly it was hard to continue, but he forced the words out. "My brother Ivrulion—Ivrulion Lightbrother—was mad. He wanted Caerthalien, you see, and it was supposed to go to him, he had been raised to believe that, and it was true; Lord Bolecthindial had given him a sword that year for his Naming Day, and . . ." He stopped, realizing his mouth was dry with so much talking and that he was swaying with exhaustion. He forced himself to concentrate. This wasn't what Leutric wanted to know.

"The final battle between the Alliance and the High King came. Ivrulion cast a spell to raise the dead from the battlefield to fight on. To do that, he drained Janglanipaikharain—the Ghostwood—to dust."

Runacar's words fell into silence, and in their wake, no one spoke. He had no idea how much of his speech they had understood.

"Why did he not simply kill you, if he wanted your place?" the Bearward shamaness asked.

"He was Lightborn," Runacar said. "Because of that he could not have Caerthalien. But in the heat of the battle . . . he could force the War Princes to set that aside." *And because he knew, when they were victorious, when they executed Lord Vieliessar, I would be dead. And so he saw a way to gain the prize his festering ambition had coveted since before I was born.*

"Did these princes agree to the death of the forest?" Leutric asked.

"No." That much was true enough. "They didn't know what Ivrulion would do to gain them victory. He didn't tell them."

"But he did not gain them victory," Leutric said. "And now your Vieliessar has made herself High King over all. Did she agree to the death of the forest?"

Runacar stared at Leutric in disbelief. "She was *on the other side*," he finally said.

Leutric waited, and finally Runacar realized he was still waiting for an answer.

"No. No, she did not agree. She was Lightborn before she was High King. She would not do that. She always honored the Covenant."

Vorlof stepped closer to Leutric, speaking so quietly Runacar could not hear. Leutric nodded—a magisterial gesture with those enormous horns—and Vorlof walked the length of the room to where Runacar stood. Behind him the rest of the courtiers were now talking to one another, their voices merged and blurred by the sound of Vorlof's hooves on the wooden floor.

"Come," Vorlof said, gesturing toward a nearby door.

Numbly, Runacar followed Vorlof along a narrow path through the forest. When he reached the other side, he was standing on a hillside overlooking a river. Below, he could see a village, surrounded by plowed fields, at the river's edge.

"What . . . ?" Runacar said, stopping. "What is this place?"

"Home," Vorlof said. "Mine, not yours, Elf."

He'd heard of Centaur villages—everyone had—but he'd thought of them as squalid collections of mud and sticks, such as the Landbonds built for themselves. This . . . This looked like a place where *people* lived.

"Come," Vorlof said again, and led him down the hill and along the village's outskirts, to a building that at least looked familiar. A barn. The Centaur unbarred the door and opened it. "Go inside," he said. "Stay here."

Runacar went inside.

There was a row of stalls, each with its manger, all empty. The floor was scattered with clean straw. The upper storey of the barn was filled with hay, but instead of a ladder, there was a long turning staircase of shallow steps leading up to it. He climbed them. There was a hayloft above, its doors open. Escape would be easy enough.

*And where would I go?* he thought to himself.

He spread his cloak on the nearest pile of hay and lay down.

❦

It was dark when he awoke, and he only roused because Keloit was standing over him. He sat up slowly, and saw that Nielriel's saddlebags were at Keloit's feet.

"I brought your things," Keloit said. "I thought you'd want them."

"For what?" Runacar asked blankly. Keloit wrinkled his muzzle in confusion.

"For . . . Because they belong to you?" Keloit said. He didn't sound certain.

"When am I being executed?" Runacar asked next.

"What?" Keloit responded. It took several ridiculous rounds of speaking at cross-purpose for Runacar to grasp what was obvious to Keloit: Leutric was finished with him, and he was free to go anywhere he chose.

He found it unbelievable. Keloit found his disbelief incomprehensible. Leutric had wanted to know what had happened to Janglanipaikharain Flower Forest. Runacar had told him. And apparently it didn't occur to anybody—even Vorlof—to hold him responsible for what his brother had done.

He was free.

He had no idea what to do with his freedom.

✥

On the other side of the Mystrals, on a rare afternoon of mutual idleness, Thurion Lightbrother walked with Komen Helecanth through the Vale of Celenthodiel. The High King was attending the Princes' Court, where the Guildmasters of the Lords of War could numb her ears with their complaints about the idleness and disrespect of the Landbonds, and Thurion took the opportunity to explore their new land in good company, though he knew Komen Helecanth did not find the Vale as strange as he did.

In death, the Lords Komen went to ride eternally with the Starry Hunt, but the Hunt only accepted those who died in battle. For generations of Lightborn, it was the Vale of Celenthodiel to which their spirits went after death—the Warm World, they called it. The Land of Light. And now they knew that had only been a myth.

A dream. Celenthodiel was as real as bread. As real as the warning that had sent Vieliessar here to find it.

"I am as happy not to be there," Helecanth said, breaking into Thurion's thoughts. "The Great Lords have ever believed that wisdom comes from the application of a whip."

"So every Landbond knows," Thurion answered. "It is a wonder we—they—are not masters of wisdom by now."

It was an odd friendship that had grown up between the two of them, but a true one. Helecanth was the commander of Vieliessar's personal guard. Thurion had neither rank nor title. He was not even Vieliessar's chief Lightborn. He loved her. That was all.

Helecanth snorted. "If they were, they would be second in wisdom to the Great Lords' own children."

"That explains so much about the komen," Thurion said dryly. "Landbonds have never beaten their children."

"Perhaps they should start," Helecanth said, "since by the High King's own word, no one else is to be allowed to."

Thurion did not answer. His own words were echoing through his head.

*They or we? Am I what I was born as, or what I have become? When Vieliessar looses the chains of custom and throws down the old ways, she oversets not merely injustice, but our conception of ourselves . . .*

He had been born Landbond, and become a Sanctuary Mage. When Vieliessar asked him to join her cause, he came gladly—but all his Landbond family saw was that Thurion lived in unimaginable luxury—luxury they had been let to share in by Bolecthindial's gift of freedom and land—and that now he meant to take it away. Foolishly. Selfishly. Until that moment, he had not thought his years at the Sanctuary and in Caerthalien's Great Keep had changed him. In that moment, he saw they had. He was no longer one of them. No longer Landbond, and the child of Landbonds.

"It must be strange," Helecanth said, looking sideways at him, "not to be what your parents and siblings have been."

"I think it is," Thurion said quietly. "I do not think any of us will ever again be what our parents have been," he said quietly.

"But perhaps we will be what our great-parents were," Helecanth said. "Those who fled this place so long ago." She gestured toward the spire that held Amretheon's city.

"Perhaps," Thurion said. "I don't know what they were like. I think Vielle does. I think that's why she's so sad."

"No War Prince was ever happy except when they were riding into battle," Helecanth said. "And she doesn't like fighting." She shrugged. "No wonder she's sad."

"She said she would be High King, and she is," Thurion said.

"And that is not enough to bring her joy," Helecanth said bluntly. "Tell me," she added. "Do you believe she is Child of the Prophecy?"

"For any reason beyond her succeeding at what Amretheon foretold only the Child of the Prophecy could?" Thurion asked. "I do. Of course I do. I've never made any secret of it."

"Then when do we ride to battle again?" Helecanth asked. "And against what enemy?"

"You know I don't know that," Thurion said tartly. "Scholars have been seeking that answer since time immemorial."

Helecanth shrugged. "I only repeat what many have said. And to you I will further say what they will not: How long do we await this enemy? To train forever to fight a battle that never comes . . . that destroys an army as surely as an enemy does. And while she prepares for battle, she does not rule."

"You can tell her that, if you're brave enough," Thurion said. "She already thinks the Enthroning is a complete waste of time, and I was in favor of that."

"She should be grateful to you for the peace you have gained her," Helecanth answered. "Her lords will not pester her to take a consort until after it is done."

Thurion made a sour face, but he knew Helecanth was right. Without a consort, without an heir, Vieliessar's *king-domain* rested upon one fragile life: hers. She was the last of Farcarinon; there was no lineage, no matter how long and torturous, that led to another heir.

*Save one. Nataranweiya's line was Caerthalien. All their Line Direct and Lines Collateral are extinguished except for Runacarendalur Caerthalien and the child of the Banebringer. Rondaniel can't marry Vieliessar and nobody knows where Prince Runacarendalur is. Or to be precise, everyone thinks he's dead. But if he were, Vieliessar would be dead, too.*

Thurion's Keystone Gift was True Speech: there were few secrets he did not know or could not discover. But it had taken no Magery to discover that Runacarendalur Caerthalien was Vieliessar Farcarinon's destined Bondmate: Vieliessar had told him, despairing.

*"And no one will believe it isn't a lie, a trick, a bone thrown to quiet the whining of Caerthalien dogs! I won't be his consort. I can't take him as mine—"*

True then, and true now. And Helecanth knew it as well as Thurion did: Runacarendalur had told her before he fled. They had never spoken of this aloud. There'd been no need.

"She must wed," Thurion said helplessly. "There must be an heir. An heir of the body; the War Princes will never stand for anything else."

"They won't stand for that, either, if she dies leaving a child behind her," Helecanth said. "I could not hold the Throne intact for a regency. Could Rithdeliel? Could you?"

"I don't think Pelashia Herself could," Thurion said. "Or Amretheon returned from the sky. Or the Lord of the Starry Hunt. And then it will all have been for nothing."

"Then we had better hope for an enemy," Helecanth said. "Or a consort. Or a miracle."

"If he came back . . ." Thurion said, very softly.

Helecanth fixed him with a blazing glare. "I am the High King's sworn vassal," she said stonily. "Caerthalien is erased. If any of its line came back from the dead, I must name that one coward, and oathbreaker, and slay them for my liege's honor. He will never come back," she added in a softer tone. "It is only by the mercy of the Silver Hooves that I may look upon the king each day and know that he yet lives."

There was nothing Thurion could offer in answer to that. Helecanth loved Lord Runacarendalur as steadfastly and hopelessly as Thurion loved Vieliessar. And for all their sakes, he must hope they never met again.

## CHAPTER EIGHT

# RAIN MOON TO SWORD MOON: TO GAIN SANCTUARY

*Every war begins with its own hero tale, as if it were a great lord who had lived a long life and now has a story-song crafted to be sung over its funeral pyre. And any prince who clings to that story-song after a campaign begins will drink to drowning of the cup of defeat and loss, for a war is not a warrior, and no mortal prince can force the world to follow their whim as if they wear the cloak of the Starry Huntsman.*

*—Arilcarion War-Maker, Of the Sword Road*

In Ice Moon, the Battle of the Shieldwall Plain was fought. In Storm Moon, word reached the new High King that the Western Shore was embattled, and had already sought help from the Sanctuary of the Star in vain. In Rain Moon, two grand-tailles of Lightborn went west on an arrow-straight track toward the Southern Pass. Rondithiel, oldest among them, was their leader, and there were few of them to whom he had not given their first lessons in Magery at the Sanctuary of the Star, for Rondithiel taught Mosirinde's Covenant, without which there was no lawful Magery. He had sought Vieliessar out early in her campaigns; he had been there when Luthilion Araphant was slain at Laeldor and Magery was used in battle for the first time. Vieliessar had sworn that she meant to uphold the Covenant, and that her act did not violate it, but if Rondithiel had not been there to agree with her, she might have been defeated in the midst of her earliest victories. But Rondithiel knew better than anyone else in the land that Mosirinde had never forbade the Lightborn to fight. The Covenant only circumscribed the sources from which they might draw their power. To draw power from death—even the death of a tree, or an insect—was the forbidden thing.

When Vieliessar had made the Lightborn into the Warhunt, Rondithiel had been among the first to join. And no one else could lead this party of the Warhunt into the west, for what Lightborn remained there would trust no one else.

Their road led them through the Ghostwood.

⊰⊱

In life, it had been a larger Flower Forest than any of them had ever seen. In death, it was a wasteland that led the three hundred to travel with their faces shrouded against the dust. A simple spell might have blown their path clear of the powdery filth, but there was no Light here to draw upon. Ivrulion had taken it all.

"Beastlings lived here," Bramandrin Lightsister said, nodding toward the skeleton of a Dryad. "I wonder where they went?"

"Anywhere else," Harwing Lightbrother answered. "If any survived, I hope they kept running. There isn't Light enough in this place to raise Shield, and Innate spells won't do us much good."

A Lightborn's innate Light was enough for the smallest and simplest of spells, such as Fire or Silverlight. Anything greater required a Flower Forest to draw upon. Even with the boundary stones down throughout most of the Uradabhur, there was no available Light: the Lightborn had drained those reservoirs nearly dry.

"Even a Beastling wouldn't stay here," Bramandrin said, looking around at the dead forest. She knew as well as the rest of them that without Magery they had little hope of defending themselves if they were attacked.

"Once we reach the Mystrals, the western Flower Forests will be open to us," Rondithiel Lightbrother said encouragingly. "The fighting there was not as hard as it was here. We will have Light to speed us on our way."

But though his words were encouraging, his thoughts were not. *We fought for survival, and for the High King's victory,* Rondithiel mused as they rode through the desolation. *I do not think any of us imagined what might follow it. I only pray there are still Lightborn between the Mystrals and the Angarussa, for if there are not, the West is in trouble beyond the High King's power to ease it.*

❧

"This is our last night on the Southern Pass Road," Rondithiel said.

It had been with a sense of relief that Rondithiel's party entered the Mystrals. Here in the mountains it was possible to forget the things they had seen and done since the war began. As Lightborn, they had seen the aftermath of many battles, and many of them had wished the War Princes and their courts to be gone forever. But now all of them knew from bitter experience what a land stripped of its governing nobles became.

They were camped in the high hills above Sierdalant. The horses and pack mules wandered freely, browsing on the new grass, for there was enough Light to draw upon here to Call them back in the morning. The tents and simple shelters they'd brought with them from Celephriandullias-Tildorangelor formed windbreaks around a dozen cookfires, but after the evening meal was done, Rondithiel had called the three hundred together, for there were things he knew he must say. He hoped, by presenting information, they would draw the conclusion he wished without him having to speak it aloud. Rondithiel had been a teacher for far too long to easily abandon old habits.

It was a great many folk to address quietly, but the night was still and the Lightborn knew how to listen.

"One can see a great distance from the top of the pass," Rondithiel said gently. "And from here, we can see all the way to Sierdalant's western border. You know as well as I what we have not seen."

"Light," Dinias Lightbrother—who sat close beside him—said. "Not, oh, you know as well as I do I don't mean *Light*-light. But—"

"Cookfires, campfires, lanterns, torches, even a lighted window," Isilla Lightsister said. "It's dark."

"It is only to be expected, one supposes," Rondithiel Lightbrother said, still gently. "The Alliance would have gathered their armies at the foot of the Mystrals before heading through the Dragon's Gate. It is true that Vondaimieriel lies north of here, but the Alliance armies drew heavily upon all the domains at the foot of the Mystrals."

"And Farmfolk aren't stupid," Isilla said. "They knew they'd been abandoned by the time the weather turned."

She gestured westward. Before the sun had set, one of Sierdalant's Border Keeps had been visible in the westward hills. No light shone from it now.

"Everyone's gone," Bramandrin said. "But where did they go?"

Rondithiel allowed silence to build behind her question. The answer was clear, though it was not the final conclusion he needed them to draw.

"Gunedwaen— We knew the Alliance Houses were riding in their normal battle array when they followed us. That meant komen, Lightborn, and servants. The Landbond, the Farmfolk, and most of the Craftworkers would have been left behind. They didn't follow the

Alliance, and anyway, the weather turned within a fortnight; they couldn't have if they'd wanted to. And they aren't here," Harwing Lightbrother said sharply. "So they went west and south. I would. It's warmer there."

"They just . . . left?" Bramandrin said, shocked. "But their homes were here."

"And if we find a single farm on Sierdalant's manorial lands intact, I'll eat my mule," Harwing said. "It's going to be the Uradabhur all over again. Outlaws and refugees."

"And there's nothing we can do about it, is there?" Peryn Lightsister said slowly.

"No," Isilla said. "Not and reach the Western Shore quickly enough to do Amrolion and Daroldan any good. And they're why we've come."

"But—" Dinias said, then fell silent.

"We must cross the West to reach the Shore," Rondithiel said gently, for it was a hard truth he was leading them to. "We know the Sanctuary of the Star remains—"

"Or at least no Lightborn has Farspoken any of us to say it does not," Harwing said. "And that is the other reason the High King sent us." He looked around at his companions, a bitter smile on his face. "Oh, don't tell me you think we're here because Iardalaith asked her to honor her treaties with Amrolion and Daroldan? We're here because Iardalaith knows his cousin Ciadorre went as envoy to the Sanctuary as soon as the roads were passable, and Ulvearth Lightsister went with her, and he has had no word of either of them since."

"The Sanctuary does not answer any of us," Dinias pointed out. "And it isn't because we've all suddenly forgotten how to Farspeak."

Every Lightborn here—every Lightborn trained since Celelioniel was Astromancer—had been trained in Farspeech by Momioniarch Lightsister. Any of them could Farspeak her, and many of them had done so all along—until Ice Moon, when the Sanctuary had ceased to answer.

"If the High King wants to find out what's happening at the Sanctuary of the Star," Isilla said, directing her words toward Harwing most of all, "then so do I. So do all of us. It's the only place in the West that can be, well, a *sanctuary* for everyone left there. We all know Hamphuliadiel is mad. But if he wants to be a War Prince, then let him care for the people as a War Prince should. And if he isn't—or can't—or won't—"

"Or he's dead," Dinias said helpfully.

"—then we will Farspeak Aradreleg Lightsister, and tell her so," Isilla finished.

"And ride on," Harwing said with quiet savagery. "That is what Rondithiel Lightbrother means. Isn't it, Rondithiel? When we go riding westward, and the people come flocking to us for help, we can't do anything for them."

There was a stunned murmur of voices at Harwing's words, some angry, some disbelieving, some merely sad. Though they had all, even Rondithiel, worn simple sturdy homespun on their journey, each one of the Lightborn had carried their robes of Lightborn green with them, and had expected to don them when they crossed into Sierdalant, for even now, a Lightborn's robes carried with it the promise of immunity from attack or enslavement by princes and komen of the Hundred Houses.

Or it should.

"Iardalaith would be here if he could." It was Pennynorn Lightbrother, born in Daroldan, who spoke. "And I would rather these words came from him. But I think he and I may be the only ones of all of you who come from the Shore. Iardalaith is the son of a prince, but I . . . my parents were fisherfolk. We Lightborn are *all* the children of Farmfolk, Landbonds, Craftworkers, and none of us—even Iardalaith, I promise—would weep if all the nobles and the Lords Komen fell dead between one breath and the next."

Quiet laughter and sounds of agreement greeted his words.

"I would rather help the Landbonds of Daroldan's greatest enemy than any prince," Pennynorn went on. "But if we do not reach the Western Shore quickly, it will not be princes who die. It will be all the folk—folk like us—in Amrolion and Daroldan both. And when they are dead, the Beastlings will come east. And there will be no one to stop them."

"So you will turn your back on those who ask us to help them?" Harwing asked quietly.

"Your House was Oronviel," Pennynorn answered. "Tell me you have no experience in choosing between 'bad' and 'worse.'"

Harwing's only answer was silence.

"We will cross the West as quickly as we can," Rondithiel said. "We will use the Light to hide ourselves from discovery as much as we can. If the High King's folk seek us out, we must send them away. We cannot delay to aid them."

"But what do we say to them?" Bramandrin said plaintively into the silence that followed Rondithiel's words. "Don't they have as much right as anyone to claim aid from Vieliessar High King?"

"Not this time," Harwing said bitterly.

⚔

At first they had kept to the Flower Forests as much as they could to keep from being seen, but those places that had once welcomed them seemed now to bear the Lightborn a special hostility. Small items went missing, brambles went out of their way to trip them, and everyone's sleep was troubled with strange whispers. When they began to lose horses and pack-mules as well, Rondithiel chose to risk taking them across the land instead, but the suppliants they all expected to meet did not come.

Sierdalant, Vondaimieriel, Aramenthiali, Oronviel, Ivrithir, Caerthalien were all deserted. If the folk who had been left behind were foregathered in the Great Keeps, the Lightborn did not know of it, for Rondithiel made certain to keep far away from them.

It took the Lightborn nearly six sennights to reach the vicinity of the Sanctuary of the Star.

⊰⊱

"This doesn't look good," Dinias said in a low voice.

It was late afternoon. He, Harwing, and Isilla stood just inside the shelter of Arevethmonion, gazing out at the landscape beyond. Arevethmonion was one of the few Flower Forests in the West where the Light hadn't been drained to dangerously low levels—Lady Arevethmonion had her own boundary stones, to reserve her Light for the exclusive use of the Sanctuary of the Star.

They'd entered the Flower Forest near its easternmost edge, moving warily along narrow deer-tracks and constantly alert against discovery. They'd seen the changes that had been made to the Sanctuary itself on their approach: outbuildings gone, walls heightened. As if someone feared attack to the Sanctuary. *But walls keep people in as well as out,* Harwing thought to himself. *Prisoners, or just Lightborn who want to go home? Not that any of our homes are still intact.* The fact that no one inside the Sanctuary was willing to Farspeak anyone outside it was the thing that worried Harwing most. It implied that once you went in . . .

*A geasa is a simple thing to set. If I were Hamphuliadiel, I'd Bind the Lightborn from using Farspeech at all. It would have some drawbacks, but the main use for it*

*is speech over distance, and he clearly doesn't want*
*that. I wonder how many people are in there? Oron-*
*viel didn't send Candidates last year, and* nobody *sent*
*any this year, but by the same token, I'm pretty sure*
*nobody who was here—or who came here—like Ulvearth*
*Lightsister—left.*

"Yes and no," Harwing answered absently. "At least
someone's building something."

"*Hamphuliadiel* is building something," Isilla said.
"A War City, like the one Lord Vieliessar built in Oronviel."

The village was clearly new, and yet it was already
being expanded. Harwing wondered how many people
Hamphuliadiel meant to cram into his War City—or
were the current structures something other than cottages or dormitories? The three of them had seen how
much land was now under cultivation here—there'd be
need of barns and silos to hold the harvest,

"And it looks like it holds as many people as a Great
Keep—or a War City," Dinias said. "There used to be a
regular forest behind Rosemoss Farm, and now there's
nothing but fields."

But it didn't matter how many fields Hamphuliadiel
put under tillage if he meant to gather so many people
in one place. The Great Keeps hadn't survived on their
attached farms alone: the entire domain had sent tithes
to their storehouses. They'd had to. The castels had held
thousands of people . . .

*Most of whom are on the other side of the Mystrals*
*now. Hamphuliadiel can't think to make himself a War*
*Prince in truth. Can he?*

If he did, Vieliessar would smash him as completely
as she had every domain that had not immediately declared for her.

*When she comes back. If she comes back. If the Shore*
*doesn't fall.*

If.

"Fields as far as the eye can see," Harwing agreed. "Just as well Rondithiel didn't follow his first impulse and come himself."

Rondithiel had suggested it, of course. They were a war party bound for the relief of the Western Shore, but the first duty of the Lightborn had always been as envoys between the War Princes. It was only right and proper for them to bring the formal notification of Vieliessar's victory to the Sanctuary and the Astromancer. It had been Harwing who pointed out that if the Sanctuary Lightborn weren't willing to Farspeak their kindred, they might not be following the Codes of War, either.

"What could he possibly do against two great-tailles of Lightborn?" Dinias asked.

"There are always some things it's better to wonder than to find out," Harwing said grimly.

"Well, somebody's going to have to go up to the door and knock," Isilla pointed out. "All we can tell from here is that Hamphuliadiel's building a village. Which does not—as Rondithiel would be the first to tell us—violate Mosirinde's Covenant."

"I'll go," Harwing said. "I'm the logical choice."

"No, you aren't," Isilla said. "My Keystone Gift is Overshadow. They can't make me do anything I don't want to."

"Except die, once they listen to your thoughts," Harwing said.

"That . . . isn't exactly . . ." Dinias said.

"It's so much fun to listen to the two of you pretending that anybody's paying attention to either the Codes or the Covenant any more," Harwing interrupted irritably. "The Codes say that any spell cast is considered the equivalent of a blow struck, which means it's a cause for war."

"Unless lawfully set upon a vassal, an outlaw, or a beast," Isilla finished impatiently. "You talk as if the Astromancer is a War Prince."

"Isn't he?" Harwing asked. "As for the Covenant, it only says we can't take Light from any source other than the Flower Forests, nor in such quantity as to harm by the taking. That leaves the Astromancer plenty of things to do—if he sees cause. But my Keystone Gift is Heart-Seeing."

"That just means he won't be able to force you to speak the truth," Dinias pointed out. "Not that he can't eavesdrop."

"I'm good at guarding my thoughts," Harwing said. "Better than you are, Talks-to-Rocks."

"Transmutation is a useful spell!" Dinias protested.

"Unless you're dealing with people," Harwing said.

"So what are you going to do?" Isilla asked. "And how long do we wait for you?"

"Not even a candlemark," Harwing said, getting to his feet. "Go back to camp and tell Rondithiel to leave at once—and to stay clear of anything that looks as if the Sanctuary's claimed it. Tell him I don't think Hamphuli-adiel's going to give us any help, and may do us much harm. I'll catch up to you if I can, and I'll try to Farspeak you. Listen for me at dawn for as long as you can."

"Until I see your body laid upon its pyre," Isilla said fiercely, rising to her feet and giving Harwing a swift hug. "May Pelashia defend you."

"And, uh, the Silver Hooves, too," Dinias said awkwardly. "They watch over all battles."

That made Harwing smile sadly. "If I ride with the Silver Hooves, I will see Gunedwaen again," he said quietly.

"Then let it be so," Isilla said. "But not soon."

❊

Harwing crouched down again once they were gone. Once word of his presence reached Hamphuliadiel, the Astromancer would certainly order a search of Arevethmonion no matter what Harwing told him, so he'd give Isilla and Dinias time to get well away before he drew attention to himself. He looked back out over the fields, letting his mind wander as he waited. Almost Sword Moon now; the fields were lush and green. There were a few folk moving among the young plants, checking for predation or weeds, but it was clear the harvest would be a good one. Enough grain to keep not only the folk here but all their animals through the winter, though it would be a few years yet before the new orchards were bearing their plums and apples, unless the Lightborn forced them by Magery. The town wasn't walled; clearly the villagers didn't expect to defend themselves—though there was certainly something here they needed defense from: he could see the bright patches where roofs had been partly rethatched, the blotching of new limewash on rebuilt walls.

*A fire, certainly, perhaps a raid, and not that long ago. Pennynorn said he'd seen a lot of signs that the Beastlings moved west in force recently: since neither komen nor commons would attack the Sanctuary of the Star, that's the only possibility left. And I will not know more until I go and see.*

Harwing resigned himself to the knowledge that he might well become one of those who went in to the Sanctuary and never came out again. But that, too, was information of a sort. Rondithiel would pass it to Vieliessar, and she would know what to do with it. *As she did with my Gunedwaen, who bought her the victory with his own life.* It was for that reason that Harwing could not love her, though he would serve where his oath had been given.

*What you seek determines who you must be to go searching for it. Who you are determines how you will go. The tale of that seeker starts years before the first step.* His first, best, lessons in the true craft of the Swordmaster: gathering information by subterfuge. Who should Harwing be, to learn what he'd come to find?

*I am Harwing Lightbrother. That much must be, when I return to the place where I was trained and the teachers who trained me. I am of Oronviel: they know this as well. I rode east in Fire Moon with all Vieliessar's grand array—as a Lightborn of Oronviel, I would have no choice. And now I come alone to the Sanctuary of the Star.*

*Why?*

*Because Gunedwaen is dead.* The thought, and the realization of what he meant to do with it, made Harwing catch his breath. But it would work. He thought of what Gunedwaen would have said, if he brought him this plan. The smile of astonished surprise. The joyful laugh at the cleverness of it.

*Gunedwaen is dead, and Vieliessar threw him away on the battlefield, nor did she send him to ride with the Starry Hunt with honor, for his body was left to lie as food for ravens and worms. She casts down the War Princes as she has said, and she casts aside Arilcarion as well. I will not serve such a one. And so I came away—*

He paused. Alone? He shook his head slowly. He must assume Rondithiel's party had been seen or spoken of.

*—and so I took my chance, and came west with the Lightborn Vieliessar sent into the west. But I left them behind, and I know not where they are now.*

That much was true. He could say they rode to aid the Western Shore, since Hamphuliadiel already knew it was embattled—at least, if Ciadorre and Ulvearth had reached him, and there was no reason to think they had not. None of the Lightborn with Rondithiel had ridden wearing Lightborn green; Hamphuliadiel would believe him if he said most of the party—should he know its size, or should Harwing be forced to tell it—was Lightless.

He frowned, concentrating, thinking of the tale he must weave into a cloak that would both conceal his true nature and direct his actions.

*And so we came west, through the Southern Pass, into Sierdalant. And we found it a ghostlands, and all to its west as empty as Farcarinon. And so I came here. When I saw the village and the fields, I didn't know what to think. I went to see what I could learn, for I feared to face you, knowing I had disobeyed your word by serving Vieliessar.*

Yes. That would serve. Enough truth to persuade. Enough to explain why he'd gone to the village instead of to the Sanctuary—for that was the first place his story would logically bring him. He would go as just another refugee. His hair was no shorter than any Landbond's, and the refugees who reached here probably had no idea of where they were. It wasn't as if the commonfolk ever saw the Sanctuary of the Star, just to begin with—to them it would be just another lesser keep. If he could find out all he wanted to know without ever going inside the Sanctuary gates, well and good. He'd slip away and Farspeak what he learned to Isilla as soon as he had the chance.

If he couldn't . . .

*Then I will serve Hamphuliadiel with as much loyalty and faithfulness as he could ask from one who has repudiated the madness of Vieliessar Farcarinon. And I will not take the first chance or the second to escape. I will count them as I count the moonturns, and take not the first one, but the best.*

He settled himself more comfortably. If Hamphuliadiel had foresters, they would find this spot, and know it was a place where someone had watched and waited, gathering up his courage to approach the village. Such a timid suspicious soul would wait until twilight, when he could cross the fields without being seen. And so Harwing would sit, and wait, and think only that he longed for comfort and safety, shelter and hot food. A place in a world he understood.

And he would hope Hamphuliadiel would believe it.

❧

When it was dark, and the windows of the few stone buildings of the village were lit, Harwing Lightbrother made his way toward it. On most farms, the fields were separated by hedgerows, but not here. Here, there were narrow footpaths between the fields, where incautious travel would not crush the growing plants. This land had been meadow and open forest when he had been a Postulant at the Sanctuary. Had the Lightborn helped in clearing it?

He reached out, cautiously, but could feel no residual trace of Light. All done by Lightless labor, then. He supposed it had been a great deal of work. It couldn't have begun before the False Parley last Sword Moon at the earliest, for only after that could it have escaped the War Princes' attention. Harwing supposed Thurion might be able to assess how much work these fields represented with absolute accuracy, but Harwing had never gotten closer to the fields than when he'd turned the horses out to graze after the harvest was in; his mother had been one of the grooms in Thoromarth's stables. He'd been lucky enough to come home to her after his time at the Sanctuary; few Lightborn ever saw their parents again after they took the Green Robe. Some never even saw again the domain they'd been born to, if they had been part of a war forfeit or a tithe . . .

He wove the cloak of idle thoughts about his mind, and looked around him with wide eyes. While he had obviously entered the village itself, there were no stone houses here, or even timber ones. Here the structures were crude huts made by weaving branches together. Some were covered with turves. Others stood exposed. Landbond huts: holes dug down into the ground with a covering of branches. Anything more elaborate was the work of generations—or of a Farmholder willing to give his chattels time and materials to build better. Clearly Hamphuliadiel was not such a master.

"What are you doing here?"

Harwing stopped at the sound of the voice. "Looking for shelter," he answered, equally quietly.

The person who had hailed him was Landbond. Former Landbond, since Vieliessar's decree, but the thing about making decrees was that then you had to enforce them. *Truths matter less than facts, and always will*, Gunedwaen's voice said in his memory.

The Landbond laughed harshly. "You'll beg your shelter and your bread from Light's Chosen, then?"

Harwing approached cautiously. The Landbond sat on the ground, in the doorway of his hut. "Is there a keep near here?" Harwing questioned in turn. It was a reasonable question from someone who didn't know where he was: the only places Lightborn lived were in keeps and large manor houses.

"'Keep,'" the Landbond answered. "Oh, aye, someday. And houses for all, and warm fires and hot food." He held out his arms before him, inviting Harwing to look. He had only one hand. The other was a long-healed stump. "For those who can work."

"I can work," Harwing said, taking it as an invitation to squat down beside him. "My name is Harwing. I used to work in a stable."

"Lodo," the Landbond answered. He regarded Harwing steadily. "In the morning you should go to the gate. It will be better for you that way."

"I don't understand," Harwing said. "What gate? What village is this?"

"Areve," Lodo said. "The master of the Light's Chosen made it. We came, because it was Sanctuary."

"I went away. With the army," Harwing answered.

"Wars are not for Landbonds," Lodo said. He shrugged. "High King promised freedom. But she left. And the lords left. Some said this was freedom, and followed. But the winter was cold, and the wolves came, and there was no food."

"And now?" Harwing asked cautiously.

Lodo simply shrugged again. "You should have stayed with your army. Unless your master was killed."

"He was," Harwing said simply. They sat in silence for a while.

There were a number of questions Harwing wanted to ask. *How many people live here? Why did you leave your lands? How far did you walk to get here? What does Hamphuliadiel promise? How are you taken care of?* But all of them would raise too much suspicion. And Lodo might not know anyway. Was this hole in the ground the extent of Hamphuliadiel's charity? Or were these living conditions a sign of Areve's quick expansion? *Perhaps the people will build better houses after the harvest is in,* he thought hopefully. The fields out there were the only source of food for both the Sanctuary and village. But it seemed just as likely that Hamphuliadiel cared as little for the people relying on him as the War Princes ever had.

He untied the cloak he wore and held it out. "Here. Take this. I'll go to the gate in the morning."

Lodo regarded it with suspicion. "You'll need a place to sleep."

"I'll find one." He'd learned as much as he could here. He'd circle around to take a closer look at Rosemoss Farm, and then perhaps try the center of the village.

Lodo reached out. Not to take the cloak, but merely to touch it. "A fine cloak," he said doubtfully. "Too fine," he said. "How should I come by it without stealing?"

"I'm sorry," Harwing said. He had little else, and Lodo was right. After a moment's thought, he undid his belt and slipped off his knife in its sheath. "Here," he said. "Take this. You can hide it. You've been kind to me, and I have nothing else to give you."

Lodo took the knife, and slipped it loose, one handed, to test the edge. He nodded, and tucked it into the front of his tunic. He got to his feet with slow care. "Don't steal," he said, the advice clearly payment for the gift. "They know. Some tried. They vanished."

Harwing got to his feet as well, picking up his discarded cloak. Vanished? He swallowed back a surge of nausea. If Hamphuliadiel was using the Light to kill . . .

But no. He would have sensed it. He hoped.

"I won't steal," he said. "I only want a safe place."

"Then Leaf and Star watch over you," Lodo said.

Harwing turned and walked back to the little path. He was more worried than he wanted to admit to himself. Perhaps he'd just take a look at the farm and leave—an incomplete report was better than none. He moved quietly and carefully until he passed the edge of Areve, then circled around behind the Sanctuary. The walls had been built up to rooftop height here as well, but they hadn't been extended to cover the buildings themselves. At first he thought the ground-floor windows were still where they had been, until he took a closer look and saw that their wooden shutters had been Transmuted to stone, sealing the windows as surely as bricks and mortar would have. Aside from a few windows low in the Astromancer's tower, the whole of the Sanctuary was dark. He went by as quickly as he could.

Rosemoss Farm had been a small manor farm, the sort of place that would house several generations of a

Farmhold family. It hadn't been large enough to either have Landbonds or a separate section of farmworker cottages attached to it. Bellion had kept his two horses in the Sanctuary stables, as Harwing remembered. He wondered if Farmholder Bellion was still here.

The farm, at least, was lit as it should be at this hour. Silverlight lanterns hung over the doors of the house and the stables, honest firelight shone from within the house. Where the woods had once come up nearly to the back of the house itself, all there was to see now was open land. The old barn was gone, and the clutter of outbuildings had been replaced by a stables that would not have been out of place in the shadow of a Great Keep. There was a fenced pasture behind it, and there were several horses turned out in it. Palfreys or destriers? It was worth a closer look.

Harwing circled around carefully, knowing that if the alarm was raised, the nearest cover was too far away to reach. He had just crossed into the shadow of the stables when the first body struck him.

He fell to the ground stunned, smelling the scent of dog and hearing the panting of breath. But even now, the beast did not bark. Beasts. More than one, a pack, quarreling amongst themselves in a terrible silence. The leader had his arm in its jaws, its teeth sunk into his flesh. He could not cast Shield with no space between them and in another moment one of them would go for his throat.

*Light.*

The spell he cast was not the gentle glow of Silverlight, but the raw bright flare of a lightning strike. It was enough to make the pack recoil enough for him to cast Shield.

He heard voices shouting in the distance.

He turned to run, then realized he would have to drop Shield to do so. And if he did, the pack would attack once more.

He was trapped.

※

He'd been brought into the Sanctuary, where Momioniarch Lightsister Healed his wounds and gave him tea. He'd been treated better than a War Prince would treat an enemy komen, not as well as one might treat a friend. A servant brought him Lightborn robes. His own clothing had been taken away, but even if they cast Knowing upon the garments, the spell would not tell them anything to contradict his story.

And when Harwing had changed his clothing, Momioniarch brought him to Hamphuliadiel.

"Harwing Lightbrother, once of Oronviel. I confess I am surprised to see you abandon your High King."

He stood at the foot of Hamphuliadiel's throne. The Astromancer's audience chamber was the most opulent thing Harwing had ever seen; its treasure enough to buy the contracts of all the vanished Free Companies and not be visibly diminished. Harwing let his amazement and confusion rise to the top of his thoughts; there was no reason to conceal them.

"I thought it would be different when she won," Harwing said grudgingly. The sight of this place and all it contained told him so many things about the state of Hamphuliadiel's mind that Harwing quietly began to doubt he would ever leave the Sanctuary alive.

*Let it be so. My death will tell Rondithiel much of what he needs to know.* He buried that thought deeply, below so many layers that even Thurion could not have teased it out.

"And now you see that I was right," Hamphuliadiel said archly. "But it does not tell me why you are here."

Harwing allowed himself to swagger a bit, as a masterless Lightborn might. His keen senses had not missed Sunalanthaid Lightbrother standing, silent and self-effacing, at Hamphuliadiel's side. "I didn't have a choice. Your Lightborn brought me."

"Don't play games with me," Hamphuliadiel snapped. "Your life is in my hands now."

"Then kill me," Harwing said simply. "What do I have to live for? Vieliessar Farcarinon has won. The Hundred Houses have pledged to her. The commonfolk love her, and whether the Lords Komen do or not really doesn't matter, does it?"

"Doesn't it?" Hamphuliadiel asked. "Don't you think others will do as you have done? Leave her?"

"And go where?" Harwing asked, shrugging. "Perhaps you do not know what the Uradabhur is like just now."

"Then tell me," Hamphuliadiel said. "You will not find me too proud to listen to your words. As Astromancer, my first care is for you. All of you, my Lightborn."

"Then you are the only one in all the Fortunate Lands that places us first," Harwing said, allowing bitterness to tinge his words. For more than a candlemark he spoke, telling the tale as if Hamphuliadiel knew none of it, from the first battles in Jaeglenhend through the terrible winter's war that followed, to the Battle of the Shieldwall Plain.

"I grieve with you at what Ivrulion was forced to do," Hamphuliadiel said. "Vieliessar's madness bred madness in all she drew into her web."

"He turned a Flower Forest the size of Caerthalien to ash," Harwing said flatly. "He fed his magic with the blood of his own son. It was his choice alone." *For victory, and to set the true heir of Caerthalien aside so he might become War Prince as well as Light-Prince.*

"And yet . . . He would never have dreamed of usurping Runacarendalur's place if Vieliessar had not begun this war," Hamphuliadiel said silkily.

"I suppose," Harwing answered grudgingly. "He did it because the Alliance was losing. And they still lost. All he managed to do was kill half the Lightborn there.

And now she's sent most of the rest to the west." He took up the balance of his tale, telling what had happened in the brief sennights between her victory and the granting of Iardalaith's petition. "She couldn't send ko-men, and Iardalaith said the Shore needed Lightborn more. So she sent them—us—with Rondithiel as our leader. I'd made up my mind to go anyway, but it was safer to go with a large party. Easier, too. No one asked 'why' any of us wished to go—it was enough to volunteer. Rondithiel was the only one who went because he was ordered to. Sending him was meant for proof, I suppose, that she had not abandoned Mosirinde's teachings."

"Or perhaps she took the chance to send away the only Lightborn who could rebuke her for such transgressions," Hamphuliadiel said. "Where is Rondithiel and his party now?"

"I don't know," Harwing said. "I slipped away when we neared Arevethmonion. He wanted to avoid the Flower Forest. They've been unlucky for us."

"Unlucky?" Hamphuliadiel's voice sharpened. "A Flower Forest?"

Harwing shrugged. "We came through the forest and over the Southern Pass—the Dragon's Gate was opened so wide the ice there probably won't melt until Harvest. Rondithiel told us we could not stop to aid any refugees we met, as we must reach the Shore as swiftly as we could. We meant to keep to the Flower Forests, but . . . supplies went missing. We all felt as if we were being watched, constantly. Pennynorn Lightbrother said it reminded him of Delfierarathadan. I suppose the others have gone on to Cirandeiron. Pennynorn said he knew the trick to let them cross the Angarussa."

"I find it odd that Rondithiel would not come to the Sanctuary," Hamphuliadiel said. "Surely he would seek what aid and shelter we could give?"

"Your silence disturbed him," Harwing said frankly.

"As did Iardalaith's tale that Amrolion's envoy and the komen with her vanished within sight of your walls."

Hamphuliadiel shook his head sorrowfully. "Vieliessar's poisonous counsel has spread farther than I could have believed. Do you wish to speak to the Lightsister, Harwing?"

"You say that as if you're trying to convince me of something," Harwing pointed out.

"Trust begets trust," Hamphuliadiel said. "Why should I trust you? You've told me a preposterous story. You didn't mean to come to the Sanctuary. You were captured. You're a spy for Vieliessar. You believe her lies."

A thousand questions, ideas, conclusions tried to come to the surface of his mind. Harwing forced them down, along with the consciousness of his danger. He was Harwing Lightbrother. He'd fled the High King's array.

"That's the trouble, Astromancer. They aren't lies."

"So you admit you are her creature?" Hamphuliadiel said, with a strange smile.

"*They aren't lies,*" Harwing repeated, more strongly. "She said she'd take the Unicorn Throne. She has. She said she'd free the Landbonds. She has. She said she'd make one justice for everyone. She has. I don't like the results. But she hasn't lied."

"She says she is the Child of the Prophecy," Hamphuliadiel said. "Do you believe it?"

Of course Harwing knew *The Song of Amretheon.* Every Postulant studied it. Gunedwaen had said—

"*She* believes it," Harwing said sharply.

"Do you know what we do here, Lightborn?" Hamphuliadiel asked. "You've seen Areve. Do you know why it is being built?"

"The refugees . . ." Harwing began.

"*She has broken the world!* They have no one else to turn to—but us! The Lightborn! We are all that stands between Mosirinde and Arilcarion and the Darkness! *She* is the Darkness! She! Vieliessar!"

Hamphuliadiel was on his feet. The transition between calm questioning and shouting rage was so abrupt, so unexpected, that there was room in Harwing's mind for only one thought.

*Gunedwaen never believed. He served her out of loyalty to Farcarinon. But he never believed she was the Child of the Prophecy.*

And suddenly, it all seemed terribly possible.

*She did not win her wars because anyone believed. She won by spellcraft and promises. She said she'd free the Landbonds and the commonfolk. She told us she would keep Mosirinde's Covenant if we would fight beside her. She gave everyone who followed her what they wanted: Thoromarth and Atholfol, relief from clientage. Iardalaith, the chance to go to war. Rithdeliel, his honor. And once the High Houses had allied against her, everyone was afraid of their anger. We Lightborn would be exempt from their punishment—but not our families.*

"She betrayed us," he groaned aloud. "She manipulated us until it was too late for any of us to turn back—there is no place for any of us now—"

"No," Hamphuliadiel said gently. "There is always refuge for the Lightborn in the Sanctuary of the Star. And forgiveness, too."

Harwing dropped to his knees and covered his face with his hands. "The West is a ghostlands. The east is an abattoir. Astromancer, how can I ever—" His voice was thick with tears.

Hamphuliadiel placed a gentle hand upon his head. "Hush, my child. While the Sanctuary stands, there is hope. With time and care, we can rebuild what she has broken."

"How— She would not even let us build pyres for the dead! Gunedwaen—! How can we—?"

"We will find our way together," Hamphuliadiel said kindly. "Our first duty is to those helpless innocents she abandoned, but we will speak of that later. You are weary. You must rest. We are so few, now, and the task is so great—"

"I will do anything I can," Harwing said hoarsely. "Anything. I am so ashamed—"

"No," Hamphuliadiel said, raising Harwing to his feet. "It is I who am ashamed. I had Vieliessar in my care, and I was unable to save her. I failed her, and in my failure, I failed all who depend upon my wisdom and care. But there is no need to speak of that now. Now you must rest, and recover from your journey."

With a gentle arm about Harwing's shoulders, Hamphuliadiel walked him to the door of the audience chamber. Harwing looked about himself as if with new eyes. How could he ever have thought this place a grasping display of wealth? It was the visible token of the trust and respect the War Princes had given to the Light. Not to the Lightborn—he knew, now, he'd been wrong. Yes, they were servants. Vassals. Subservient to the commands of their masters, yes, but their purpose was to wield the Light so that the Lightless could see it manifest in the world. To help them. To guide the Lightless, as the Lightborn were guided by the Light.

The door opened. Momioniarch stood waiting.

"Take Harwing Lightbrother to his room. He is weary," Hamphuliadiel said. "But now he is home."

❧❧

It took you long enough to bespell him," Hamphuliadiel said when Momioniarch returned.

"His mind was strong, and his thoughts were guarded," Momioniarch said. "It is difficult to change the heart of one whose Keystone Gift is Heart-Seeing. Without the cordial I added to his tea, it would have been impossible."

"But you did it?" Hamphuliadiel demanded.

Momioniarch smiled. "As I took him to his chamber he offered to seek out Rondithiel and bring him here."

"And it will be a proof of my good intentions that I do not ask that of him," Hamphuliadiel said archly.

"The Astromancer is both wise and merciful," Momioniarch said, bowing. "What *will* you ask of him?"

"Nothing," Hamphuliadiel said. "Nothing but loyalty—and service."

Momioniarch bowed again at his gesture of dismissal, leaving Hamphuliadiel to his thoughts.

If loyalty could be gained by spellcraft, the Hundred Houses would have ended their fighting long ago. Overshadow could make its subject a helpless puppet—but only for as long as its caster held the spell. Illusion could deceive for only as long as its victim believed in it. Spells to manipulate the emotions were commonplace, and as finite as any *geasa*. Every spell ran its course, and reached its end.

*But doubt . . . ah, let someone first doubt everything they had once believed to be true . . .*

And such a spell would never be undone, for its subject, Lightborn or Lightless, would recast it daily out of their own fear or guilt.

Momioniarch's delicate work could never have been performed in a War Prince's court. Lightborn had spied upon one another as assiduously as they spied on—and *for*—their masters, and such manipulation was held to be as direct an act as a sword blow. Unthinkable against an enemy. Madness against a vassal, for it could never be kept secret.

But here it need not be. All trace of the spell would be gone by sunrise, but Harwing's doubts would remain. Doubts Hamphuliadiel could manipulate as easily as he wove the Light.

*It is no transgression of Mosirinde's teachings to open the minds of the deluded to the truth,* he told himself.

*I save my Lightborn from Vieliessar's madness so that we may rebuild what she has shattered.*

When Vieliessar returned to the west—*if* she returned to the west—she would discover it had slipped through her fingers. The Sanctuary of the Star would become a rallying point for all who had realized her madness too late.

And Hamphuliadiel Astromancer—*Lord* Astromancer, Prince of Areve—would be the one who would lead them.

## CHAPTER NINE

# THUNDER MOON AND BEYOND: THE ART OF WAR

*Then did Amretheon Enslaver slay the heart and hopes of the folk, and then did Pelashia's children flee to the West. And it was a dark time, yet all consoled themselves that it was not the darkest time, for that would only come when the Children of Stars set over themselves a new High King in Amretheon's place, seated upon the throne of his shame.*

— *Chronicle of the Nine Races*

It had been a gift unlooked-for when the Children of Stars took their quarrels beyond the mountains and went with all their folk to fight their battles there, and the Otherfolk took quick advantage of it. It had taken the Nine Races millennia to understand that even Pelashia's sacrifice couldn't gain them peace while the Children of Stars lived. From the Red Winnowing to this eve of the Red Harvest, they had tried so hard to reach the Children of Stars. To make them *hear*. And never with any success—only pain, and tears, and loss upon loss.

Only when the last of the Children of Stars was gone from the world would Leutric dare to give up the knowledge that would rouse the Bones of the Earth. Those were the only weapon that might protect the Otherfolk and the Brightfolk from the Red Harvest—and only the bloodline of Pelashia could wield them. That knowledge had been in his keeping since the day he reached adulthood, when his father showed him the way and the signs, and warned Leutric just as his own father had warned him:

*The Bones of the Earth have no conscience. They have no loyalty. Whoever takes them up will own their power. See that it is not turned upon you.*

And he had promised, as his father had promised, but his father had not lived in such times as Leutric did, to see each sign and portent appear telling that the time of the Red Harvest was near.

And so Leutric sent scouts eastward, and in time, his scouts returned, bearing with them two things: the news that every living thing in the land hastened westward—and the Child of Stars who had seen the southern Flower Forest die. His name was Runacar, and he was a prince of his people. Runacar did not know how narrow the knife blade was upon which he stood when he spoke before Leutric and his court to say that it was his brother who killed the forest and its people—his brother alone, at no one's order. And he told Leutric something else, something whose importance he clearly did not understand.

*"The Hundred Houses have lost. The High King has won. Vieliessar Farcarinon is High King over all the Fortunate Lands."*

The Fortunate Lands belonged to the Otherfolk, but Leutric did not say so. Nor did he say that this was the last of the signs given to the Otherfolk, that now the Red Harvest was a thing only sennights, not Wheel-turns, away. And most of all, he did not say that Runacar must die. The Otherfolk did not kill as casually as the Children of Stars did; let this Child of Stars find his own way in the world, and his own fate. Leutric had much to do, now that the last sign had come, and he went off to do it.

And three moonturns later, Runacar came to him again.

❧❦❧

Leutric was constantly on the move, seeing what must be seen, giving tasks to those who would accept them. When he found that Runacar had followed his track, Leutric was mildly surprised to find him still alive, for just because Leutric did not choose to order his death, few of the Otherfolk had any great love for the Children of Stars. But then he remembered that Keloit had seemed fond of him—and Keloit's mother, Frause, was a great Spellmother. Perhaps she had been sent a vision. Perhaps it was simple kindness. Perhaps it was wholly an accident that the Child of Stars still lived.

But Leutric was curious, and so he sent for him.

❧❦❧

Runacar stood before Leutric in the center of Alqualanya Flower Forest, where Leutric sat upon a stone to hold court. By now Leutric's people had seen the inside of many of the great buildings of the Children of Stars, so Leutric understood that his own place of rule would look to the Elven Prince like nothing more than a forest glade. So be it. Leutric was King-Emperor, and Runacar had come seeking speech with him. Leutric would hear what was to be said.

"You're fighting a war," Runacar said.

"That much should be obvious even to you," Leutric rumbled. "This was our place before it was yours. You took it from us once. We will not let you take it a second time."

"Forgive me, lord King-Emperor, but I did not say what I meant," Runacar answered. "You're fighting a war *badly*."

"'Badly?'" Leutric asked. "We're winning."

"You're losing," Runacar said flatly. "Your people are scattered from here to Greythunder Glairyrill. You build towns that a child could sack. Keloit says you mean to take the Western Shore away from Daroldan and Amrolion, and in the next breath he tells me that all you're doing is driving them away from Delfierarathadan."

"And we will drive them into the sea," Leutric said. He was more curious than affronted.

"No," Runacar said. "You won't. What will happen is this: Damulothir Daroldan will make common cause with Leopheine Amrolion, if he hasn't already. Leopheine will bring his people north—I would; the Kashadabadshar is nothing to have at your back when you are besieged—and together they will fight. If they must, they will go north, through the Medharthas, around Delfierarathadan, and come into the west."

He waited expectantly.

"And they'll be gone from the Shore," Leutric said. "That is victory."

"No," Runacar said. "That is a skirmish. Two War Princes, with all their households, with all their array, with every single one of their folk, will gather what's left of the West behind them faster than you can imagine. They will call for aid, if they have not already, and the High King will send it, for they have been her vassals from the beginning, and she will not stay in the east forever. And when she comes, you will not face a hundred armies more interested in fighting each other than fighting you. You will face one army, King-Emperor Leutric. One army with one mind and one voice, an army made not of komen, but of every one of her people." He stopped speaking, looking as if he were overcome by the sense of his own words. "What will you do then?" he added at last.

Leutric thought of a hundred things he might say. *That day may never come. That day is far in the future. The Red Harvest will bring an end to such foolishness.* But instead he said: "Why do you come to say these things to me?"

"I like being on the losing side," Runacar said bitterly, staring at the ground. Then he raised his head to gaze into Leutric's eyes. "Your people don't know how to fight a war. Mine do. *I* do. If there is one thing that is still true, it is this: I know how to make war. I can teach you. With my help, you can win—whatever victory means to you."

Leutric frowned thunderously "Your people have called us Beastlings. Abomination. You've killed us. Burned our homes. Worn our skins as clothing. We have been delicacies for your table. You cannot even look at us without flinching, because the shapes we wear are different from yours. Why would you help us?"

"Because—" Runacar swayed and nearly fell. Now Leutric could see he had not sought this audience lightly. Weariness and strain etched the lines of his body. "Sit," Leutric said, motioning him toward the ground. "Whatever great state your people keep, ours do not."

"So I discover," Runacar muttered. He went ungracefully to his knees then sat heavily, hunched forward, his elbows on his knees.

Leutric waited in silence, and at last Runacar spoke.

"I don't know," he said at last. "You're monsters. So I was told. Why shouldn't I believe it? I believed my father when he said Caerthalien deserved the Unicorn Throne. I believed my brother when he said he was content to be Lightborn. I believed my mother when she said Farcarinon was tainted and corrupt—" He broke off with a weary laugh. "I didn't believe Vieliessar when she said she would be High King. And she is. And . . . I think she has destroyed us. I just want to save something. Even if it's you."

Leutric did not believe him. He did not disbelieve him, either, for the Children of Stars lied so readily they did not know how to recognize truth even from their own lips. Instead, he kept Runacar by his side as he moved through the West. Sennight after sennight, Runacar attended every court, heard ever report, every petition, and always Leutric tested him, asking his advice, asking what he would do.

He did not follow Runacar's advice at first, but as the days passed, he came to realize that Runacar was more often right than wrong. When a plan of Leutric's failed, it failed in much the way Runacar predicted.

And so one day Leutric said: "Give me the Shore."

Runacar answered: "I will. But first I will give you the West."

⊰⊱

It was, of course, not that simple. If Runacar meant to destroy the remaining strongholds of the Elves and harry their occupants from the Western Reach, he must have the fighters to do it. But while Leutric might be Emperor of the Otherfolk, he had less authority over them than Caerthalien's chief castellan would have had over the kitchens of Aramenthiali. Though Leutric sent out a call for volunteers to join an impromptu war band, Runacar realized that without his sennights of acting as Leutric's military advisor in the sight of all who came to the King-Emperor's court, no one would have been willing to answer that call—except, perhaps, Keloit.

Even before his first volunteers arrived, Runacar was planning out what he would do. The Otherfolk would have begun with the obvious targets, the Sanctuary of the Star, the Western Shore. If they had thrown the whole force of their people into such a battle, they might even have prevailed, but brute force against craft and skill would buy any victories at far too high a cost. Runacar meant to begin with the smallest and easiest targets he could find, but before that, he and his war band would have to find out what they were. Leutric had gotten reports, but they were all-but-useless to Runacar.

And even that must wait upon discovering who would follow him.

By now Runacar knew that the Otherfolk divided themselves into two groups. One—called the Nine Races, though there seemed to be far more than nine of them—was what Runacar knew as the Beastlings; the Otherfolk upon whom the Hundred Houses had eternally waged war. The other group were called the Brightfolk. They lived only in the Flower Forests and were—at least to him—silent, invisible, and intangible. Even the few he could see or hear—like the fairies—he could not understand. In the end, it didn't much matter who or what they were: the Brightfolk would not fight.

In fact, *most* of the Otherfolk would not fight. It had taken moonturns, but Runacar had come to realize that everything he thought he knew about the "Beastlings" was completely wrong. Not only were the Otherfolk not the monsters Runacar had been told they were, they weren't even a really credible threat to an Elven army. If the Hundred Houses had ever been able to agree on anything, they could have slaughtered all of the Otherfolk centuries ago, because the Otherfolk would have—could have—offered no organized resistance. War was Runacar's trade and profession, and when he had been Prince Runacarendalur of Caerthalien, Runacar had been a master of war.

The Otherfolk simply weren't any good at war.

The Gryphons, far from being the terrifying aerial killers immortalized in many of the Windsward ballads, were shy and rather skittish, interested in creating and reciting long poems and songs. The fact that an adult Gryphon could carry off a horse in its talons did not translate to battlefield aggression. The horse was *food*—and despite the centuries of warfare between them and the Elves, the Gryphons still hesitated to kill sentient beings: Gryphons were pacifists.

Bearwards looked terrifying. They would attack Elves if they were threatened. Their Spellmothers were fearsome sorceresses and fearsome foes. But the Bearwards lived in the forests which they tended, did not gather in large groups, and when offered the choice between attack and retreat, Bearwards nearly always chose retreat.

Hippogriffs were scatterbrained and easily bored, more interested in playing tricks upon an enemy, or showing off, than they were in fighting. They were savage fighters when attacked, but as soon as the immediate threat was gone, they lost interest.

The Minotaur clans were widely scattered, reluctant to leave their families, reluctant to organize.

Nobody but a lunatic would put a Faun in charge of anything.

And so it went, race after race. Individually they were dangerous. Certainly they had strong ties to family, clan, and—at least in the case of the Centaurs—villages. Certainly there had been no season since the Hundred Houses came to be that did not bring news of some Elven death at the hands of the Otherfolk. But to drive Elvenkind out of the West, the Otherfolk needed to be an army, not a disorganized collection of individuals. Until Leutric became King-Emperor, they hadn't even had a leader.

Many of the first volunteers were Centaurs, for the West had once been their territory. Some Bearwards came out of curiosity and for the fun of it. Leutric had enough sway over the members of his own clan to convince some of the Minotaurs to join—including Audalo, who was, Runacar discovered, Leutric's heir. Radafa came, though he said firmly he came only to watch and to learn more of the *alfaljodthi*. But the most surprising recruits to Runacar's nascent war band were ... Elves.

They named themselves Woodwose, and swore that Elves were another race entirely. Woodwose had lived beside Otherfolk—and among them, in Centaur villages and Bearward hidels—not just for centuries, but for millennia. Most of them neither knew nor cared how they'd come to live among the Otherfolk, but Radafa's people, the Gryphons, were great storytellers, and he told Runacar enough for him to make a Loremaster's story of it. Runacar wondered how often one of the Woodwose was the last sight a huntsman or a forester saw, for there had never even been rumors of their existence—at least, rumors that rose as high as a War Prince's court.

Woodwose averaged a little taller than Landbonds, but with that same willowy strength. They wore tunics and leggings, the items painted rather than dyed, and braided ornaments into their hair, which they often dyed in garish colors. It was ironic that the element of his army most like him in form and heritage was the element Runacar could least depend upon. The Woodwose were kin, but kin who loathed the "Houseborn" who had discarded them, or their ancestors, like worthless refuse. In battle, he would not be able to trust them to hold a position: they would see the enemy and go running toward it. Or disappear into the forest to ambush knights who would never arrive.

But at least they would fight.

◈

To scour the West as he had once scoured Farcarinon would not be the work of a moonturn, or even a Wheelturn, but it could be done—if there was no leader who could unify and rally the leaderless Landbonds, Farmfolk, and Crofters.

Runacar took his two tailles of volunteers east. His array carried what it needed on its backs—even the Woodwose did not ride horses—with a few light pushcarts for the heaviest items. Once he had some idea of the scope of the task before him, he began training his most unmartial of levies by sending them against the easiest targets he could find, for his new partisans lacked even the basic theory of war. *"It is not enough to destroy an enemy if you cannot hold what you have taken from him,"* Arilcarion War-Maker had written in *The Way of the Sword,* and so Runacar believed. Under his command, farmsteads were overrun, border steadings erased, abandoned Keeps were opened to the wind and the sky and cleansed with flame.

At first, Runacar was certain time was the one thing he did not have. A few moonturns after the Battle of the Shieldwall Plain, Vieliessar had sent a grand-taille of Lightborn westward. Leutric—at Runacar's suggestion—had let them pass unmolested. They had vanished across the Angarussa, and no more followed. He'd been certain that the High King's army would come again by Fire Moon, but she did not—nor had she come by Harvest, by Frost, or by Rain. Nor could Runacar send scouts across the Mystrals to survey and report: the Gryphons or the Hippogriffs could reach the Shieldwall Plain and return in less than a handful of days, but they simply would not go, saying the Red Harvest had begun. Runacar had no idea what the Red Harvest might be, and all Radafa, or Keloit, or even Audalo would say was that it had been "prophesied."

Runacar was sick of prophecies. He didn't ask further.

He spent the moonturns of the first deep winter that followed—the few moonturns when snow and cold made skirmishing impossible—among Keloit's family in a forest through which he had hunted as a boy, for it was on Caerthalien lands. Caerthalien Keep was utterly deserted. Whoever its caretakers had been, they had fled long before Runacar arrived.

Spring came, and the war band—now doubled in size by an influx of new recruits—returned to its task, and worked from Storm to Hearth. Runacar spent that winter at one of the new Centaur villages somewhere in what had been Domain Brabamant. Pelere's family lived there—she and Keloit were his most promising students.

Spring came again. His forces regathered. And over moonturns and Wheelturns—slowly, painfully—he turned his tiny War Band into an army. Not the sort of army he had once proudly commanded in his father's name, but one well suited to its current task: to take the Western Lands as its own. He had promised Leutric the West and the Shore, and he meant to keep that promise.

And still the High King did not come. She was not dead—there was no place far enough away that Runacar, her unwilling Bondmate, would not mirror her death with his own—but she did not come west, and he did not know why. Even though they had been destined enemies from the moment of her birth, they had had the same teachers. Even though she had far outstripped those teachers, she had certainly not rejected their basic principles. *Move quickly. Secure resources and defensible structures. Do not give your enemy time to entrench and prepare.*

Yet she did not come.

As the Wheelturns passed, Centaurs built villages and farms in the shadows of disparaged Great Keeps. Woodwose and Bearwards planted saplings at the edges of Flower Forests, Fauns frolicked through the forests where Bearward families made their homes, Dryads filled the orchards, and the Minotaur clans carved great mazes into wide, serene meadows. The land grew peaceful, fruitful, and populated.

Runacar's army grew from one taille to two, to four, until he led eight tailles of folk used to rough and tumble banditry. It was no form of warfare that Mosirinde or Arilcarion would have recognized, let alone Caerthalien's own Warlord and Swordmaster, but it was effective and deadly. He also had a handful of true apprentices in the art of war. Any Warlord might have a thousand students, but true apprentices were rare, yet Keloit and Pelere, Audalo, the Woodwose Tanet, and even Radafa, scholar and pacifist that he was, had become Runacar's most able students.

The most important thing he tried to teach them was that the purpose of war was to gain peace.

⚔︎

W hat is that?" Pelere whispered. Pelere was fair, with wheat-colored hair and a flaxen tail to match. Her slenderness made her lower body appear more horselike than that of many Centaurs, and her roan hide was polished to gleaming. She wore a hooded jerkin of exquisitely soft undyed leather, completely embroidered in a design of twining vines covered with berries and flowers.

Beside her, Keloit—clad only in a necklace and a wide belt—shifted uneasily. In the Wheelturns since Runacar had first met him, Keloit had grown up, gaining most of his adult height and mass; where once Runacar could look him in the eye, now Keloit towered over him when he stood. The last time Runacar had been to Keloit's home, Frause had introduced him to Keloit's future bride. (Helda was a Healer, not a Spellmother, to Runacar's obscure relief.) It was a sobering reminder that many of the Nine Races did not share *alfaljodthi* longevity: aside from Radafa, his first friends among the Otherfolk would be dead of old age in a scant handful of decades. *If any of us live that long,* he thought mordantly.

The third of his students, the Woodwose Tanet, stood unmoving, nearly invisible in his painted leathers, ornamented with beads, shells, and feathers. His hair, dyed to the color of ash, formed a spiky corona about his head.

Runacar raised a hand, silencing the Centauress. The scouting party was almost a league south of the forest road that led through Arevethmonion to the Sanctuary. There should be nothing here but wilderness. Instead, Runacar looked out over farmland that ran to within a bowshot's length of the Flower Forest. Fields stretched into the distance; some being plowed, some already planted, some holding flocks of sheep or herds of cattle.

He had kept his war band away from the Sanctuary of the Star while they had cleared the lands between it and the Mystrals, and now he was glad that he had. It was second nature for him to count the people in the fields, and to estimate how many people the strange vast village outside the Sanctuary of the Star could hold.

Hundreds.

Thousands.

They should not be here.

*None* of this should be there. He had known that the Sanctuary had expanded, that a village had grown up near it, but he had never imagined the sheer size of it. He was glad, now, that he'd chosen to make his approach through Arevethmonion. The Dryads and the other Brightfolk would protect them and give warning of any discovery or pursuit. He could not think of the Brightfolk without thinking of the Ghostwood, and there were nights when the memory of it allowed him very little sleep. But to set against that were days like today, filled with sun and growing things and the deep, sacred hush of the Flower Forest.

He motioned to his companions and they retraced their steps, moving silently back the way they had come. Tanet moved like a shadow among the trees and Pelere moved as gracefully and as quietly as a deer among the saplings and fallen leaves. Otherfolk knew how to hide.

"What's going on?" the Centauress repeated when

they had returned to their campsite deep within the Forest. She stamped a hoof impatiently.

"They're farming," Runacar said.

Keloit snorted, wrinkling his snout. "We can all see that they're farming! But what does that mean?"

Runacar sat down on a fallen log. "I don't know," he said.

"That's helpful," Pelere grumbled. "You're supposed to know. If you don't, what good are you?"

"Are you just now beginning to wonder that?" Tanet asked silkily.

Runacar smiled without warmth. He was never sure whether the Woodwose hated him—or to be frank, *how much* Tanet hated him—or if he was simply pragmatic enough to want to learn all he could, regardless of its source. "I'm the Elven general who's going to give you everything from the Mystrals to Great Sea Ocean. And to do that, I need to see what we have to get rid of." As he spoke, he turned to the pack resting against the trunk and pulled out a large scrollcase. He tipped its contents out and shuffled through the sheets of vellum until he found the one he was searching for.

"Here is the Sanctuary as it stood before the High King's War," he said, smoothing the sheet over the trunk and bringing out a stylus. "I know it's accurate, because I drew it myself. Sanctuary, gardens, Guesthouse, stables, and Rosemoss Farm to provide everything that didn't come with the tithing wagons. But nobody's tithed for five Wheelturns now, and even before that the tithes were short—"

"Because you were at war," Keloit said.

"Going to war," Runacar corrected absently. "After the False Truce in Fire Month, but Oronviel had belonged to Vieliessar since the previous Harvest—"

"What good is telling us what we already know?" Tanet demanded.

"It tells us what's going to happen next," Runacar said. "If your people had paid more attention to things like that, mine wouldn't have been burning you out of your villages since the fall of Celephriandullias. Now," he said, as Pelere swished her tail in impatience, "no tithes, no Candidates, no War Princes to keep order—and no High King returning to restore order. So Hamphuliadiel sets himself up not just as Astromancer, but as War Prince. He builds a higher wall around the Sanctuary garden, dismantles the stables and the Guesthouse, expands Rosemoss Farm, and builds a very large village. What does that tell us?"

"That . . . he's got a lot of free time?" Keloit suggested, his ears perking up hopefully.

"Or that he's as mad as all Houseborn," Tanet suggested. "But clearly you don't think so."

Runacar laughed shortly. "Hardly. The outbuildings were torn down to improve the sight lines. The new wall forms a line of defense. The village is vulnerable, but a couple of Lightborn casting Shield could protect it easily. Hamphuliadiel's expecting a war. With who?"

"Us?" Pelere suggested hopefully.

"Why not the High King?" Runacar asked gently.

Pelere frowned as she struggled to think of the answer to his question. "Well . . . The High King's on the other side of the mountains," she said. "She isn't here."

"True," Runacar said encouragingly. "But she might come here. What then?"

"Wouldn't she win?" Keloit asked tentatively. "She has more knights than there are stars in the sky—Mama says—and witches, too. The Green Robes."

"Witchery won't save anyone from an arrow through the throat," Tanet said, touching the quiver at his hip. "Or a dart—if it's poisoned." The Woodwose fought in forests, from ambush; their weapons were sling and dart-pipe, bow and bolo, javelin, garrote, and sharp curved dagger.

"But this is where they come from," Pelere protested. "All the Green Robes come from this place." She looked hopefully at Runacar, but he would not give her the answer. His apprentices had to learn to find the answers for themselves.

"It's a bower-bird nest!" Keloit exclaimed. "You know: they build them with all the prettiest flowers they can find, as big as they can. That's what this is! Only what does he want to come?"

"Not us," Pelere said firmly. "But bandits won't attack Green Robes," she said, dutifully reciting her lessons. "And we won't, because King Leutric says we are not to show ourselves within a hundred leagues of this place, and so we haven't. The High King isn't here. So there *is* no threat." She stamped her hoof again and frowned. "Only *he* doesn't know we won't attack . . ."

"That's right," Runacar said encouragingly. He glanced at Tanet, but the Woodwose's face was expressionless. "Hamphuliadiel means to hold the Sanctuary against you—*us*—and perhaps against the High King if she comes. For that he needs an army. He cannot summon one, for the Astromancer has no such authority. But he can lure one with this display of wealth and order."

*And he has the only Lightborn between the Shore and the Mystrals, so he has something everyone needs . . .*

"Do you think it's worked?" Tanet asked archly.

Pelere grinned bloodthirstily. "Let's find out."

"Soon," Runacar said. "For now, we'll go and tell the others what we've learned. What is the first lesson every scout learns?"

"Never risk losing what you have learned of your enemy before you can tell it," Pelere and Keloit chorused. Tanet merely grimaced.

—⁂—

The war band's camp at Araglion Flower Forest was tiny by the standards Runacar had once known, but immense by the reckoning of the Otherfolk, for there were nearly a hundred souls gathered here.

Andhel appeared from nowhere less than a quarter-mark after his party entered Araglion. She stood blocking their path. There were a number of Woodwose with the war band, but Runacar had never deluded himself that they followed him—none of the Woodwose trusted him. Tanet was their leader, and most of them pretended Runacar was invisible—except for Andhel. The Woodwose was one of the camp sentries—running away, Andhel said, was a prized skill when you were a sentry or a scout. Like Tanet, she wore painted buckskin, but hers was stitched and appliquéd with horsehair and feathers, artful trailing ribbons and tattered scraps of cloth. Her long straight hair was dyed the green of forest moss, and her face was painted with an elaborate design of dots and spirals.

"So, Great Prince Runacar, what did you find?" Andhel demanded. She seemed to take an unfailing delight in mocking him at every possible opportunity. And while Tanet actively wanted to learn what Runacar had to teach, and confined himself to occasional moments of snark, Andhel took a passionate delight in baiting his temper. He wasn't sure why she had joined his experimental Free Company in the first place.

"That Hamphuliadiel has decided to become War Prince," Runacar said shortly. Usually he found her bickering entertaining, but not today.

She snickered. "That's what you all want, Houseborn."

"I have said—" Runacar began.

"That you are Runacar-of-no-House," Andhel singsonged, "but its stones will be in your bones until you die, Houseborn." She smirked at him triumphantly.

"Yes, if you say so, Andhel, I am certain it is Pelashia's own truth," Runacar said. "I have stones for bones. Now, where is Audalo?"

"Where else?" she answered, pointing deeper into the forest. Runacar looked—he could not see the camp from here—and when he looked back, Andhel had vanished.

"Why doesn't she like you? Tanet likes you," Keloit said. Runacar had long since discovered that Keloit liked everyone, and was always surprised to discover his view of the world wasn't everyone's.

Tanet said nothing very loudly.

"Tanet hopes that someday Runacar will become Woodwose in his soul," Pelere said. "And then he can declare victory over all the Children of Stars."

Tanet smiled. "Ah, I see someone has figured me out, pretty one."

Pelere tossed her head and ostentatiously looked away from Tanet. Runacar shrugged and walked in the direction Andhel had indicated. Pelere and Keloit followed.

"No," Runacar said, swooping up the Faun who'd darted from cover to grab at his boot-dagger. He tossed the little creature up into the air and plunked it on Pelere's back.

"Hey," she said, turning to look over her shoulder. The Faun grinned at her.

It was a creature the size of a young child, with long, tufted, pointed ears, tiny golden nubs of horns, and disconcerting brown-red curls on its head. Above the waist, at a distance, it might be mistaken for one of the *alfaljodthi*. Below the waist, it was goat-like, in the way Centaurs were horse-like and Minotaurs bull-like.

"Flary likes you," Runacar said hopefully, as the Faun began trying to search Pelere's pockets.

"Flary likes anything shiny," Pelere said. She plucked him from her back and tossed him gently to the ground.

"Run along," she said kindly. "You don't want to play with Runacar today. He's in a bad mood."

Flary scurried off. Runacar suppressed a scowl. At the moment, he thought he'd give a great deal for someone—someone other than Andhel or Tanet—who was in a bad mood. Or at least properly *worried*. The Otherfolk were fighting for their lives. He knew it. They knew it. But—

*They don't think like Elves. They don't fight like Elves. And you miss people who do.* Even the Woodwose didn't think like his people. No matter what they looked like, they thought like Otherfolk.

⚜

The encampment was scattered among a dozen clearings. Audalo was sitting on a tree-trunk in the central one. He'd stayed behind on the scouting expedition because there was simply no way for a Minotaur to *skulk*.

Beside Audalo, insubstantial as smoke, stood a Dryad. She was speaking to Audalo, but Runacar couldn't hear her. He stopped where he was, watching. She was beautiful.

He thought of the twisted, wooden bones in the Ghostwood and gritted his teeth.

*If we'd known . . . would it have made any difference? I keep asking myself that, and it's always the same answer: no. Because we did know. And we killed them anyway.*

Her report finished, the Dryad faded away. Runacar glanced around the clearing, trying to figure out which tree was hers.

"Runacar! You're back!" Audalo rose to his feet in greeting, his leather creaking. Like most Minotaurs, Audalo went barefoot, but that didn't mean he wasn't dressed. Wide leather bracers covered his arms from wrist to elbow, and again from elbow to shoulder, their surfaces elaborately painted, carved, and studded. His tunic was of good heavy linen, dyed with a pattern of bars and swirls in grey and green—the design looked purely ornamental until Audalo vanished into the forest without taking more than a step or two. It fell to mid-thigh and was secured with a wide belt holding pouches and weapons. His great ivory horns were gilded in a spiral pattern interwoven with small red and blue dots: Minotaurs were known for their decorative skill and their main trade items were decorated pottery and designs, which others could translate into cloth or other woven goods.

"We had to make sure we weren't followed from the Sanctuary. But I saw some things there that will interest you," Runacar said.

"By that he means you should be worried," Keloit said irrepressibly.

"Bah!" Audalo scoffed. "With Leutric for our King and Runacar to lead our armies, we are certain of victory!" He smiled to show it was meant in jest, and indicated Runacar should sit beside him. "What have you learned?" he asked.

Audalo was Runacar's apprentice in the art of war, but he was also King Leutric's heir. Runacar concentrated for a moment, organizing his report in his mind, just as he would have given it to Lengiathion or Elrinonion, or even to Bolecthindial, when Caerthalien still stood. "The Sanctuary of the Star is going to be a problem."

Audalo cocked his head in inquiry, a gesture that still mesmerized Runacar every time he saw it. The first time, he'd wondered why the Minotaur simply didn't fall over, pulled by the enormous weight of his horns. It still seemed so likely that he might.

"The drawings I made for Leutric are no longer true," Runacar said. "What I thought was there was something we might easily have ignored while we took the Shore. But now—"

He told all of what he remembered and what he guessed of what Hamphuliadiel had done. The Sanctuary itself, made defensible. The land for leagues around put under plow, and a great village built to hold those workers.

"It will keep growing," Runacar said. "Any Landbond who didn't go running after that damned— To join the High King's army—or who we didn't chase over the Mystrals or into Delfierarathadan—wants protection. Keloit suggested Hamphuliadiel was building a lure to entice the surviving masterless komen to join him. I think he's right—we haven't seen much of them east of the Sanctuary, and we should have. The Astromancer means to build an army."

"What do you think he means to do with it?" Audalo asked, after a pause.

"I don't know," Runacar admitted. "What I do know is this: we'd better find out. And that means trying his defenses. If we do not know what he has, and what he plans, we will once again find ourselves caught between hammer and swordblade." He had long feared a leader rising up to unite what was left of the Western Reach. If Hamphuliadiel was that leader . . .

"See the brave Houseborn fleeing from shadows!" Andhel said scornfully, stepping to Audalo's side.

"See the brave Woodwose who has never faced Lightborn in battle!" Runacar answered caustically. "Let us see how Hamphuliadiel will defend what is his before we make our plans."

⊰⊱

It was a few candlemarks after midnight. There was nothing to see but a few lights burning within the Sanctuary itself. The village was dark. The moon was a tiny sliver, giving no light.

Runacar had planned and led raids and skirmishes

most of his life. He'd been the favored son, the Heir-Prince, meant to rule over Caerthalien when his father went to ride with the Starry Hunt. There was no reason to be nervous, he told himself.

The difference was that this time, he would not be leading the raiders. He wouldn't even be a big part of the fight. Without a horse, he could not keep up with the Centaurs or even the Bearwards. And the initial attack depended on speed.

Runacar did not intend to attack the Sanctuary itself. Even if he'd possessed ten times the numbers at his current command—and even assuming he were able to instill anything approaching field discipline into them—it would be an affront to the Silver Hooves to attack Their shrine. The village beside it was a different matter.

The plan Runacar had made was simple. It had to be. The Otherfolk were strong, fast, and smart, but they did not wage war as Runacar understood war. *Lengiathion and Elrinonion would laugh themselves to scorn to see me now. But Lengiathion would also say that the warrior fits himself to the war, and not the other way around. If these are my knights, then my tactics must serve them as well as they can.*

He tried to push the feeling of wrongness from the surface of his thoughts. Every instinct told him he should be astride a destrier, in full armor, the heavy weight of a helm on his head to match the weight of the sword at his hip. To ride forward into the eternal dance that was half prayer, half promise, its every move an offering to the Silver Hooves and the Starry Huntsman. An offering of the beauty of war to Those Who watched and judged.

It was something he would never have again, thanks to his destined and unbeloved Bondmate. Now he wore leather armor and Centaur-made chain. His sword was

short, something that would not impede a man on foot.
He carried a small round shield, its weight and heft
awkward and unfamiliar.

Around him, behind him, stood his war band,
waiting.

He took a deep breath. *Remember who you were*, he
told himself fiercely. He forced calmness over his
thoughts, and his hands were steady as he opened the
gate of the tiny dark lantern. One—two—three pulses
of light. It was the signal.

There was another moment, in which Runacar imagined a thousand things to have gone wrong. Then, suddenly, there was a blaze of light as the Centaurs whipped
their torches aflame. The ground trembled with the
thunder of hooves as two tailles of Centaurs charged
from the woods. They had sixteen furlongs of open field
to cross before they reached the town. Plenty of warning for anyone on guard.

That was the point.

"Archers, move up," he whispered. To whisper was
reflex only: he could have shouted without betraying
their position, for the Centaurs were howling their battle cry, a sound that struck chills down his spine. "Do
not loose until I give the order."

"Does it feel good to give orders, Houseless?" Andhel asked, as she stepped to his side. She carried a walking bow nearly as long as she was tall: the archers were
the first line of defense.

"Ask me again when we've won," he answered, and
Andhel laughed soundlessly as she moved beyond the
tree line to take her position. The archers were in the
first rank, backed by the rest of the Centaurs.

The running Centaurs had nearly reached the village.
The windows of the Sanctuary began to fill with light,
one by one, like slow fireflies.

"Radafa."

Runacar stepped back as the Gryphon came forward.

Radafa stepped into the open space and began to run, a gleaming shape in the darkness, his feet soundless over the plowed earth. Runacar heard the sharp sound as his wings unfurled, the muffled drumbeats of them as the Gryphon clawed for altitude.

The Centaurs thundered through the village. Light flared as their torches kindled thatch and timber. There were screams, as the villagers awoke to their peril.

*No watch,* Runacar noted automatically. *Hamphuli-adiel doesn't defend the village; there might be a sentry somewhere inside the Sanctuary, but they don't know what they're watching for and they're too slow to sound the alarm.*

He drew his sword and began to run.

The rest of his War Band followed.

An alarm bell began to ring at last, jangling instead of tolling, its rope pulled too fast by panicked hands. A rush of Silverlight spilled into the Sanctuary courtyard. The Lightborn were coming and neither Code nor Covenant prevented them from using their spellcraft against Otherfolk. It had been done for centuries.

*But not by these Lightborn,* Runacar thought with a wolfish grin. *All the Lightborn willing or able to fight are east of the Mystrals or west of Delfierarathadan. That's why we'll win.*

Keloit and the other Bearwards passed him, running full out.

Runacar could see the Sanctuary entrance clearly now. He saw green-robed figures come racing through the gates. A cloud of Silverlight cast its radiance over them as if they stood in full moon's light. A few stopped just outside the gates—probably the ones casting Shield in front of their fellows. But Shield was a stationary spell; the wall before the running Lightborn appeared, vanished, appeared a few paces further on, over and over, a pale flicker against the glow of the fires. Half the town was burning now.

Runacar counted under his breath: a hundred count, no more, from the first torch thrown to the retreat.

The sky began to boil. Someone was about to summon Lightning.

The Centaurs appeared again, fleeing the way they'd come. This time they were visible against the firelight. They scattered, no longer a compact group, but wide-spaced running figures.

From around the far edge of the town came a band of mounted riders. Chain shirts and palfreys. Guardsmen, perhaps. Not komen. Two or three tailles at most. *Clever,* Runacar thought approvingly. *A horse can outrun a Centaur over a short distance.*

A wall of Shield appeared before the fleeing Centaurs, cutting off their retreat.

And Radafa dove out of the sky, screaming—a raptor larger than an ox, with a wingspan wider than the length of a Great Hall. Foreclaws with razor talons longer than a komen's arm and a cry like a stormwind. The gathered Lightborn screamed and scattered, flinging themselves prone to avoid Radafa's presumed attack. The violet wall of Shield vanished. The clouds began to roll away.

The horsemen were having enormous trouble controlling their mounts in the presence of the Gryphon; when the Bearwards reached them, the animals simply bolted. Some left their riders behind on the ground. Runacar saw one of the horsemen rise to fight, only to be struck down by a single, open-handed Bearward slap.

The Lightborn had regrouped, but they were running toward the burning village and a task they understood. The flames guttered and died with unnatural speed.

The Bearwards followed the Centaurs back to the safety of the woods.

Now came the thing Runacar had hoped for. The sound of a war-horn. The thunder of destrier hooves.

Hamphuliadiel had gathered komen to his banner after all. Eight of them. Runacar saw the flash of the war-horn in the leader's hand, and felt a terrible clutch of grief at the sight of what he'd once been and no longer was.

Their tabards were purple and gold—Haldil's colors—barred with a slash of Lightborn green. More proof of Hamphuliadiel's princely ambitions. The komen came up past the Sanctuary gates. *Probably quartered at the old manor farm. And I know to the heartbeat how long it takes a komen to armor and arm.*

Audalo charged past Runacar and stopped, striking a pose. Making sure the komen saw him. *The enemy is in sight. The enemy flees. Pursue.* The sound of the war-horn was sweet and wild. Audalo turned and ran. The komen followed.

The tearing-silk sound of arrows cut through the night, followed by screams of knights and horses, as the Woodwose archers loosed, killing every single one.

⊰⊱

It was dawn by the time the war band rejoined the rest of their people at Araglion. The whole war band then swung north, on a salient that would lead them across Farcarinon to Ullilion's bounds. There had been no casualties and few injuries, most minor. Enough to slow them, but not by much. They went on until midday, when they found a Flower Forest and were granted permission to enter. By then, the reports from the Woodwose scouts trailing the war band had come back: there had been no pursuit.

Not that pursuit had been likely. Who could Hamphuliadiel send? They'd just killed his komen, and guardsmen on palfreys were very little threat: an Elven destrier might stand against a Gryphon, and perhaps a Bearward. A lesser beast would not.

The mood among Runacar's war band was jubilant,

if confused. For himself, Runacar was simply glad to stop walking. War should not be conducted afoot.

"I don't see why we didn't just kill all of them," Pelere said. "We could have." She handed him a steaming tankard filled with a mixture of tea and mulled ale. Runacar didn't think he'd ever get used to the taste, but it was hot.

"Yes," Runacar said patiently. "But this was a test of strength, not a massacre."

"So you said," Pelere answered. "I still don't see why."

"Audalo!" Runacar called. "Why didn't we kill everyone at the Sanctuary?"

"Because you're afraid of your gods?" the Minotaur asked, shouldering his way over to Runacar and Pelere.

"They love blood and death," Runacar said. "And if They cared enough to strike you down, you'd have been gone a long time ago."

Audalo laughed, a deep booming sound, and shook his great head. "Your gods fear the Great Bull, Rune. And the Herdsman. And King Wind."

"I doubt it," Runacar said. "I think your gods have as little interest in us as mine do—in giving either of us victory, at least. But tell me, Audalo. We've attacked. What happens now?"

"Now they cry out for help," Audalo said. "But no help will come, for your great army is far away."

"And the High King seems to have other wars to fight," Runacar said. "If Hamphuliadiel calls, all that will answer him are those ancient pensioners who did not ride with the Grand Array and whom we have not driven east. We have slain those komen he's already drawn to him, and as I thought, there were not many. But now he'll do his best to build an army. And he'll keep it close."

Pelere smiled. "He will not send his army to the Shore."

"No," Runacar said. "He won't. He'll protect the

Sanctuary. If we raid them every few moonturns, as we did tonight, they'll always stay close. And once we clear the West from Farcarinon to the Angarussa, we can attack the Shore."

"Not the Sanctuary?" Tanet asked, walking into the clearing. He had a tankard in his hand and a loaf of bread under his arm. He tore it in half and gave one piece to Pelere; she tore her portion in half and shared it with Runacar. Tanet made a face.

"No one holds the Sanctuary in vassalage, but the High King holds Amrolion and Daroldan. If she does not send aid when they call, her oath to them is broken, and they are no longer her vassals," Runacar said. "That is a rebellion she cannot afford."

"She sent them Lightborn," Audalo pointed out.

"Wheelturns ago," Runacar answered. "We need to know what she will do *now*. And if she does not come . . . The Shore will become an anvil, and we the hammer. And Hamphuliadiel will be the blade caught between us."

## CHAPTER TEN

# HARVEST MOON: THE RED HARVEST

*Even as we reckon time, our history is long—so long its beginnings have been worn away by the passage of time. Long before Man came to be, we were. It could be said that our history begins with the Endarkened, for that terrible conflict scoured away all that we had been before it, leaving us one purpose: Survival.*

—Peldalathiriel Caerthalien, *Of the Reign of Great Queen Vieliessar*

A new War Prince lit the pyre that consumed their predecessor's body and held a feast in the Great Keep to mark the beginning of their rule, but the new High King could not follow that tradition. Vieliessar's predecessor had been dust for thousands of years and Vieliessar had been High King from the moment Ivrulion died. She'd taken the oaths of her War Princes already, and all she need do now was rule them.

But it was also true that it was proper to mark the end and the beginning, and so she would do in the sight of all what she'd sworn she would do from the first. The daughters of her people had flown their kites in Flower Moon, the sons of her people had leapt the fire in Fire Moon, and in Harvest Moon Vieliessar would take her seat upon the Unicorn Throne of Amretheon Aradruiniel in the sight of all her folk.

There was no great hall vast enough to contain the multitude that wished to witness this day. The Enthroning would be outside, in the great plaza. And afterward, Vieliessar would hold Harvest Court beneath the open sky to reassure her people that not all things were to be new.

*Let us hope it will not be as exciting as the last Harvest Court Lord Thoromarth held,* Vieliessar thought wryly. It seemed as if that day had happened in some other lifetime, but it was just two Wheelturns since she had taken Oronviel and began the road to the Unicorn Throne.

The last eight moonturns had been as full of work as the Wheelturns she'd spent fighting to do all Amretheon had asked of her. Not only the struggle to survive, and feed, and shelter her folk in a land that had lain deserted for ten thousand turns of the Wheel of the Year, but the work of undoing much of what her victory had created. Vieliessar's army had spent the summer fighting ardently to bring order to Houses that were already sworn to her.

If the whole of ten Windsward Houses and Shanilya Thadan, War Prince of the Arzhana, hadn't come through the Nantirworiel Pass the moment it was passable, the task would have been impossible. But now the bones of a new city rose up in the shadows of the old one, and for the first time since she had ridden forth from Oronviel to war, Vieliessar slept within stone walls and beneath a stone roof. Harvest Court and her enthronement would celebrate true victory and not its faint reflection.

⚔

"Just think; once you're done with this bit of nonsense, your War Council—and everyone else—can start badgering you about who you should marry," Annobeunna said, sliding yet another jeweled bead into place and fixing it with a drop of alchemical gold. Annobeunna and her attendants had roused Vieliessar before dawn to begin the process of dressing her for Court. Every inch of her body had been scrubbed and painted and perfumed as her impatience grew and her temper shortened. At last Annobeunna had sent the others away, announcing she would finish the High King's preparations alone. "Oh, hold still! You'd find this much easier if you didn't wear your hair as short as a Landb— as short as a Lightborn's. You'll have to get used to courtly finery sooner or later. You've won, now you have to reign."

Vieliessar snorted rudely and said nothing. She and Annobeunna were alone in the single room that must serve Vieliessar as bedroom and dining hall and presence chamber until the whole of the new Keep was ready. Though it was small, its walls were hung with silk and its floors laid with rich carpets—as befit the High King—and when Vieliessar walked through the door, she would do so garbed not as Lightsister or ko-men or general of armies, but as High King. Every stitch and jewel must reflect that power.

"I haven't won yet," Vieliessar said after a few moments of silence.

Next springtide—she had said to her War Council, and would say again today in the sight of all—she would send her army to relieve the Western Shore, and go herself to the Sanctuary of the Star to settle matters with Hamphuliadiel. Here in Celenthodiel, she meant to create a Sanctuary of the Sword to match the Sanctuary of the Star, where any who wished, regardless of birth, would be trained in the arts of battle by the best Warlords and Swordmasters of her people.

But even as she shaped these thoughts, she knew they were empty fantasies, a child's wistful hopes of what might be. The victory she celebrated today was a lie. *I haven't won at all.* The Unicorn Throne had never been her goal. Nor was it now. *"While Darkness breeds in lands unknown and marshals armies bought with blood . . .*" She had fought not to gain a throne, but to gain an army. The Fortunate Lands' greatest battle was still to come. *And I do not know how long I have until that day. The candlemarks of my days are filled with pledges and plowing and lawgiving! I build a city and I do not know if I will ever live in it.*

"Of course you've won," Annobeunna said chidingly as she paused to inspect her work. "You hold the West, the Shore, the Uradabhur, and the Arzhana. Soon they will prosper and flourish once more. What more is there?"

"Haldil," Vieliessar said grumpily.

For a little more time she would be able to hold her people ready for battle. Gonceivis had given her that, little though he might wish to aid her. After the coming turn of the Wheel of the Year, they would have one last War Season. She would take Haldil's so-called Windsward Kingdom; she could send Rithdeliel to do that, while she led the rest of the army west for the final relief of the Western Shore. She could winter in Caerthalien Great Keep, if she chose, a final triumph.

And what then?

"P'fft," Annobeunna said. "You fret because a handful of Windsward Houses haven't sworn to you? They will. They just want to see if somebody's going to kill you first. Gonceivis will sue for peace at the Midwinter Truce. Mark my word on this."

*It doesn't matter whether he does or not,* Vieliessar thought mutinously. For Wheelturns she'd always known what she must do next. Unriddle the Prophecy. Escape the Sanctuary. Become a knight. Become a prince. Become a *King.* Now she didn't know what came next. And she was afraid.

It was moonturns without counting since she'd been afraid.

⚔

*T*he time of the morning meal at Caerthalien was a good candlemark away and the Great Hall was empty except for those bound for the Sanctuary of the Star. When young Varuthir saw Ladyholder Glorthiachiel, she hoped for reprieve; when Glorthiachiel beckoned her over, she was certain it had come. But the words Ladyholder Glorthiachiel spoke to her instead were as sharp and painful as a swordblow.

"So, today you leave us and my vengeance is complete. You are the last of House Farcarinon. Fare you well, Vieliessar Farcarinon," Lady Glorthiachiel said mockingly. "And live a long, long time."

The geasa compelled her to walk sedately and silently to the bay palfrey that would carry her to imprisonment and exile, but inside she was screaming in rage and fear. What would become of her? What would happen to her now?

⊰⊱

*W*hat?" Vieliessar asked vaguely. She hadn't been listening.

Annobeunna laughed. "I see I should have been asking you for lands and honors rather than speaking of your victories to come! But truly, my lord: you have won."

"I'm glad *you're* confident," Vieliessar grumbled.

"You're thinking entirely too much for a day of celebration," Annobeunna said, holding a transparent silken veil gently in place as she settled the narrow band of elvensilver Vilya blossoms over it. "Well, I've done all I can for you. When I swore fealty to you, it was to fight, not to be your Mistress of Robes. Just try not to look as if you've mislaid your sword and are wondering where your horse and armor are."

Vieliessar got carefully to her feet. "Annobeunna, you know that today I reward those who aided me," she began slowly. The War Princes who had sworn to her had lost much—wives and husbands, children, friends, wealth and lands and even—some of them—their lives. But Annobeunna had lost Keindostibaent twice over, for her Consort Prince Vithantael had taken her throne from her when she had announced she would pledge to Vieliessar, and then Keindostibaent had been turned to a ghostlands by the Winter War. Vieliessar would not favor her friends and battle companions above her former enemies. But she wanted her gifts to her friends to be richer, in her care if not in their cost.

"And your enemies as well, just to confuse them," Annobeunna said firmly, cutting off Vieliessar's next words. "And to keep your promise that you wouldn't buy the Unicorn Throne with rich gifts to those who helped you to it. But you owe more to the dead than to the living. When you can figure out how to pay that debt, you must let me know. Now come. Your people wait to be astonished by you."

Vieliessar got to her feet, careful and a little awkward in the elaborate gown. She had worn such garb so few times in her life that she could count them upon her fingers, and she could not say which she missed more: the cool heavy sweep of a Lightborn's robes about her ankles, or the weight of a sword at her hip.

In the outer chamber, Helecanth waited. Of everyone gathered here, only Rithdeliel and Helecanth—her Champion and the captain of her personal guard—bore swords; today Vieliessar's guard was for honor only. Two twelves of her people waited to escort her to the Unicorn Throne, but of those in armor, three had once been the most notorious bandits and mercenaries in the west, one was the Landbond-born leader of her Lawspeakers, and one was the Lightborn commander of the Warhunt Mages. Her honor guard was made up of all of her people, Lord and Landbond, Craftworker and Commonborn.

"My lord, you truly bear the semblance of kingship," Rithdeliel said, bowing.

Vieliessar inclined her head. She didn't know what kingship should look like. No one did. All she could do was hope Amretheon had left her enough time to learn it.

*Mistress Maeredhiel would have laughed to see this day,* Thurion said silently, meeting her eyes. He did not speak the words aloud, but True Speech brought them to her clearly.

*Yes. She would have,* Vieliessar thought sadly. *You were my first teacher, Maeredhiel. And the first to tell me the whole of my true heritage. Pelashia grant you knowledge of the tapestry you have woven.*

"My lord King," Helecanth said. "Your people await you."

"You have all brought me here to this day," she said quietly, letting her gaze fall upon each of her escort in turn. "You as much as any here, Lord Ivaloriel, Lord Sedreret."

Ivaloriel Telthorelandor bowed minutely. Sedreret Aramenthiali kept his face a careful blank.

"It is time to begin," Rithdeliel said.

Vieliessar nodded, and Helecanth opened the outer door.

Sunlight struck bright fire from the jewels and silks of the nobles who lined the path, but among them, standing as equals, were her commonfolk, splendid in the richer softer glow of wool and linen. The carpet beneath her feet was green and silver, its design of running unicorns taken from the carving on the walls of the Fireheart Pass. The air was filled with the scent of flowers, and the sky was flawlessly blue.

Her people filled the plaza all the way to the wall of the pass. Some had climbed the steps that led to Amretheon's city to get a better view: the whole of the staircase was filled with people. As many as could be physically present had come. All wished to say to their children and their great-children: *I was there upon the day the High King took her throne.*

They greeted her with silence rather than cheers, as if she were something so new and unknown that all they could do was stare. And if a candlemark hence there would be a return to plotting and scheming, this moment was the fulfillment of a wondertale.

Aradreleg stepped out in front of her. The Lightborn's green robes were the precise shade of the carpet beneath her feet. Aradreleg began to pace forward slowly: the High King's Chief Lightborn leading the High King into court. Vieliessar counted six steps and followed, matching her pace to Aradreleg's. She concentrated on walking slowly and ceremoniously. Maeredhiel had taught her that: the serene graceful gait of the Sanctuary servant.

*"If you're going to run, girl, never do it where someone can see."*

*I won't, Maeredhiel. I promise.*

Behind her, she heard the rustle and chime as her escort followed, pacing slowly behind her. Helecanth first. Behind Helecanth, Thurion and Tunonil. She had given her Landbond councillor pride of place and refused to listen to the wrangling and arguments among the War Princes about who would walk behind him. It did not matter. She would dedicate her life to building a world in which it did not matter.

In the distance, the Unicorn Throne awaited her, raised up upon a long platform set with chairs of state. The thousand steps that would bring her to it were only the last steps of a journey she'd been making every day of her life—as Varuthir, as Vieliessar, as Vieliessar Lightsister, Vieliessar Farcarinon, Vieliessar Oronviel, High King Vieliessar. She walked it in silence. A few times someone began to cheer, but the sound of their lone unaccompanied voice made them quickly silent. It seemed as if this moment was too strange, too holy, to be marred with blatant celebration.

She reached the dais. Here, her Law Lords in their tabards of blue and gold lined an open space to hold back the crowd and to make a place where her petitioners would be able to approach when Court began. Behind them stood her Lightborn, a second line of protection. Aradreleg had stopped at the foot of the steps, waiting for Vieliessar to ascend.

*Blessed Pelashia, let her not forget her skirts—!*

Aradreleg's thought was so heartfelt that it broke through the background hum of thoughts as Vieliessar reached her side. She wanted to smile reassuringly, but it was almost as if she had forgotten how. She had bowed before the weight of Prophecy like a sapling in a storm for as long as she could remember: now its weight upon her shoulders was so heavy her limbs trembled with the strain.

Three steps. Vieliessar gathered her skirts carefully and stepped up. Now she stood before the Unicorn Throne, and for a moment she could not move. It was as if she confronted some living presence, a power beyond her own to which she must offer fealty. *Such a little thing for so many to die for.* Then she turned, careful of her skirts and her veil, and took a half-step backward, silently letting out a breath she hadn't known she was holding.

She was seated upon the Unicorn Throne.

The stone of the unicorn's chained necks was hot under her hands, the Throne itself was hard and smooth beneath her hands and body. Not a comfortable seat; it seemed more as if she bore its weight than that it bore hers. If the weight of rule, as she had learned, was a heavy one, then the weight of kingship was heavier. Both she and her people must learn to bear it.

Now she could see the order of those who followed her. She held her face still with an effort, wondering by what threats, bribes, and miracles of trickery Sedreret had been induced to walk at Nadalforo's side. When Helecanth reached Aradreleg, they stepped up together, each taking her place behind Vieliessar's throne.

The cheering began at last, spreading back through the crowd from those who could see clearly, growing louder as it spread. It went on as her council took their places behind her. Rithdeliel grinned at her as he moved past her. Thurion seemed dazed with relief. In a moment more, Aradreleg would step forward and Harvest Court would begin.

The cheering began slowly to die, but at the same time its quality changed. *No,* Vieliessar realized, *it isn't that.* Those facing and flanking the Throne cheered as before. But those crowds gathered behind the dais had stopped.

"What *are* those?" Annobeunna demanded, just loud enough for Vieliessar to hear. She was looking skyward, and sounded more annoyed than anything else.

"Not Beastlings," Thurion answered, sounding confused.

"*Thank* you, Green Robe. If you'd like to tell me everything they aren't, we can occupy ourselves through Midwinter," Annobeunna said tartly.

Vieliessar rose to her feet. The northern sky had been stainless blue and empty when she had ascended to the dais. It was still blue, but no longer empty. Through it came a flock of creatures too large to be birds, their wings ribbed and leathery. She knew of no winged Beastling with a shape so like a Trueborn's. Nothing with great ribbed wings and a long barbed tail.

None with skin the color of blood.

"Clear the court!" Vieliessar shouted. "Sound the call to arms!"

But it was too late. She felt a tide of foulness rising, a terrible echo of Ivrulion's Banespell. The other Lightborn felt it, too. She could see the horror on their faces.

The first of the fliers folded its wings and dropped into the crowd, too far away for her to see what happened next. The knight-heralds were already relaying her orders, and the sound of horns mingled with the sound of distant screams.

Aradreleg clutched at her arm. "My lord, we must get you—"

"A horse!" Vieliessar snapped. A Fetch-spell summoned her armor to her; she drew the dagger at her belt and began cutting away her gown.

*There is no time.*

More of the creatures dropped from the sky. The sounds of the horns cut through the shouts and the screams, but there were too many folk packed into too small a space. "Storm!" she shouted to the Lightborn. "We need cover!"

Naked now, she swore and struggled as she thrust herself into her aketon. Annobeunna snatched up her helm and thrust it at her, then grabbed for the chain mail coat. The Vale of Celenthodiel had gone from court to battlefield in a matter of heartbeats, and it was a battlefield Vieliessar did not control. Even retreat was impossible. Only the edges of the crowd had any freedom of movement. The courtiers with her on the dais were leaping down, pushing through the crowd as best they could, trying to clear a space.

*The Darkness. This is the Darkness.*

Vieliessar was only half-armored when one of the winged things landed in the widening space before the throne. Nausea surged around her with its nearness, making her vision blur for a moment until she fought it back.

Time seemed to stop. The enemy was female. Perhaps half again as tall as Vieliessar was. Her skin was redder than blood, her features a distorted mockery of Elven-kind's. Her pupilless eyes glowed yellow; enormous ribbed wings arched above her back. In her way, she was beautiful, and that was an abomination, for she radiated something that was the very antithesis of the Light. But worst of all, the creature was jeweled and ornamented as if for a feast. Her long black hair was braided with jewels. There were rings on her talonned fingers. The horns that jutted from her brow and curled back over her skull were gilded. Vieliessar stared, frozen in the horror of the Prophecy's nebulous warnings made real at last, and saw that the monster's eyes held more than bloodlust. This was no beast, but something as knowing, as aware, as Vieliessar herself.

*We are not ready!* Vieliessar thought despairingly, raising her sword.

Helecanth rushed forward, drawing her sword. The woman-thing laughed, wolf teeth gleaming, and batted her aside with a single blow.

"High King," the woman purred, locking eyes with Vieliessar. "Shurzul bids you welcome to the day of your death."

Dimly, Vieliessar could still hear the screams rising in pitch as her people became a mob. There would be time later for shock, for horror, to try to make sense of what she saw. She felt the surging tide of Light rise around her as her Lightborn tried to calm the rising panic and Fetched weapons to arm the komen. The pieces of her armor stood scattered about her, but this was not a battle for swords. Vieliessar struck with all her power at Shurzul. Shield to contain her, Fire to burn her, Command to bind her for a killing blow. . . .

But even as the violet fire of Shield enfolded her, Shurzul laughed. She spread her arms wide, and Shield warped and twisted at her touch. Vieliessar felt the touch of alien sorcery as Shurzul set her power against the Shield, but Vieliessar had all of Tildorangelor to draw upon, and her Shield held. She enveloped Shurzul's body in flame. The space inside the column of Shield flared torch-bright—

And then both Shield and Fire were gone.

Shurzul's stood before her, her body covered with molten gold. Her skin was charred and oozing. But it began to heal even as Shurzul shrieked and clawed in pain at her ruined finery. For a moment she was distracted, and Vieliessar felt a savage surge of triumph. If they could be hurt, they could be killed. She raised her sword and started forward, only to fall heavily against the Throne as Rithdeliel shoved her back.

"Rithdeliel!" she shouted in fury, but he was already moving to the attack. Helecanth had regained her feet and was moving forward as well. Shurzul turned to face them.

The light shifted, going coppery and dark as the storm the Lightborn had summoned boiled up over the ridge. The rain struck like another swordblow. Steam rose from Shurzul's body, washing ash and charred gems from impossibly healing flesh. Vieliessar saw her laugh.

*"My lord! Come! You must come now! Vielle!"* Thurion clutched at her, shouting in her ear, begging her to run.

*I can't.*

Komen in festal dress fought their way toward the Throne, striking down anyone who stood in their path, foe or vassal. There was a clamor of warhorns rising over the screams and the roar of the storm. Some signaled for attack. Some for retreat.

"If you die we all die!" Thurion dragged her backward, behind the Throne, across the dais, and then she was falling—

*—falling—*

The sudden silence was deafening.

Rain pattered down through the leaves of the forest canopy. She could feel the eternal Springtide of the Flower Forest washing away the taint of Shurzul's magic. Annobeunna and Aradreleg were behind her; Aradreleg must have sensed Thurion's spell and dragged

Annobeunna through Door with them. They had been the two nearest to Vieliessar and Thurion when it was cast.

Thurion fell to his hands and knees among the wet leaves, gasping. They were in a clearing. At its center were four stones: one large and flat, the other three tall and grouped around it.

"*What have you done?*" Vieliessar shouted.

"Door—" Thurion gasped. "Flower Forest—Tilinaparanwira—the Shrine—"

Rage filled Vieliessar like the fire she had summoned moments before. She raised her sword. At that moment, she would gladly have made him a sacrifice to Tilinaparanwira, spilled his blood upon the stones and made of his death a prayer for victory.

Annobeunna grabbed her sword arm. "No!"

Vieliessar lowered her sword. Annobeunna released her instantly and stepped back.

Thurion raised his head and met her gaze. "Without you we are lost," he said quietly. "You are the only one who knows what enemy we fight."

"I know *nothing!*" Vieliessar cried, flinging her sword away in fury. In this moment, she didn't care who saw. Annobeunna, Aradreleg—let all the princes of the Hundred Houses witness that nothing—no death, no loss, no betrayal—had prepared her for this moment. She was not ready. Her people were not ready. How could they face an enemy such as this? How could they *win*? She sank to her knees, terror and shame mingling with her anger. She had abandoned her people to slaughter. "This— This—"

"Then we die," Aradreleg said quietly. She went to kneel beside Thurion. He pushed himself to his knees, but did not get to his feet. "Because only the Child of the Prophecy can save us," Aradreleg finished.

Vieliessar wanted to weep. She wanted to scream. "What am I going to do?" she whispered.

"Lead us," Thurion said.

Vieliessar turned away. The forest around her hushed every sound. She could not hear the sounds of battle.

*This is why you were born.*

For the last time, she railed against her fate and begged for her freedom. She thought of the creature that had named itself Shurzul. And in that moment, her hope of freedom died forever. She was the Child of the Prophecy. It was for this that Vieliessar Farcarinon had been born.

"Then let us go back," she said steadily. "And see if I have anything left to lead."

⊰⊱

He was becoming a connoisseur of hopeless retreats, Rithdeliel decided. He didn't know whether to bless the rain or curse it. It covered their movements, but it concealed the enemy. *We would all be dead by now, if our foe weren't insane.*

He and Helecanth hadn't slain their attacker. Again and again the two of them had landed what should have been mortal blows—and weren't. And then the winged woman simply abandoned the fight as if she'd gotten bored. Rithdeliel had dragged himself into concealment with Helecanth as best he could.

The dais was, improbably, still standing, a bare expanse of splintered wood. The ground around it looked like a slaughterhouse. He had thought the plains of Ifjalasairaet after the battle had been the most terrible sight he had ever seen, but the slain that had covered it had died in battle, of honest wounds.

These bodies had been torn apart.

One of the monsters was wallowing in the flesh, so covered in blood and ruined meat that it was difficult to tell what it was.

*They're playing,* he thought in horror. *This is not a battle to them. This is sport.*

The mob was driving itself toward the creature as the people tried to escape. Those at the front, seeing what lay ahead, tried to turn aside, to flee, but the press of bodies behind them made it impossible. The flying woman pounced on them as a dog might pounce on a rat.

Another one—a male—joined her.

And then Rithdeliel saw something that gave him hope.

At the far edges of the fleeing *alfaljodthi*, folk were running toward the safety of the Flower Forest. In the last half Wheelturn, Vieliessar's folk had cut down most of the woodland that edged the Flower Forest to build their new city, but of course the Flower Forest had been left untouched. Many of those trying to escape were struck down, to be added to the . . . playground. But there was an invisible line the creatures did not cross. Even though the escapees were still in plain sight, they chose other targets.

The Flower Forest was sanctuary.

"Helecanth," he said, his voice a rusty croak. "I have a plan."

❈

Sedreret was armed and armored, by his lady mother's grace. As soon as the fighting began he had found her. Aramenthiali still kept itself as a war camp: he had ordered his vassal komen to armor and to stand to horse for the Enthroning: he could not break his oath of vassalage, but he could show Aramenthiali's displeasure with the High King's new ways.

He rode onto the rain-drenched battlefield with a thousand komen behind him, and as he did, he saw a glorious sight. One of the creatures was high in the sky, great wings beating. It clutched two Lightborn in its arms.

As he stared, momentarily fascinated, all three bodies

burst into flame. In the next moment, a bolt of lightning sizzled from the clouds above, striking them. And when the flare had passed, there was nothing left.

He shouted with delight. The monsters could be killed. He'd seen it. Soon this annoyance would be swept away, and in its aftermath, dissent and rebellion would find a fertile field. Everyone would ask why the High King had not protected them—and Sedreret Aramenthiali would have answers. *It is the Beastlings. They have followed the Windsward Houses here. They have been brought here by Vieliessar. She is your doom. Aramenthiali will save you.*

But where was the foe? It must be seen by all that Aramenthiali had ridden eagerly into battle as a force led by its rightful master should. He peered into the storm, searching for the patterns that would tell him where the Beastlings engaged. For a moment he wished he had brought his lady mother with him onto the field: she was Lightborn. It was no violation of the Covenant for her to use her Light against beasts.

But Lady-Abeyant Dormorothon was no komen, to ride to battle on a destrier. The palfreys were wild with fear, and even the destriers were fretful, sidling and dancing as people ran toward them. It was the perfect chance to settle old scores and to clear the path for Aramenthiali ascendance—accidentally, in the press of battle—but Sedreret could not make out any useful targets. With an impatient sigh, he led his meisne in the direction of the Throne. His fleetness and quick thinking had let him reach his encampment before panic had set in, but swift movement was impossible now, even with his komen to clear the way.

"How am I to engage if I cannot find the foe?" he shouted in exasperation.

"I don't think you'll find that a problem, little Elfling."

A table creaked as a body dropped to it from the air. Giant—winged—scarlet-skinned—but far more Elven in appearance than any other Beastling Sedreret had ever seen. And lushly female.

*You will make a fine trophy,* he thought, and drew his sword.

"I *like* you," the creature purred. It sprang forward even as he spurred his destrier to attack. The stallion reared, then shied, and the creature landed on its back. Sedreret's mount lashed out, trying to dislodge the extra weight. The creature raised a fist and brought it down.

Even over the sound of the rain and the shouting, Sedreret heard the sound of the impact as the blow struck the stallion's neck. It went down, carrying Sedreret with it. For an instant, he thought the stallion would wallow to its feet again. Then he knew it was dead.

"I'll be back, darling. Never fear."

The creature crouched beside him for a moment, furnace eyes glowing and lips twisted in a terrible parody of a smile. It kissed his armored helm, and Sedreret smelled blood on its breath. Then it sprang to its feet and bounded away.

At first he struggled to free himself, but realized it was impossible. He was pinned in the midst of chaos unimaginable. Destriers reared, fighting their riders. The komen who dismounted to protect him never reached him. The creature had armed itself from the weapons of the dead. It held a sword in each hand, and every blow it struck cut off a limb.

Or a head.

"Retreat!" Sedreret cried. His voice cracked. In the tumult of the battle, no one heard.

⊰⊱

"The Flower Forest is safe," Rithdeliel said, gesturing toward it.

"It is also defended," Helecanth answered. She stood fully erect. There was no point in trying to hide.

"The enemy is few," Rithdeliel answered grimly. "They can't be everywhere. Send enough folk toward the Flower Forest and some will reach sanctuary."

"If it *is* sanctuary," Helecanth said quietly.

"If it is not, I shall see you this night in the Huntsman's train," Rithdeliel said. He raised a hand in salute and turned away.

⊰⊱

Ivaloriel had been War Prince of Telthorelandor since before Serenthon Farcarinon's father had been born. Since the day Serenthon wed Nataranweiya, the world had been changing, and it seemed only Ivaloriel could see it. Like Serenthon's, Ivaloriel's bride was his Bondmate, but unlike Serenthon, he had not set aside a betrothal and strained ancient alliances he would later break: Lady Edheleorn had been born to Telthorelandor, daughter of a distant connection to the throne. As soon as they discovered the Bond, he had gone to his mother and liege-lord to tell her. Morwaenir Telthorelandor sent apologies and gifts to Cirandeiron, and Ivaloriel's previous betrothal was dissolved before his affianced Cirandeiron bride ever left her own keep. He had wed the woman of his heart and soul, a woman who was his match and his equal in every way. In time his mother had died, and Ivaloriel placed his cool hand upon the web of marriage alliances his sisters and brothers had made, and waited.

Serenthon rose and fell, his alliance a hasty passionate thing easily broken by another alliance. And still Ivaloriel waited, for the daughter lived, and when she rose from her exile at last, she reached for the High Kingship in a way no one had done in ten thousand years.

Neither by alliance nor by force of arms, but by right.

It was a gossamer strand, and she rightly did not rely upon it. But it was there. Even when Vieliessar won, the others did not see what Ivaloriel saw: if one thread of the tapestry she had woven was true, the whole of it was.

Child of the Prophecy. Harbinger of the foe they had awaited since the fall of Celephriandullias—the unknown foe. Ivaloriel could read a scroll as well as anyone: The Song of Amretheon contained nothing more than garbled warnings. If there had been more to know, she would not have been the only one to know it: there were thousands upon thousands of Lightborn in the Fortunate Lands, all trained just as their new High King had once been.

And so, when the flying creature appeared in the sky, Ivaloriel ceased to wait. He rose to his feet with all the others, but as they wondered and argued, he moved.

Off the back of the dais. The Law-Lords and the Lightborn parted to let him pass. The front ranks were a tight-packed mass, but further back there were pathways between them, just as if all this mingled folk were an army on parade, and he began to run. He gave no warning as he passed; there would be panic soon enough, and speed was essential. Let those who saw him think the High King had sent him upon some urgent errand; it would explain his haste. Through the Bond he could feel Edheleorn's worry and confusion; a Bond was nothing that would allow more, but he matched her emotions with his own. She would know what to do.

At least she was near.

If this had been Telthorelandor, his next actions would be obvious. But there were no gates to seal, no walls to defend—there was not so much as a manor house or a border tower here: they still lived in the pavilions they had taken to war. The city on the spire was too far to reach. But he had planned. Not for this, but for disaster. Treachery, war—it did not matter. It was inevitable. He had moved Telthorelandor's encampment as far down the valley as he could without raising questions.

What a pity most of its folk were gathered here.

The commonborn moved quickly out of his way. The Lords Komen did not, but there were few of them so far distant from the Throne, and those who had elected distance over a blatant show of loyalty were gathered by House.

Behind him he heard screams. He did not look back. He could question the survivors later. He would lead his komen in support of the High King as he was sworn to do. But he was sworn merely to follow her orders, not to anticipate them. When she arrived to give them, he would be ready.

It began to rain.

The crowd was moving at last, a tidal beast with a multitude of limbs and very little mind. To make his way through it was harder now, but finally Ivaloriel reached a place where there were only scattered groups of people. Some had brought food and drink to make their own festival. Now they milled uncertainly, unable to see what was going on, not even certain anything *was* going on.

"To the Flower Forest!" he said urgently. "Go there at once!"

They were not his folk, but they were commonborn, trained to obey. Some began to move at once. Others stood their ground defiantly.

Let them.

Tildorangelor was an ancient forest. It held one of the Ancient Shrines. It had stood untouched for a thousand lifetimes. It was the only shelter there was. He could only hope Edheleorn reached it as well, for their lives were in one another's hands.

❧❦❧

Thurion was too exhausted to cast Door again, but with Tildorangelor's power to draw upon, Vieliessar could do it easily.

She did not.

To simply appear in the place from which she had been taken would place her in the thick of the fighting. *Each element of an army moves as if it is one body, and all the elements which make up an army move as one body as well. When a single komen is a single body and nothing more, the army is merely a mob doomed to defeat.* Arilcarion had written those words, and it was not until this moment she'd truly understood them. Even if she returned to the battlefield, her army would be a disjointed puppet. They would not know where she was. She could not command them. And no one—even she—knew the nature of their enemy.

She must have more information before she fought.

"The Lightborn camp still stands, does it not?" she asked quietly.

"Yes," Aradreleg said slowly. "After Rondithiel Lightbrother's embassy left for the Western Shore, you never ordered us to return to our households."

"You knew I would not," Vieliessar said. She took a deep breath, the weight of rule settling over her shoulders once again. "And it lies near the edge of Tildorangelor, and from there we may see . . . what is." She did not know Tilinaparanwira's location within the Flower Forest. Perhaps Thurion had explored enough to find it. Perhaps he had merely sensed it when he set his spell. But she could find the Lightborn camp easily.

Annobeunna stepped over to Vieliessar, the High King's discarded sword in her hands.

"Mark this place well, both of you," Vieliessar said to the Lightborn. "We will need it soon. I think only the Starry Hunt can save us from what has come."

"Are these the vanguard?" Thurion asked, coming toward her. "Does a larger force follow?"

Vieliessar laughed jaggedly as she sheathed her sword. "You know Amretheon's Prophecy as well as I! But I know one thing more," she added. "We can survive this day. And we can win."

Thurion stopped in his tracks. "How can you say that?" he demanded. Astonishment warred with hope in his voice.

"Because Amretheon could not warn me about them if they had never come before. And so they must have. And we are still here. Now come."

She held out her hands. Annobeunna took one, and Aradreleg the other. Aradreleg held out her free hand to Thurion, who clasped it gingerly. Vieliessar summoned Door. As she did, she could feel the ripples in Tildorangelor's Light. Somewhere her Lightborn were fighting.

One step, two, and they stood in the middle of the Lightborn encampment.

Shouts of terror greeted their arrival. She heard the rasp of a drawn blade, and drew her own in reflex.

"No!" Annobeunna said, stepping in front of her. "It is the High King! She lives!"

They stopped. Annobeunna was still in her courtly finery, easy to recognize.

The people approached at the sound of Annobeunna's voice. One of them rushed to Thurion and flung his arms around him. *Denerarth. He is Thurion's friend.*

Everyone began talking at once, demanding answers. Orders. Vieliessar raised her hand for silence, but it was slow in coming. She looked around. It was less than a quartermark since the attack had begun. There were perhaps two dozen people here—no Lightborn, since she had called them all to help keep order—but some of the Lightless who lived among them had stayed behind. More people were moving through the trees toward them. She saw one of her Law-Lords and a few of her lesser nobles. No Lightborn. None of her council.

"Take up all you can easily carry, and quickly," she said, gesturing at the camp. "Thurion, Aradreleg, lead them as deep into the forest as you can."

"Where do we go?" Aradreleg asked instantly.

"Toward the Shrine. Go as far as you can. I will find you," Vieliessar answered. "Stop for nothing, and do not turn back."

"I will not leave you," Annobeunna said instantly.

"You will stay here and direct everyone who comes to follow Aradreleg," Vieliessar said sharply. "Who among you here can tell me what is happening?"

"I saw." A young noble stepped toward her. "Beregur of Niothramangh, my lord." He wore festal garb in the red and yellow of House Niothramangh; his cloak brooches showed Niothramangh's three red foxes. "I was late—my servants—"

"What did you see?"

"Winged— Beastlings with wings—out of the sky— killing without swords—the Lightborn could not stop them—"

More survivors arrived. They were ragged, disheveled, bruised. Some were bloody—not as if they were wounded, but as if they had bathed in blood. All looked terrified.

The Lightborn camp was being looted in haste. Tents toppled. Some people began to fight.

"Stop!" Vieliessar shouted, raising her sword. "There's no time for this! Go!" She turned back to Beregur and Annobeunna. "Keep order here," she commanded, handing Annobeunna her sword.

"Where are you going?" Annobeunna demanded, her voice tight with fear.

"To see," Vieliessar said. She pulled off the pieces of armor she'd managed to don in the chaos, and handed her chain mail shirt to Beregur.

"You cannot risk yourself," Annobeunna said, eyes blazing.

"I've already risked all of you," Vieliessar answered sharply. "Follow my orders."

Annobeunna opened her mouth to protest. Vieliessar cast Cloak over herself and walked away, invisible. Behind her, she heard Annobeunna shouting for her to return, calling to Thurion and Aradreleg to find her.

Vieliessar broke into a run. There was no time to argue. She hoped the Flower Forest was a true refuge, and not merely the illusion of one.

The folk who entered the Flower Forest ran like hunted stags, sprawling as they tripped on branches, colliding with trees they did not see in their terror. They were a tiny fraction of those who had gathered to see her enthroned; commonfolk and Landbonds, those who would have been toward the back of the gathering. Vieliessar headed directly south to get out of their way, but there were people entering the forest at every point and she spent much of her energy dodging them. At last she shed her spell of concealment—no one would recognize her—and moved forward warily. This far toward the edge of the forest, she could tell that the storm she had ordered had stopped: she did not know whether this was a good omen or a bad one. She could still feel the Light rippling around her as her Lightborn fought.

But against what enemy? Her heart told her this was the vanguard of Amretheon's "Darkness," but she had seen only a handful of the creatures, and that was hardly enough to have set in motion all the architecture of the Prophecy. No matter how powerful they were, they could be killed. Her people had slain Aesalions, Gryphons, Minotaurs, and all were formidable quarry. The Bearwards had shamanesses whose spells were as powerful as the Lightborns' own.

*We will win. We must.*

She was still too deep within the forest to see the open space beyond, but its sounds came to her clearly. They were . . . wrong. She knew the sound of the battlefield.

This was nothing like it. There was no clangor of swords, nor sound of horns. Only the frantic shouting of a mob.

In her mind, she assembled a map of Celenthodiel. Tildorangelor Flower Forest was vast, beginning near the great plaza. It extended all the way to the curtain wall on its northern side, and they had not yet found its western boundary. The pavilion encampments in which most of her folk still lived were set along the eastern and southern boundaries of it.

She'd never thought she would have to fight in Celenthodiel itself.

*Even if the komen can reach their tents and arm, they cannot ride. There are only a few thousand destriers here. The rest are pastured, or run free for lack of stabling and servants to care for them. Those who fight, fight on foot. There is no castel to retreat to against this save one.*

Tildorangelor itself.

The Enemy had not followed them into it; she must believe it was safe. Her new city was only half built and indefensible; Celephriandullias was a ruin—and the enemy had wings. But desperate folk might do anything, including risk the long exposed climb up the winding stair. And perhaps they would lure the enemy toward it. As the thought entered her mind, she realized she had made her plan of battle. Today was not a day to fight. Today was a day to retreat. She must save as much of the army—of her *people*—as she could.

Vieliessar stepped from the cover of the trees. The ground was sodden with blood and churned to mud. It was littered with bodies—some bearing the wounds of claws, some trampled by those who fled. She could smell smoke. The Fireheart Gate was jammed with folk trying to escape: over it the winged things soared and wheeled like monstrous birds of prey. They dove, over and over, into the mass of bodies, rising up each time with one or two in their grasp. They soared into the sky, holding them.

And then they dropped them.

She could see two more creatures above the city on the spire. The staircase was crowded with people. As they struggled to climb to safety, the creatures dove at them, causing hundreds to fall with each pass they made.

She took in the sight with a single despairing glance as she prepared her spell.

Call.

A simple spell. Every Lightborn knew it. But what could be used to summon sheep and goats could summon people as well.

*If I am wrong, and Tildorangelor is no sanctuary ...*

She dared not doubt.

She sent forth her spell. In her mind, she held the image of the Shrine deep within the forest. The place to which her magic called her people.

Suddenly she was snatched into the air.

"Pretty," her attacker cooed. Its talons sheared through the aketon that was all she wore, piercing the flesh beneath. "Pretty little Elfling magician. Pretty toy."

Bile surged up in Vieliessar's throat and she fought to keep from choking. She was cut off from the Light. The heartbeat of the world no longer coursed through her veins. The creature's touch was profanity.

*Darkness.*

She struggled in its grasp. With each beat of its wings, it flew higher. There was no escape. A fall from this height would kill.

"Who are you?" she gasped, though even speech was agony. "What do you want?"

For a moment a look almost of surprise crossed the creature's face. "You are strong," it said. "Your death will be long and glorious. Arzhugdu of the Endarkened promises you this."

For a single instant, a petty and ludicrous irritation at the misleading poetry of *The Song of Amretheon* swept aside all other thoughts. Amretheon hadn't been trying to warn his descendants against darkness. He'd been trying to warn them against these creatures who called themselves *the Endarkened*.

And if Vieliessar could not manage to survive this moment, that warning would be in vain.

Arzhugdu did not seem to expect her to struggle, and for the moment she seemed to want Vieliessar alive. Vieliessar hung limp in the Endarkened's grasp, gathering her will against the miasma of foulness that surrounded her.

*Retreat.* It was the plan of today's battle, the only hope of living to fight another. But how? Already the peaks of the mountains were below her, and the air was sharp and thin. Vieliessar was no eagle, to take flight if she broke free.

There was one hope. And it was a thing she must do in a heartbeat, or fail. Door. But even if she could cast the spell, her captor must be made to move through it. And that meant Arzhugdu must fall.

She arched her back and swung her legs up, though her chilled muscles screamed in protest. She kicked with all her strength. It was little enough, but the blow disrupted the rhythm of Arzhugdu's wingbeats. The Endarkened rolled through the air, diving to regain speed. It was a maneuver Vieliessar had seen a thousand times as she watched birds soar above a battlefield.

It was enough.

*Door.*

Suddenly sky was replaced by trees. Captor and captive struck the ground with bruising force.

Arzhugdu shrieked in agony and released her. Vieliessar scrambled away. The Shrine was just behind her. Vieliessar dragged herself to the center stone, clutching at the standing stones for support. Her blood smeared

them, and she wept, helplessly, because Tilinaparanwira
was screaming. She felt her heart slow with each beat,
as if her life and Arzhugdu's had been bound together.
She saw the creature's skin crack and blister. Leaves fell
like rain as the trees around them withered. Arzhugdu
sprang at her, but the Endarkened's movements were
spastic, disjointed. Arzhugdu's yellow eyes stared sight-
lessly as she flailed. Her feet left bloody prints in the
grass, and the living soil beneath it turned to lifeless
dust.

"*Elfling!*" Arzhugdu shrieked. "*You will spend a
thousand years begging to die!*"

In another moment the Endarkened would seize her.
To cast Door over such a distance had taken all she had
to give; Vieliessar had no strength left with which to
fight. Arzhugdu was dying, but she would manage to
live long enough to end Vieliessar's life. Even the Shrine
itself would not be enough protection to keep that from
happening. Blackness crept in at the edges of Vieliessar's
vision, pulsing in time with her heartbeat. She could no
longer feel the stone beneath her knees.

Then Arzhugdu screamed more loudly than before,
and her cry held, not rage, but terror.

Vieliessar forced herself to see.

For a glorious impossible moment she was certain
she had died without knowing. Before her stood the
creature she had glimpsed only once before.

The Unicorn.

It was the living form of the creature her ancestors
had carved into the Plaza fountain, had enchained in
the carving of the Unicorn Throne. It shone with a silvery iridescent radiance that seemed to emanate from
its thick feather-soft fur. It had a long slender neck like
a deer's, but a mane roached and bristling like a plow
horse's. Its tufted tail lashed like a cat stalking prey. The
last time she had seen it, she had been spellbound by
its beauty. This time she was transfixed with as much

terror as love. Its spiral horn glowed as red as forge-heated iron, and she had barely registered its presence before it launched itself directly at the Endarkened.

"Don't—" she gasped. In that moment, she would have given her life to protect it from harm.

Then its horn touched Arzhugdu, and the Endarkened fell dead. The foulness of that presence was instantly wiped away. It was a relief as great as healing, a pure uprush of goodness to offset the horrors of this terrible day. And as consciousness left her, Vieliessar heard a voice where no voice could be, speaking words that made no sense to her.

"He said there were more of us. Surprise."

## CHAPTER ELEVEN

# HARVEST MOON: THE BEGINNING OF THE GREAT SILENCE

*When the Darkness was revealed at last, we did not know how to fight it, for who can fight what they cannot understand? It was not an enemy that wanted what we had: It was an enemy who wanted no one to have anything.*

— Thurion Pathfinder, *A History of the High King's War*

The Endarkened had not been meant to create life—that had been the work of King Virulan's great spell, the first sorcery any of the Endarkened had worked. Even though they were now male and female, they did not spawn as the beasts of the Bright World did.

Once the spark of life was kindled in an Endarkened womb, it drew its mother's magic to itself, feeding upon it. Such a process was normally a slow one, spanning centuries, but with enough pain and fear to feed upon, a new Endarkened could go from spark to squalling newborn in the blink of an eye—and here, today, there were both pain and fear in unimaginable quantity. Endarkened after Endarkened had to break away from the slaughter to fly with swollen, gravid body back to Obsidian Mountain to expel their burden.

Xennara flew homeward, her thoughts on one thing: to rid her body of the parasite it carried. Then she could return to the Harvest, safe from interruption once more.

It was only a handful of Risings ago that she had lain with King Virulan. It was a dangerous honor, but such only added spice to the encounter, and the wounds had quickly healed. Almost as soon as the Endarkened descended upon the Elflings, Xennara could feel the nauseating sensation of life moving within her body, and at last—reluctantly, angrily—she left the killing ground.

*There are so many! Surely some will remain by the time I return!* The thought did not console her. Altruism was not an Endarkened trait. What Xennara could not take for herself, she could not have, for no one would consider giving her charity.

Upward she flew, scarlet wings straining, until the killzone was only a tiny blood-red speck on the ground below. Higher and higher, until the blue darkened and the air thinned and she flew onward as much by sorcery as by wings. At the utmost pinnacle of her flight, she drew in her wings, folding them tightly about her, and dove. Her lips peeled back in a savage grin of joy. Her hair streamed out behind her, the wind of her passage stripping its ornaments away. That same wind whistled over her skin and in her ears, singing a high frantic song like the music of terrified screaming. Below her, Obsidian Mountain grew from a dark speck in the midst of an icefield to the tallest mountain in a jagged chain. Soon she was close enough to see every fold and cranny of its surface, and in the moment when it seemed she would dash herself to death on the rocks, she unfurled her scarlet wings with a sharp *crack!* and glided in through one of the cave entrances.

The entrance was guarded, as always, by several of the Lesser Endarkened. They scrabbled to open the enormous doors of black iron that barred her way into the deeper caverns, and closed them behind her just as quickly. Now she was in absolute darkness, but no Endarkened needed the light of the daystar to guide them.

A few steps, and she found a shaftway to lead her directly to her goal. Without hesitation, she flung herself into it, her huge scarlet wings brushing against the glass-smooth sides with a keening whisper as she fell. Though the Penance Chamber was deep within Obsidian Mountain, it lacked the glorious ornamentation of other deep-mountain chambers. This was not a place the Endarkened came by choice, and one which they left as quickly as they could.

As her feet touched the floor, a cramping spasm made Xennara growl and hunch over. Wetness slicked her thighs and trickled to the floor: in a fit of impatience, she ripped the remaining ornaments from her body, flinging them as far from her as she could.

The clicking of hooves on the glass-smooth floor heralded the approach of one of the Lesser Endarkened. Xennara gasped as another spasm took her. For a race that took such delight in the pain of others, the Endarkened took little joy in their own. The fastest way to be rid of the puling parasite she carried would have been to slit open her own belly, but the pain would be unbearable. So she squatted and strained, hoping her shame would be over soon. By now she was ringed by a circle of the Lesser Endarkened. It was to them that the newborn would be entrusted; they who would feed it and raise it until it was old enough to join the society of the Endarkened as an equal, for any of the Endarkened who could not defend themselves from their brethren quickly died.

Her barbed tail lashed and her great ribbed wings opened to their fullest extent as she pushed. She dug her talons into her skin and her sharp white fangs drew

blood from her lips. At last the head of the infant appeared between her legs, then one shoulder. One of
the Lesser Endarkened darted forward to grasp the infant and draw it free. Xennara howled at the new spasm
of agony and lashed out against the Lesser Endarkened,
but the creature had already dodged out of reach. Birth-
waste rushed from her body, spattering the floor. Xennara forced herself upright, breathing deeply. It was
over. Praise to *He Who Is*.

"Mistress, what are we to name your daughter?" the
Lesser Endarkened midwife asked.

*A daughter to share my curse.* Xennara forced the
rage at King Virulan down and away. The Endarkened
did not feel loyalty or togetherness or even unity, but
there was one truth the female Endarkened all agreed
on, whether Born or Created-and-Changed: the King
would never be allowed to know how absolutely they
hated him for making them what they were. *Not until
the hour of his destruction.*

"Savilla," she said. "Call her Savilla. Send her to me
when she is grown."

Xennara strode from the chamber, ignoring the
birthing-mucus caked on her skin.

Blood would wash it away quickly enough.

Tzurliat had never imagined it was possible to get
tired of killing, but no matter how much of the
*meat* she ripped apart with fangs and talons, there was
still more to kill. She was almost glad that some escaped
into the Flower Forest where she and her kindred could
not follow. Meat was stupid and had short memories.
Soon enough it would venture out again.

Pain and fear hovered over the killing ground like a
red fog. Even the painful brightness of the day could
not mar her pleasure. With each breath she took, Tzurliat felt reborn. She gorged herself on the pain of her

victims; reveled in the inventiveness of her brethren. Here, someone plucked a child from its mother's arms and hovered above her, dangling the child tantalizingly out of reach for a few moments before dashing the infant to the ground with so much force the body bounced and skidded in the red mess leaking from its flesh. There, another of Tzurliat's fellows hamstrung a warrior then used magic to peel him, layer by layer—armor, under padding, skin, flesh—as he tried to drag himself to safety. There were so many delicious variations to try.

And best of all, the day belonged entirely to the Born—just as Hallorad had been given to the Created-and-Changed. The King and the rest of the Created had come to watch, but the killing belonged to their children, in acknowledgment of the Cycles of privation and sacrifice that had lulled the *meat* into a false sense of security.

The Elflings had thought themselves so very safe and sheltered. Today the Endarkened proved that they were wrong, over and over again. From now until the end of the Red Harvest, the Endarkened would move from sea to sea, destroying every living thing in their path. The tireless, immortal Endarkened could fly and fell and feed without stopping, moving westward until they returned to this very place, and when they had . . .

The task that *He Who Is* had set them would be done.

Behind them would come the abominations of King Virulan's Cold Nursery, and between them they would ensure that nothing, down to the smallest insect and blade of grass, survived. *But never will there be such glorious slaughter as there is here today,* Tzurliat thought wistfully.

And yet . . .

There were whispers. Barely rumors at all. But these vague sourceless hints all spoke with one voice: delay.

*But what of the Born?* the rumors whispered. The Born were tainted by the crime of every enemy of *He*

*Who Is*: they were Created Life, and many of them had created Life in turn. If the rumors were true, the Born would be the last to die here in this terrible place of light and life—but they would still die. There would be no glorious communion as their selves were re-absorbed into the eternal Nothingness of *He Who Is*.

Everyone knew the price of rebellion or even of displeasing King Virulan. The Endarkened were masters of torture and the sweetest and most wonderful expression of that mastery was to use their arts on one of their own. Tzurliat had seen such an execution once. The traitor's death had encompassed Cycles of unendurable agony—an agony that no Endarkened wished to experience for themselves.

But if the Born no longer ruled . . .

*Yes,* Tzurliat decided, launching herself into the sky with her latest captive. *In delay, there is enough time for anything to happen. Anything at all.*

To think such thoughts was not treason, not rebellion. It was only truth.

❊

The sun set over the Vale of Celenthodiel and the moon rose. In its light, the stones of the courtyard, the meadows and fields surrounding it, were black with Elven blood. The Endarkened soared and wheeled in the night winds over the killing ground. They circled over the Spire of Celephriandullias, above the Fireheart Pass, out over the wide plain of Ifjalasairaet.

Hunting.

Some of the Elves had found some other hiding place than the Flower Forest. Night became day again, became a dozen days, as Endarkened searched them out and took them away to the World Without Sun. Those who could not claim the glory of an Elfling captive vented their spite upon every other living thing they could reach: horses, oxen, cattle, mules, sheep, goats.

But they could not enter the Flower Forest to claim the treasure they knew was hidden there.

They tore at it with storms, rained fire down on it from above. The winds did not break the trees, and the flames died quickly. King Virulan sent for Lesser Endarkened and forced them into the forest to drive the Elflings out. The Lesser Endarkened did not return.

The King of the Endarkened was too wise to concede defeat or even to indicate that he imagined such a thing. Before his subjects could become frustrated, he summoned the Endarkened back to Obsidian Mountain, there to enjoy the fruits of their victory.

⊷✤⊷

The Heart of Darkness glowed with torchlight. The flames made the figures in the wall murals seem to writhe in an agony that mirrored that of the Elfling stretched upon the cunning golden frame set before the Dark Throne. The victim could not live much longer, even with Khambaug's magnificent artistry to delay his final moments.

Virulan sat upon the Throne of Night, the Crown of Pain upon his brow, his fangs bared in an approving smile as he watched. The banquet tables and playrooms of the World Without Sun were glutted with shrieking playthings, and the Endarkened gorged to satiation on Elfling flesh. No longer were captives given only to Virulan's favorites. Now he gorged his darlings upon blood and pain as if he wished to rouse their appetites to new heights: he had made it his new custom to begin court each Rising with some entertainment. All the Endarkened understood that message: it was the promise of the glories to come.

And all knew Virulan could grant—or withhold— these pleasures at his whim.

Khambaug's subject was beyond screaming now. Its every breath was a sob. With glittering tools of obsidian she made the delicate cuts in the skin of his torso. The Lesser Endarkened beside her handed her each new tool almost before she could reach for it. Skin was delicately teased away from the muscle beneath as her audience murmured its praise of her deftness. Muscle was delicately extracted without destroying the delicate web of veins, nerves, and arteries, and the watching Endarkened gasped in awe and wonder. Not even a talon-scrape or a wing-rustle disturbed the beautiful music of the Elfling's pain.

At last bone stood exposed, and beneath it the glistening tissue of straining lungs and spasming heart.

Khambaug looked to Virulan, who nodded his permission. She made one last careful cut, and then pulled the ribs apart as if opening a treasure box.

"And still it lives!" Lashagan murmured in delight, for even now, the Elfling's heart still struggled to beat.

Khambaug bared her fangs in triumph as she plunged her hand into the Elfling's chest cavity. The mutilated body spasmed once as she closed her fingers around his heart and pulled. She raised it high above her head in triumph, and then knelt submissively before Virulan, holding it out to him on her cupped palms.

Virulan smiled as he accepted it from her. The still-pulsing muscle crunched faintly as he took a bite. Blood dripped down his chin and from between his fingers.

"Beautifully performed," he said, tossing the remains back to her. Khambaug lowered her gaze demurely even as she gulped down the treat. Virulan gestured, and the room exploded into sound as the Endarkened cheered.

*He is clever,* Uralesse thought, in grudging admiration. He guarded his thoughts carefully: Virulan trusted him least of all his subjects, for Uralesse was the only other of the Created who was still as *He Who Is* had shaped them. The World Without Sun was a place of plots and scheming. Loyalty was something the Endarkened neither possessed nor valued, and Virulan's great magic had increased their numbers a thousandfold. The plots and counterplots, the cabals and conspiracies, reached to the foot of the Dark Throne. But there they stopped.

The beginning of the Red Harvest had been a thing unequaled even in the memories of the Twelve. Even when some of the Elflings escaped, Virulan had not allowed that to mar his victory. Uralesse knew, too, that Virulan had created tools to go where the Endarkened could not and the Lesser Endarkened would not go. He remembered the occasion, less than a hundred Risings ago, when Virulan had summoned them all, Created and Born, to witness his genius.

⬧⬥⬦

*M*y *dear comrades, my fellow children of* He Who Is, *I know that you are as eager as I for our Red Harvest to begin. As it will be the last hunt, it must be perfect—a fitting offering to* He Who Is. *I know you are impatient, but is it not truly more artistic, more delightful, more . . . just . . . to aid the Brightworlders in their own destruction?"*

*The silence that followed did not indicate agreement, Uralesse knew. What it meant was power. He watched as Virulan paused for a moment to savor that fact.*

*"I do not mean to leave our great crusade to those who are weak, merciful, incapable of utter annihilation. No. It shall be ours. But before it begins, I mean to raise their hopes of survival. To show them a tiny danger and let them hope to overcome it. And then to dash those hopes entirely."*

*Now there was a murmur of approval, and Virulan smiled. "Come, my darlings," he said. "Come with me and see the rich gifts I have for those who dwell beneath the sun."*

⬧⬥⬦

*I*n Ugolthma, where the World Without Sun lay, nothing lived and nothing grew, and so Virulan's Cold Nursery had been placed far enough to the south that the sun rose and set each day, plants grew upon the ground, and Bright World beasts existed in sufficiency to feed Virulan's newest children.

The Endarkened were gathered upon a high ridge at twilight. Below a herd of snow-elk—creatures larger than horses, with fearsome branching antlers—were gathered by the thousands to graze, trusting in their numbers to protect them from ice tiger and snow lion.

"Watch," Virulan commanded. "Watch my Coldwargs at the hunt!"

The snow-elk scented danger and began to run just as the first of the Coldwargs crested the low hill above them. Soon the whole herd was in flight. The Coldwarg pack followed. They did not attack the stragglers; instead, the Coldwarg swung wide of the herd, paralleling its flight to encircle it. The herd began to curve away from the line of running Coldwarg, but it was too little, too late. The pack had outrun them. The herd turned back upon itself, and the Coldwarg charged.

They flung themselves into the mass of horns and hooves, and as they ran, they killed. A single snap of their great jaws could rip out belly or throat. Uralesse watched, delighted in spite of himself, as blood ran and steam spilled from the half-frozen earth. Not one of the thousands of snow-elk was permitted to escape. When there was nothing left to kill, the Coldwargs began to feed.

"So beautiful . . ." Orbushnu breathed, her scarlet wings trembling with the force of her emotion.

He has them, Uralesse thought, careful to keep his thoughts entirely shielded. I had believed—hoped— there might be rebellion if he continued to delay. No longer. "They are beautiful in their savagery, my lord Virulan," Uralesse said aloud. "I would expect no less.

*But . . . a better wolf . . . ?"* He let his voice trail off, as if he were honestly puzzled.

"Wait. And watch," Virulan said, baring his long white fangs in a terrible smile.

The scene below looked like a battlefield. Suddenly the Coldwarg leader raised her dripping muzzle from the belly of the snow-elk upon which she was gorging, and threw back her head to give a short imperative howl. Almost as one, the Coldwargs retreated.

"I see something coming!" Gholak cried excitedly. She turned to Uralesse, her face soft and flushed with the slaughter she'd witnessed. "What is it?"

Virulan chuckled paternally. "My losels come."

If the Coldwargs had been impressive, the losels were not. They were grey-furred, nearly invisible in the deepening twilight, perhaps a cubit long, resembling weasels or otters.

But there were so many of them.

They came in a mass a mile wide, a carpet of fur that stretched off into the distance. The small beasts of the tundra fled before them. The mice and hares and other creatures outran the losels easily . . . but Uralesse had the uneasy sense that the living carpet of hunger would not stop.

The losels reached the killing field, and spread out over the dead. Soon all that could be seen was the losels themselves. The sound of their gnawing upon the bones of the snow-elk was the loudest sound that could be heard, and the grinding popping crunching was pleasant to the ears of the Endarkened. The living carpet continued to advance, and the concealed carcasses writhed and twitched at the assault.

"They will feed until not even bones remain," Virulan said.

"I wonder that there is anything for us to do, with such efficient weapons in your arsenal, my lord King," Uralesse said, now making it seem as if he merely jested.

"I was most artful in their creation," Uralesse answered. "Generation upon generation they seem like any other creature of the World Above. Scavengers. Solitary beasts. Then suddenly—" here he smiled "—and mysteriously, they begin to breed, and breed, and breed. And then they gather together to swarm, as you see, and every living thing flees before them. But that cannot continue forever. They do not breed when they swarm, and so the swarm will age, and starve, and only a few survive. It would be a century or more before you might see this sight again."

"But of course, the Brightworlders do not have a century," Uralesse said.

"No," Virulan said. "They do not. But look—I have not done showing you wonders!" Suddenly Uralesse smelled the hot scent of sorcery. Whatever creature Virulan now offered possessed it in some small degree.

"Losels are easy enough to breed, and more than one swarm would spoil our sport," Virulan said. "And so I have created these to . . . control them. Aren't they charming?"

As the first of the creatures clawed its way to the top of the writhing mass of losels, Uralesse had to agree. They were indeed charming. They were superficially similar to the Lesser Endarkened, though they were a good bit smaller. Their smooth skins were colored like rotting meat, and their arms were half again as long as their torsos. Their huge pale eyes glowed in the gloom, seeming to wink on and off again as they blinked. If that were all there was to them, Uralesse would not have been the only one to question Virulan's fitness to rule.

But then he saw one of them open its enormous jaws and stuff one of the losels into its maw as the creature struggled and bit. It chomped down, swallowed, and reached for another. And another.

"What are they?" Marbuglor asked in awestruck tones. "Can I have one?"

"*Of course you can, my dear. I call them goblins,*" Virulan said proudly.

The losels were intent upon feeding. So were the goblins. The swarm of losels continued to move forward, intent on food. They were as willing to eat the goblins as to eat the dead snow-elks, but each time they swarmed the goblins, the goblins simply vanished.

"*Where are they going?*" Uralesse asked quietly.

"*I bred them from water-creatures who possess a certain amount of magic in their own right,*" Virulan said. "*And so my goblins have the ability to move through rock and earth as if it is no more substantial than water. They are poisonous as well,*" he added idly, as one of the goblins, unwilling to flee, spat at the losels trying to swarm it. The thick green spittle spattered over their fur. The losels died instantly.

More and more goblins appeared, and soon the field was a roiling swarm of goblins and losels. The losels surged forward even as the voracious goblins devoured them. It is like watching a boiling cookpot filled with maggots, *Uralesse thought.*

In the end, there was nothing left but goblins. Some died and were eaten by their fellows as efficiently as they ate everything else. Every bone, every sinew, ever drop of blood and scrap of fur—everything that had been the slaughtered herd of snow-elk, the voracious swarm of losels, was gone.

"*It's a pity they can't bear light,*" Virulan said regretfully. "*But one can't have everything.*"

With nothing more to eat, the goblins vanished as well. The plain was bare and silent.

"*Show us more!*" Marbuglor begged. "*Show us everything!*"

All through the night Virulan showed them the wonders of the Cold Nursery: icedrakes, serpentmarae, hellsprites, hordeblights, poisondancers . . . some *rare and solitary, some unable to endure warmth or light, but all creatures to delight the Endarkened heart.*

"Now you have seen all my treasures," Virulan said, *as the sky began to grey again with approaching dawn.* "And now I shall loose the spells that bind them here *and let them roam as they will. They will drive every-thing in their path before them."*

Directly into the path of the Elfling armies. It is an inspired plan. If it works. *Uralesse thought of the uni-corns, whose lightest touch could kill the Endark-ened. Who knew what else lay within those forests no Endarkened could enter?* King Virulan will drive all of Life into places where we cannot reach it. And what then? Our people will not endure the thought that the Red Harvest is to be accomplished by . . . others.

"All hail King Virulan!" *Uralesse shouted.* "Truly he is the wisest of the Endarkened! All hail his power—his wisdom—his skill!"

And let the day his stupidity is revealed come soon.

*The winds rang with the terrible shrieking cheers of the Created. Virulan spread his wings and threw back his head, glorying in the praise, the adulation, the wor-ship.*

"And while we wait, let there be feasting, games, a carnival of pain!" *Virulan shouted.* "Let the caverns of the World Without Sun run wet and slick with blood! Let us claim the most isolated of the domains of the Elflings and all it holds as the first fruits of our coming triumph!"

In the Vale of Celenthodiel, Harvest Moon became Rade, Woods, Hearth. Rain washed the land and snow cloaked it, and the tiny crawling things feasted upon the dead until only bones were left. No light showed within Tildorangelor, and no *alfaljodthi* was seen to venture from its borders. Silence and solitude reclaimed Amretheon's lost city.

And ten turns of the Wheel of the Year passed.

❖

Areve endured and grew, defying all who would destroy it, though its foes were many. In the first Wheelturns of its existence, reivers and sellswords turned bandit—unwilling to swear fealty to Hamphuliadiel Astromancer—had tried to take by stealth what they could not take by force, and even bribery had not been unknown, but Areve stood firm against them, and soon such attacks ceased. In these times, the folk who came to Areve pledged their fealty with whole hearts, for Beastlings roamed the land unchallenged.

The refugees spoke of a Beastling army ravaging the land, seeking out and destroying every Elven enclave it could find. The Lord Astromancer promised safety, and so far the Sanctuary had kept that promise. When the Beastlings attacked Areve—as they did frequently—Lightborn and Lightless fought side by side for the safety of all, for everyone knew the Beastlings would slaughter every soul within Areve's boundaries, leaving nothing behind. Each year the walls of Areve were expanded further—there was talk that someday even Arevethmonion Flower Forest would lie within them and be cleansed at last of Beastling taint.

Hamphuliadiel's ambitions were as great as the wise Astromancer himself was humble: a simple Lightbrother who had set his hand to what must be done when the evil days came upon the land. Harwing Lightbrother had never regretted his decision to join him. Not once, in all these Wheelturns.

The time before Harwing had returned to the Sanctuary was a hazy jumble of guilt and loss. Healer Momioniarch had been unable to lift that veil, but Harwing was not troubled, for by the grace of the Light and the compassionate assistance of the Astromancer himself, Harwing had been able to piece the tale together.

Vieliessar Farcarinon, once Lightborn, had rejected all the Sanctuary's oaths and even Mosirinde's Covenant to gather an army in quest of the Unicorn Throne. The Hundred Houses had risen up against her, so crazed with rage and jealousy that they had abandoned their domains and their people to pursue her into the uttermost east. The battles had been vast and costly—and in the end, they had been futile, for the two great armies had destroyed each other. Harwing and others like him had fled the battlefield to seek sanctuary in every sense of the word. Someday, Hamphuliadiel swore, Areve would be strong enough to risk sending scouting parties eastward to see what had become of the two great armies, but Harwing knew that day was far distant. There was much still to do here. Far too much for him to waste his time dreaming about, or worrying about, what the future might hold. So long as Astromancer Hamphuliadiel bore that terrible weight of responsibility, no one else need trouble themselves.

As he did each day, sometimes several times a day, Harwing wished Hamphuliadiel a long, long life.

⊰⊱

The World Without Sun hummed with a purpose and an energy it had not possessed since time out of mind. These were the days of the Red Harvest, filled with slaughter and feasting, and the knowledge burned in every brain that soon the great task set them by *He Who Is* would be complete. The slave-pens were filled with victims enough that every Endarkened could refine their skills, extracting the last possible erg of agony, terror, and despair from their subjects. There were feasts and games, contests, competitions of artistry and of skill. It was a joyous time. A time of festival.

And yet, one Endarkened paced the jeweled and

tessellated floor in the Heart of Darkness with an un-
quenched restlessness. He wore the Crown of Pain. He
sat upon the Throne of Night. The Tree of Night enfolded him within its roots. But Virulan was . . . uneasy.

Three times before, he and his then-brothers had
scoured the world of Life. Four times, Life had been reborn. This time, Virulan had made careful plans that
Life would not be reborn again. This time, the destruction would continue until there was nothing—not the
stone beneath his feet, not one fragment of Ugolthma
itself—to say that any form of Creation had ever been.

So why was it taking so long?

For a moment, he wished that Rugashag still lived.
She had hated him and plotted his death, but she had
also been clever. When there was anything to know
within the World Without Sun, Rugashag had known
it first.

Of course, she would almost certainly have not told
him what she knew, so perhaps he did not regret her
being dead after all. And it was utterly and completely
true that her death had been a work of art, a thing still
spoken of in hushed whispers. It was right, Virulan
thought, that he should have the power of making and
unmaking over his subjects, for though he was a tool
of *He Who Is*, they were the tools that *He Who Is* had
given him.

It was not right that they should die by any other
means.

And yet they were.

Time was meaningless in the World Without Sun, its
passage marked only by Virulan's descent into deep
contemplation and his return from it. Yet many Risings
had come since the beginning of the Red Harvest and
the Bright World Life was not yet extinguished. And
Endarkened died.

The Endarkened could not feel compassion or empa-
thy, nor could they feel grief as the Bright World under-

stood it. When Virulan contemplated his dead subjects, the emotion he felt was rage. The Endarkened had been created to be immortal. Eternal. *Perfect*. Even those that were, by harsh necessity, born instead of created shared that aspect of Endarkened nature. They were not meant to die. But they *were* dying—dying at the hands of Bright World filth.

Of course, those lives were easily replaced, and the Endarkened made up in undoubted superiority of form and mind and power what they lacked in superior numbers.

And yet.

It was true the Endarkened could make themselves invulnerable by magic—but the spell must be cast. It was true that they could heal any physical injury—but again, the spell must be cast. They were naturally immune to both disease and poison—but what lunatic would pause in the heat of battle to offer his enemy a snack? And what fool would accept it?

And so Virulan's children, despite knowing they were utterly superior in every way to the meat they hunted, continued to die of sword cut and arrowshot, by knife and by fire, crushed beneath stones and trees and lured into traps that used every one of those methods at once. The vermin were quick to adapt.

Such thinking only brought Virulan's mind back to the initial cause for irritation: the vermin were living long enough to be able to adapt.

*"Why are you not all dead?"* he roared to the deserted chamber. The echoes of his bellow came back to him, a susurrant sound that chimed from the gems and obsidian, gold and bones, that ornamented his throne room. The venting of his fury gave him no ease.

*I will have answers,* he thought grimly.

Uralesse was the logical one to consult. He was nearly as powerful in sorcery as Virulan himself and had engendered many of the Born. But Virulan knew well that to ask a question meant exposing the need for an answer, and any such need would rightfully be seen as weakness—a weakness that Uralesse would exploit ruthlessly. No, Virulan would ask his questions, but not of Uralesse, and he would do it in such a way that it would seem he asked only to test, and knew the answers already.

It was, so he congratulated himself, a very clever plan.

⊰⊱

The captives the Endarkened took were carefully separated from their own kind, lest the presence of a parent, a friend, a sibling might strengthen their will to resist. Captives were graded and sorted as coldly as gems: this one to the feasting table, that one to become a worker under the rule of some Lesser Endarkened, another to become teaching material for some young Endarkened only beginning to learn mastery of the Way of Pain and Sorrow. Only a very few were worth reserving to the higher ranks of Endarkened nobility and their pleasures, and of these, only a scant few had the makings of proper slaves.

"Please! It is so dark! I cannot see!" The child's voice, roughened by tears, broke upon a sob. "Mama! Are you there? *Mama!*"

The Elfling child had not yet learned that begging was useless, though any intelligent creature would have realized that from the moment of its capture. The creature's eyes were intact for the moment, but the darkling beauty of the World Without Sun was closed to it, for its inferior senses could perceive nothing of the glory that surrounded it. Shurzul reminded herself yet again of the pitiful inferiority of *meat*. She doubted this Elfling would survive to become a slave. Slaves were utterly pliable, possessing no will of their own. They accepted everything that happened, everything that was done to them, with utter passivity. They did not rebel. They did not demand. They did not *beg*.

Its ceaseless keening was one of the reasons she had chosen it as part of her share in the spoils of the last raid. The others its age had already fallen into silence and despair. This one still fought. There were other uses for meat than lives of slavery.

With a wave of her hand, Shurzul caused the braziers in the corners of the chamber to kindle with an unnatural scarlet flame. The Elfling blinked and squinted, putting its hands over its eyes to shield them. Shurzul nodded in approval of her own intelligence. It had beauty of form that was nearly Endarkened in its quality. Even though it was encrusted with blood and feces, the skin beneath was smooth and flawless, the bones beneath that skin finely-shaped and smooth. The combination of beauty and rebellion was intoxicating to her.

Now it lowered its hands and gazed around itself in horror. Shurzul imagined what it saw: to its weak eyes, the red flames would give only dim illumination. The Lesser Endarkened who ringed the chamber—the servants who had brought the meat from the slave pens— would be nothing but glowing eyes and hideous shadowy forms.

And she. . . .

Shurzul knew well her own beauty. Her beauty—and her inventiveness—had been enough to lure King Virulan to her loins, just as it had given her victory in the hunt. Today her bare breasts jutted proudly, her nipples jeweled and gilded, the scarlet flesh unconfined. Her long hair, as scarlet as her flesh, was braided with gems no Brightworlder eyes had ever seen, for these were the living jewels of the deep earth. Her hands sparkled with rings, her wrists and ankles chimed with bracelets, her throat was garlanded with a chain of fire-clear diamonds. She knew herself to be an impressive sight.

Indeed, the child's gaze was drawn to her, and therefore did not linger where it should have, upon the racks and cases of instruments glinting at the edge of the firelight. Its eyes grew round with horror; it was young enough to have been born after the beginning of the Red Harvest, to never have known an existence as anything but hunted prey. It took a step backward, the sight of her momentarily stilling its endless mewling.

Shurzul squatted on her haunches, bringing herself to its eye level. "Come, child," she said throatily. "There is no reason for fear. I will not harm you."

She did not mean it, of course. But raising hope only to betray it, gaining trust only to break it, were sweet and heady appetizers to the great feast the Way of Pain and Sorrow promised.

"Where is my mama?" the child whispered into the silence Shurzul had allowed to grow.

"Why, I do not know," Shurzul said, forcing herself to sound innocently confused. "I will find out, of course. Would you like that?"

Her heart sang to watch the child regard her with wary hope. It nodded fractionally.

"Then so I shall," Shurzul said fulsomely. She held out a hand. "Come to me, little one. I promise I will keep you safe. Come. Tell me your name."

To her concealed delight, the child ran forward and flung itself into her arms. "My— My name is Hazaniel," it said, its face pressed between her breasts. "Mama's name is Thetarara. Please find her!"

Shurzul's nostrils flared at the heat and stench of the body in her arms, even as she carefully stroked Hazaniel's back in a soothing fashion. She sent a speaking look toward one of the Lesser Endarkened; the servant hurried off to discover if the Thetarara-meat was still alive. Great sport could be had if it was, but if was not . . .

Shurzul was certain that little Hazaniel was hungry and thirsty, and would welcome a bowl of nourishing broth.

A shift in the air warned her that she was no longer alone, and Shurzul straightened slowly to her feet, resting one taloned hand upon the filthy head of her toy. A moment later, King Virulan entered the room, and Shurzul immediately knelt, bowing low and furling her wings tightly around herself.

"Rise, my lovely one," Virulan said, placing a finger beneath her chin to tilt her head upward. "I wish to speak with you."

Again Shurzul got to her feet, bowing her head in acquiescence.

"Take the— Take dear Hazaniel and see that he is bathed and fed," she said over her shoulder. "Be certain there is light for his eyes, for I do not wish him to be afraid. I will send for him."

There was a scraping scuttling sound behind her as the Endarkened moved forward.

"Do not fear," Shurzul said lovingly to Hazaniel. "These are my most trusted servants. You will be safe with them." She smiled inwardly as the meat tremblingly nodded.

The moment it was gone, she bowed low again to Virulan. It was the most delicate of balancing acts to flatter the King without throwing away the work she had already put in on the meat. "I beg your forgiveness, my lord and my King. I do not wish to spoil this one. It shows great promise. Enough, perhaps, to amuse the Court."

To amuse its king, they both knew she meant. Virulan smiled and took her arm, drawing her closer to him. "Your constant thought for our ease and pleasure warms my heart," he said. "I shall look forward to the day when you present it. You are a notable artist," he added.

"My skill is but a poor shadow of your own mastery,

King Virulan," Shurzul said modestly. "But I beg of you: please tell me how I may serve you."

There was a pause as King Virulan led Shurzul from the Lower Workroom and even deeper into the World Without Sun. In the Bright World the meat might build high towers and accord the highest point to the highest rank, but in the World Without Sun, the highest rank had the lowest depth: deep within the rock, far away from Life. When he reached one of the long galleries that led to the Throne Chamber and its gardens, Virulan paused.

"Tell me, my delicate, firebrand darling," he said. "How goes the destruction of all Life?"

"My lord King must know far better than I," Shurzul parried, allowing her tail to curve seductively about Virulan's ankle.

"And yet your answer would be of interest to me," Virulan responded neatly, spreading his wings to mantle her shoulders as well as his own.

"Then I would say it is glory beyond imagining to act in accordance with the will of *He Who Is*," Shurzul responded. "To take to the sky when we choose, to hunt where and how we choose—by the King's command, of course—and to fill the slave-pens with the brief beauty of living treasure."

"And now the slave-pens overflow," Virulan said. "And you, clever huntress, tarry here among those treasures."

Though not phrased as a question, the statement demanded an answer.

"But of course," Shurzul said, her brow wrinkling in pretty confusion below its curled golden horns. "After so many centuries of discipline, of hiding, of keeping the Bright World filth from believing we were anything more than a myth, is it not good to savor the pleasure of their extinction? It was you, King Virulan, who showed us the way: Do not your glorious creations

sweep across the land from the Uttermost East, driving
before them any they do not devour? Have you not created splendid monsters to course the surface, to fly
above it, to burrow beneath it, and to swim in its waters? Should not we, your people, exert ourselves to
mirror your great art, though we may never equal it?"
She beamed upon him, her jeweled ivory fangs brilliant
even in this utter absence of light, her entire expression
that of delight and expected praise.

*But why are you taking so long?* If he were not both
Endarkened and King of the Endarkened, Virulan
would have expressed that thought in a wail of frustration. Shurzul had said nothing to which he could take
exception, yet her words only increased his disquiet.

"We all long for the day our task is done," he said
briefly.

"Who would not wish to be once more enfolded in
the glorious, sterile, mindless embrace of *He Who Is*?"
Shurzul answered. "To become once more one with the
essence that sent us forth, knowing we have acted as
an extension of *His* Glorious Will? When that day
comes, *He Who Is* will have no cause to feel we have
exerted less than the last uttermost erg of our being to
do *Him* honor." Her eyes closed in rapture and she drew
a deep shuddering breath. "And you most of all, lord
King. All that we do is done by your will and at your
word. The greatest credit, the greatest magnificence,
splendor, and fame—these are yours most of all."

Virulan's eyes narrowed in suspicion, for no Endarkened praised another—even as subject to King—without
having some clandestine purpose in mind. Yet, try as he
might, he could determine no falsehood or treason in
Shurzul's words. She spoke not only with propriety,
but words of uttermost truth.

"It is precisely as you say," he said, ignoring his own
unease. "Well done, thirdmost among the Endarkened."
Shurzul's eyes widened as if she was astonished by

such praise. "My lord King, such praise is a heavy weight to bear, and I will endeavor to be worthy of it. And yet, in this moment of your pleasure, may I beg of you a boon?"

"Speak, Shurzul," he said. And when she did not continue: "Your King listens."

"King Virulan," Shurzul said, nestling beneath his wings and caressing his thigh with her tail, "I can only wish—should it please you—that you will lead us often upon the hunt, so that we may see—in the sky, in the slaughter, and in the disposition of the captives—the standard to which we, your people, can only aspire."

Virulan considered her statement warily, but—no matter from what angle he regarded it—he could see no trap. He had held back from taking part in the Red Harvest, though it pained him deeply, as a way of keeping control over his subjects. He let it be known that he denied himself this pleasure so there would be more for them, slaking his lusts merely upon the first fruits of the slave pens.

Perhaps it was time for a change.

"It shall be done," he announced. "We shall give them a moonturn to grow incautious and to hope, and then I will lead you against them once more."

"Well do I remember the glorious days of the Winnowings," Shurzul breathed throatily, gazing into the King's blazing yellow eyes. "Well do I remember the beauty of your slaughters, the mastery of your kills. To once again be witness to such . . . my heart sings as if I bathed in the tears of a thousand Bright World children."

"I have no doubt of your ability to elicit such tears," Virulan said. "And even in my passion, I would not keep you from your art."

"The child will be only the readier for more uncertainty," Shurzul said. "If there is some way by which I may serve my King . . . ?"

"You need not ask," he growled hungrily, pulling her body against his own.

❦

I had wondered why you chose to absent yourself from the hunt," Virulan said to Uralesse a handful of Risings later, as Virulan and his most favored courtier walked once more in the Garden of Tears.

"I am certain my reasons were much like your own," Uralesse replied cagily. "Favored" did not mean "trusted." Not among the Endarkened.

Virulan responded with a smile that bared all of his not-inconsiderable teeth. "The power lies often not in claiming the sweets of victory, but denying oneself those very pleasures," he said, neither agreeing nor rebuking. "And yet, I did wonder . . . if the lack of leadership caused the Red Harvest to proceed less swiftly than it might have."

"Your perspicacity astounds me," Uralesse answered, carefully keeping the irony he held in his heart from reaching his voice. "We are, of course, perfect as *He Who Is* made us. But is it possible, do you think, that those whom we created in our turn, and those they thereafter made, could be . . . *less* than perfect?"

"Certainly not!" Virulan snapped instantly. "If they can make Brightworlders into submissive slaves, how can it be that we shape them with any less skill? Yet . . . they do require guidance. This much I know. And so I shall lead the next hunt. And perhaps others to follow. I have not yet decided."

"My King! My brother!" Uralesse gasped, as if overcome by the thought. "Surely you could not risk yourself so! The vermin of the Bright World are but brief cattle—yet they have managed, through luck or treachery, to end Endarkened lives. And if their cousins should choose to come to their aid . . ."

"You think I am not stronger than any of you? Faster

and more clever? My powers are enough to withstand anything such puny mortals may do!" Virulan shouted.

"I only—" Uralesse said, groveling.

"I have made my decision and I will not be swayed from it!" Virulan said. "This will be not merely a Cleansing pleasing to *He Who Is*, but a work of art the like of which will never be seen again—and *I* shall be in the foremost of its creators!"

"My lord King," Uralesse whimpered. "I am your most loyal and devoted servant!" He flung himself to the ground, beating his forehead against the chill black stone, and crept forward until he could rain kisses upon Virulan's feet. He did not even try to dodge the kick that sent him rolling away, and left him with a gashed and bloody mouth.

"Then serve," Virulan growled, "in silence. I forbid you to speak in my presence until I again give you leave. I had thought to command you to accompany me upon the hunt, for we have been friends and comrades since the moment of our creation, but now I see it would be a favor you did not deserve, faithless coward. Go! And do not allow me to gaze upon you again until I summon you!"

In silence, Uralesse backed away, crawling on his belly, until one of the pillars of the Garden of Tears hid him from Virulan's sight. Only then did he turn and begin to crawl forward—still on his belly—and only when he had left the Garden entirely did he dare to rise to his feet.

But an observer—had there been one—would have noted that he did not seem particularly disheartened by this latest punishment from the creature who might choose upon a whim to kill him.

In fact, Uralesse looked very content.

*It is just as I have long known. Virulan is steered by opposites. Had I praised his plan, he would have found some way to get out of it. Having expressed my horror and displeasure at his idea, I have only made him more obstinate and unwilling to reconsider. Let him lead our hunts against the Brightworlders. In fact, let him attack them and slay them while we others merely watch. One Endarkened can die as easily as another.*

*Even if he is King.*

## CHAPTER TWELVE

# RAIN MOON:
# A MONTH FOR WAR

*In those days, leading the Otherfolk to war was like go-*
*ing on a picnic—you took a blanket and as much food*
*as you could carry and trusted to luck for the rest.*
*When the Otherfolk attacked, they attacked like rov-*
*ing bands of brigands. Drunken brigands. Their tactics*
*were those of small war bands and their notions of*
*strategy were vague at best.*

*They were also very effective.*

— Runacar Warlord, *A History of the Western Shore Campaign*

⁂

W hen Runacar pledged himself to King Leutric he'd been certain the High King's army
would come again by the next War Season.
It didn't.

Five Wheelturns, and everything east of The Sanctuary of the Star was emptied of Elvenkind. Four more,
and Farcarinon, Ullilion, and everything to the banks
of the Angarussa belonged to the Otherfolk. And each
time Leutric asked when Runacar would give him the
Shore, Runacar smiled and said: *"Soon."*

In the ninth Wheelturn of Runacar's exile, Leutric
asked him when he would give him the Shore. And
Runacar smiled and said: *"Now."*

⁂

T he Goldengrass—what the Children of Stars called
the Grand Windsward—had once been the home

of Leutric's people, and when Runacar had scoured the Western Reach clean of Elves, Leutric had moved his throne rooms from the Flower Forests to open ground where the sun could warm his old bones. It gave him the greatest of pleasure to make his place in the stronghold of his enemies and to take the sweets they had once commanded for his own. In the middle distance stood what had once been Cirandeiron Great Keep, now utterly empty but mostly intact. Nearly everything about it affronted his sensibilities, but it was too big to burn and too massive to topple, and stone didn't rot overnight. It was just going to have to sit there, Grass and Star alone knew how long.

He turned his thoughts to happier things. The orchards had gone from blossom to leaf over the past sennight, promising apples, cherries, and peaches in due time, and the spring day was bright and warm. The archivists and message bearers necessary to a court on eternal and unending pilgrimage moved fearlessly and contentedly over the open ground. There was no need to fear the *alfaljodthi*. Not here.

Much had changed.

The Centaurs were expanding the acreage under tillage and there was talk of building towns. The Dryads were working to expand the Flower Forests and the Bearwards were doing much the same for the less-magical forests. And after centuries of having to hide in their own rivers, the Selkies would soon be able to once more make their pilgrimages to the sea.

None of that particularly called for any King-Emperor management. The only thing that really required Leutric's attention at the moment was the plan for the new Minotaur city. The western slope of the Mystrals was only lightly forested and it had been agreed that it would be given to his people, as the Mystrals and Medharthas would be given to the Folk of the Air. Their ancestral lands—the Goldengrass and the soaring Icewild mountains—could not be reclaimed.

*We plan for the future as if we think there will be one,* he thought gloomily.

It had seemed so simple when he'd started. Another Red Winnowing was to come, and Leutric meant its scythe to fall upon the *alfaljodthi,* not the Folk. The Elves had cooperated by starting another of their endless wars and going across the Mystrals to fight it. Then Runacar had come, to bring with him the bitter and the sweet. The bitter was the omens that said this was not to be merely another Winnowing, but the Red Harvest, the end of days. The sweet was Runacar himself, with his understanding of how the Children of Stars made war, and his generosity in yoking that understanding to Otherfolk needs. And so Leutric dared to hope.

*Perhaps the prophecies are wrong. Perhaps this is only another Winnowing, and not the Harvest. Perhaps the Darkness will glut themselves on the Children of Stars and go back to sleep.*

He could hope for that, at least. And all the other news was good.

"If everything is going as you desire, Leutric, why don't you look happy?"

The voice startled Leutric up from his seat with a roar of shock. *"Melisha!"* he shouted, loud enough to scare the birds out of the trees. The courtiers and judgment-seekers glanced around, saw the unicorn, and moved courteously away to give her space to approach Leutric.

"Who else?" Melisha stepped daintily from behind a tree. Her back was covered with fallen apple blossoms, their whiteness seeming dark against her gleaming fur. "I've come to see if you're ready to talk to me yet."

Leutric glanced around. Everyone was busy—or wished to look that way—and well out of earshot, save for the tumble of Fauns that had been playing some incomprehensible game all morning and now lay in a happy slumber amid the trees. He looked back at Melisha.

"No," he said simply.

"You're being very difficult," Melisha answered, switching her tail.

"I'm being practical," he said. He wanted to get to his feet and pace, but that would make things difficult for Melisha. He sighed and stayed where he was. "You say that our only hope—by which you mean 'the hope of everything living all the way down to butterflies and angleworms—'"

"I've always considered butterflies to be more beautiful than angleworms, haven't you?"

"Don't change the subject. 'All the way down to butterflies and angleworms' to survive this ... Winnowing ... is to make common cause with the Children of Stars and surrender the Bones of the Earth to them."

"Oh good. You *do* remember what we talked about."

"You've come to me every time the seasons change since before I became Emperor as well as King," Leutric grumbled. "You will come to Audalo with it when he takes my place, I am certain. And it's just as impossible now as it ever was."

"Why? You've already got one of the Children of Stars. He likes you. I admit, he isn't best placed to persuade the others, but—"

"And here I always thought unicorns were realists."

"And *I* thought Minotaurs were practical. Calling the Red Harvest a mere Winnowing does not change what it is. You want to live. They want to live. If giving the Children of Stars a way to fight back helps you both do that, then why not?"

"Because if they did not use the Bones against us at first, they would use them against us at last," Leutric said. "And even if they did the impossible and agreed to let us live among them, the best we could hope for would be the status of livestock, not equals. I'm not willing to let *Elves* decide they know how to run my life. Not even if that is the only way to *have* a life."

"And the others?" the Unicorn asked softly. "Have you asked them?"

"Who shall I ask?" Leutric said. "The Gryphons, whose feathers have gone to ornament Elven cloaks? The Selkies, trapped and skinned so a highborn lady can stay warm at night? The Dryads, whose groves have been cut down for firewood? The Centaurs, herded into their own barns and burned alive? Or my own ancestors, killed for their ivory, or as trophies, or as *food*. There are so many of the Folk to take counsel of, I don't think I can manage it before we're all dead," Leutric snarled.

"Yet you let them plan for the future," she said, nodding in the direction of the rest of the court.

"It passes the time. And maybe I'm right and the Darkness will be satisfied with the Elves alone. Fitting, don't you think, since it was a Winnowing that began our grief? Or do you think a second Pelashia will rise up among us and go as our ambassador to their High King? You know as well as I do that Pelashia failed."

"A thing I know far better than you," Melisha said softly. "And yet I still say this: we must join together with my cousins in this battle, or there will be no one left to argue about whether the idea will work."

"It cannot be done," Leutric said, his voice as low and as sad as hers had been. "I have thought about your madness—"

"I thank you for that assessment of my counsel, old bull!"

"—since the first time you came to me with it. I will not give up the Bones of the Earth unless I know the Elves will not turn their power against us. And how am I to make certain of that? Since the days of the White Mare and the Sword-Giver they have believed that anything not in their own shape must be their enemy. It is hard to argue otherwise when you have a swordblade through your throat."

"That much is true," Melisha said. "And yet, a way must be found."

Leutric drew breath for a bellow of exasperation, looked around, and let it out in a gusty sigh. "Why?" he asked again. "If the Darkness will be satisfied with half, let that half be the Elves. If this time it means to have the whole, what can it matter whether we are together or apart?"

"Because of the Bones of the Earth," Melisha said, stepping as close to him as she could. "Only one of the Children of Stars can awaken them."

"*Only* if I lead them there—and I won't," Leutric said firmly. "Elves are no improvement over the Darkness if the Elves want us dead."

"That is as true as the fact the Darkness comes for us all this time, Leutric," Melisha said seriously. "But the hearts of the Elves is a truth we can change. If we—Elves, Unicorns, Brightfolk, Otherfolk, *all*—are united as one people before the Bones are awakened . . ."

"That won't happen," Leutric said, glancing away for a moment. "And so—"

But when he looked back again, Melisha was gone.

"Unicorns," he said with a sigh. "I'd trust in hope sooner than in the hearts of the Elves," he said, louder, as if she still might hear.

❈

To take the Western Shore was a task that a war band could not accomplish. For that, Runacar needed an army. Because of all he had done already, when Leutric sent word to the Otherfolk that an army was needed, the Nine Races answered in their thousands. Bearward—Woodwose—Minotaur—Centaur—Hippogriff—Faun—all the folk he knew to name had come. Radafa had managed to persuade several Gryphons to join him, though only to scout, not to fight. Even an Aesalion had come.

⊰⊱

Blackwheat Gate was a manor house in Cirandeiron that commanded a view of both the Delfieraratha-dan and the ruins of Cirandeiron's Great Keep. If Runacar had any home now, it was here, but in truth he viewed the manor house as a convenient place to come in out of the rain and train his horses; a place to gather his forces at the beginning of each campaign. It had been beautiful once, but its upkeep required the labor of many hands, and now it was falling slowly into ruin. *Still, it should outlast my need for it.*

The day was warm and he had moved his desk outside to take advantage of the light. His generals were gathered round: Keloit and his wife Helda dozing in the sun, Audalo reading scrolls from a basket at his side, Pelere doing something complicated with a wax tablet and stylus. Gunyel and Radafa were on the wing above and Tanet . . . was somewhere. Runacar was going over lists of tally sheets, trying not to grind his teeth while doing so. This "war season" would be unlike any other since he had come west, and it required endless planning.

The Otherfolk had never, not in living memory—not in Gryphon memory, which went back to a time before there were Elves in Jer-a-kalaliel at all—put an army into the field. When the Centaurs had fought, it was because their farms and villages were being overrun. When the Fauns and Minotaurs played deadly pranks upon supply caravans wending through the Flower Forests, they were doing so practically on their own doorstep. The idea of going to a place they'd never been for no reason other than to fight—and carrying food and shelter with them to do so—was something they had no experience of. Certainly the Otherfolk traveled, and for such purposes would carry necessities with them. But they were far more likely to build an encampment out of materials that came to hand than use a tent. Gryphons, Hippogriffs, Aesalions were used to ranging for leagues in search of a meal, and Gryphons literally slept upon the wing.

The Angarussa formed the eastern boundary of Amrolion and Daroldan. On its western bank, Delfier-arathadan Flower Forest ran from mountain to desert, thick and wild. North of Daroldan, the Medhatara Range rose up, range after range of impassable icy peaks. In the south, the red sands of the Kashadabad-shar promised death to any who attempted to cross them. This was the theater across which Runacar must wage his war, and to do so, he must find a way to supply his force without use of wagons, sledges, oxen, or mules, without a portable city to follow the army as its sanctuary and haven.

"Hello. You're having a war. That sounds like great fun! What's a war?" The voice was deep, unfamiliar, and came from something . . . large.

"A war?" Runacar said in bewilderment. He looked up. There was . . . someone . . . perched on the roof, looking down at him.

The newcomer was as large as an ice-tiger. Its body was felinoid, though winged. The wings were iridescent black, with bars of red and yellow. Its fur was the pale grey of wood smoke, except for four blood-red socks. It had a disturbingly Elven face—disturbingly large as well—rather than the animalic muzzle the tigerish shape implied. The furless skin was grey instead of Elven ivory, making Runacar think of dead knights who had lain all winter beneath a lake's ice before their bodies were found in spring. Its face was ringed with a mane of red and black fur that covered its head and throat.

Audalo instantly got to his feet. "This person is

under the protection of King-Emperor Leutric," he said firmly.

Runacar could see that everyone in the garden—even Tanet had appeared from somewhere—were all on their feet and gazing roofward with identical expressions of wariness. That was not reassuring.

The creature on the roof pouted toothily. "I'm not going to *break* him! I want to play." It spread its wings and glided to the ground, and when it landed in front of him, Runacar was able to identify it at last. Because he could see its tail.

As long as an ice-tiger's, it ended in a black, chitinous, clublike barb—a scorpion's sting. That poison barb could pierce Elven armor and bring instant death. This was an Aesalion, and according to *Lannarien's Book of Living Things*, Aesalions had the ability to influence the emotions of their victims, broadcasting terror or grief and then settling down to be entertained by the results. Of course, Lannarien *also* said that all Aesalions were male, so Runacar wasn't sure how much of the entry was true.

"Is a war fun?" the Aesalion asked.

"No. It is not," Radafa said, coming in for a hurried landing. "You are far from home, Drotha. I thought the Aesalions had chosen to stay in the east."

"I got bored," Drotha said simply, looking at Radafa. "And I heard you were going to have a war. So I came to see what that was."

Drotha's great head swung back toward Runacar, and now Runacar was caught in the Aesalion's gaze. He'd thought, at first sight, that its eyes were as black as any Elf's, but now he could see they were not. They were green—violet—yellow—blue—red . . . He took a step backward, feeling the sour taste of fear in his throat. He could feel his heart hammering in his chest. It had all been a trap. These weren't his friends. They'd lured him here, lulled him, so Drotha could come and kill him. He had never wanted so badly to run in his entire life—but if he ran, the Aesalion would pounce, would sting, would rend the flesh from his bones . . .

*"Fear is the komen's first enemy. Fear of pain, fear of defeat. Fear is the enemy that must be defeated before the komen steps onto the battlefield. And it will ride with him on every battlefield."*

Runacar took a deep breath. He could not marshal his wits enough to speak, but he vowed he would not run. He had stood on Ishtilaikh when the *mazhnune* had risen, and *he would not run.*

"Leutric will not wish to learn you are our enemy," Audalo said with deceptive mildness, and suddenly the fear Runacar felt was gone as if it had never been. Drotha's eyes were black once more.

"If you break your toys, you don't get to keep playing with them," Runacar said evenly, holding Drotha's gaze. "Play nicely and I'll let you come with me to the war."

*"Rune!"* Pelere protested.

"Deal!" Drotha cried. He bounced across the clearing like the largest housecat Runacar had ever seen and stopped so close Runacar could feel the heat of his body. He beamed at Runacar merrily and quite madly.

"Is this wise?" Tanet asked, his voice almost a whisper.

"No," Runacar said. "It's war."

And so Drotha came to live at Blackwheat Gate, and the planning for the campaign went on.

⚔

The Otherfolk would come when Leutric called, but they would not follow an *alfaljodthi.* Runacar's knowledge of war had given Leutric this decade of victories, and it was Runacar's generalship that would give the Otherfolk the Shore, but not all of them were as sanguine about Runacar's change of heart as King Leutric was. Cooperation among the various peoples of the Otherfolk was a new thing that did not even predate Vieliessar Farcarinon's initial claim of the Unicorn Throne.

For this war, Runacar needed numbers, and if that meant others were his army's generals, well, his pride had been trampled into the dust long ago. So his war band became his captains, and his apprentices became his generals, and those who came to fight followed them, not Runacar. Runacar, Warlord to King-Emperor Leutric, became merely an advisor to Pelere, Keloit, Tanet, Audalo, and others. If he could convince them of the value of his ideas, they would present the plans to his captains—who, in turn, would consider them before attempting to persuade their followers to obey.

And that was only the beginning. When they reached Great Sea Ocean, his generals must win the agreement of the Ocean's Own to join in the war. The Nisse, Keloit said, were sorcerers nearly as powerful as the Bearwards. The negotiations with the Queen of the Nisse—who was, so far as Runacar understood matters, the Empress of the Ocean's Own—had been going on for moonturns, and all that Leutric had gained was the promise of a meeting.

Still, Runacar had little choice in the matter.

*"Take the Shore, and we'll hold everything from here to the Mystrals. The High King will never get them back."*

"We will attack from the south," Runacar said firmly.

It was Flower Moon in the tenth Wheelturn since the Battle of the Shieldwall Plain—*nearly War Season,* a quiet ghost in Runacar's mind whispered—and the fire in the great stone fireplace of Blackwheat Gate's Great Hall sent out a welcome heat. Once its mantel and surround had been carved with fanciful representations of

Gryphons and Minotaurs: those ornaments had been smashed to anonymity.

"Even coming up from the south we'll still run into Amrolion sooner or later," Pelere said, tapping the stone floor with her forehoof in an absent gesture. "We've pushed them into Daroldan's lap with those raids you said were so useless, but that doesn't mean they're gone."

"No," Runacar agreed. He ran a hand absently through his hair. There was no one left to read the stories of victories woven into his battle-braids and no one to braid it for him, so he wore it in a simple queue. "And that's the point. Push them hard enough up into the Medharthas, and Amrolion and Daroldan will abandon the Shore to come east—and end up in Hamphuliadiel's lap. And before they do, they'll squall loud enough to get the High King's attention."

"If she's still listening," Helda commented dryly. "It's been a decade, you know," the Bearward Healer pointed out.

"She's listening," Runacar said grimly.

"They won't get far if they run," Audalo rumbled. He shook his head and the great curved horns branching from his brow flashed in the firelight.

"Oh, but they will," Runacar said, smiling ferally. "They can't go west—there's nothing west but ocean, and the Ocean's Own hold that. Eastward, there are only a few roads through the Flower Forest, and none of them designed for the passage of large numbers. They know the Flower Forest is deadly to them, and they won't risk breaking out through it until they have no other choice. So we'll give them no other choice."

"They could just keep going north—and not cross the forest at all," Keloit pointed out. Now that he had reached his full growth, he truly towered over Runacar. Keloit was one of Runacar's most able generals, but he was here also as his mother's deputy, for among the

Bearwards, the women led. What Keloit knew, his mother would soon know, and what Frause knew, all the Bearward Spellmothers would know.

"Into the Medhataras? Idiot!" Andhel said. "Nobody goes there and lives." The Woodwose gave Runacar a deadly glance, as if agreeing with him was physically painful.

"Which is why—when they run—they'll turn east through Delfierarathadan, or run along its northern edge," Runacar said patiently. "They won't want to, and that's why they'll go north first. But they can't go west, and we'll be in the south, so their only hope will be to go east."

"So they enter Delfierarathadan and don't come out," Audalo said, puzzled. "But you just said they do. How is this a victory for us, Rune?"

"It's a victory for us because as they flee we will strip them of everything they have. Seed grain, saplings— every herd beast, every hunting hound, every horse and mule—we'll take them all. Two War Princes and all their people will enter the Western Reach as poor as Landbonds. And they will go to the Sanctuary of the Star."

"So we want to give the green-robed witches an army, do we?" Tanet said mockingly. "I may dance at your funeral yet, Houseborn."

"You may," Runacar said, "but not this Wheelturn. I'm not going to give Hamphuliadiel an army. I'm going to give him an enemy. Daroldan and Amrolion are sworn to Vieliessar. They won't ally with Hamphuliadiel. They'll fight him."

"I'll help!" Drotha crowed. "If they don't want to fight, I'll *make* them!"

"So the idea is that we chase them," Pelere said, tactfully ignoring the Aesalion. "That clears the Shore, but then we have a great herd of them next to Arevethmonion." The Centauress pondered for a moment, swishing her tail absently. "Hm. Yes. That could work."

It was not decided that easily. The Otherfolk did not view time the way the *alfaljodthi* did: their sense of it was tied to the Wheel of the Year and to the long cycles of slumber and rebirth that were the heartbeat of the Flower Forests. Runacar was resigned to spending another Wheelturn gathering a force and convincing it that his strategy was sound, but he was overly pessimistic. At the start of Rain Moon, the Otherfolk army assembled itself in the shadow of Caerthalien Great Keep and headed west.

Runacar had even managed to recruit a second Aesalion.

⊶⊷

The Gryphons, the Hippogriffs, and both Aesalions—to persuade Juniche to tolerate Drotha's presence and Drotha to tolerate Juniche's presence might be the greatest achievement of all Runacar's campaigns—were already airborne.

Runacar closed his eyes, taking a deep breath. It was perhaps an hour before dawn. Late in the springtide. Perfect weather and a perfect time for war. For a moment he could almost believe that none of it had happened—no Vieliessar, no Winter War, no shattering defeats. He could close his eyes and imagine his brothers and sisters here somewhere, each commanding their own grand-taille, while Bolecthindial Caerthalien, War Prince of Caerthalien, led the army as a whole.

The fantasy was strengthened by the fact that—for the first time in a very long time—Runacar wore armor and rode a destrier. When the war band had taken Caerthalien, he had found the armor he now wore in one of the Great Keep's unlooted storerooms. It had clearly been the prized possession of one of his greatfathers, and Runacar had asked Keloit and Helda to store it in their hidel in anticipation of a day such as this. It was beautifully made, some forgotten Craftworker's masterpiece, gold enamel over engraved and gilded plate. Wearing it, Runacar glowed like the sun come down to earth. Pelere's family had woven the fabric of his surcoat and saddlecloth as luck gifts and crafted his warcloak from velvet that was another of the many spoils of war. From sword to spurs, he was armed and armored as befit the hero of a wondertale.

As for his mount, the Alliance had not taken with it every horse in the West when it had marched, and by a few Wheelturns after The Battle of the Shieldwall Plain herds ran wild all across the Western Reach. The breeding programs of centuries had been cast into disarray, but enough pure-blooded animals had remained for Runacar, with the help of the Otherfolk, to capture a few likely mares and breed them. Hialgo had been the result. The destrier had seen four summers. He was a pale grey, the sort of animal a General of Armies might ride, and his training had been worthy of his breeding.

Arilcarion had once written that a true knight should not only be able to wage war but ornament it; they must be able to forge every element of their gear, from destrier to the standard they would carry into battle, and when the battle was done, they must be able to memorialize it in poetry and song. Arilcarion's ideal was one that most Elvenkind could only aspire to, but Hialgo was the equal of any Caerthalien-bred beast Runacar had ever ridden—better, perhaps, since the great grey stallion had lived among Otherfolk from the moment of his birth, and the forms, sounds, and scents of Gryphons and Bearwards did not disturb him in the least.

Hialgo's saddlecloth, Runacar's surcoat, and the war banner he carried were all emblazoned with the symbol of the King-Emperor's Great House. There was no such symbol, of course, so Runacar had needed to create it himself. After long deliberation, he had chosen a Vilya, proper, surrounded by a moon, argent, a star, argent, and a single leaf, vert, all on a cobalt field. Leaf and star, ocean, tree and sky: the things all the Otherfolk held dear were represented here.

He thought the banner would annoy the War Princes of the Western Shore a very great deal.

He sighed deeply, opening his eyes. His family was dead, and now Runacar led an army not out of legend, but out of nightmare, and did not examine his motives all that closely. He raised his arm and flourished the banner, raising its staff and pointing it forward. Hialgo danced in place, eager to go, and behind him Runacar felt the army begin to move.

❖

They gave the Sanctuary of the Star a wide berth, though not wide enough, by intention, that they would not be seen and noted. Perhaps the size of the array would be large enough to give the Astromancer more than a few sleepless nights. Runacar sincerely hoped so. Radafa told him that Areve was expanding again and that Arevethmonion seemed to have diminished since the last time the war band had scouted this way. Perhaps they were pushing it back so that the Sanctuary Road no longer ran through it: he could not imagine that any gaggle of Green Robes, no matter how misled, would want to make the whole thing go away. It blocked expansion to the east, true, but there was plenty of room at the other nine points of the compass.

*How many more souls can that village hold—or should I be asking, how large can it grow? It already holds the population of a great army—and I know exactly how many hectares of farmland are needed to feed a great army. How will they go on farming if it takes them from sunrise to sunfall to reach their fields? And if they build homes closer to their fields, they will not be one village, but many villages that no longer live beneath the Astromancer's eye, and I do not think Hamphuliadiel will like that.*

Runacar shook his head ruefully. He had been his father's child, not his mother's: it was Glorthiachiel who saw reasons behind reasons, plots within plots, Bolecthindial who had seen a goal and the most efficient way of reaching it quickly. But now that they had both gone—to Void or Hunt, he did not know—it seemed he was taking heed of his mother's lessons at last. Hamphuliadiel hoarded people as a miser hoarded wealth, uncaring that the wealth amassed would burst the bounds of the counting room—or city walls—and overflow. But people were not grain or gold, nor would they patiently stay where they were put.

Another puzzle for the future.

※

Once Runacar had gotten them across the Angarussa, which was broad and shallow this far south, and through the Temeryll Hills, the army was in the Kashadabadshar, the great red desert that formed the southern bounds of most of the Western Reach and the Western Shore. Not even the Otherfolk knew how far the red sands stretched: the winged ones enjoyed the spiraling updrafts, but even the Gryphons said they could see no end to the sands. Runacar's plan was to traverse the Kashadabadshar to the coast, meet with the Ocean's Own, and then turn northward. The domains would be expecting any attack to come from the landward side, not the seaward, and probably through Delfierarathadan.

It took his army most of a sennight to make the desert crossing, and they were very low on water by the time they saw the ocean in the distance. The little water they'd found along the line of march needed to be purified by the Spellmothers before it was drinkable: it extended their supplies, but not by much. The Spellmothers and the Earthdancers both said the same thing: you could not call water if it was not there to call. Even Radafa agreed, saying you could not call rain to a place where it did not rain.

Runacar could have crossed a hundred miles to the north, and evaded that problem. But the Kashadabadshar crossing did what he intended it to: it gave the army its first lesson in relying upon one another.

❧❧

What if your friends don't come out to fight, Houseborn? Will you be sorry?" Andhel walked beside Runacar's destrier as had become her habit, her bundle of javelins resting lightly on her shoulder. None of the Woodwose—so they said—knew how to ride, and try as he might, Runacar had not been able to convince any of them to learn. They attacked on foot from deep cover, with throwing spears, the short bow and the long bow, slingstones, and darts. There was—so they said—no place for a horse in all of that.

For this journey she'd dyed her hair the color of the Kashadabadshar sands and her leathers had been replaced by a tunic and leggings of pale homespun. The ribbons sewn along the arms and across the back of the tunic made her look as if she had wings.

"No," he said briefly, and Andhel smirked. "You know as well as I that our purpose here is not to kill them, but to drive them eastward. If they lock themselves up in their keeps, we have to get them out. But if they choose to run, I'll be grateful."

"Unwilling to kill your own kind? You've been willing enough to kill us." The "us" in her remark was the Otherfolk, of course: Andhel lost no chance to remind Runacar that no matter what she looked like, she was not Elven.

Runacar laughed. "I've been killing my own kind since before you set foot to earth, girl."

"Let him be, Andh'a. You've been sounding that same horn since he came to us, and I'm tired of the song," Tanet said.

Runacar didn't trust Tanet any more than he did Andhel—at least, he didn't trust Tanet not to slit his throat if it was convenient; he certainly trusted his generalship—but at least Tanet didn't spend all his time baiting him.

"Doesn't mean I'm wrong, Tan," Andhel said.

"Doesn't mean you're right, either," came the response. "Besides, all the other Houseborn want him dead, too. So you and they have that in common."

Runacar touched his heels to Hialgo's flanks and the grey stallion trotted forward until he was out of earshot. He'd heard the start of this argument before, and knew that the bickering would go on for hours, the matter only dropped when the participants grew bored.

⁂

The vanguard of the army crested a last hill and Runacar saw the ocean for the first time in his life.

He'd known what an ocean was, of course: a large body of water like an enormous lake, and salt instead of fresh. But nothing had prepared him for the fact that it seemed to stretch on forever, its surface a shifting dance of blue and gold and green. It was edged by a beach of white sand as fine and smooth as if it, too, were made of salt; a border of sea-wrack showed the highest point of the tide, and its endless waves curled up to break upon the shore with a crashing hissing sound as rhythmic as a heartbeat. He stared in wonder, inhaling air that was briny and fresh at the same time.

Sea-birds wheeled over the water's edge and stepped delicately through the surf, hunting dinner. A band of shore-apes, startled by the arrival of the army's vanguard, fled, shrieking and barking indignantly. Runacar barely noticed them.

Ever since he had taken sword and spurs at his father's hand, Runacar had only considered a landscape in terms of how easy—or how difficult—it would be to fight across. Even the Flower Forests had meant nothing beyond that: Otherfolk hid in them and Lightborn needed them. But Great Sea Ocean was something he could not ride across, nor was it something he could ignore. It simply *was*.

"—Runacar. Runacar. *Rune!*"

He blinked, coming back to himself, realizing that Pelere had been trying to get his attention for some time. "Sorry, I . . . What?" he said, shaking his head to break the ocean's spell.

"Should we make camp here?" she asked.

"Yes," he said. "Yes, of course."

⌁

The army, as usual, made camp by the simple expedient of stopping in its tracks and wandering off. *Ah, if only the Hundred Houses had ever embraced such refreshing simplicity*, Runacar thought. The coastal air was mild and warm, the salty bite of the ocean was an unfamiliar but welcome scent, and so far as he could tell, nobody had ever farmed these lands at all.

The following day, the delegation to meet with the Sea Peoples left the camp a few candlemarks past midday. No one had told Runacar how long the discussions might take, and he suspected nobody, not even Audalo, really knew. In addition to Runacar, Keloit, and Tanet—which probably meant Andhel as well—there would be Frause, Audalo, who would speak on behalf of Leutric, Pelere, and Radafa, since the Gryphon could fly out over the water to let them know whether anyone was coming to shore. Probably they would be accompanied by a dozen Fauns, since Fauns were always everywhere and obeyed no orders. Runacar doubted that so large a group could agree on any matter whatsoever, but for once that was not his problem.

He had ridden Hialgo down to the shore, at least partly to discover the destrier's reaction to the Ocean's Own. Now he swung his leg across the stallion's back and dropped lithely to the ground, proving once more that a suit of Elven armor was so flexible its wearer could dance while wearing it, or fight afoot. Collecting the banner-stave from its rest on the saddle, he followed the others toward the water's edge.

Before he'd covered half the distance, he revised his opinion of the armor and its craftsman unfavorably. It was clear that four legs were better than two on this terrain, and the shifting salt-white sand seemed to be slippery, fluid, and inflexible all at once. He found himself needing to use the banner-pole as a discreet walking-stick more than once, but fortunately, the wet sand at the water's edge was firmer.

By the time he reached it, he could see a roiling disturbance offshore. The sea bubbled like a cauldron. Suddenly it exploded in spray as something breached its surface.

Horses.

No, not horses. The creatures were three times the size of even the largest plow horse, while as graceful and delicately-made as the finest racing high-bred. Their coats and manes were as white as seafoam, and as they made their way shoreward, he realized they weren't horses at all—or not entirely. Just behind the ribs, hide turned to scales, a dorsal ridge appeared upon the spine, and instead of hind legs and a flagged tail there was a scaled, sinuous, alabaster length of . . . body . . . terminating in a wide double-lobed fin.

With them, some holding to their manes for support, others free-swimming beside and behind them, came other creatures. Some he had seen before—the otterlike

Selkies—and others were unknown to him: men and women who looked nearly as familiar as any Wood-wose or *alfaljodthi*, save that their hair was silver, or green, or blue, or gold, and their bodies below the waist terminated in fishtails of a number of rainbow hues. *The Nisse,* he thought to himself. They were garbed in ornamental armor and brilliantly gleaming jewelry, and he wondered if they traded for such items or if they had some magic that let them forge metal underwater.

"Aejus and Meraude, here to speak for the Ocean's Own, accompanied by members of their court," Audalo said quietly. "The seahorses are their guardsmen. The Selkies you know; they are here as observers for those races who will gain the most from access to the Western Shore. Those others are nixies."

Runacar looked where Audalo indicated. Sporting through the foam around the royal party were perhaps a dozen creatures so near to Elven shape—and at the same time so far from it—that they gave him an uneasy pang of aversion.

If they were standing, they would, he thought, have been as tall as a child old enough to serve as an Arming Page. But they were slender to the point of emaciation, and their arms and legs were far too long for their height. Their hands—he could not see their feet—were as outsized as their limbs, and their long, delicate fingers were webbed like a duck's foot and had far too many joints. The other things outsized were their ears, so large and long that the points rose above their heads like horns; their outer edges were finnily frilled. In the bright sunlight, he could not tell the color of their skin at first: it was only when one of them leaped onto the back of one of the sea-horses for a moment that he could see the skin was greenish-pale and iridescent like bad meat left in the sun. One called out to another, the sound hushed by the rushing of the waves, and the teeth in its mouth were as pointed as a cat's.

But it was the nixies' eyes that made them utterly unsettling. Even the Gryphons' eyes were something Runacar recognized himself in, eyes that held life, and humor, and awareness. But the nixies' eyes were round as the eye of the serpent is round, and absolutely and utterly black. Reflexively, he reached down to tousle the hair of the Faun beside him.

"They're strange, perhaps, to land-dweller eyes," Audalo said, for Runacar's ears alone, "but the sea holds many strange things. And their hearts are good—even if their attention span is short."

"Like this fellow, I suppose," Runacar answered wryly, sending the Faun on its way with a gentle push. "I'll try not to shame you by acting like a Houseborn."

Helda, standing at his other side, made a soft rude sound. "The Children of Stars would already be firing arrows and yowling for their witchborn."

These were the conversations Runacar found most unsettling. It was hard not to see the Hundred Houses through Otherfolk eyes when one of them said things like that. After all, *The Art of War* taught the sons and daughters of the Hundred Houses to think like the enemy, and he had been a good student. But seeing the world through Helda's eyes, through *Otherfolk* eyes, left Runacar confused not only about who he was now, but who he had been then. Had Runacarendalur of Caerthalien—Prince Runacarendalur Caerthalien—lived a good, and honest, and honorable life? His ancestors said yes. The Otherfolk said no. And somehow both were true. He shook his head, setting the unsolvable quandary aside once again. Now he must meet with their allies; discover if they would accept his presence, and discover what aid they could—or would—offer.

He stabbed the pole of Leutric's standard into the soft sand hard enough that it would stay upright, and walked forward.

The two gigantic sea-horses had planted their fore-hooves in the sand at the tide line, resting on their bellies in the packed sand. Aejus and Meraude stood, or lay, or whatever people with fishtails did, beside them, each grasping a handful of mane to hold themselves upright. The nixies twittered and hissed like sea-birds, clearly daring each other to move further up the sand.

Pelere, Audalo, and Frause approached the court first, giving their names, and extending the King-Emperor's greetings.

"And where is the general of whom the very winds speak?" Meraude asked. "I would look upon that one."

Runacar walked to the edge of the sand and bowed, equal to equal, for though Meraude was Empress, he was not her vassal. "In the name of Leutric, King-Emperor, I greet you," Runacar said.

"You are the Woodwose who would sweep the *alfaljodthi* from the land?" Meraude asked. Her tone gave nothing of her thoughts.

"I was born to a prince of the Hundred Houses," Runacar answered. "I am *alfaljodthi*. All my kinfolk are now my enemy."

"Ambitious," Aejus said, peering at him. "Come closer, *alfaljodthi* rebel." The sea-king held out his hand to Runacar.

Cautiously, Runacar stepped into the water. The sea-horses turned their great heads silently to watch him, and he wondered absently whether they could speak any language he could hear. The water found every small gap in his armor; his cloak and surcoat clung to him soddenly, and he would need to give serious attention to both armor and weapons once this was over. But somehow, in the utter derangement of his life since the Battle of the Shieldwall Plain, this was something familiar. He set his feet carefully and bowed again.

"The King-Emperor sends his regards," Runacar repeated. "To him I have proven my loyalty through a service of many seasons. I do not command here, merely advise those I have trained, and Leutric sends his heir to stand surety for me, his life to be forfeited beside mine do I offend or betray." He gestured toward Audalo. "In my own place, I would be styled Warlord, he who sets what talent he has at the service of his prince, holding no ambition of his own. The plan we have made is a plan approved by all. All of the landfolk," he added hastily. "And so we now set it before you, our allies and kin, for it benefits you as well as us that the Western Shore be ours again."

*Thank Sword and Star for Radafa and his love of history!* Runacar thought feelingly. At first, he'd found Radafa's tales not just boring, but meaningless, but it was unwise to tell someone to shut up when they could snap you in half with their beak. Eventually Radafa's stories had started to form a linked picture in his mind of migrations, and alliances, and first meetings. And without them, he would have had no context for the hatred between the Ocean's Own and the Hundred Houses, since it was hard to imagine them fighting over land, or fish. But the great rivers that began in the Mystrals and surged ever westward found their ends here in the sea, and as the creatures of river and lake were barred from Great Sea Ocean, so the Ocean's Own were barred by Amrolion and Daroldan from using the rivers to travel inland.

"And do you say this is a thing that you shall do, King Leutric's Warlord?" Meraude asked.

From the corner of his eye, Runacar could just glimpse one of the nixies slithering slowly toward him through the water.

"*We* say it is a thing *we* shall do," Runacar answered. One of the first lessons he had learned in his new life was that the Otherfolk acted out of consensus, not fiat. Leutric might well style himself their King-Emperor, but if he had tried to unilaterally command any of the

Otherfolk clans—even his own—he would have found himself utterly ignored.

"Yet you ask for our help," Meraude pointed out.

"We come to ask your counsel, and to tell you our plans," Runacar answered. "And to ask if you will fight beside us to gain what will benefit all." This was not the strangest parley he'd ever participated in, but it came close.

The nixie had been joined by two of—his?—her? companions. None of them seemed to be carrying weapons, but Runacar wasn't certain what to do about them. He could easily defend himself, but he did not have the least notion whether doing so would be a good thing . . . or an utter disaster.

"Then we will listen," Aejus said, just as the first of the nixies reached Runacar.

Runacar heard more than felt the skittering scraping of their claws over tasset and fauld and cuisse, then one began to climb him as if he were a tree, while the other two simply dug their fingers into his cloak—and pulled.

He'd expected them to be strong, but they were also surprisingly heavy. Fortunately, any war-cloak would tear loose before strangling—or trapping—its wearer. It did. The two who had hoped to claim it as their prize found themselves imprisoned in a dozen ells of water-logged velvet. He plucked the third one free as it reached his shoulder, holding it beneath the ribs and trying to duck its thrashing legs and claws as he held it out.

"Yours, I believe?" Runacar said blandly, and Aejus roared with laughter.

"Brainless sea-lice," one of the sea-horses said. "You should eat it."

Runacar didn't even blink.

⊱✦⊰

Once the initial greeting was out of the way—it had been a test, as Runacar well knew—the Ocean's

Own moved closer to the shore, and the Landfolk came down to the tide line. The meeting turned from parley into briefing and negotiation, and Runacar found himself kneeling to draw illustrative diagrams in the wet sand with his dagger.

"Amrolion and Daroldan can put less than thirty great-tailles of komen into the field between them," Runacar said. "That is not a large force, I grant you. But their foresters are deadly foes, and I cannot say how many of those they have, as they were never required to count them as knights of the field. And their Lightborn are—"

"Used to fighting us," Meraude said silkily.

"—used to fighting you," Runacar agreed, with a small smile. "But while the Keeps can't be taken by force—perhaps you know that better than I—they're still vulnerable. No matter how many resources they have, a siege will starve them out eventually. I am hoping it does not come to a siege, because we want them to run—at least, we want some of them to. There's another keep, inland, and with enough refugees fleeing to it for safety, its defenses will be weakened, and we shall take it as well. Once it falls, the power of the *alfaljodthi* in the West is ended forever."

"And you think they will run?" one of the sea-horses asked.

"I think you underestimate how very afraid of you they are," Runacar said quietly.

"Well, fear is all very well," Meraude said briskly, "but kraken cannot dance. What of their witches?"

"I will match my power and that of my sisters against the Houseborn witches—and we will win!" Frause said firmly. The gems and talismans on the necklaces she wore glittered in the bright spring sunlight.

Aejus looked politely skeptical. "You have never done so yet," he said at last.

Frause glanced toward Runacar, and curled her upper lip in a Bearward smile. "Ah, but we have never had a Master of War to lead us before," she said. "You will see."

⧉

The Ocean's Own agreed to permit the war to take place, and to harry the enemy if the Folk of the Land could entice them down to the ocean's edge. There was a discussion of what kinds of magics they could provide; those seemed to be concentrated on weather, illusion, and—surprisingly—healing. Runacar was grateful for Spellmother Frause and his apprentices—it meant he did not have to involve himself in another discussion about magic.

They spent three days discussing tactics—once the strategy had been agreed upon—and sharing information. Aejus said that the Ocean's Own could summon up a waterspout if the landfolk could lure the enemy close enough to the water for it to be effective. Once it had been explained to Runacar what a waterspout was, he agreed that this would prove a useful tactic. It was one the Shore Domains had seen before, but they probably wouldn't be expecting one in the middle of a land attack. Meraude said that if they were lucky, they might be able to use a waterspout to awaken the kraken. Nobody explained to Runacar what a kraken was, and he did not ask.

The Ocean's Own were also able to give the army a great deal of useful information on what the Western Shore had been doing while Runacar had been scouring the Western Reach. Meraude told them that the Shore Domains had not been strengthened beyond the meisne of Warhunt Lightborn that the High King had sent nearly a decade of years before, and that as soon as Leopheine Amrolion realized no more help would be coming, Amrolion had made a fighting retreat northward to join with Daroldan, leaving most of Amrolion deserted except for frequent patrols in force. Since Runacar had been expecting to face a combined meisne, the news did not worry him much, but it was a sobering reminder of how hard it would be to make the two War Princes run. Both Western Shore Domains had the same motto: *Isterya Adzab*. "I hold." The High King had only gained their fealty by promising them she would not ask them to send komen to her army so that they could continue to do so.

When the discussions were over, the army marched northward.

⊰⊱

To be perfectly fair, the only thing accurate about that statement was the direction of their travel. Aside from the Centaurs, who had taken easily and happily to the discipline and organization of a traditional army, the rest of Runacar's force might be best described as a collection of hostile individuals ambling vaguely in the same direction. Since he didn't expect anything else, Runacar was not disturbed when elements of his forces made detours into the Flower Forests or vanished entirely for a day or two. Some of the Ocean's Own—usually the sea-horses, accompanied by the usual pack of nixies—were paralleling the landward army's course along the coast, and Radafa carried messages back and forth between the groups. The shore-apes had lost much of their fear of this new invader, and trailed the army close to the water's edge, barking and scolding, and running when anyone took a step toward them. Aside from some of the Fauns blundering into snares in Delfierarathadan, they hadn't found an enemy force to engage, but by now Runacar could make a good guess about when and where the first attack by the domains would come—and why.

Runacar had received many reports that Amrolion Great Keep still stood, seemingly untouched and undefended, and that would have made the Keep a tempting target for any previous Otherfolk sortie. It was almost certainly a trap. None of his people disagreed. Runacar hoped that the trap had been baited and set for what Amrolion had expected: a great-taille or so of Otherfolk raiders, not an army of thousands. To make use of the trap against the present force, Amrolion would have to drive the invaders into it—and that meant attacking them only when the Keep was close enough to seem a safe haven for retreat.

And so for a sennight, the Otherfolk marched northward unopposed.

⊰⊱

By the time Vieliessar gained the Unicorn Throne, the war had stripped the Western Reach of its armies. Damulothir knew there was little aid the High King could send, but he asked anyway, because he was her pledged vassal, and because his people needed help.

She was more generous than Damulothir could have imagined, but by the time Rondithiel Lightbrother arrived with his Warhunt Lightborn, the foretellers of Damulothir's court were speaking of Beastlings rising like a vast army of darkness, led by a warrior cast out by the Starry Rade, a warrior who had torn his own heart from his chest in return for power . . .

Most of it, as Damulothir told Leophrine Amrolion, was absolute and utter nonsense, except for one thing: the Beastlings somehow had found a general who could wage war. Reports—and a few desperate refugees—came from the Western Reach to say the Beastlings were scouring the land and toppling the Great Keeps with terrifying efficiency. Nine Wheels of the Year passed, and upon the tenth, that dead-alive general at last turned his attentions to the Western Shore.

The Western Shore made its plans accordingly.

⁂

The attack came late in the afternoon. There was almost no warning. One moment Runacar's attention was caught by a flicker of light on metal in the underbrush edging the forest. The next, a meisne of knights rode out of concealment, aiming for the fantail of Runacar's army. The knights' charge was a feint, cover for mounted Lightborn and foresters armed with walking bows.

⁂

Hialgo wheeled automatically to attack as the enemy knights charged. Runacar imagined more than heard the high singing sound his sword made as he drew it from its sheath and flourished it in a signal to the Ocean's Own who should be watching offshore. He knew he could not control the battle. There were no drums and war-horns, no inviolate messengers, no *rules*. All he could do was what he had already done: make certain that everybody in the army knew what the objective was and how to achieve it.

The Centaurs moved to take the brunt of the komen's attack; they were armored and equipped with hammers and maces, and their targets were the warhorses, not the knights. Runacar spurred past them, giving them time to set themselves against the charge of the enemy.

The enemy komen let him get far too close—*they think I am one of their own*—before belatedly realizing that no matter what Runacar looked like, he was the enemy. Only after he struck the first blow did they turn to close with him.

Runacar was glad he couldn't see the faces behind their helms.

Hialgo began a whirling spinning dance as three attackers—two in the blue and silver of Amrolion, one

in Daroldan's grey and gold—tried to find an opening
in his defense.

More attackers appeared out of the forest. The air
was filled with magics: Runacar saw Shield and Lightning deployed in the first few moments—other spells,
he well knew, would leave no visible trace.

And all the time, the Otherfolk were being herded toward Amrolion's Keep.

*"Show a man a thing, even a thing disguised, and he
will expect it to behave in accordance with the thing
he knows."* So Elrinonion Swordmaster had taught
Runacar long ago, and been—as he so often was—
correct. The Western Shore had been fighting Otherfolk
for centuries, and were very good at what they did.
But Runacar hadn't shown them a roving band of
Otherfolk—he'd shown them an army, and so, irresist-
ibly, they had responded as if it *were* an army. Amrolion
and Daroldan's combined force expected Runacar's to
stand its ground, and counted every ell of ground they
dispossessed it of as a victory—and not a tactic.

When the Hundred Houses had still existed, running
battles such as this were rare, for the battlefield was determined ahead of time by negotiation. But that did
not mean Runacar was any stranger to such battles, for
there was always a need to hunt down bandits and outlaws, and after the Scouring of Farcarinon—an extensive campaign of itself—the number of raiders had
increased twelvefold.

A running battle was the sort at which his new army
excelled.

It was as if several completely unrelated battles, with
differing objectives and different tactics, were taking
place on the same spot. Only one thing remained constant: the battle was, like all battles, very loud. The most
conventional Otherfolk element involved was the Centaurs, who had no ability to use magic, though they

could be affected by it. They charged the mounted knights, killing and crippling both men and horses. Those they did not finish off, the Fauns scampering among them did.

But if he had expected a mage-duel between Lightborn and Otherfolk, Runacar was disappointed. The Spellmothers and the Earthdancers were focusing on the Ranger archers, while the Bearward berserkers, led by Keloit, charged the Lightborn in hopes of stampeding their horses. Oddly, the horses did not react to the Bearwards at all.

Radafa led a wing of Gryphons in a low pass over the fighting with no more effect than the Bearward charge. It was clear that the Lightborn had bespelled the horses so that they saw and heard only what their riders wished them to see and hear.

*Fight your own battle or you will not live to know how they have fought theirs!*

Feint and turn. Hialgo lunged tualthally as Runacar leaned far out in the opposite direction. At the full extent of his reach, he set the point of his sword against his foe's breastplate and pushed. Hialgo finished his turn just as the knight swayed off balance. Setting his forefeet, the destrier kicked back strongly. The other destrier staggered at the blow and the knight toppled from the saddle.

Destriers were trained for war almost from birth. In melee they were an extension of their rider's will; if the knight was unhorsed, their mount became their guardian. The riderless destrier quite properly took a position over its downed rider, prepared to defend its position with teeth and hooves—and in doing so, it became an obstacle for Runacar to exploit. He backed Hialgo and the other two attackers followed eagerly. Then Runacar did the unthinkable.

A knight was a mounted warrior first, last, and always. Elven armor might be as flexible as fine buckskin, but that was to aid the knight in the saddle, nothing else. Runacar had learned better. He remembered a favorite saying of the High King's: *"The purpose of war is to win."* He intended to win.

He cued Hialgo with his heels, and as the grey stallion reared, Runacar vaulted from the saddle. Leaping forward, he grabbed the reins of one attacker's mount, hauling down as hard as he could. A dagger buried in the side of its neck gave him a convenient handhold as he forced his way into its saddle and flung its rider to the ground. The komen he'd originally unhorsed was on his feet now, and Hialgo was doing all he could to force his riderless destrier away from him. As he did, Runacar used his borrowed mount to stamp its rider to death.

Now the two Amrolion destriers were trying to attack each other, and Runacar caught the third and last of his attackers between them as Hialgo, still riderless, herded Runacar's mount forward. The three horses were too close together for the mounted knight caught between them to be able to use his sword against Runacar, but Runacar was not so encumbered. He turned in the saddle and brought his sword around in a great sweeping blow, catching the knight just below the backplate, where his body was shielded only by the vulnerable tasset-plates. They crumpled as if they were made of paper, and the knight began to thrash agonizedly in his saddle, dying.

*Arilcarion would call that an illegal strike,* Runacar thought absently.

Hialgo appeared beside him. Runacar kicked free of the stirrups of the wounded destrier and jumped back to the saddle of his own warhorse.

The engagement had taken mere heartbeats.

He rode free and took a moment to catch his breath. The air felt thick with Magery—he didn't know what was going on, but he hoped the Lightborn were getting the worst of it. He glanced seaward. The sky and the ocean were both still clear, and his heart sank.

*"Where in the name of the Rade is my waterspout?"* If Aejus and Meraude couldn't—or wouldn't—do what he expected of them, this battle would not end as Runacar intended. He turned Hialgo and galloped back into the thick of the fighting.

❧

At the same time most of Runacar's force "fled" toward Amrolion Great Keep, a good portion of it was disappearing into the forest. It should look like desertion to the foe, but in reality the Otherfolk were sweeping the Flower Forest for enemies and preparing to attack the enemy's rear guard. They couldn't do that until the enemy was reduced in numbers, and the enemy would not be reduced in numbers if that damned waterspout he'd been promised didn't arrive. The enemy had exposed the majority of its force to fight this pitched battle, just as Runacar had hoped. If the Ocean's Own did not do their part, Runacar's force would be cut to pieces.

The Otherfolk were in the outer precincts of the castel now—the outbuildings and false walls that led up to the drawbridge and the main entrance. Warlord Challaron of Amrolion would have designed his trap with the assumption the enemy knew Amrolion Great Keep had been deserted . . . but oh how temptingly, how seemingly *accidentally*, the chains upholding the drawbridge gangway had snapped, leaving the way open into the inner precincts.

This Keep was constructed in a style far different from those of the West and the Uradabhur: squat, smooth, monolithic, and large. Rather than a dazzling and complicated curtain wall meant to confuse and entangle Lightborn spells of Farseeing or Fetch, this outer wall was smooth and seamless, the viewing slits in it so well recessed that they were nearly invisible: a fortress that expected to have to face assaults of strength, *in* strength, with depressing frequency.

And before another candlemark had passed, most of the Otherfolk were going to be penned inside it or crushed against its walls if the Ocean's Own had abandoned them.

⌁

B y now the battlefield looked like nothing Runacar could once have imagined calling a battlefield. A riot. A rout. A nightmare. A thousand instants imprinted themselves on his mind:

A Minotaur, one great horn broken away, body studded with arrows, reached an Elven Ranger, impaling the body on his remaining horn as he sank to his knees in death.

Two knights, one unhorsed and clinging to the stirrup of the other, trying to flee the field.

A Hippogriff, its wings chopped away, head thrown back in agony, flailing as it died.

Four Centaurs caught in what must be a Lightborn spell, bleeding out from every pore and orifice.

Woodwose swarming a mounted knight as if they were rats, hacking knight and horse to pieces with their knives.

Madness.

War.

And the Otherfolk were winning.

Runacar jerked Hialgo to a stop as one of the two Aesalions—he thought it must be Drotha—landed amidst the taille of knights harrowing them northward. Runacar hadn't dared count on the Aesalions remembering to join the battle instead of watch it, and was only glad they seemed to remember from sunturn to sunturn which side they were fighting for. Drotha laughed as he disemboweled a horse with one swipe of

his back claws and skewered its rider with the poisonous barb in his tail, then reared up on his hind legs,
wings fully extended. He emitted a deafening roar and
every destrier that could still move fled mindlessly, for
no amount of Lightborn spellbinding could be enough
to ward an animal against an Aesalion's ability to project any emotion it chose. Runacar was only glad he and
Hialgo was spared the effect.

"It's a pity you can't do that to the whole army,"
Runacar said, as Drotha bounded gleefully up to him.

The Aesalion grinned toothily. "I could try," he said.
"But I won't have to. Look."

Runacar looked seaward. Far on the horizon, there
was a smudge of black. The waterspout?

"They've taken too long!" Runacar cried in frustration.

Drotha laughed. "You'll be surprised at how fast it
moves."

⊰⊱

He was.

⊰⊱

By the time Runacar fought his way to the vanguard of his army the waterspout had gone from a
distant smudge of black on the horizon to an enormous, churning column. It moved faster than a running
horse and made a roaring sound that rendered both
hearing and being heard an impossibility, but that
didn't matter. No orders needed to be given. No one
who knew the Western Shore wanted to be anywhere
near that waterspout.

The enemy began to disengage. Instead of rushing toward the safety of the Keep, the Otherfolk turned as
well, heading toward the safety of Delfierarathadan. To
reach the forest's edge they had to scale a long rise cov-

ered with slippery sea-grass. It would have been suicidal—Arilcarion warned constantly against attacking a foe who held higher ground—save for the fact that the other part of Runacar's strategy was working. The elements of the army of the Western Shore that were gathered at the forest's edge to drive the Otherfolk into Amrolion Great Keep found themselves set upon from behind. As their foe vanished from before them and appeared behind them, the Elven army realized that the Otherfolk had taken the Flower Forest from them.

The waterspout approached, and the Great Keep would provide them no shelter. The Elves did the only thing they could: they fled northward, hoping to outrun the disaster. Riderless horses ran with the retreating army, both destriers and Lightborn palfreys. Some knights rode double. It was a true retreat, however, not a rout: the enemy meisne engaged any Otherfolk they could reach.

Runacar spurred Hialgo up the hill toward the forest, now in the army's fantail. He could sense the great stallion's energy was flagging: in a battle from Before, Runacar would have left the field several times already to change to a new mount. He could not do that here, but it didn't matter. All he had to do was reach Delfierarathadan and the sanctuary it represented.

He nearly didn't make it. The wind rose to a howling gale. The light shifted, first to grey, then to green. The grass waved wildly in the wind and the branches of the trees thrashed, shedding leaves and blossoms. By the time Hialgo reached the top of the slope the wind was filled with sand, for the waterspout had reached the shallows and begun ripping up the sea-bed. Urging Hialgo forward, Runacar risked a look back.

The waterspout walked up onto the land and struck the outer wall of Amrolion Great Keep. There was a sound louder than a thousand thunderclaps. And the Keep . . .

*Dissolved.*

Walls, roofs, and towers softened and collapsed as if made of wet mud. Flashes of silver, purple, and green danced over the shifting edifice as the interlocking web-work of spells that had both destroyed and maintained it was triggered by the collision. The ground shook with the impact, and mature trees at the forest's edge whipped back and forth as if they were slender saplings; some toppled and fell. Hialgo danced madly, desperate to keep his feet. He lurched sideways, slamming his shoulder against a tree, and it took all of Runacar's strength and skill to remain in the saddle and keep the stallion from hurting himself further.

If he'd led his army into the Keep there would have been no survivors.

The waterspout collapsed abruptly with a sound like dough tossed into hot fat, dousing what had been the Great Keep with thousands of tons of water. The wave curled as it raced forward, capturing the whole of the beach and the battlefield, and racing up into the outskirts of the forest itself before it retreated.

When it did, the battlefield was swept clean of both the wounded and the dead. Nothing remained behind.

Hialgo stood quiet at last, sweat-covered, sides heaving. The clouds were breaking up and the westering sun showed itself in a sky of perfect blue. Runacar slid from the saddle, groaning at the manifold aches and bruises he felt. He hoped all the Otherfolk were safe inside Delfierarathadan, but he didn't *know.* What he did know was that the enemy was far from finished, and if he could, Runacar had to marshal his forces to resume the attack. He staggered to the edge of the hillside on unsteady legs, Hidalgo's reins in one hand and his sword in the other.

A cloud of multicolored sparks appeared, swirling about his head. He swatted at them reflexively, before recalling what they were. "Tell the others to come at once!" he said to the fairies. He was unable to understand any response they made: when they spoke, it sounded to him like hawking bells chiming. Nor was he sure of how much of his speech they understood. But he was a pragmatist: using them to carry messages and orders worked.

Suddenly he heard screams.

Just beyond where the Great Keep had been, where a half-circle gouged into the shore marked the site of a deep tidal pool, the remains of the combined army of the Western Shore was mustered. The damage done by the waterspout and the bespelled Great Keep had been local enough; whoever had planned the battle had meant to catch the Otherfolk in a classic hammer and anvil pattern, and while the "anvil" had been obliterated, much of the "hammer" was intact.

At least for a few more moments.

The water in the tidal pool churned as if it were being boiled, and he could see the silver flash of fish as they leaped into the air, trying to flee. For a moment Runacar thought that the waterspout had somehow, improbably, forced a new island to appear in the bay.

Then he saw the sea-foam was tinged with blood, and realized that the "island" was the long dark body of some immense living thing. Its back was the bronzy-brown of sun-dried dates; its tentacles were the same color, save on the undersides, which were a startling shell-pink, covered with row upon row of quivering white suckers.

Those tentacles, like snakes or horribly-animated roots, writhed among the Western Shore army. Runacar watched as two of them—one holding a destrier, the other its rider—lifted themselves fully from the water, curling as they dropped their burdens into an open circular maw whose entire gullet seemed lined with gleaming teeth. There were too many tentacles to count, so many that it did not matter how many the defenders severed. Only distance made them look slender; at their tips they were as thick as an Elven body, and thicker by far where they joined the body of the beast.

By ones and twos, by tailles and meisnes, the creature scooped knights, horses, armor, into its tireless maw, plucking them from the sand just as a pampered lordling would choose sweetmeats from a tray. Those who tried to flee were captured. Those who tried to fight back were crushed. Some it tore in half. Some it drew beneath the water alive.

He felt the warmth of another body as Keloit moved to stand beside him. Blindly, he put out a hand and fisted it in the thick gold fur. Keloit made a sad sound and shifted closer to put an arm around Runacar's shoulders. "Oh," the Bearward said softly. "I don't know what that is."

Runacar stared at the carnage, numb inside. Who should he hope would be the victor? Which side was he supposed to be on? Was *this* what the Ocean's Own had summoned up as their ally?

"Kraken," he said, almost whispering.

He recognized it now. *Lannarien's Book of Living Things* was a scroll present in nearly every War Prince's castel. Hunters used it because it listed every beast of the land and bird of the air, and the moonturns and seasons in which it was lawful to hunt them. But beyond those beasts of venery, the *Book of Living Things* listed all creatures, from Aesalion to Unicorn . . . many of them noted as "almost certainly imaginary."

Right now he wished that were true. It was one thing to attack and to kill in the hot blood of war, and to laugh together afterward at the victory feast. It was quite another to stand, cold and aching, and watch knights and honorable warriors slaughtered with less dignity than the castel cooks gave to the chickens they slaughtered for stew.

*This is the price of a war fought with magic,* Runacar

thought. He felt numb inside. Vieliessar's War Magicians had been children playing with their first wooden swords compared to this.

A handful of komen escaped. The sand was sanguinary and churned by the time the kraken withdrew. Not even its own severed limbs remained. It had eaten those, too.

The sun, setting at last, turned the surface of the ocean to blood and gold.

## CHAPTER THIRTEEN

# SWORD MOON:
# THE REBOUNDING STROKE

*Since the moment of their founding, the Hundred
Houses held half the Otherfolk hostage without knowing it. Every creature of forest, pond, and river was at
their mercy—they could have asked any terms they
chose, and the Otherfolk would have had no recourse
but to accept. But hostages and parleys are part of the
Code of Battle, and the one thing the Hundred Houses
were never willing to believe was that their enemies
were people.*

— Runacar Warlord, *The Other Way of War*

The vanguard had been primarily Minotaurs and
Centaurs—both relatively slow-moving—while
the fantail had been almost entirely Woodwose
and the Bearward Spellmothers—Runacar was not
sure what Amrolion and Daroldan would think when
the reports reached them of "Elves" fighting beside
Otherfolk, but anything that added to the enemy's confusion was to the Otherfolk's benefit. It would take a
score of candlemarks for all those scattered elements to
regroup. Keloit led Runacar deeper into the forest; the
fairies that had come to him just before the kraken's attack had been trying to tell him where the camp was.
He suppressed a groan of relief at the sight of Pelere and
Audalo among those gathered around the tiny cookfire
built in the center of the clearing. His generals—his
*friends*—had survived the day.

"Sit down," Pelere said briskly, coming over to him. "You look terrible." She took Hialgo's reins from his hand. "Enbor will take care of your better half," she added, making a long-familiar joke as she handed the reins to the Centaur beside her.

"We saw the kraken," Keloit said helpfully.

"Oh," Pelere said. "Radafa said it had come."

"Is he all right?" Runacar asked, as she bullied him toward the fire.

"None of the Gryphons came within a bowshot of the ground," she answered. "We lost several of the Hippogriffs, though. Gunyel is trying to gather her flight and find out the tally." She pushed a tankard into his hands. "Drink this. You'll feel better."

"I have to—"

"You have to let us do what you trained us for, Houseborn," Tanet said, walking into the clearing. "If we don't know by now how to end a battle as well as begin one, you are even stupider than most Houseborn. Oh, and Andhel said if I saw you, to tell you she is alive. She does not wish you to gain too much joy from this day."

That startled a laugh out of Runacar. "Tell her I am grief-stricken at this news, and next time I will set her in the vanguard." He was gratified to see Tanet smile.

❧❦❧

As the sun set and the night deepened, the army slowly drew itself together again. The Ocean's Own had recovered much of the gear belonging to the land-based force—it had been swept into the sea by the wave—but their provisions were lost. This was no real impediment—Amrolion could feed them, and what the land couldn't provide, the ocean would.

Dozing by the fire, Runacar woke to take reports throughout the night as his generals and captains came to share information. He ached from combat, for there were no Lightborn Healers to make the injuries sustained in a day of war conveniently vanish, and the salves, poultices, potions, and charms the Otherfolk used didn't work nearly as fast. But the news made up for that. Their losses had been minimal: Otherfolk dead numbered roughly a grand-taille, or one out of every twelve who had taken the field. An early report had given him the initial count of the enemy—Daroldan and Amrolion had taken the field jointly and in force with fifty great-tailles made up not just of komen, but Rangers and Lightborn as well—but the information Runacar really needed was how many were left. The only true metric of victory was the number of enemy dead.

Near dawn, Pelere finally came with the answer. "Radafa said 'not many,'" Pelere said. "Ten hands. Perhaps twenty. At least more of them than us died."

Runacar knew that to a Centaur, a "hand" was a count of five. He multiplied the numbers, converted them to tailles, and was shocked by the total.

*Sixteen. Sixteen tailles*—perhaps—*out of the grand meisne fielded by two War Princes. Fifty great-tailles took the field . . . and that's all that are left.*

"Was this a war?" Drotha asked, breaking into Runacar's grim thoughts. The Aesalion sounded confused for the first time since Runacar had met him.

"No," Runacar answered softly. "This was a slaughter."

❧❦❧

Three days later the Otherfolk were ready to march again. They continued to move northward, this time within the Flower Forest itself. The weather stayed fair, and the sortie parties that moved between forest and ocean—so the Ocean's Own could be kept informed, and their help called upon at need—did so unmolested. Delfierarathadan fed them, sheltered them,

and gave them spies Daroldan and Amrolion could not
equal. And if Runacar had to receive their reports
through intercessors who could see and hear them while
he could not, well, his pride had been killed along with
the Ghostwood.

A sennight after the Battle of the Kraken, the line of
march (such as it was) covered several hundred hectares at any given time. Outlying elements of the Otherfolk force began to report clashes with Rangers and
Lightborn—information-gathering skirmishes at best,
tests of force at worst. Runacar spent candlemarks pondering how he was going to convince Leopheine and
Damulothir's folk to flee east, even after such a shattering defeat.

With their forces so diminished, it was unlikely the
Western Shore would choose to stage another conventional battle, though they would certainly continue to
fight. Since this was not war as the War Princes understood it, it was difficult to imagine them suing to surrender. *Or attending a parley under a flag of truce.* The
very thought made Runacar laugh bitterly. The last formal parley he'd attended had worked out so well,
hadn't it?

*I wonder what they will try next?*

On the tenth day after the Battle of the Kraken, he
found out.

✦

Runacar awoke in the middle of the night to the
smell of smoke. By the time he was fully awake and
reaching for his boots, he knew that this was not a matter of a badly-tended cookfire. The smoke was thick
enough to haze the air, though he could see no fire.
Colored lights flitted agitatedly in the air above him,
then arrowed off, seeking folk who could hear what
they had to tell. Around him, the Woodwose and the
Centaurs were up, moving, lighting lanterns, packing

up blankets and bedding. Runacar hunted until he found Pelere.

"The witches have set fire to Delfierarathadan," Pelere said without preamble.

"That's impossible," Runacar said in disbelief. "Without the Flower Forest, the Lightborn don't have any power."

"But Delfierarathadan is large enough that they could burn half of it and still have enough left to use," Audalo said, joining them. His expression was grave and worried. "And it's certainly burning. Some of the witches flanked us and went south almost to Kashadabadshar. Runacar, what do you want us to do? The fairies are asking."

Suddenly, in his mind, it was not now, but then. The Flower Forest wasn't Delfierarathadan, but Janglanipai-kharain, the Ghostwood. And Runacar stood in the center of a clearing choked with tiny skeletons, staring at the bones of a Dryad's tree.

Bile filled his mouth until he choked and spat. Every living creature ran from fire—*but some couldn't run*. The Lightborn had no idea of how thoroughly the Flower Forests were inhabited—Sword and Star knew *he* hadn't until he'd joined the Otherfolk. And if they had, they wouldn't care, would they? They'd set this blaze to kill the ones they *did* know about. Anything else would just be a bonus.

He could keep marching the army north. With this much head start, they could almost certainly outpace the blaze. Damulothir would almost certainly quench it or divert it once it got close to Daroldan Great Keep.

And meanwhile, everyone caught in the fire would die. Nearby Otherfolk would do what they could to help, but if the Nine Races had little idea of how to cooperate as a fighting force, they had less notion of how to act as one people. Aid would be local and sporadic.

The army—organized, disciplined, and *here*—was the

best hope of those caught in the fire. But to help them, Runacar would have to abandon the attack.

If victory was the only important thing, Runacar wouldn't have been here at all.

"We have to stop the fire," he said. "You know how many of the Brightfolk are mobile—find out what they need to leave their homes and make them do it: they aren't safe where they are. Send them north; Damulothir won't burn the forest near his castel; it wouldn't be safe. Have the fairies warn everyone that they can. Find out exactly what's burning, and where, and—who can work weather besides the Ocean's Own?"

"The Gryphons," Pelere said slowly. "And the Hippogriffs, maybe, a little."

"*We* can't," Audalo said, speaking of the Minotaurs. "If you wanted to shake the ground, our Earthdancers could do that, but if you want to work the weather, you'll need the Ocean's Own. They'll be near the shore at noon. We can talk to them then . . ."

"We can't afford to wait," Runacar said. Vieliessar had used fires as weapons when she'd fought in the west, and every domain feared fire season at summer's end. He knew that a forest fire could move faster than a galloping horse and double its size every candlemark. "Pass the word as fast as you can," he said to Pelere. "We march south at once. Get everyone out of the forest who doesn't need to be here—we'll move faster along the shoreline."

"South?" Pelere asked, switching her long tail nervously. "That's back the way we came. It will give Daroldan more time to prepare."

"And if we don't rescue everyone we can," Runacar said evenly, "then why are we fighting at all?"

❧

T he wind blowing landward from the sea swept the air clean of smoke taint. The ocean gleamed with faint phosphorescence where the waves spilled over the sand. The stars filled the sky, sweeping down to meet the ocean at the horizon—the absence of stars was the only way to tell where the sea began.

But when he looked southward Runacar could see the orange gleam where the flames of the burning Flower Forest illuminated the smoke that rose from its burning. The whole army was not yet on the move, but Runacar, Keloit and his Bearwards, and a couple of troops of Centaurs were already heading south.

It was still a candlemark before dawn when Radafa arrived—he must have seen the unusual movement below. When Runacar saw the familiar shape wheeling through the pre-dawn mist, he reined Hialgo to a halt. The Gryphon landed in the shallows, backwinging to stop himself, then bounded up the sand.

"I thought you'd be here, Runacar," Radafa said. "I smelled the smoke. The Elves are burning the Flower Forest."

"I know," Runacar said. "We're going to stop them. And stop the fire." *Somehow,* he added mentally. "And for that, we need magic. The Ocean's Own should see the fire soon and come to find out what we're doing, and I'll ask for their aid, but . . . I know your people have weather magic—can you help as well?"

Radafa clacked his beak unhappily. "It is true that we have . . . some magic. But it is a magic of wind and cloud only."

"Clouds make rain," Runacar said stubbornly. "And if wind can blow out a candle, it can blow out a fire."

"I can ask my kin," Radafa said slowly. "Such an undertaking would require the consent of the many, for it is not a thing to do lightly. The weather affects all—even the Folk of the Air and the Ocean's Own. But I can take your request to the Ascension, if you wish."

*Even if they agree, and agree quickly, how much can*

*they do? It isn't the season for rain here—something I'm
sure Daroldan and Amrolion took into consideration
before ordering this . . . abomination.* Runacar ran a
hand over his hair in frustration. "If only I could see
what's going on! I'd have a better idea of what to ask
the Ocean's Own to do!"

Radafa cocked his head and regarded Runacar sideways, his beak hanging open. While the expression
looked vaguely ridiculous, Runacar had learned that it
meant Radafa was thinking very hard.

"I could carry you, I think," he said at last. "And you
could see what I have seen."

Even in the midst of this disaster, Runacar was astounded. Whatever the Otherfolk might look like, they
weren't animals, and they certainly weren't beasts of
burden. He would no more expect to ride Radafa than
he would have expected to ride Elrinonion Swordmaster of Caerthalien, had Elrinonion been here.

"Are you sure?" he asked carefully, and Radafa emitted a harsh caw of laughter.

"You do not weigh nearly as much as a horse or a
stag," he said, "and I can carry off either one. Sit as close
to my neck as you can, and I think we can manage. Besides, I can always catch you if you fall."

Looking at Radafa's long, razor-sharp talons, Runacar decided that the thought wasn't nearly as reassuring
as Radafa *perhaps* meant it to be.

"Then let's do it," he said, beginning to remove his
armor. *And the Hunt spurn all cowards to the endless
Dark!*

❧

The first lesson a young knight in training learned
when he or she passed from the hand of the Swordmaster to the hand of the Warlord was that the bridle
and reins their destrier wore were tools for the use
of someone else. The *komentai'a* rode by balance and

signaled their destriers with knee and heel and shifting weight. Hands were for grasping sword hilts, not
reins.

It was fortunate for Runacar that he'd been trained
so thoroughly that such reflexes were as automatic as
breathing, for of course Radafa wore no saddle, and
there was nothing for Runacar to cling to—if he
wrapped his arms around Radafa's neck, he'd strangle
the Gryphon. He thought of a hundred reasons why this
was insanity, and a thousand reasons why this was the
best idea he'd ever had, as he swung himself carefully
onto Radafa's back and settled his weight as near the
Gryphon's neck as he could.

And then Radafa spread his great wings and began
to run.

On the ground, a Gryphon wasn't very fast. They
moved in a mismatched flurry of fore and hind legs, and
looked both comical and clumsy—and certainly the ride
Runacar experienced was the most jolting he'd had in
a long life spent a-horseback.

Then Radafa took flight.

It began with a long, rising spiral out over the ocean,
using the unfailing sea-winds to gain altitude. Runacar
was dressed in nothing more than aketon and boots and
expected to be cold. But the Gryphon's body radiated
heat like a furnace; Runacar was too warm, if anything.

All there was to see was the blackness of Great Sea
Ocean and the luminous vault of the heavens—he dared
not risk vertigo by looking down. He'd thought he'd be
buffeted by great winds here in the sky—as if he were a
sort of war-kite—but despite the sense of speed, the air
seemed still, for they were moving with the winds, not
fighting them. The only sound was a faint whistling
through the Gryphon's great wings, the ever-changing
song of its passage.

For a moment Runacar forgot his worries, his shame,
and his guilt, living only in this miraculous moment.

He imagined this was how it must feel to ride with the Starry Hunt along the star road: this glorious sense of freedom and invincibility. No matter what was to come, he knew he would always treasure this moment. This gift of flight. To see the world as only hawks and eagles saw it—to soar effortlessly, even if through the exertion of another, upon the wind, riding as the Hunt Itself rode—these were treasures too great to imagine, let alone to take by force. Precious, in a way he had no words for.

Runacar had been raised to become War Prince of Caerthalien: he had learned law and custom, war and geography—not philosophy. Even so, the thought remained: Why did the Hundred Houses and the Otherfolk fight? The Otherfolk fought because the Hundred Houses attacked, of course, but why? Where had it begun? *How* had it began? They had so much to offer one another . . .

Radafa banked—Runacar compensated for the shift unthinkingly—and far in the distance he could see a glowing white-orange scar in the blackness. The gleam of moonshine on the familiar loop of the Angarussa told him exactly where he was.

The Kashadabadshar grew from a faint pale line on the horizon to an endless expanse of featureless sand as they flew south. Radafa swung out over the ocean when they reached the fire. The shape of the flames was like a great clawed hand digging its talons into the Flower Forest. It was far worse than Runacar had imagined. The entire southern edge of the Flower Forest was burning. Thin pioneers of flame raced ahead, feeding on grass and brush, while stands of ancient trees held back the fire elsewhere.

But not for long.

*If there's a strong east wind, Cirandeiron will catch like a basket of oil-soaked rushes, just as Araphant once did because Vieliessar willed it so,* Runacar thought in horror. *This is Fire Season—once the fire leaps the An-garussa there will be nothing to stop it from burning everything from Cirandeiron to the Mystrals—and every living thing from the Red Sands to the Medharthas.*

He tapped Radafa on the neck and pointed downward, hoping the Gryphon would take his meaning. A moment later, Radafa banked again and spilled height in a stomach-twisting descent. The fire seemed to rush up at them, and suddenly the silence was broken by the roar of burning, and the blackness of the night by skirling sparks and red-glowing smoke. The furnace-hot updraft flung Radafa skyward again, but that brief vertiginous glimpse was enough to show Runacar what he wanted to see—and to give him an idea.

"North!" he shouted.

The fire receded abruptly and silence fell once more. Radafa descended until they were skimming just above the waves. Far ahead, Runacar could see a fleck of fire at the edge of the beach; Audalo must have lit a signal fire in hopes of summoning the Ocean's Own. From a distant spark it grew rapidly in size, and then he and Radafa were earthbound again, the blaze about a mile distant.

Runacar slipped from Radafa's back, barely catching himself before he patted the Gryphon's neck as he would that of a good horse. He began to walk toward the fire, moving down to where the wet sand gave firm footing. He could tell, by the faint noises behind him, that Radafa followed.

"You're very quiet," Radafa said, after a time.

"I'm wondering why the *alfaljodthi* and the Otherfolk ever went to war," Runacar said, stopping and turning to look at him. Radafa's face was not built for displaying expression, but Runacar thought he looked sad.

"That is something not even the greatest historians of my race could tell you with certainty," the Gryphon answered sorrowfully. He was a scholar and the entire business of war disturbed him deeply. He turned his head to gaze out over the sea for a moment, then looked back. "Did the seeing help?" Radafa asked.

"I think so," Runacar answered slowly. Whatever the causes of the beginning of that ancient war, this was a chance to end it. *Vieliessar Farcarinon said she had come to end war by fighting one, and now here I am doing the same thing. If all of us just made a pact to kill ourselves in the same candlemark in the same moon-turn, we could accomplish the whole thing much more easily.*

"They're counting on the fact we're a fortnight's march away from the fire, but that doesn't matter as much as they think it does. I need to ask the others a few questions to decide if my plan can work, but as far as the Ascension . . . if you can get the winds to blow south and west, it will slow the advance of the fire. And rain would help, too." *I might as well ask for miracles while I'm asking for magic,* Runacar thought.

They walked on in silence.

"Rain here out of season will mean drought else-where," Radafa said after a while. "As will shifting the winds as you ask."

"Do whatever you can," Runacar said awkwardly. The vision of the Ghostwood rose up behind his eyes again. *So much death . . .*

❦

Pelere and Audalo were watching over the signal beacon just as Runacar had expected. Several of the other commanders were gathered around them as they waited—Frause, Tanet, Pendor, Bralros, a few others.

"Nothing yet," Audalo said, as Runacar and Radafa approached. "They don't pay much attention to the land when it's night."

It was light enough now to tell sea from sky, but the morning mist was rolling in and the sun would not rise for candlemarks yet.

Runacar turned back to Radafa. "Go now, if you can," he said. "And return as quickly as you can, no matter what news you bring. I need to know what I'm going to have to work with."

"I shall," Radafa promised. He turned away, and leapt into the air in a single graceful bound.

Runacar turned back to the group by the signal fire. "We have to start making plans at once. If we can create a firebreak too wide for the fire to jump, it will die. The Angarussa is to the east of the blaze, and Great Sea Ocean to the west. The fire burns now at the edge of the desert, and the forest is thin there, but if it gets much farther north it will be harder to stop. And if it reaches the place where we are now, we won't be able to stop it at all: there's plenty in the way of orchards and vineyards to give the fire a path around any firebreak we can manage."

"What good is stopping it if the witches only rekindle it?" Bralros demanded.

"Do you just want to give up?" Pelere snapped at him.

"I want to be realistic!" the grizzled Centaur barked. "The more time we spend fighting fire with hope, the longer the forest will burn—the only way to get those rats out of the granary is to stand on their doorstep until they run!"

"We'll do both," Runacar said, as Pelere drew breath for an even louder reply. "Bralros is right: as long as there's a Lightborn left, they can start another fire. You know better than I how far away they can set a Fire spell, but it doesn't matter—a Landbond with a torch could manage much the same. We need to put out the fire and while keeping them too busy to start another one."

"And I'm sure you have some hoary Houseborn wisdom on how we can do that," Andhel mocked, arriving with another bundle of sticks for the fire. "How fortunate we are to have a Houseborn here to save us!" She flung the bundle to the ground with an angry gesture.

"Feel free to pitch in at any time, Andhel," Runacar answered evenly. "I could use some help. My plan is this: we go south, and help any of the folk to escape who can't do it on their own. At the same time, we prepare to divert the Angarussa into the forest. With a little help, it will carve a new bed and flow down to the sea there, instead of north of Daroldan. We use it both as a firebreak and a way to help the folk escape."

"And what are your Houseborn brethren going to be doing during the many twelves of seasons you will need to turn the river?" Andhel asked after a moment's pause. She sounded almost stunned.

"Running from whatever else we can send against them," Runacar answered grimly.

❧

The Angarussa was said to be deep enough to drown the whole of a Great Keep, and even if it were as deep as that, it was still wider than it was tall. It was no placid water: the river rushed and roared, kicking up fans of spray where the water hit rocks, its dark surface a pattern of waves and churning currents. Anyone who fell into that water was swept away, and either drowned or battered to death. It could be neither forded nor swum, and while it could have been bridged or dammed, one of its greatest values to Cirandeiron lay in its impassibility, giving her one border as secure as if it was topped by a thousand-cubit wall. But at the same time, it was a barrier that needed to be passed, and frequently, for Amrolion and Daroldan lay on the far side.

The solution to that problem was both simple and

amazing: the western reach of Cirandeiron was riddled with caves, and so some ancient artificer had paved the bottom of the riverbed for some distance and then contrived to make an outlet through that paving that opened into the caves below.

An outlet that could be opened or shut at will.

Once, during the early moonturns of The High King's War, Runacar had seen the ford opened. A counterweighted catch, sheltered by a small stone building, was released—something that required no sorcery at all—and as the counterweight swung up and back, it lifted with it a great section of the paved streambed. The water immediately began pouring into the chasm with a roar and hiss, and as it did, the level of the river dropped abruptly.

The bed of the river was too deep simply to jump into and out of, but as the level of the water dropped, two sets of shallow stone steps were exposed, one on each side of the river and offset from each other, so that whoever crossed had to do so on a salient—and quickly, for once whatever chamber the river filled became full, the counterweight would swing back, and anyone still in the river's bed would be swept away by the resurgent waters.

Runacar's plan hinged on two Brightfolk races: stone-sprites and gnomes, which he had been told of but never seen. The two races lived in stone, so far as Runacar could figure out, and were able to shape it as easily as a Lightborn might. Between that, and the secret of the Angarussa ford, there might just be a chance. If the Otherfolk could divert the river *permanently*, that and some weather-magic might be enough to save most of the Flower Forest and all the folk that lived within it.

He didn't want to think about the level of despair that had caused the Western Shore to set Delfiriatha-dan alight. *It is true, one does not count the cost in en-*

*emy lives when one makes war,* Runacar mused. *But one also does not expect to expend the whole wealth of one's domain to buy the victory.* In Arilcarion's *The Way of the Sword,* such a tactic was called "The Rebounding Stroke"—you won, but you might as well have lost. Were this a game of xaique, Runacar would applaud the strategy: with its army much reduced, the enemy used the terrain itself as a weapon.

Rats in a grainary, Bralros had called the *alfaljodthi,* but it was Bralros and all the Otherfolk who were being treated like vermin. And when you were fumigating a grainary, you didn't show mercy, you didn't parley, and you did everything you could to kill them all.

⊰⊱

As Runacar waited for someone to locate a group of Otherfolk who had regular dealings with the gnomes and the stone-sprites—and for the Ocean's Own to arrive—he was far from idle: he had to meet with his commanders—he had to *find* his commanders, just to begin with—and discover which of their forces would be willing to continue northward, and what they would do as they marched. He would offer suggestions where he could. But most of all, he had to convince all of them that what he had in mind was a good idea.

The first thing, obviously, was to evacuate the whole of Delfierarathadan. There were enough Flower Forests in Cirandeiron to accept the Brightfolk refugees, and even most Dryads could abandon their trees if they had to . . . and had enough time to. That meant finding those in the army who were best suited as envoys and messengers and sending them to warn the Brightfolk over an area larger than Caerthalien and Aramenthiali combined.

But every time he made a suggestion, he was greeted with "Maybe," and "Perhaps," and "We must ask if they are willing." With forlorn exasperation, he wished for the intricate hierarchy that characterized a High House meisne—all that was necessary to cause a thing to be done was to give the order, and it spread swiftly by twelves down to the least hedge-knight in the field. For a moment, he envied the High King her throne—at least Vieliessar could give orders and know they would be obeyed—but he might as well wish to be High King himself as to wish for the Otherfolk to operate with such efficiency. They weren't one people, they were a hundred different peoples, and none of them had any concept of war on a grander scale than a High Festival brawl. *And if only I had thought of calling the Other-folk to Caerthalien's banner in the very beginning, why, I could have far outstripped Vieliessar's draggled meisne of Landbonds and sellswords and be seated on the Unicorn Throne at this very moment.*

By the time the envoys of the Ocean's Own appeared, Runacar felt as weary as if he'd spent a full sunturn in combat.

Drotha had volunteered to fly out over the ocean and keep watch, and Runacar had accepted gratefully. He doubted that even the Aesalion would be able to see anything until the fog lifted from the water, but that wasn't really as important as keeping Drotha occupied. The Aesalion was easily bored, and what he did when he got bored could have been referred to as pranks if not for the high death toll. Some of the Otherfolk, Runacar had come to accept, were people much like the *alfaljodthi* wearing different shapes. Others—like Drotha—were not.

The only warning he had of Drotha's return was a disturbance in the mist followed by a thump on the sand as the Aesalion landed.

"They're coming," Drotha announced. "They'll be here soon."

On the heels of Drotha's words, Runacar heard the

low moaning note of the horns the Ocean's Own used to announce their presence. A moment later, Meraude appeared, this time riding one of the seahorses.

"I greet you, cousins," she said. "I already know your trouble, for Amrunor told it to me."

"*Amrunor* couldn't help noticing," the Sea-horse said archly, flaring his nostrils, "because I haven't smelled such a stench since the last time a kraken died ashore. The question is, what does it mean to our little undertaking?"

There was a long moment of silence until Runacar realized everyone around him was waiting for him to speak. So much for the pretense of him being nothing more than an advisor to Leutric's chosen generals. He wondered if anyone had really been meant to believe it.

"It will be no impediment to driving the *alfaljodthi* eastward," Runacar said. "But we also hope to save the forest, and those who live there."

"Ah," Amrunor said, as if suddenly enlightened, "you are a great sorcerer, able to do two things at once."

"What else is an army for?" Runacar answered, deliberately matching Amrunor's tone. He wasn't quite sure whether the sea-horses were as otherworldly as the Aesalions, or if Amrunor simply had a flaky sense of humor.

"Since you have such a vast army, why call upon us, cousin? Surely our puny aid is nothing you cannot triumph without," Amrunor said, clearly prepared to play this game for candlemarks.

"We need rain." Incredibly, Andhel was taking Runacar's side. "You can make it." She slanted a sideways glance toward Runacar, as if to remind him she still didn't like him.

"What do you need this rain to do?" Meraude asked.

"Slow the spread of the fire," Runacar said. "Or stop it entirely, though I don't think that's possible. I saw a forest burn once. All the rain did was make steam."

"I would gladly send you another waterspout," Meraude said. "But it cannot be done without the kraken, and the kraken sleeps now and cannot be roused for many moonturns. But if it is rain you wish . . . know that the rain comes at a price," she finished.

For a moment Runacar thought she was asking to be paid somehow, but then he realized she was merely saying the same thing Radafa had: interfere with the way the Wheel of the Year turned, and there would be a price to pay. It was no different, really, than if you overtaxed your Farmholders and their Landbonds starved to death—the price you paid for that was famine a year or two later.

"Is it a higher price than the lives of everyone who will die if Delfierarathadan burns to ash?" Runacar responded, realizing mid-sentence that he wasn't asking a rhetorical question. "If it is, then we'll find another way," he finished.

Meraude and Amrunor regarded him with identical expressions of assessment. Runacar had long since gotten used to seeing eyes that might be any color at all: bright gold or red-amber or grey or even blue. But the two pairs of eyes gazing at him now were not merely green, but a green that shifted and swirled as water did. It was mesmerizing—so much so that when Meraude spoke again, it startled him.

"It is a high price, but not as high as that," she said at last. "But you must know . . . water can quench fire, it is true. But the *alfaljodthi* witches can set even a stone ablaze."

"Then I need to make sure they have other things to think about," Runacar said grimly.

## CHAPTER FOURTEEN

# THUNDER MOON: FIRE AND THE FOLK OF THE AIR

Show someone a thing, even a thing disguised, and they will expect it to behave in accordance with the thing they know.

— Elrinonion Swordmaster of Caerthalien

Audalo, which party shall I accompany?"

The Minotaur battle-leader had been a stripling when Runacar had first seen him, but that had been many Wheelturns ago and now he was in the prime of his strength, his coat sleek and glossy—and soon, as Elves reckoned time, he would be dead of old age, for Elves' lives were long, and those of most of the Nine Races were not. All the friends Runacar had made in this decade of exile—save the Gryphons, perhaps, who counted their lives in centuries—would die long before him, whether they died in battle or not.

It was midday by now, and the day was so beautiful that a part of Runacar ached that it could not be used for fighting. Sea-birds wheeled and cried overhead, the sunlight sparkled on the sea, and the air was scented with an exhilarating mix of salt and flowers. Everything was brightly and sharply beautiful in a way he associated with the moments before a battle began, when life was sweetest because it might abruptly end. It was odd to feel that sensation here and now, with no battle in the offing.

"And why, in the name of Leaf and Grass, do you ask *me* such a question?" Audalo answered.

"You're the highest-ranking general," Runacar answered dryly, and was rewarded with a mocking snort.

"*You* are the one my cousin-uncle says can drive the Houseborn from the land and bring us peace at last—or as much peace as the Darkness will let us have."

Runacar ignored Audalo's mention of "the Darkness"—he'd never gotten an enlightening answer about what it was from anyone he asked. And besides, whatever it was, it wasn't going to attack today.

"And not even the Woodwose trust me," Runacar answered.

"But Keloit does," Audalo answered inarguably. "And Pelere does. And so do I."

Runacar waved that aside. "I am grateful for your trust, and for theirs. And that is beside the point. I'm asking you whether I should go south to help evacuate the Flower Forest, or continue north with you."

"I suppose you should do as you think best," Audalo said. "And before you start making faces at me like one of the shore-apes, let me ask you this: Where would you be more useful—telling the army how to fight in a way none of us have ever done, or blundering around among the Brightfolk you can't even see?"

Put that way, the choice seemed obvious, but Runacar was tired and in a contrary mood. "Tanet is taking a meisne of Woodwose south," he said.

"The Woodwose can see the Brightfolk," Audalo said, sounding almost . . . ashamed.

*That's impossible. Woodwose aren't Otherfolk— they're alfaljodthi just like me.*

"Melisha says it is because they have always known about the Brightfolk," Audalo added. "Perhaps . . . if you had been raised in a Flower Forest, you, too, could see them."

"I doubt it," Runacar said curtly. *Those of you I can*

*see are more than enough for me.* "Well, if I am to go north to take Daroldan Great Keep and drive its folk into the mountains, I had better find out who will come along to keep me company."

❧❦❧

A rilcarion wrote of war waged on land, for it was the only sort of war the Hundred Houses had ever known. The diversion of a river, the flooding of a battlefield, these did not alter the essential thrust of Arilcarion's doctrine: war was fought on land. No matter what barges or skiffs Elvenkind built to navigate the lakes and rivers of its domains in time of peace, they had never built warships, for they never looked to the waters when they prepared for war.

And equally, they never looked to the skies.

Should any Warlord of the Hundred Houses ever have been asked to imagine such a campaign as Runacar was now engaged upon, their first thought would have been to use the winged Otherfolk as aerial cavalry mounts. Runacar had been fighting such campaigns for nearly a decade of Wheelturns now. When he thought of the winged Otherfolk, he thought of scouts, messengers, skirmishers. The reconnoiter of the burn-site had taken candlemarks, not sunturns. The speed of the army, in terms of gaining and disseminating information, was not the speed of a running horse, but the speed of a bird on the wing.

It was an advantage Runacar intended to make the most of.

❧❦❧

T he Ocean's Own made good on their promises to send rain, and by the following day the sky—even this far north—was grey and cloud-choked. The cloud-cover did a little—not enough—to cut the ever-present stench of burning, and when the sky broke forth in incidental showers, the rain that fell was black and greasy.

The two armies diverged. The Hippogriffs and both Aesalions—no surprises there—were staying with the northern army. The Bearwards were dividing by gender: the Spellmothers and Healers were going north; the Berserkers, south. Individual Centaurs, Woodwose, and Minotaurs were choosing their destinations by some mysterious standard known only to them, though Pelere and Audalo were both remaining with the northern army. The southern army would travel within the Flower Forest, for added protection, while the northern army would advance along the tide line, both to draw the attention of the enemy, and to be in close proximity to the Ocean's Own. The waters offshore were churned to milk by the presence of so many bodies, including an entire herd—or perhaps "school" was the better word—of sea-horses.

Since the few Gryphons who had joined his army had gone with Radafa, Runacar intended to use the Hippogriffs as messengers to coordinate with the southern force. Gunyel and her flight complained constantly about being asked to fly through the smoke-tainted clouds, but they did. The Hippogriff leader reported that even the monsoon the Ocean's Own had called down upon the southern Flower Forest was only slowing the rate of the fire. Keloit sent word that they had contacted the gnomes and the rock-sprites and both races were willing to help, but it would take a fortnight or more for them to complete their work—if it could be done at all.

Runacar's task was to buy them that time—and to keep the enemy from setting more fires.

One of the doctrines of war as laid out by Arilcarion was that the path to victory lay in controlling your foe's thoughts just as you controlled the battlefield. A foe who thought the cost of war too high would sue for peace instead of risking a costly defeat. If Daroldan and

Amrolion saw that all they would get—even if they won—was a wasteland, they would think even harder about the consequences of losing, especially to an enemy with whom there could be no truce, parley, or parole.

So, since the northern army wasn't going to march in a highly-organized, well-drilled formation *anyway*, Runacar suggested to his commanders another task to be performed as they marched.

*Destroy everything.*

The Western Shore did not contain the extensive manors and Farmholds of the domains east of them. Here, all the people lived inside the Great Keep. But property, the domains still had, though in the wake of the domains' retreat, the tall, wooden watchtowers that overlooked the fields stood empty, as did the fields, the dovecotes, the cow byres and sheepfolds, the orchards and vineyards. As the Otherfolk army passed by, all were destroyed: the vineyards dug up, the orchards despoiled of their harvests, the watchtowers and every wooden structure smashed to bits to provide wood for cookfires.

Three leagues spanned the distance from the shoreline to the forest, and three leagues was the width of the army's line of march. It swept over the works representing centuries of labor and husbandry from Farmholder, Landbond, Craftworker—and unmade them all.

Of course this meant their progress was slow, for everything that had been abandoned was catch-trapped in one way or another, often with magic, and that meant the magicians who had stayed with the northern army must occupy the vanguard. In other circumstances, Runacar might have chafed at the constant delay—but now the slowness of their progress was a part of his strategy. He would give Damulothir and Leopheine time to see they had already lost, and show them that

their only chance to save their people was not to fight,
but to flee.

❧❧

Look! They're coming!" Pelere said, gesturing skyward. It had been a sennight and more since Runacar had sent Radafa for help. Now the Gryphon had
returned, and it looked as if he'd brought his whole Ascension with him.

Runacar glanced skyward just as the first winged
forms broke through the overcast. They flew in an ar-
rowhead formation just as birds of passage did: wingtip to wingtip, as steady and precise as a grand-taille of
knights in formal procession. Their shadows raced
across the ground before them, and their wings and
their bodies blotted out the sky. They were too many
to count, and the sight was . . . impressive.

The Ascension flew once over the line of march, then
began to land down by the water's edge, backwinging
in the way any large winged thing must. The shore-apes
foraging among the tide pools fled amid a raucous
chorus of scolding yelps—they were timid things, but
endlessly curious, and would be back within the sunturn. In a few heartbeats, the whole Ascension was
down, looking even more numerous than they had in
the air. Of course the marchers had come to a stop once
the Gryphons arrived, and of course anything resembling order immediately disintegrated, but Runacar had
long since given up caring about appearances. They'd
hear whatever news the newcomers had brought, then
march onward. (He very much hoped someone in Daroldan was Scrying or Farseeing every move the Otherfolk made.)

He looked for Radafa, but couldn't spot him. Not
that Gryphons were identical, because they weren't—not
only was there a wide variation in color and pattern
among them, but several of them had crests of dark

feathers as well. No, there were just too many to make out any individual . . . though he thought the two smallest, the ones with the dappled haunches and vividly barred feathers, must be the youngest.

Before Runacar gave up and asked Pelere to point out Radafa, the Gryphon came bounding out of the surf toward Hialgo.

"Horrible weather!" he said happily. "Clouds halfway to the Mystrals, and all the way to the Kashadabadshar!"

"We still need anything you can do to help," Runacar said.

"Come!" Radafa said, gesturing with a foreclaw. "Riann wants to meet you."

Runacar dismounted and tossed his reins over his saddle—Hialgo would stand until he returned for him—and moved in the direction Radafa indicated, with Pelere at his side.

The Gryphons were milling about. Some had gone to seek out friends among the gathered Otherfolk, others were conversing quietly with one another. The two children were splashing enthusiastically in the shallows, chasing fish. He tried to put out of his thoughts how much this resembled the arrival of a noble family at Caerthalien Great Keep, but he couldn't. It looked just the same, Gryphons or not. He wondered just when he'd started seeing them as people, and not as monstrous animals that talked. He wondered if it indicated madness, or sanity, or just exhaustion, and realized it really didn't matter.

One of the crested Gryphons—female; apparently that was what the crest indicated—turned toward them as they approached. Runacar stopped at the tide line, having no desire to spend half the night drying and re-oiling his boots and armor.

"You are the Star-Child who has turned against his people?" Riann asked.

It was certainly not the first time he had faced that accusation. "My people are dead. I turn against those who killed them," Runacar said patiently.

"So you seek revenge?" Riann asked.

Runacar sighed, wondering what Radafa had told her. Just because he was used to the questions didn't mean he liked them. "Revenge has to have a *point*," he said. It was hard to explain a thing when he didn't completely understand it himself and half the Otherfolk didn't even have the concept. "My family is dead. The High King has destroyed everything I know and love. I have nothing left to fight for—so I might as well fight *against* something."

Riann regarded him without speaking for what seemed like an eternity. "Poor Runacar," she said at last, and though it was impossible to discern any emotion in the harsh hissing whisper of Gryphon voices, somehow Runacar knew she was not mocking him. "Have you ever considered not fighting?"

The very idea made him laugh. He'd been born in the midst of war and spent his whole life fighting. He would almost certainly die the same way. Fighting was who he *was*. But he didn't want to try explaining that to Riann. "Not today," he said briefly. "You wouldn't have come if you didn't intend to help," he added. "The Ocean's Own have brought rain, but it isn't enough. The forest is still burning. And the fire is spreading."

"The Gryphons command the winds only," Riann said gently. "We will take counsel with the Ocean's Own, so our efforts do not work against theirs. But all that is within our power to do, we shall do."

"Thank you," Runacar said humbly. "And—if you will permit—I have thought of another way you can aid us. Without shedding the blood of any," he added, remembering Radafa's aversion to violence.

⊰⊱

It had been Drotha's idea originally, and the Aesalion wasn't averse to shedding blood at all. He'd been listening as Runacar had been discussing with Pelere and Audalo how to make the best use of the one asset the enemy would not know how to combat: the power of flight.

"I don't want to ask the Gryphons to actually kill anyone," Runacar said, "and the Hippogriffs tend to be a little scatterbrained." As well as not particularly threatening: eagles and horses were both things the *alfaljodthi* knew well, and if you combined them, the result might be a monster, but it wasn't a particularly threatening one.

"They can drop rocks," Drotha suggested, getting to his feet and stretching. "Then they wouldn't *know* they'd killed someone."

"Drop rocks?" Pelere demanded, turning toward Drotha. "What in the name of the Great Herdsman are you going on about *now*?"

Drotha stretched again, elaborately, reminding Runacar of nothing so much as a particularly malicious cat. "Drop. Rocks. Why is that so hard to comprehend, turnip-eater? You pick up a rock. You fly up into the sky. You drop the rock. Anything underneath it goes 'splat.'"

"How long could you keep doing that?" Runacar asked curiously.

"Until I got tired, I suppose," Drotha said. "Or bored."

*Which would take less than a candlemark,* Runacar thought to himself. *But Gryphons are more patient. And a rock doesn't need to hit anything to force the Lightborn to hold Shield against it.*

Even if the rocks hit no one—which would please the Gryphons—they would still be annoying (at the very least), and it would remind the defenders that worse than stones might fall from the sky. Because most of all,

Runacar wanted his enemies to *worry*. To give up the Shore as lost. To flee to the only place of safety and shelter remaining: Areve.

When the time came, he was going to *enjoy* smashing Areve.

⊰⊱

He outlined his plan to Riann—fly over Daroldan Great Keep, far beyond arrow-range, carrying a rock, which did not need to be any larger than a knight's helm, and then drop the rock on the castel. It would make a booming noise, possibly damage what it hit, and even perhaps scare the livestock sheltered within the castel. And the Lightborn would have to Shield against the falling rocks, and that might keep them occupied enough that they would set no more fires.

Riann listened without speaking, and when Runacar was finished, said: "A good plan. See, Runacar? It is not that hard to be civilized. It just takes a little effort."

Runacar found it hard to decide whether he was flattered or insulted. "It doesn't mean no one will die," he felt compelled to add. "But you won't have to kill any of them."

Riann fluffed out her neck feathers in gentle amusement. "Oh, Runacar. If I see it and don't stop it, I am as complicit as if I did it myself. And no matter what happens here, they are all going to die, anyway. Just because we chase them into the Darkness and hope it will take them and leave us does not mean our feathers are clean of blood."

*It doesn't mean it will work, either. You don't know the Darkness—if it exists—will stop with the* alfaljodthi. *Vieliessar didn't think it would. And if it will be satisfied with my race alone, will your Woodwose nobly sacrifice themselves as well? You don't know any more than I do. You have hope and I have none. Which of us sees more clearly?*

"Do what you can," he said. "That's all I can ask."

"I know." Riann lowered her head and rubbed her face against his. Her beak was smooth and cool, and her feathers were soft and warm. "Poor child. You were never raised to think of such things, were you?"

"I was raised to fight, and to win," he answered. "And I will." *This time, though, it will not make up for the battle I lost.*

"And we shall help. But first, we must speak with the Ocean's Own, and call the winds."

Riann stepped back and gave a long harsh cry. The scattered Gryphons gathered around her again, and then the entire Ascension took to the sky in a great rush of golden wings. They circled once, and then began to fly seaward.

"There's an island a little ways offshore," Pelere said. "They'll meet there, I guess. What should we do while we're waiting?"

"Keep going," Runacar said, walking back up the sand to where Hialgo stood patiently. "And keep on breaking things."

❧

Runacar told himself he was not worrying over the outcome of Riann and Meraude's discussion, but even though he knew Gryphons did not fly at night, Runacar was still up and watching before the sunrise. In the early-morning fog the air was wet and bitterly cold. He walked to the edge of the camp and helped himself to a mug of tea and a piece of bread at one of the sentry posts, greeting the two Bearwards who watched there and taking their reports. The night had been quiet. If the enemy were on the march, or massing to attack, the Brightfolk would have seen it and brought word. In one sense, the sentries were unnecessary, as the Flower Forest was friendly to the Otherfolk in a way Runacar had never imagined. In another, sentries and sentry-posts were as vital as they were in any other war Runacar had ever fought, for the Bright-folk could only see and warn—and even among the Otherfolk, not everyone could understand their meaning.

He continued down to the shore, thinking idly of the strange mystery of the sun. It was something he would never have known to wonder about without the Light-born, but when Caerthalien had ridden to put down the Windsward Rebellion, much of their planning had been done through Lightborn, sent ahead and using Farspeech to make their reports. And so Runacar knew that even though the brightening sky held no glimmer of sun, on the vast golden plains of the Grand Wind-sward, it had already risen. It was as if the Grand Wind-sward and the Western Shore were two different realms, each with its own sun, instead of being all one place across which he could ride over the course of a handful of moonturns.

*Or I could have done so, once. Does anyone remain to hold the east? Or have they all flocked to the High King's banner? What joy she must have found in Hal-dil and Bethros and all the rest of those ill-starred cattle. I wonder if she . . .*

Something flickered among the clouds, a dark smudge of body, there and gone in an instant. Runacar put his hand on his sword, frowning in puzzlement as he gazed upward.

Then the first Gryphon knifed through the clouds. It was still too dark to see anything other than shape, but even blurred by fog, that shape was clear. A strong downward sweep of wings, and the Gryphon vanished into the clouds again. Barely had it done so when two more appeared. Their paths crossed, then they were gone again.

The sky continued to lighten.

Four appeared next, then two. Then four again, and eight. Sixteen (it must be, to keep the pattern) and eight.

And then there were too many, moving too fast, for him to count their appearances and departures. Slowly Runacar began to understand what he was seeing. A dance. Not a dance merely of back and forth, but a dance of up and down as well—as if the Gryphons were fish who swam in air instead of water. He followed the path each individual Gryphon took with the ease of one who has watched mounted komen drill in formation since before he could walk, and slowly a great latticelike image began to shape itself in his imagination.

The sky lightened further, though of course the clouds remained. The elaborate dance of the Gryphons expanded in width and depth. A hundred times it looked as if a collision was about to happen; a hundred times such a collision was avoided. And as the dawn wind freshened, and the low fog began to break up, Runacar at last realized what the dance was for.

*No wonder Radafa told me a whole Ascension must agree on a spell to be worked. It takes a whole Ascension to cast one.*

For the first time in sunturns, the sky was scrubbed clean of clouds. And then the Gryphons were all rising, soaring, towering above the earth until they were nothing more than a single speck against the bright colorless sky. The tiny speck burst into a myriad dots, each flung away in a different direction, and then it was true day.

⊰⊱

 How does it look to the south?" Runacar asked, over a bowl of breakfast porridge. Those of his generals who were not with the southern army were gathered with him—as were many of the other veterans of the war band—but as friends gather, not as a War Prince and their staff.

"The forest still burns," Radafa said, looking as despondent as a Gryphon could look.

"Steams, say rather," Pelere said, switching her tail back and forth as another might drum their fingers upon a tabletop. "Many are dead—but fewer than would have been without your intervention," he added, addressing this last directly to Runacar.

"The wind will blow for a moonturn, Riann says," Radafa added. "But such fires as this can burn for far longer."

"If the little glittersparks have not found the wit to run to safety in a moonturn, then they never will," Drotha said sweepingly.

"The Angarussa will have turned by then," Pelere said, ignoring the Aesalion. "It will keep the fire from going north, though I would not wish to have the farmland below the burnt-over place."

"We'll be at Daroldan High Keep in a moonturn," Runacar said thoughtfully.

"And how is that more important than the lives of the Folk?" Andhel asked. "Oh! Of course! The affairs of Elves are *always* of more importance than the lives of beasts!"

"It's plain to see you know nothing of farming," Runacar said mildly to the Woodwose, startling a snort of amusement from Pelere. "But my thought is this: Damulothir Daroldan wishes to hold the Shore at all costs, but neither his Warlord nor his Swordmaster are fools. I would wager it's Martenil Swordmaster of Daroldan who was behind the fires—a dangerous gamble, since Delfierarathadan is the wealth of the Shore—and by the time we are at Daroldan's walls, he will see that it has failed."

"Leaving us to besiege the castel and take down its walls," Audalo said. "Well, that is easily enough done. You have said all the Children of Stars will be gathered inside it."

"That has been the accepted military doctrine since Elvenkind first took the Shore," Runacar answered, "for your people have never had the organization or the numbers to besiege a castel long enough to force it to fall. And while that has changed, to slaughter all of Daroldan is not in our best interests."

"Because the holy *alfaljodthi* mean to extend the hand of alliance and comity to we poor and humble outcasts?" Andhel asked with poisonous sweetness.

"Because Damulothir can't fight Hamphuliadiel for control of Areve if he is dead," Runacar said, just as sweetly. "And we must destroy Areve next, and . . . deny the use of the Sanctuary of the Star to the *alfaljodthi*." *Somehow*, Runacar thought. *To profane the Shrine of the Star is not a thing I would dare to risk, but the Lightborn who serve it are Elves, not gods. There must be a way.* "Which means we must convince Damulothir to run rather than fight."

"I'd like to see you convince a Houseborn of anything," Andhel scoffed.

"But I shall," Runacar said. "First I am going to throw stones at them for a fortnight or two. And then I am going to offer to parley."

"Throw stones?" Pendor asked, just as Andhel said: "Parley!"

"Stones," Runacar said. "Very large stones, falling from very high up. And while it's true the War Princes won't meet with Otherfolk under a truce-banner, I think they will meet with Runacarendalur Caerthalien."

⚔

It was the tenth Springtide since the start of the High King's War, the ninth since the founding of Areve. In all things, today should have been a day for calm rejoicing, but Hamphuliadiel could not rejoice. Tonight he would go into the Shrine.

When he took up the mantle of Astromancer, Hamphuliadiel had held all the secrets of the land—only to find them bitter fruit, for what was knowledge without power? But the stars aligned, and Hamphuliadiel spun secrets into power, and the thought that the War Princes might return to take away all that Hamphuliadiel had gained was like a cold stone in his belly.

But the War Princes did not return, and his power continued to increase. Areve, his *king-domain*, grew and flourished—as did all the land, for over the Mystrals poured the beasts of field and forest—both wild and tame—and with them, the birds of the air. It was as if a great fire raged in the east, and all things that could flee, fled west.

But there was no fire.

Hamphuliadiel's disquiet grew. Why had Vieliessar not returned to the West to rule? Why had none of her vassals come to rule in her name? Why had no War Prince returned to reclaim their lands and chattels? Why, of all the living things the world held, was Elvenkind the only one that did not flee over the Mystrals into the west?

These unanswered questions formed an insoluble riddle. But even the most irresolvable riddle could be deciphered by someone. The Sanctuary of the Star held the Shrine of the Star, where sacrifices were given to the Starry Hunt, where favors could be asked and Foretellings could be granted. It had been the custom of the Hundred Houses to make sacrifices at the Shrine of the Star for luck in War Season, and again at Harvest for victories granted. With the Hundred Houses vanished, the springtide and harvest sacrifices ceased. The summer sacrifice—made for matters other than luck in battle—had also been in the hands of the Hundred Houses, and it ceased as well. Only the Midwinter Sacrifice had been traditionally performed by the Sanctuary alone, and none had been made since the Snow Moon before Vieliessar's victory.

No one noticed, for certainly Hamphuliadiel had done nothing to give any of the folk he ruled—either

Lightless or Lightborn—any reason to believe the sacrifices were not being made. But among the many changes made to the Sanctuary of the Star since the beginning of the High King's War had been to move the entrance to the Sanctuary, so that the great bronze doors of the Shrine were no longer the first thing a visitor saw upon entering. The Shrine of the Star, which by ancient custom was open to any who had the courage to enter it, had been locked away as carefully as Hamphuliadiel had locked away the Great Library ... but it was still here. And Hamphuliadiel knew that the Silver Hooves could give him the answers he sought—if he dared to ask.

In his time, Hamphuliadiel had scoffed at many things and named them folklore, falsehood, and country superstition—from a secret truth in *The Song of Amretheon,* to the idea that an Astromancer might only reign until the fragrant Vilya flowered, to the idea that the Code and the Covenant must govern every act of Lord and Lightborn. Among his inner circle, he called Pelashia Flower Queen and the paradise of the Vale of Celenthodiel the wondertales of Landbonds ... but though he wished to say that the Starry Hunt was more of the same, he could not quite bring himself to do it.

Hamphuliadiel had only been inside the Shrine once: on the night he became Lightborn. It had been long ago, and he remembered nothing that had happened there. He knew he did not wish to go back, but if he sent someone into the Shrine with a petition, he would have to trust them to give an accurate report of what followed, and Hamphuliadiel trusted no one.

The only alternative was to go himself.

It took him Wheelturns to admit to the necessity of consulting Them. Still longer to reason his way to the unpalatable truth that he could not send anyone in his place. And longest of all to admit that no time was

better than another for the doing of this thing he so
very much did not want to do at all.

And so at last Hamphuliadiel bowed to necessity.

❧

He had already chosen his sacrifice: two colts,
twins, of Mangiralas lineage and destrier blood-
lines. They were a year old, identical in every way, and
without flaw. They had been brought into the walled
garden, and were being carefully watched over by Lightborn who were themselves from Mangiralas. All was
ready.

In the Hour of the Wolf, Hamphuliadiel set forth
from his private chambers to keep the appointment he
had never wanted to make. He went first to the garden,
where the young Lightbrother on watch silently handed
him the colts' lead-ropes, and then through the garden
gate to a door only he could open. It was on the western face of the Sanctuary, looking like nothing more
than another panel of the decorative limestone clad-
ding. This, and the equally-hidden entrance in his personal chambers, were now the only two entrances to the
Shrine. Hamphuliadiel had enchanted both so that only
his touch could open them—should some future Astromancer wish to enter the Shrine, let them build their
own entrances, as he had.

The young stallions, bespelled to docility, followed
him as meekly as dogs into the gently curving corridor,
the sound of their hooves muffled by the thick straw
matting that covered the floor. Silverlight cast on crys-
tals mortared into the wall glowed just brightly enough
to show the way. There was no door blocking the far
end of the corridor, and the Silverlight that had been
cast by generations upon that chamber's walls and ceiling was so bright that Hamphuliadiel narrowed his
eyes against it as he emerged from the dimness of the
corridor.

To the left stood the cyclopean bronze doors of the Shrine with their deep-carven images depicting the Starry Rade. To the right, the radiant curving wall swept onward around the circular chamber, the doorways which had once interrupted it erased as if they had never been. The hooves of the colts clicked as they passed from straw to marble, crossed the mosaic floor inlaid with its compass rose, and stepped beneath the ceiling inlaid with the star-pictures edging the Hunt-road.

Hamphuliadiel stopped before the doors of the Shrine, so close he could easily reach out and touch them. Once he opened them, there would be no turning back. He hesitated, wishing yet again that there was some other way. In that moment, if he had possessed the power to speak across the years to his younger self, he believed he would have set Hamphuliadiel of Haldil on a different path—on *any* path that did not lead to this moment and this place.

But here he stood, the prince he had made of himself with vision and ambition, and if all he had amassed was not to pass into dust and ash, there were things he must know. They were things he would have paid any price to obtain if that meant he did not have to come here, but he had at last learned there were things neither power nor wealth could buy.

He took a deep breath and reached out to touch the tuathal door.

Both doors immediately swung noiselessly inward—a thing that needed no magic, he reminded himself, just engineering and careful counterweighing. The warmth and scent of a Springtide forest rushed out as if to draw him in, for there was neither roof nor floor in the Shrine. The chill pale radiance of the moon at midheaven shone down, showing him three tall stones beneath the open sky. A fourth flat stone was set into the ground between them, for the Sanctuary had begun as a wall about the Shrine, built so the stones could never be moved.

*Nine Shrines are given to the* alfaljodthi; *nine places where the breath of first creation still can be felt upon the skin. Nine where the Powers must hear us when we call.* Arevethmonion was first among them by custom only: all of the Nine were equal.

Hamphuliadiel just barely remembered to remove his slippers before he stepped across the threshold. He could not repress a shudder as his bare feet sank into the soft, fecund earth.

Slowly, cautiously, he led the colts into the Shrine. For a moment he thought he saw a light glimmering through the trees—but that could not be. The Shrine occupied less than a twelfth-hectare of ground, and was surrounded by the Sanctuary's stone walls. He told himself that the darkness all around him was because the doors had closed noiselessly behind him. He told himself he did not hear the wind rustle through nonexistent branches where no wind could be. He was Hamphuliadiel Astromancer: he knew what tricks and illusions both the Light and the pretense of the Light was capable of.

He took the last few steps forward, until he stood before the standing stones. He felt as if they somehow exerted a tangible pressure upon his body, as if at any moment they might rush forward and crush his body between them.

No. He would not give himself over to fantasy.

He took a deep breath, and cast the spell that caused the twin colts to step forward and kneel placidly upon the flat stone; to continue to kneel as Hamphuliadiel withdrew a blade of black glass from his sash of office and cut first one throat, then the other. Hot blood spurted out, splattering the standing stones, pooling upon the stone between them. Hamphuliadiel dropped the knife of sacrifice, a further gift, into the pool. The raw scent of meat and metal rose up from the gouting steaming blood, and it seemed to Hamphuliadiel that the blood was too red, too bright, for something illuminated only by the moon's light.

Then he glanced skyward, and the well-rehearsed words of his petition died in his throat.

The moon was red.

Red as blood, redder than any eclipse had ever rendered it. In its light everything was red. Hamphuliadiel raised his hands—to gaze upon them, to block out the sight, even he did not know—and they were as red as if he'd bathed them in the blood of the sacrifice. Warmth and wetness—impossible quantities of blood—covered his feet, rose to his ankles, soaked the hem of his robe. There was a soft sound as the bodies of his sacrifices, dead beyond spellbinding, collapsed limply to the sodden earth. As he looked, the blood rose up around them, staining them, covering them. It was everywhere, a black lake stretching into impossible distances, sparkling in the light of the blood-drenched moon, its surface punctuated only by the death-pale trunks of a dead forest. The wind was cold now, and held no scent of anything but blood.

It came to his mind, with the insistent absolute knowing of a dream or a vision, that the stones of the Sanctuary were gone, its walls and doors were gone, that the Shrine was walled in not by limestone and granite, but by a bleached and desiccated tangle of bones rising higher than even the Astromancer's Tower. Here in the Shrine of life there was only death.

He would have run if there was anywhere to run to. He, who had spent every sunturn of his life seeking knowledge, hoarding secrets, would have cut this knowledge from his mind if he had possessed the means, but the knife was somewhere beneath the sanguinary tide he shuddered to touch. The liquid continued to rise, past his calves, past his knees, thick and greasy and stinking and warm, and as it did Hamphuliadiel saw all, everything, the answer to every half-formed question, every unarticulated wondering, answered now and forever.

The Darkness of Amretheon's Prophecy was real, and it had come. It was not black, this Darkness, but red as the blood in which the Darkness would drown the whole of the world until there was no other hue nor shade nor color anywhere in the world. The Darkness swept from east to west as if it rose in the heavens with the stars, and every creature possessed of breath and heartbeat fled from it.

*They* were coming.

> *"When stars and clouds together point the way,*
> *And of a hundred deer one doe can no longer*
>   *counted be,*
> *When peace is bought with maiden mother's blood,*
> *And those so long denied assert their ancient claim,*
> *When scholar turns to sword, and warrior to peace,*
> *And two ford rivers swelled with mortal gore . . ."*

Serenthon had been right. Celelioniel had been right. *Vieliessar* had been right. But if they had been right . . .

A grief as compelling as nausea rose up in his throat, and Hamphuliadiel gagged. All was lost. The whole world, lost. All of his subjects, lost. *He* would be lost. His agile mind, his glorious wisdom, his compelling leadership—all snuffed out like the embers of a dying fire. Gone. Lost. *Not* because he had been wrong—no, never that! He had been right. He had always been right. All was lost because the enemy was too vast, too powerful, for any one, any *thing*, to prevail against it.

That was it. That had to be it. Not that he was wrong, had failed, had hindered his only chance of survival. No one could win. Any resistance was futile, because no one could win.

He retched and fell to his knees, sending a vast rip-

ple through the lake of blood. He struggled to rise—*oh
precious Light, do not let me drown in this unnatural
lake!*—as his throat closed, strangling the harsh choking braying sounds of terror and grief.

*Is there nothing that can be done? Nothing?*

Once again Hamphuliadiel was the child of the disgraced kitchen slave, cowering against the hearth, his
body aching with kicks and beatings, his stomach
cramped with hunger and shame. He was of noble
blood, scion of Bethros, his mother Einartha betrayed
into slavery in Haldil by her sister, the woman she had
trusted most in all the world, the knight to whom she
had been Sword Page . . .

His plans, his ambition of gaining revenge, of gaining the rank that was his by right of birth and bloodline, all were subsumed in the terror of a child alone in
the dark.

> "*When two are one, then one may speak for all
> And in that hour claim what never has been
>     lost . . .*"

The words of that damnable Song echoed in his ears
as if he were remembering rather than discovering.
Now his inward-looking sight saw a cavern beneath the
earth, so deep it took sunturns to reach it. There lay the
weapon to stem the rising tide, there lay the promise of
victory over the Darkness! He reached out to it greed-
ily, eagerly. *He* would save them all! Vieliessar would
kneel weeping at his feet and beg him to take the High
King's place. He would be worshipped as their great ancestors had been, and his shrine would never lack for
offerings . . .

But suddenly the vision came clearer. In the darkness,
great yellow eyes and leathern wings. Anguish, and
tears, and grief, a vast aching immeasurable grief . . .

Hamphuliadiel screamed, over and over, clawing at his face, his neck, wallowing in the vast rising tide of blood.

⊰⊱

Harwing Lightbrother woke abruptly. He sat up, gazing around himself in the darkness of the dormitory. What had awakened him? His brethren slept on undisturbed all around him. Yet Harwing was certain he had heard screaming . . .

*A dream. That's all it was. An evil dream. Something from the past that Healer Momioniarch says you do not wish to remember.*

The phantom screaming echoed in his mind, but still no one roused. He eased his body cautiously from his bed and gathered the bundle of his clothing from the basket beside it, then crept to the door. He opened the door only wide enough to slip through it and closed it softly behind him. The stone of the corridor was chill beneath his feet and he dressed quickly, then hurried through the familiar halls and down the steps until he came to the door that opened into the garden. The way was more labyrinthine than it had been when he had been a Postulant, but the Astromancer had explained that the changes to the Sanctuary were to protect the Shrine of the Star from the Beastlings, so certainly the small inconvenience was worth it.

*. . . isn't it . . . ?*

Harwing frowned, pausing just short of opening the garden door. How did sealing off the Shrine and the Great Library protect them from *Beastlings*? The whole of the Sanctuary was their protection. And surely, if anything was anathema to the wrongness the talking animals represented, it would be the Shrine of the Star. All the changes had done was seal both places off from any person who might wish to visit either . . .

Harwing shook his head in self-reproach. That was

ridiculous! Why would Hamphuliadiel do such a thing . . . ?

*Because he is tainted and twisted and power-mad. He is the High King's enemy, and Gunedwaen was her most loyal lord until the candlemark of his death. If for no other reason, that is why you must choose her as your liege and lord.*

Harwing ran both hands through his hair, closing his eyes very tightly. The headache that was fast building behind his eyes had blotted out the phantom screams.

*Gunedwaen.*

He had not thought of his beloved in . . .

He took a deep breath.

*Control, dissemble, this may be a trap as well. You awoke in the night and went to walk in the garden lest you disturb the others in your dormitory. The cause of your wakefulness you do not know.*

He set those thoughts upon the surface of his mind, where anyone who looked could see them, pushed open the door, and stepped into the garden. Above, the sky was darkly blue, filled with stars and the elvensilver ribbon of the Starry Road. Below, the high walls turned the garden into a piecework of light and shadow. The night was silent, but a mere twelve Wheelturns ago, the Sanctuary would have been busy at this time of year, for the new Candidates would have just arrived, and the War Princes would have come to make their sacrifices to the Starry Hunt for favor in the coming War Season. The Guesthouse would have been full to overflowing, and the pavilions of the latecomers would have been set all across the fields . . .

*No one has even asked if the sacrifices are still made even without any War Princes to make them.*

*Are they?*

Harwing frowned. He could not remember Hamphuliadiel saying anything one way or the other, in his frequent public exhortations to the Lightborn. Certainly he had not said that he did *not* make the sacrifices . . .

*But he has not said he does, either. Perhaps they are made at another of the Shrines—there are eight—nine, because Tilinaparanwira the Lost isn't lost anymore . . .*

He gasped in shock as the whole of his pent-up memories rushed free. Gunedwaen. Vieliessar. The Domains of the Western Shore. Rondithiel had led the two grand tailles of Lightborn to their aid . . .

Ten Turns of the Wheel of the Year ago.

*And we crossed the Mystrals and entered the West, and I knew as well as Rondithiel did that the High King wanted news of the Sanctuary of the Star and so I came to see what I could learn . . .*

And had stayed, because Hamphuliadiel had told him Vieliessar was the Darkness prophesied in *The Song of Amretheon* and Harwing had believed him. He had *believed* him. He, whom Gunedwaen Swordmaster had taught to believe no words and few sights.

Why?

*Never mind "why." "Why" is not the business of scholars, scouts, and spies. You* did *believe him, and you stayed, toiling away as his patient drudge and never questioning any orders he gave you.*

Suddenly he heard someone walking toward him, the motion but not the sound hidden in the shadows. "Who goes there?" Harwing whispered.

"Only I, brother." A tiny ball of Silverlight formed on the hand of the speaker, illuminating his face.

"Irchel," Harwing said in relief. "So I am not the only one to go sleepless tonight."

"Did you not come to relieve me of my watch?" Irchel asked, puzzled. "There is no need of it now, for the Astromancer took the colts to the Shrine not a quarter-termark past."

"The twin destriers foaled last spring?" There had been talk almost from the moment of their birth of their suitability as a sacrifice, for twin foals were rarely born and even more rarely survived. Harwing could not decide whether he was relieved that Hamphuliadiel had made the Springtide sacrifice, or . . .

*Or terrified by all that you forgot. Of course, why remember it when you were here in the place you belong?* he added firmly, in case someone watched his thoughts.

"Yes, Arja and Tarja," Irchel said. "It is wrong to be sad that they are chosen, I know, for now they will run with the Starry Hunt, young and strong forever. But I would have liked the training of them."

Irchel Lightbrother had been born to a horsegroom in Mangiralas and had worked with the great herds until he'd been Chosen by the Light. *And no wonder he thought you were to relieve his watch, for you were born in Thoromarth Oronviel's stables . . .*

"There will be others," Harwing said gently, reaching out to touch Irchel's shoulder. "But I do not wish to keep you from your bed. I will stay here for a while, and hope that sleep will favor me again before morning."

"As you wish, brother. Go with the Light."

"And you as well," Harwing said.

He breathed a tiny sigh of relief when Irchel Lightbrother was gone, and walked on along the white stone path toward the edge of the garden. The garden was bound around by a wall more than twice Harwing's height. Its surface had been smoothed by Magery until it was slick as glass. Hamphuliadiel had said it was only so that the stoneworking Lightborn would have something to practice on before trying their skills elsewhere, but it meant the wall was impossible to climb. In that moment, Harwing knew the thought that had been growing in his mind since the moment he awoke.

*Flee.*

But Gunedwaen—*oh Beloved! I miss you so!*—had

told him over and over not to follow the first thought, but the best thought.

He had come to gain information, and he had. But he had spent too long a time at it—*far* too long a time—and he had no idea what to do now. His information was worthless by now, and after so long he had no idea who to deliver it to. Following Rondithiel and the others to the Western Shore would be difficult if he tried to do so on his own—and who was to say any of them were still alive? That Amrolion and Daroldan were still there? Harwing's knowledge of the world and the events which transpired in it now stopped at the edge of Areve's pastures and ended ten Wheelturns ago.

Struggling to control both his thoughts and his emotions, Harwing wandered until he came to the bench set beneath the ever-flowering Vilya. He remembered the last time the Vilya had borne fruit—he had still been at Thoromarth's court then.

*But* this *Vilya did not fruit. Hamphuliadiel spellbound it so it would not, so he could use that as a legal pretext to remain Astromancer. And who will challenge him, with the Hundred Houses gone, and Vieliessar . . . ? Where is she? The High King has not come west in all this time, and the last of the refugees we took in came two Harvests ago, and they were from domain Cirandeiron, and that is on this side of the Mystrals. . . .*

She had won. He remembered that. She might take a Wheelturn, or two, or even three, to consolidate her victory, but there should have been scouts sent over the Mystrals, and whether they reported back or simply vanished, the result would have been the same: the next Wheelturn, or the Wheelturn after, the High King's army would have come west.

*So she is dead.*

But he did not believe that, either. If she were dead, her War Princes would have swept back into the west to retake their old domains and enlarge them at the expense of their neighbors. And if they did not, then the Houses of the Uradabhur, the Arzhana, and the Windsward certainly would have.

*No war lasts a decade.* It made no sense. And it left him floundering.

*"When you don't know what to do, do nothing. Sooner or later you will know—or you will know you should have been running away all along."* Gunedwaen had said that to him every time Harwing had fretted with impatience and the need to act. Tears prickled at the memory. Gunedwaen had been his *world* . . .

Suddenly what he must do was clear.

Gunedwaen had died because Ivrulion Light-Prince had been rotted through with ambition—the same ambition that marked Hamphuliadiel's every act. Ivrulion was dead, but Hamphuliadiel was still alive.

That could be remedied.

He would have to plan carefully, because nobody amassed this much power without amassing protections and guardians for it. It wouldn't do to fail because of haste. He would only get one chance.

But he had one sterling advantage that gave him a near-certainty of success.

He didn't care whether he survived.

✢

As the morning sunlight upon his face woke him, Hamphuliadiel Astromancer inhaled deeply and automatically, smelling the mingled fragrances of sundried linen sheets scented with lavender, of ripe naranjes sitting in a silver bowl beside his bed, of cedar and sandalwood clothing chests, fresh flowers, pine resin set out in bowls to sweeten the air . . .

*It was a dream, all a dream . . .*

Relief surged through his veins as he opened his eyes

to regard his familiar bedchamber. A dream. The sacrifice must be tonight, then. And he had dreamed of it, nothing more.

Though it had all seemed so real . . .

*But of course, as Astromancer, my dreams are more vivid than those of ordinary souls,* Hamphuliadiel told himself. He would meditate upon what it had revealed before going to the Shrine tonight. That was proper and correct; behavior no one could whisper behind his back about. Or . . . perhaps he need not go at all? Perhaps the dream had been a warning, to tell him that entering the Shrine would be futile, and perhaps even dangerous . . .

The surge of relief he felt convinced him that this was the correct interpretation. So be it. Perhaps he would send someone else in his place. Young Harwing Lightbrother, perhaps. Or that Lightsister from Daroldan; what was her name . . . ?

Still pondering, he sat up in bed, reaching for the bell to summon a servant to bring him his morning *xocalatl*.

And with that motion, the last of his dream world faded. He saw the grit and mud that covered the bedclothes. He felt his hands covered with blood and earth, sticky and rough. He smelled mud and dried blood and black water and offal. He threw back the coverlet and saw that his whole body was covered with a dried slurry of filth. His face burned where he had clawed at it, and every muscle in his body ached as if with prolonged misuse.

Hamphuliadiel whimpered despite himself, his gaze darting frantically about his cluttered and opulent bedchamber. Whether he was looking for aid, or reassuring himself that no one was here to see him, even he could not say. But what he saw made him wish there was someone here—someone *else*—upon whom he might blame the sight that greeted his gaze.

The carven smokewood screen that masked the concealed doorway leading down to the antechamber of the Shrine lay on the floor where it had fallen. Bloody handprints marred the smooth whiteness of the wall, as if left by someone groping blindly to find their way. The rug between the door and his bed was marked with a line of bloody footprints and splashes of mud. His robe, no more than a sodden wad black with dried blood, lay beneath the window. It had struck the wall and slid to the floor; he could see the streaky brown stain.

He had made the sacrifice already. Last night, as he had thought, on the first full moon of the Springtide, as custom demanded. And then he . . .

The images of the night before tried to push themselves into his consciousness, and he thrust them brutally away. *No.* He would not permit himself to think of that. It was not real. If it was real, it was not true. It was a false vision, an evil vision, no true Foretelling at all. There was no Darkness. There was no threat so baleful and real that Vieliessar Farcarinon had torn all Jer-a-kalaliel apart because of it. There was a normal and ordinary explanation for everything that had happened. Only what he could see, and touch, and taste was real. The Silver Hooves had not come. The power of the Shrine had not awakened—*no!* The Shrine had no power *to* awaken. It was a myth, a fantasy, the Silver Hooves a survival from the days of ancient savagery. Not true Powers. Not real. The Starry Hunt, the Shrine of the Star, all nine Star-shrines, were nothing more than a hoax, a dream, an ancient custom given unnatural weight. He had been right to seal off access to the Shrine. It was only a trap for the gullible. The Light existed without it. The Light was created in the Flower Forests for the *alfaljodthi* to use—as much a commodity, a resource, as fields of wholesome grain or streams of sweet water. It was not capricious. It was not . . . sentient. The Light was all they needed.

All *he* needed.

Hamphuliadiel forced himself to get to his feet. He walked with unsteady steps toward his bathing chamber. The bath that had been filled last night in anticipation of his return from the Shrine still steamed, scented with fragrant oils. Hamphuliadiel lowered himself into it gratefully, wincing as the hot water laved his battered body.

This was here. This was real. Last night was not. He would rise above darkness and superstition. He would show his people the road leading to a new world free of such moldering beliefs. He was Hamphuliadiel Astromancer, Lord of the Sanctuary of the Star.

It was as simple as that.

And when he had bespelled away every trace of dirt and blood in his chambers and reduced everything it contained to ash, he rang for a servant and demanded the chamber be swept and scoured, and new furnishings brought immediately.

New furnishings . . . and hot honeyed wine.

⊰⊱

Harwing Lightbrother did not know how long he had been back at the Sanctuary of the Star, or—so the thoughts that lived on the top of his mind told anyone who wished to look, and he knew—down deep where no one could see—that they *did* look. Frequently.

And so, to all outward and inward eyes, he went on as he always had, a loyal servant of the Astromancer and the Sanctuary. He did not know how the veil over his mind had been ripped asunder, only that on the night the twin colts were sacrificed, he had come back to himself.

*And Hamphuliadiel fell ill afterward. No one ever spoke a reason—of course they didn't—but a rumor was started—somehow, somewhere, as these things al-*

*ways are—that he had valiantly defended us from
Beastling sorcery, and taken harm of it.*

It wasn't true, of course. Even if the Beastling sorcerers were to be so rash as to attack Areve and the Sanctuary, they could not possibly strike down someone within the Shrine itself. But that it was a lie—and what that lie concealed—didn't matter to him. The only thing that mattered to Harwing now was to somehow get close enough to the Astromancer to kill him. And that meant gaining his confidence. Being allowed to join his inner circle. To do that, they must believe in him—and Harwing must believe in himself.

## CHAPTER FIFTEEN

# THUNDER MOON:
# A WAR LIKE NO OTHER

*Amrolion and Daroldan were bordered on one side by
the largest Flower Forest in the Fortunate Lands, and
on the other by Great Sea Ocean. Like the Domains of
the Arzhana, they did not fight with each other. Like
the Domains of the Windsward, they considered themselves always to be embattled. Like the Domains of the
Uradabhur, their strength lay in coalition. In truth, they
were one Domain, not two, for they both had the same
motto: Isterya Adzab: I hold.*

—Runacar Warlord, *A History of the Western Shore Campaign*

R unacar had never imagined presiding over such
a substantial battlefield. It stretched along the
entire Western Shore from the southern desert
to the northern mountains. Such a vast area would be
impossible to oversee without a mount a hundred
times faster than the swiftest horse ever foaled. Of
course he could delegate control of any of these opera-
tions to one of the Otherfolk battle leaders—and in
practice he did so, for every one of them had once been
a member of his war band, and they had learned from
him. But if he was to craft the overall strategy of the
campaign, he needed to *see* what he was working with.
Reports were not enough.

Even if the Gryphons did not fight, they were the key
to the Otherfolk's victory. The night Radafa took Runacar to see the scope of the blaze in Delfierarathadan

was merely the first time they flew together, not the only time. Today, the seventh sunturn after the fire had been set, Radafa and Runacar had flown south again.

The Gryphon-called winds and the Nisse-called rains had made an uneasy alliance. Though one could smell the burning even in the vanguard of the army, both smoke and steam were blown southward by the unfailing wind. The smoke rose up to coat the bellies of the low-hanging rain clouds so that when the hard soaking rain fell, it was black. Where the fire had passed, the rain drenched the grim skeletons of charred trees and glutted the ash-choked mud with moisture until the thick black slurry seeped all the way to the water's edge, staining the sand and the sea black as well. The contours of the earth itself had been reshaped by furious heat and unremitting rain.

From the black mud to the red sands, there grew no tree, no flower, no blade of grass. The only thing Runacar could think of to compare the burnt-over forest to was the Ghostwood, but that had been white as death. This was as black and wet as a poisoned wound.

Yet despite the rain, the fire still raged, a furious blaze that devoured unimaginable amounts of forest every sunturn and moved as fast as a running horse. What madness could possess a War Prince to despoil their own domain more utterly than even an enemy's victory could do?

*Fear.*

Amrolion and Daroldan existed between two vast enclaves of Otherfolk, suffering constant sightings and encroachments by each, and saw themselves as the only defense of the West. Certainly the War Princes would burn Delfierarathadan if it would stop the northward march of something that had never been seen in the Fortunate Lands—an army of Otherfolk. Runacar had never thought much about the Western Shore before this campaign, nor about how its War Princes saw the world. Now, he saw that this information was as vital as anything he had known about the numbers of their komen, or the spells their Lightborn might deploy.

*I don't care what they're willing to do to win. My job is to make them run.*

Radafa circled the desolation, letting Runacar look his fill, then turned north, flying through smoke and steam, the hot wind from below making it easy for him to gain altitude.

*This is what Arilcarion tried to save us from. Vieliessar said the Hundred Houses turned war into a game— but if we did, that meant we did not ride to war over the bodies of the helpless.*

This was, perhaps, not entirely true—Runacar acknowledged that even in the midst of the thought. But it was certainly more true of the summer wars of the Hundred Houses than of what he was seeing here: a landscape turned to ash and sand and innumerable thousands dead. *Ah, but they are only Beastlings,* he thought in bitter self-mockery, *so where is the harm . . . ?*

The jarring thump of Radafa's landing brought Runacar's thoughts to the here and now. The Gryphon had landed two leagues ahead of the leading edge of the fire, where the southern contingent of the army was working frantically to evacuate the Brightfolk and the fire-teams were striving to create a swath of barren ground that the fire could not leap. Centaurs, Minotaurs, and Bearwards labored with axes and rope to fell the great trees, even hitching themselves to the fallen trees to drag them clear of the area, as if they were no more than beasts of burden. In the rain, in the mud, it was grueling, back-breaking work.

The moment he and Radafa landed, a couple of Centaurs galloped over, one carrying a waterproof cloak for Radafa. This monsoon rain was certainly not the place for anything with feathers; Runacar felt as if he was standing under a waterfall. He helped Bellor and

Randin pull the garment over Radafa's neck and wings. The Gryphon looked truly miserable, but the two Centaurs looked worse: faces and bodies covered with soot and ash; their faces masks of exhaustion. But still here. And still trying.

"I suppose I don't have to ask you how things are going?" Runacar said, looking around. He had to raise his voice nearly to a shout to be heard over the roar of the fire and the hiss of the rain.

"If the Stonekin can't turn the river, you in the north'll have the fire up your asses in a sennight," Bellor said. "This is the third firebreak we've made, by the Herdsman's Grace, and it'll jump this one, too, we think."

"The . . . people?" Runacar asked hesitantly.

"We won't know how many died here for a long time," Randin said bluntly. "I think most of the Dryads are safe. Anyone who can is running for the waterline or the river—the Ocean's Own are helping evacuate them at the sea. I can't say what's happening at the river."

Runacar shook his head numbly. He didn't even know what questions he should be asking, and he wasn't sure he'd understand the answers even if he did. A Green Robe might know—but he might as well wish for the power to wave his hand and douse the blaze as wish for Lightborn to fight beside Otherfolk.

"Do you know how soon they can turn the Angarussa?" Runacar asked, and Randin shook his head.

"No time to spend chatting with Stonekin, and they're working east of here," Randin said, gesturing vaguely. "And we'd best get back to our work, too. Stay safe, Commander—you're the one who's going to make sure the witches who did this find out what it's like to die in fire."

Runacar raised his hand in a silent salute—one of the first lessons he'd learned was that if you couldn't be confident of victory, you could at least act as if you were. The two Centaurs wheeled and trotted away.

"Have you seen enough?" Radafa asked.

"Too much," Runacar said. "But I want to get a good look at the terrain between here and Daroldan Great Keep. If the rocks aren't stopping the Lightborn from setting more fires, we need to know."

As the purpose of the bombardment was to occupy the Lightborn rather than damaging the Keep, it did not have to be constant. It had taken a sunturn or so to put the plan of bombarding Daroldan Great Keep into action, and much of that time was spent in stockpiling stones. Not enormous boulders, such as a trebuchet could hurl. These were small, perhaps the size of a loaf of bread, easily carried in talons or paws. For the first few sunturns, the Hippogriffs had rained stones upon the Keep from sunrise to sunfall, and at night the violet glow of Shield had been visible leagues to the south. When the novelty faded, they flew over the castel to drop stones less often, but the very randomness of the attack acted in its favor: Damulothir Daroldan would not know when the next attack would come, so his Lightborn must keep constant watch, always ready to cast Shield. And since the Gryphons who were aiding in the bombardment were reliable and conscientious, Runacar could be certain that at least one stone per candlemark would fall upon Daroldan.

Shedding his cloak, Radafa flew up through the clouds to where the sky was blue and the sun was shining—as much to get a break from the desolation below as for the chance to dry out completely. From above, the clouds were as white as the armor of a maiden knight.

Radafa radiated heat like a cookfire, but Runacar had been soaked to the skin while they were on the ground, and leather trews and jerkin provided scant insulation. He shivered in the icy atmosphere of the high sky.

"I can't see anything from up here, you know!" he

shouted. The Gryphon screeched laughter and tilted his wings, and they swirled down through the clouds. Here, the worst of the rain was behind them, and it was warm besides.

Radafa swept over the forest in long lazy arcs, like a hound coursing to pick up a scent, sometimes down at treetop level, sometimes far enough above that Runacar could get a panoramic view of the whole of the forest. From above, the army marching northward looked small and vulnerable. So far as Runacar could tell, there was no sign of either fire or enemy troop movements, and Radafa was not the only one acting as aerial sentry and scout. When Radafa overflew the army, he quickly picked up an escort: another Gryphon and a half-taille of Hippogriffs. A shadow passed over all of them, and Runacar glanced up to see Juniche, the second Aesalion who had agreed to fight as part of the army, flying far above.

"Seen enough?" Radafa asked.

"Almost!" Runacar answered. "Can you take me over the Great Keep? High enough that you aren't in danger," he added quickly.

"That would be too high for you, Rune—you would not be able to see, or to breathe," Radafa answered. "But if we are fast, perhaps their witches will be looking the other way."

Despite what he'd said, Radafa rose until they were in the lower drifts of the clouds, and Runacar could tell he was putting on speed. They left the Hippogriffs behind, but Juniche continued to follow, as if this was some game of Chase and Catch.

Then Radafa dropped out of the clouds, and there below was Daroldan Great Keep. It was the most enormous single structure Runacar had ever seen—a vast labyrinth of walls within walls, and the space between each set of walls was filled with refugees and livestock. He saw no sign of either Shield or Lightborn. The Inner

Close was built as a single great tower, as high as any watchtower, but large enough to hold all that a Great Keep must. Its walls were smooth, and its windows were mere slits. Upon the top of the tower, siege engines were gathered—not to batter down castel walls, but to attack a besieging force. It looked as if a number of war engines that he was used to seeing on a battlefield had been adapted for defense. There was no one in sight.

*That isn't right. Even if they've dropped Shield, there should be guardsmen on watch. This is too tempting a target . . .*

Radafa turned toward the forest. The beat of his wings was labored as he strove to rise, for the wind had turned sharply. But at last he gained enough altitude to catch one of the sea-winds to use to soar even higher. His path, of necessity, was a long open spiral.

Suddenly a blur of red and black dove past Radafa toward the tower. Juniche had clearly found the unshielded Keep to be irresistible.

"No!" Runacar shouted, knowing it was useless.

Guardsmen ran from concealment. *Bait,* Runacar thought in horror. *They're bait.* Even this far above, Runacar heard Juniche laugh as he forced them to run to the edges of the tower and leap off.

There was a flash of green as Lightborn came from beneath the siege engines, then a shimmer in the air. A net appeared directly above Juniche, falling over him, pinning his wings, driving him out of the sky and down onto the top of the tower. Aesalions were immune to magic, but Runacar had seen Lightborn use Fetch often enough to know what he was seeing: there was no Magery involved aside from bringing the net and dropping it over Juniche.

He heard Juniche scream. Whatever the strands were coated with, they clung. And they burned.

The Aesalion was trapped, tangled in the net and unable to fly, his body already a map of ugly, oozing burns. He lashed out with claws and barbed tail, but every movement enmeshed him tighter in the thing that was killing him.

His screams of agony sounded very Elven.

More guardsmen clambered to the roof, armed with axes and war hammers. It was the last Runacar saw as Radafa's path led them out over the forest, but Juniche's screams followed them, rising shrilly.

Until they abruptly stopped.

If Juniche's killers celebrated their victory, Runacar did not hear them. His eyes were blinded by unexpected tears, and he could not say why he wept. In war, people died. That was the nature of war. Juniche had shown no more mercy to the guardsmen he had driven to their deaths than the Lightborn had shown to him. *It's only fair,* Runacar told himself. *Only fair.*

"War is not a game," he whispered, over and over. "War is not a game."

❧❦❧

When Radafa landed at the waterline, the Otherfolk came running to meet him. The babble of voices filled the air, sounding oddly similar to the breaking waves. As soon as Runacar slid off his back, the Gryphon headed landward. Everyone was asking what had happened, had they seen any other fires in the forest, where was Juniche, had he gotten away . . .

*Word must have already reached them,* Runacar thought. *Or they saw Juniche fall.*

He walked away from the crowd, out onto the wet sand. He stared out to sea, toward the line of foam that marked the passage of the Ocean's Own in their procession parallel to the shore. Runacar wanted to make Juniche's death make sense in his mind, and he didn't think he could. Before the High King's War, Runacar might have been one of the fighters on that rooftop, cheering as loudly as anyone else over their success in killing one of the most dangerous of the Otherfolk. *Only you would have called them Beastlings, and thought of them—of him—as a clever and dangerous animal that needed killing. Like a rabid dog or a rogue wolf.*

As Prince-Heir of Caerthalien, he'd often fought beside people he despised, against people he called friend. It was the nature of war, and Vieliessar naming herself High King didn't change that. You didn't cheer your enemy's success in battle—but if they did well, it didn't open an aching void in your heart. And he didn't know what had changed. He hadn't liked Juniche. He'd barely known him. Even Drotha was someone he treated with friendly wariness. He didn't think either Aesalion had possessed close comrades here—and Sword and Star knew they'd despised one another . . .

"Why so glum, Lord Commander? Surely you aren't grieving over the death of a talking animal?"

Runacar did not turn around. "Go away, Andhel. This is not the time."

"Oh but of course, Lord Commander. At once, Lord Commander. Certainly your lightest whim counts for more than any desire of *my* kind."

Runacar turned to face her. She'd brought him Hialgo; he didn't know why someone who despised him so completely made so many reasons to seek out his company. The grey destrier stood just behind her, saddled and bridled. "They aren't your kind," he said flatly. Andhel's eyes gleamed with triumph at goading him to respond. "Oh? Why? Because I look like you and they don't? Because of course, how you look is the most important thing. When—"

"Shut up," Runacar said. Andhel looked surprised. "I'll tell you why they aren't your kind," he said, his voice low and soft and very even. "They aren't your kind because they can never hide what they are. They can never change it. But you? Any time you—or any of the Woodwose—want, you can leave. Approach a Farmhold or a Border steading. Make up some tale. Be accepted. You talk about being Otherfolk, but for you it's a choice, and one you can unmake at whim. So don't tell me this is about 'my' kind and 'your' kind, because it isn't. And you know it isn't. For you it's an adventure you can give up any time you get tired of it."

She stared at him, mouth gaping. It occurred to Runacar that this might be the first time he'd seen her surprised. Or maybe he'd actually managed to hurt her. He felt nothing, not even triumph.

"High words, Houseborn," she finally said, but her voice lacked its usual mocking conviction. "Even—Even if that's true, can't the same be said of you?"

Runacar smiled without mirth. "Oh, perhaps—though I doubt I could manage to hide, even among Border steaders. But there's one other difference between you and me. I know what I am. You call yourself Otherfolk—and I don't."

She flinched as if he'd struck her. Her eyes were wide and dark, and her mouth worked, soundlessly, as if she was trying to summon words that weren't there. Then she dropped Hialgo's reins and fled.

Hialgo stood patiently, waiting. Runacar walked over and tossed the reins up over the stallion's back and leaned his head against Hialgo's shoulder wearily. Then he sighed, and flung himself up into the saddle. "Come along, my friend," he said. "It's time to get on with helping the talking animals unseat the lords of creation."

⊰⊱

The northern army continued to march toward Daroldan Keep. The southern army went on fighting the fire.

It was frustrating for Runacar to have no real sense of how well his plan was working. After Juniche's death, the Gryphons and Hippogriffs had bombarded the castel without stopping for two sunturns, until it was ringed by the stones that had bounced off Shield. The Fauns made a game of sneaking up under cover of night to retrieve the fallen stones. Runacar couldn't stop them, and he didn't try.

The Lightborn did not release Shield again. There was no point in dropping more rocks until they did, though Drotha continued to do so for the sheer amusement value of making Shield flash and flare. Runacar wished he knew how much it cost the Lightborn to keep the spell in place. His brother Ivrulion had been cagey about sharing what he knew—*and now I know why, may the oathbreaker rot forever in the outer dark*—and in the natural course of things, matters involving the Lightborn were dealt with by the Chief Lightborn of a War Prince's Court. It was true that the Western Shore Lightborn hadn't tried doing most of the things that would have been useful in this situation—Lightning Strike, Thunderbolt, the more powerful forms of Transmutation. Did Delfierarathadan's burning constrain their magic in some way? He had no idea.

What he did know was that no competent Warlord would allow an enemy army to march right up to the walls of his Keep, and he was right.

❧

At the first nudge to his bedroll, Runacar was instantly awake. He blinked his eyes at the corona of colored lights surrounding Bralros's head. Though the Centaurs were all utterly incapable of doing any kind of magic—which apparently meant being unable to see or hear many of the Brightfolk—the fairies never stopped trying to talk to them. Flary, the Faun—no, this was Flary's greatson, Tilwik—was standing on the Centaur captain's back, whispering in his ear in his high-pitched voice. His stub of a tail wiggled with excitement.

"Attack?" Runacar asked in a low voice, pulling on his boots and reaching for his sword and his cloak.

"Not yet," Bralros said. "But coming."

Runacar followed them to the watchfire on the sand where the sentries gathered. Bralros was Pelere's lieutenant; he wondered vaguely where Pelere was.

"We saw Shield flicker, so I sent Tilwik to see what the fairies knew. Rather send a Bearward, but I'd have to wake them first. According to Tilwik, people from the Great Keep have entered Delfierarathadan," Bralros said. He glanced skyward to check the time, still haloed in a rainbow of fairies. "Maybe a hora ago—that's a candlemark to you. They went on foot, without armor, and there were 'many.'" Bralros made a face in anticipation of Runacar's disgust.

"Many!" Tilwik agreed. "Dressed like Woodwose. Fairies say. Brownies, too!"

Which meant dressed like Rangers, since camouflage was camouflage. "So . . . anything from a taille to a great-taille," Runacar said with a sigh. "Rangers, probably, and maybe Lightborn. It takes moonturns to get a komen off their destrier." It had been a joke the Alliance meisnes had made during that long terrible winter when they learned the power of infantry: *It takes moonturns to get a komen off their destrier—or one forester with a grudge and a bow.*

Bralros ignored—or didn't get—the joke. "They don't bring horsemen into the forest except along their Trade Road. And they don't move at night."

"Horses don't see very well at night," Runacar said mildly. Nor did many of the Otherfolk; several of the "Nine Races" were bound to the sun and could not be roused by night, or only with great difficulty. It would have been more of a handicap if their enemy had not been so thoroughly bound to tradition, confining its skirmishes to daylight.

Until now.

"We need to get an accurate count of their numbers," Runacar said. "The Flower Forest is too dangerous to risk a night attack; they're probably taking a position to wait for sunrise. When it's light, ask Riann to have the Gryphons spot them. If we know how they're moving, and their numbers, that will almost certainly give us some idea of what they're planning. You've fought Rangers before, haven't you?"

"Oh, aye." Bralros's voice was bitter. "We came up over my Da's farm, getting here. Southern edge of Delfierarathadan, no place your people cared about, even the ones who claimed it. But they were quick enough to march a fortnight out of their way to burn him out."

"Then you'll know more about their tactics than I do," Runacar said steadily. He didn't apologize for what Amrolion had done. That led to ridiculous impossibilities like apologizing to High King Vieliessar (in the unlikely event he ever saw her again) for having had a part in slaying Serenthon Farcarinon. War was war, the dead were gone, and yesterday's sworn enemy might be today's battle-comrade.

Bralros considered for a moment. "Strike and flee, that's their style. Hard to see and harder to catch." He frowned. "But where's the advantage to them in it? They must know a few dozen—even a few hundred—deaths won't give them victory."

"They don't know Gryphons," Runacar said. It sounded like an absurdity, even to him, and he blinked, shaking his head. "I was wrong. They aren't going to wait. They're risking a night assault because they're going for important targets. They'll be after the Gryphons. But they don't know that Gryphons sleep on the wing. I didn't." That made sense. It explained why a sortie party would risk entering the Flower Forest at night.

"And what you don't know, they don't know?" Bralros said dubiously.

"I was raised to become War Prince," Runacar said. "And if it isn't in *Lannarien's Book of Living Things*—"

From the corner of his eye he caught a flicker of light. It grew, a churning multicolored ball, as if all the fireflies in the world had mated with a rainbow and this was the result. The fairies had returned.

"Coming *now!*" Tilwik squealed.

"Sound the alarm!" Bralros shouted.

Runacar had already drawn his sword and was running toward the camp.

⊱⊰

Clouds of shining Brightfolk swirled between the trees, filling the Flower Forest with an eldritch opaline glow. The enemy didn't need the light, Runacar knew, as certainly as if he'd been there when the attack was planned; the Lightborn had cast Silversight upon the Rangers, enabling them to see clearly even in total darkness. And for their attackers to have reached them this quickly from Daroldan Great Keep . . . they'd used Door. Door could be used to move a sortie party hundreds of leagues in heartbeats.

He saw the sparkling clouds of Brightfolk go instantly dark, and knew the Lightborn were killing them with Magery. He heard the deadly song of the Rangers' arrows as they flew, every one hitting its target. Runacar knew how far away the archers had to be, and he knew the direction. The Lightborn would be nearby.

The Otherfolk were scrambling to arm themselves, or simply throwing themselves at the enemy barehanded. He saw a Minotaur fall, her body feathered with a dozen shafts. A Faun screamed, thrashing wildly as he clawed at the arrow that pinned him to a tree.

"Here!" A shout came from behind; he saw a flicker of movement out of the corner of his eye and turned just in time to catch the ringmail vest Pelere flung at him. He stopped just long enough to shrug it on before moving forward again. Pelere had already passed him. She held a spear in one hand and a torch in the other, and had not taken the time to don her armor.

They reached a clearing. There was nothing to see, but suddenly Pelere went to her knees with a surprised cry, blood spilling from a sudden wound. Runacar swung his blade into the emptiness. It caught and bit hard. The Invisibility Cloak—Cloak cast upon cloth was still Cloak—fell back, exposing the body that lay dying on the ground. Green tunic and leggings. Light-born green.

The Lightsister stared up at him in shock. "Caerthalien . . ." she whispered through the blood bubbling on her lips.

The clearing was empty now. He didn't question how he knew. He turned and knelt by Pelere's side.

The dagger was sunk deep into her shoulder. It quivered as she gasped in pain. But even so, she had not dropped the torch she held. He reached out and took it gently from her hand.

On the old familiar field of battle, Healers would come, draw out the blade safely, and carry its victim to the Healing Tents. There was nothing familiar in this. All he knew was that to draw the blade forth would be worse than to leave it where it was.

"Go," she said. "I'll be fine. Go."

"I'll kill them all," Runacar promised, rising to his feet.

⚔

If this was Palinoriel Warlord's devising, he was a tactician to fear, sending Rangers and Lightborn from the Great Keep in the depths of night, breaking them up into smaller groups—a taille at most—then using Door to instantly place them at the enemy's side. Strike and run. A strategy of attrition. It would have been a sweeping success if not for what Palinoriel didn't know he didn't know—that the forest was alive, and fighting at his enemy's side.

The battle was a hundred ambushes, a thousand single combats, routs and engagements with no plan or organization behind them. For Runacar, it was a night of running through the twilit forest, attacking both foes he could see and those whose presence he barely guessed at.

⬦⬦⬦

He flung his sword up, ready to attack at the sound behind him, but it was only Drotha, crashing through the trees to make an awkward landing.

"They won't run when I frighten them," the Aesalion said plaintively.

"They're probably Warded," Runacar said. *Like the ones who killed Juniche.* "They have cloaks of Cloak," he added. "Of invisibility," he amended. It was unlikely that the Aesalion was familiar with Lightborn spells.

"Do they?" Drotha asked, sounding puzzled. "Is that why some of them don't run? I caught one," he added. "He looked very surprised."

*He can see through their spells?* He knew Aesalions were immune to magic, but he hadn't realized that meant being unable to *sense* it.

"Stay with me," Runacar ordered. "You can see what I can't."

"Can I kill things?" the Aesalion asked.

"Everything that isn't on our side."

There was a flare of brightness off to the right. Runacar ran toward it, with Drotha bounding along beside him as if he were an enormous hound.

⬦⬦⬦

Runacar managed to engage two more parties of Rangers—and barely kept Drotha from bounding through a Door spell after a third. But as daylight began to filter down through the canopy of the trees, even Drotha had to admit that the enemy had fled.

"They'll be back," Runacar said grimly. "This was a test, nothing more."

"I hope so," Drotha said cheerfully. "I want to kill more of them."

"I hope you have your chance," Runacar said simply.

❦

It was full day by the time Runacar rejoined the army. The Otherfolk had gathered at the edge of the ocean. There was some semblance of order—cookfires and salvaged caches of supplies—and as far as Runacar could tell by sight, most of the army was here, sitting or lying on the sand. The water was filled with Ocean's Own of various sizes and shapes, both to stand watch, and to heal the wounded. There were open pavilions set in the shallows, and each of them was filled with floating beds on which lay the injured. Runacar looked, but did not see Pelere among the wounded.

Above them, Riann's whole Ascension and most of Gunyel's Flight wheeled and soared, also keeping watch. If he'd been right—if the Gryphons had really been the War Princes' true target—Daroldan knew by now that it had failed.

"Runacar!" Audalo said, hurrying over to him. "Thank Stone and Leaf you survive! As soon as the rest of our people reach us, we can begin to make ready."

"How many are dead?" Runacar asked, shifting the Faun who dozed upon his shoulder like a sleeping child.

"Too many," Audalo said. "Bralros said you would want an exact count, but that may take some time. I have asked the Brownies to take care of it." Brownies were one of the Otherfolk races Runacar could actually see, though there was no point in enlisting them as fighters, as the tallest of them was a bare two hand spans high. Still, he was glad they wanted to help.

"We'll have to find the bodies and move them," Runacar said. The thought of Daroldan returning to the battlefield and harvesting the bodies of the Otherfolk dead as if they were deer or berries was oddly revolting to him. "I don't know what rites you use . . ."

"We burn them, so *your* kind can't profit from them," Andhel said. She looked tired and battered, and the top half of one ear had been cut away, but aside from that she didn't seem to be too badly injured.

"We can do that before we go," Audalo said. It was the second time he'd mentioned having plans, and this time it caught Runacar's attention.

"Go?" he said. "Go where?"

"Why . . . home," Audalo said, sounding surprised. He made a gesture vaguely eastward. "What else can we do? It was you who taught us some fights can't be won—they'll just keep coming and coming, night after night—how can we stand against that?"

"You idiot." Exhaustion made Runacar's voice low and flat and ugly. "I've tried to feel sorry for you—for all of you—because of what we'd done to you, but by Sword and Star and the Starry Hunt, you've deserved every bit of it. Lose a battle and all you want to do is *run*? Where's the honor in that? Where's the respect for those who died fighting not a candlemark ago?"

"Respect doesn't mean throwing ourselves onto the pyre with them, Houseborn," Andhel snapped.

"Run away, and what they died for means nothing," Runacar said, not looking away from Audalo. "This is war, and people die. You *know* that. Yes, as long as they keep Dooring in with Rangers, our losses will be heavy until we can figure out a defense. But run away, and we'll have it all to do over again—and an enemy who's had time to learn from our mistakes."

They'd accumulated a ring of interested bystanders, he noted, and not even Drotha's presence at his side kept more from gathering.

"Houseborn get to learn and we can't," Andhel said mockingly.

"If you stop now, how not?" he answered, turning at last to address her directly. "Leutric told me to take the Shore. I can do it, but not without an army."

"Or maybe what King Leutric told you doesn't matter," she sneered, "and all you care about is seeing us die."

"Fine!" Runacar snarled. "Go. Run. Like— Oh, I don't know! But don't any of you *get it*? *We won this battle*. Yes, we lost people—but Daroldan used its most effective combatants—Rangers, Lightborn—and *we pushed them back!*" Suddenly he realized how purely exhausted he was. "Never mind. You won't listen. I'm going to find something to eat and somewhere to sleep. Don't bother to wake me when you run off. I'm staying."

He turned away. The watchers in front of him moved back hastily as Drotha stepped forward. Runacar handed the Faun he was carrying to the nearest Woodwose that wasn't Andhel, and headed in the direction of the cookfire.

Drotha grinned at him toothily. "Well, if nobody else is going to bother, I'm going to go drop some more rocks. Maybe they'll hit something."

"Maybe," Runacar said. He wished there were more Otherfolk like the Aesalion, though Drotha wasn't so much warlike as murderous. "Don't get killed."

"And miss the rest of the fun?" Drotha scoffed. He bounded away, spreading his wings, and in a few moments he was airborne.

There was an enormous iron kettle suspended on a tripod over the fire and a stack of wooden bowls beside it. Runacar dipped one into the liquid—soup, from the smell, though the kettles were just as often used to brew tea—filled it, and drank. He couldn't remember the last time he'd been this tired—and to add insult to indignity, his feet hurt. War was not a business to be conducted afoot.

He wondered where Hialgo was, and if he'd survived.

He wondered if any of the enemy who'd escaped had recognized him. By now they certainly knew about the Woodwose—what did they think of "Elves" fighting beside Otherfolk?

He dipped his bowl into the kettle again. Nobody seemed to want to talk to him, and at the moment that was the most wonderful thing he could imagine. He pulled off the ringmail vest and dropped it to the sand. It wasn't his, anyway. Its owner would probably want it back—if he or she was still alive.

Then he walked up the sand to the edge of the forest, sat down with his back against the trunk of the first large tree he saw, and slept.

⚜

He was walking through the Flower Forest, thinking: *no matter what happens in the world of the Folk, this will go on*. No matter what the season outside, it was always springtide in the Flower Forest. Season of hope. Season of plans and possibilities. He wondered vaguely why anyone would ever wish to leave such a place.

And then the ground turned soft and slippery beneath his feet, and his boot sole crunched down on a tiny delicate skeleton. The trees around him lost all color as their leaves turned to ash and blew away. Even the everliving Vilya was leafless and dead. Runacar stood in the dust and ashes of the Ghostwood—a world of bone white and ash grey—but just as it occurred to him that this was a dream—the same dream he'd had since the

Battle of the Shieldwall Plain, in fact—the colors changed.

Ivory flushed to scarlet, pale grey became fulgent black. The Ghostwood became a fleshy slaughterhouse, carnal, pulsing with unclean vigor, branches festooned with bright wet red leaves.

A woman stepped out from behind one of the trees. Her skin was the same scarlet as the leaves, rendering her nearly invisible against the blood forest, and her shining black hair fell all the way to her ankles. She was as tall as a Minotaur, but slender and wholly female, and when she smiled, she showed him a predator's ivory fangs.

"It's unfair, you know," she said, as if they were old friends encountering one another again. "If she'd never been born, how different your life would have been." The woman reached out to a branch and plucked a fruit so ripe its skin was nearly black. She bit into it, and thick red juice ran down her chin.

"Vieliessar," Runacar said. Not the woman he faced here, but the one she spoke of.

"Vieliessar," the scarlet woman confirmed. "Who is lauded for her miracles of war, her grasp of strategy, her innovative tactics. And you, who are so much more than her equal, are simply . . . forgotten. Brushed aside. You would have been the hero of your age, had she not been born. *You* would have been High King."

"At what price?" Runacar asked warily.

"Does it matter?" the woman asked. She took another bite of the fruit. "Here," she said, tossing it to him. "Catch."

He caught what she threw almost reflexively, but it was not a fruit. He did not have to look down to see he held a skull in his hands. His fingers tightened on it reflexively, and he heard delicate bone snap. Around him the blood forest was fading, becoming the Ghostwood again, and even in the dream, Runacar closed his eyes. He did not want to see.

"You shouldn't bait them."

Despite himself, he opened his eyes. The forest was neither white nor red. It was green.

And he knew who had spoken. A voice as familiar to him as his own heartbeat.

"Vieliessar."

"Why are you here?" she asked, stepping out of the shadows. "Why *aren't* you here?" she corrected herself, shaking her head. "Where did you go?"

"I went home," he answered. He knew this was only a dream, a fantasy born of his exhaustion, but he felt compelled to answer anyway. "Why didn't you come after me?" Though what he would do if and when she did he had no idea.

"I will," she promised. "I am. Wait for me."

"Forever," he answered. The words said more than he wanted them to. They didn't say enough.

⧈

When he crossed the border between sleeping and waking Runacar knew he'd been dreaming, though he did not remember the dream. (One of the benefits of being Lightless was not having to constantly scour your dreams for Foretellings and portents.) Despair, he had long since learned, had this much in common with contentment: it left you willing to simply live in the moment, unwilling or unable to influence the flow of events in which you swam.

All around him he heard the noise and clatter of the encampment, and his mind painted a picture of neat rows of pavilions, cook tents, and Healing Tents, grooms walking destriers up and down the lanes to exercise them, the distant lowing of the cattle any army must drive with it. The sun was warm on his skin, and he had the odd thought that he'd dreamed Caerthalien had gone to war in winter . . .

Then the sounds resolved, becoming not the sounds of Caerthalien's war-camp, but the sounds of the Otherfolk. The soft roaring was not wind in the trees, but waves upon the shore. He opened his eyes, blinking half-dazzled at the westering sun. Someone had thrown a blanket over him as he slept, and the vast bulk of Keloit was curled up at his side, sleeping the deep and carefree sleep of the untroubled mind. He wondered when Keloit had returned from the south, and why.

He sighed, sitting up and repressing a groan at the pull of muscles stiff and sore. He spared a reflexive moment of longing for the luxuries of a properly equipped campaign—not even Healers and wine and the luxurious meals little different from those served at the High Table of the Great Keep, but hot baths and soft beds and soft chamber-boots. It had been a privileged life, and he'd enjoyed it.

*But the cost was far too high.* He frowned, wondering where the thought had come from. True, to live like the princes they were required the toil of an entire domain, all the wealth of those vast lands trickling, drop by drop, to the top. As Heir-Prince, he'd been as familiar with tax rolls and account books as he'd been with stables and training field. But there was something here he could not quite reason his way to: some flaw in the order of battle that would cost the war . . .

Then he saw Bralros coming toward him and let the thought go.

"Wake up, you lazy lump," he said, prodding Keloit with his elbow. "Do you want to sleep the day away?"

"Already have," Keloit said, yawning. "And anyway, so have you. Got here about sunfall, and then we spent the whole night fighting, so I *deserve* a nap. Pelere sent me to keep an eye on you, to keep you out of trouble."

Runacar made an amused noise as he levered himself to his feet. *At least she is still alive.* "You can tell her you did an excellent job," he said. "I slept very well." *But no. I dreamed, I remember that much. And nothing good.* Small wonder, considering what he'd been chasing through the forest all night.

"Bralros," he said, as the Centaur stopped before him.

"You say we can still win," the Centaur said without preamble.

"No," Runacar answered. "I say we're winning *now*."

Bralros looked unconvinced. "And if we continue as we are?"

"Marching toward Daroldan Keep? We'll be there in about a fortnight, I think. If they haven't run by then, we'll have to besiege them, and it will take about a Wheelturn to starve them out—a dehora, as you reckon it."

He'd hoped to make the Shore Domains run east, but the longer he fought, the less likely it seemed that they would.

"And the attacks like the one last night?" Bralros asked.

"Oh, they'll continue," Runacar said simply. "After a few more of them they'll realize they can't find the Gryphons, and change their tactics. But attrition is a good strategy, so I expect our losses will increase."

"Then how can you expect to win?" Bralros demanded in exasperation.

"Because they can't kill all of us before we get to the castel," Runacar said flatly. The murderous exasperation he'd felt listening to Audalo had returned in full force. "But none of that matters now. Audalo intends to retreat, and I can't stop him."

"And what would you have us do?" Bralros asked. "How can you ask hundreds—thousands—of people to die? And not even for victory, but for the chance to fight again somewhere else? It's madness!"

*This is how they see you.* For a reeling, unsettling moment, Runacar saw the Hundred Houses from the outside. As the Otherfolk saw them. Their round of endless, eternal, *purposeless* wars and deaths. It was true that few of the princes and the Lords Komen died of battle injuries—but few wasn't none. There were always casualties. And the Otherfolk did not possess the Healing abilities of the Lightborn—they could Heal illness and injury, true, but not instantaneously. Most of their magics were turned in directions Elvenkind had never thought of.

"We can win," Runacar repeated. "But not if we retreat now." *I could have been the greatest hero of our age.* He wasn't sure where the errant thought had come from. He ran his hands over his hair and then gestured for Bralros to wait.

"They're using Lightborn against us," he said slowly, as the bones of a strategy began to lay themselves down in his mind. "Traditional doctrine states that if the enemy uses a resource against you successfully, you must find a way to deny him the further use of it. Bralros . . . how long would it take to evacuate all of Delfierarathadan—not just the south?"

"Why?" Bralros asked suspiciously.

Runacar smiled at him in unfeigned delight. "Because I want to burn it down."

❧❧

A moonturn. Four sennights. That was their best guess.

None of his captains had wanted to listen to what Runacar had to say until Pelere and Keloit pointed out that the War Princes wouldn't leave them alone just because they were leaving. That their losses would be equal whether they ran or stayed was clearly something the Otherfolk had not thought of.

"Then what are we supposed to do?" Audalo demanded, flinging back his head and addressing his words to the sky. The sun was setting, but it wouldn't be dark for hours yet, and the sky was filled with fire. At the edge of the tide line, pyres of the dead awaited burning. *"You have destroyed us!"*

"I never said there would not be casualties," Runacar said, keeping his voice even with an effort, his teeth clamped tightly shut. "This is war. There are casualties."

Audalo swung back toward him, gilded horns gleaming, and time seemed to stop. In that moment Runacar suddenly realized the army was not just on the verge of retreat, but of mutiny. By every metric Runacar had been raised to understand, he had been conducting a perfectly normal military campaign. The Otherfolk saw things differently. Looking back, he could suddenly see the thousand times one of them had asked him if things must be done this way. If it was necessary to take so much risk. If he couldn't find some way to better protect them.

The losses in the Battle of the Kraken had been terrible by Otherfolk standards, but the fact that the enemy had lost so much more had kept the army with him. The fire set in Delfierarathadan had angered all of them, but they had been focused on saving the Bright-folk, and part of that was continuing to march on Dar-oldan. But last night's attack had been the final straw.

*The Otherfolk don't understand war,* a small voice inside him said. *They understand raids, ambushes. Everything you did with the war band in the Western Reach was a matter of a sunturn or two, a sennight at most. And they came and helped as much for the novelty of it as because they wanted to learn war tactics. Most of them just want to be left alone. Of the half who can fight effectively, half won't. It took Leutric moonturns to gather an army large enough to take the Shore—and that was after a decade of military successes conducted nearly without losses.*

"Our whole strategy hinges on scaring the War Princes so they'll run, not just in slaughtering all of them. If that would be enough, it could easily be done. But this way is better." Runacar spoke this time with more caution, feeling his way, watching the Otherfolk around him for clues.

"You want to destroy Delfierarathadan," Andhel said. "Make up your mind, won't you? You've spent the last fortnight trying to save it."

"Not to save the forest. To save the people," Runacar said. "I don't give a damn about a bunch of trees, and if the Lightborn need them to cast spells, that's all the more reason to turn them to ash."

He thought momentarily of the Shrine in Delfierarathadan. Of course no one—meaning no one *Elven*—had ever used it, because the Flower Forest was too dangerous to wander through. Would it survive the fire? Would the Silver Hooves exact revenge against those who destroyed it? He wondered if there was anyone here he could ask.

He wondered if he cared.

"Will you two stop butting heads like stags in the spring?" Pelere demanded crossly. Her shoulder and torso were wrapped bulkily in something that looked and smelled like seaweed, and she was entirely too pale, but she had insisted on being here for the debate. "Nobody wants to see any more people dead. And this might work."

"And it might not!" Andhel said vehemently. "All of you are so englamored by the idea of a Houseborn willing to take your hand and teach you all his Houseborn ways of killing that you never ask *why!*" Andhel cried. "Why is this Houseborn so different from every one of the others—how many times did one of us beg with our dying breath to be seen as something other than an abomination and been denied?"

"Something, Andhel, you have never and will never experience."

Runacar blinked. He hadn't been the one to speak, though certainly he'd said something more than similar to Andhel not so long ago. It was Frause, who now came muscling her way into the circle surrounding him.

"It is true, what you say. True for Bearward, for Gryphon, for Centaur, for Minotaur—for many races of Folk. But not yours. It is true that the *alfaljodthi* treat their own kind worse than a Centaur treats a henhouse fox, and that the Woodwose are the children of the left-for-dead. But never would the Children of Stars deny you were people," Frause said.

Andhel inhaled as if she'd been struck, her eyes wide. Audalo put a comforting hand on her arm.

"We would, though," Runacar said, bowing slightly to Frause in acknowledgment. "Your Woodwose came from our Landbond, and we treat the Landbond like animals instead of people. Animals we don't particularly like," he added. "It's why Vieliessar won, I think. She told them they were people and set them free." From the corner of his eye, Runacar saw Andhel glaring at him with undisguised loathing.

"And none of this addresses the point," Bralros said argumentatively, folding his arms over his chest. He looked around the circle, meeting Audalo's, Pelere's, Keloit's eyes. "I say 'go' before more of us die. Audalo says 'go.' Runacar says 'stay'—and says we'll be slaughtered if we go. Do we fight or do we run? And whichever we do, how do we *stay alive*?"

"Their tactics are the same whether we stay or go," Runacar said. "So our defense must be as well. I will help you all I can—but I will tell you now, they will cut you to pieces as you run and there is nothing I can do to change that. So tell me whether you mean to let me carry out King Leutric's orders or not. He told me to give him the Shore. I still can."

"How?" Audalo asked wearily. His shoulders drooped with exhaustion.

"You want the strategy that involves the least loss of Otherfolk life. Very well. If we burn Delfierarathadan to ash—we'll still need to put out the fire in the south first, because I need the whole army here and we have to evacuate it before we burn it down—we will have destroyed the only source of Light—of *magic*—for the Western Shore Lightborn."

"But not of ours," Frause said quietly. "The witches' magic is a magic of taking, while ours comes from breath and bone, just as it always has. So we will have power and they will have none."

"And the Shrine?" Runacar asked. He didn't want to. He didn't want to hear the answer. But he refused to win by trickery and misdirection.

"How can a fire burn a thing which exists beyond Time?" Frause asked, and now she sounded amused. "It will always be, whether it is buried in ash or at the bottom of the sea. Fear not, Elf-child. Your gods will still hear you."

"They haven't listened yet," Runacar muttered under his breath.

"How does burning Delfierarathadan give us victory when the witches set it afire first?" Pelere asked. There was curiosity, not accusation, in her voice.

"Because if we burn it—and we do that only after it is empty of Brightfolk—we destroy the entire remaining wealth of the Western Shore," Runacar said. "You can't defend a thing when the thing is gone. We've already destroyed their fields. They will have nothing left to fight for, and very little left to fight *with*. They will have to flee, or starve."

He looked around the gathering. The Otherfolk closest to him he knew: they were his commanders, his students, people he'd known for Wheelturns. But in the way of the Otherfolk, they were not the only ones privy to this decision: the circle was ringed, and ringed again and again, by all those who wished to listen. Even the Ocean's Own were clustered as near to the land as they could come, listening.

"My companions, I apologize to you all," Runacar said, bowing without irony. "I attempted to conduct this war as I would among the Houseborn, without taking into account your strengths and your desires. But as a learned general of my people once said: *The purpose of war is to win.* The purpose of this campaign is not to outlast Daroldan as it kills dozens of us each night. It is to make Daroldan *run,* so that in the end we can drive them to Areve, and then drive Areve and all its inhabitants through the Dragon's Gate. That you are here today—alive—tells me it is possible to hide in Delfierarathadan. What you have done in the south tells me we can burn this forest without loss of Otherfolk life. I know that many of your folk refused to join this army that King Leutric created—will they come, not to fight, but to save Brightfolk lives? If they will, if this is what you choose, then the Shore shall be yours."

It was a performance, an act, a rallying speech such as he had given to the meisnes he had commanded more times than he could count, but it was also true. *The best lies are made of truth,* Elrinonion Swordmaster had said, over and over. And this was both. He would count anything short of mutiny as a victory today. And if he must retreat . . . well, he would learn all he could from the doing. He would not give up.

"We cannot decide such a thing in a *hora,*" Audalo said at last, gesturing toward the westering sun. "So how do we survive the night?"

"We spend it here at the waterline," Runacar said

instantly, striving to conceal his relief at discovering Audalo still sought his counsel. "We're far enough from the edge of the forest that Rangers would have to leave the forest to shoot at us. I don't think they will. In the open, we cannot be ambushed. Tomorrow . . . well, that depends on what you decide."

## CHAPTER SIXTEEN

# THUNDER MOON: RICH, BEAUTIFUL, AND CURSED

*Were the Nine Races the Hundred Houses, the Centaurs would be Cirandeiron: standoffish and reliable. The Minotaurs, Mangiralas: different from the others but dealing well with them . . . but the Woodwose would be Aramenthiali to the alfaljodthi's Caerthalien: two Great Houses alike in so many ways that they would never agree on anything.*

—Runacár Warlord, *A History of the Western Shore Campaign*

F ew slept that night. The pyres for the dead were lit, and after that, the army fragmented, each group discussing the matter among itself. Runacar collected Hialgo and those of his possessions that had survived the previous night's raid, and went off by himself to think. Whatever the army decided, there were certain things that must be done. Before anything, a messenger to Leutric, to tell him . . . whatever there was to tell him . . . and to ask for more help. The Folk who had not wanted to fight would probably assist a mercy mission, and if the Otherfolk were to have any hope of surviving their retreat, they would need that help. He had no idea what the Ocean's Own thought of any of this. So far as he knew, they had sustained no losses in the fighting.

When dawn came, he saw Riann's Ascension land, but it was nearly midday before Keloit came to find him.

※※※

They haven't decided yet," Keloit said without preamble, skidding to a stop in the loose sand. He
dropped to a sitting position; Bearwards walked upright, but to run they used all four limbs. A running
Bearward could outpace a horse over a short distance.

Runacar turned his face toward the sun. "This is a
nice place. It would be nicer if everybody wasn't fighting over it."

"You aren't listening," Keloit accused.

"You haven't told me anything I didn't know a sunturn ago," Runacar said. "What do you think we should
do?"

"Me?" Keloit looked astounded and a little panic-
stricken to be asked. "It's not my decision."

"It's not mine, either," Runacar said reasonably. "And
if one of the Rangers manages to put an arrow through
my throat, it *will* be your decision."

"Mama—" Keloit began, and stopped. "Mama won't
say what she thinks we should do. Drotha says he'll stay
even if we go. Bralros says we might be able to evacuate the rest of Delfierarathadan in under a moonturn,
if King-Emperor Leutric can send us more help, so
Radafa's gone to ask him. Riann says if we decide to
evacuate the whole of the forest, she'll ask the other Ascensions to join us."

"Meraude? Aejus? Amrunor?"

Keloit looked truly miserable. "They say they will
wait for the kraken to rouse and use it to destroy Daroldan whether we stay or go, but if we leave, they will
consider any treaty we have with them at an end."

Runacar shrugged. "That's Leutric's problem, not
mine. How long until the kraken wakes?"

Keloit uttered a sharp bark of laughter. "Maybe in
my grandchildren's time."

"So . . . not immediately useful?"

"No."

"And the Woodwose? Go or stay?"

"You know Tanet's in the south . . ." Keloit began evasively. The Bearward wasn't any better at lying now than he'd been when Runacar first met him.

"Andhel wants to leave," Runacar said flatly.

"No." Keloit sighed. "She thinks your gods might help us if we make a sacrifice at the Forest Shrine."

"You do that already, don't you?" Runacar asked idly. He knew the Otherfolk had gods, but he'd never wanted to know much more than that.

"Not living things," Keloit said simply.

"Ah," Runacar said.

They sat in silence for a while. Suddenly there was a rushing sound of wings—like a flock of doves taking flight, only far louder—and winged shadows flickered along the sand. Gunyel's Flight was racing northward. They were flying low—barely above treetop level—and were all carrying stones. Apparently they'd decided to resume the bombardment.

"They do that deliberately," Runacar said mildly.

Keloit grinned at him. "Well, sure," he said. "They're Hippogriffs. They think anybody would want to fly if they could."

"And I suppose the Ocean's Own pity those of us who cannot live underwater," Runacar said. He watched as the Hippogriffs soared out of sight.

"Probably," Keloit said. "But I don't want either feathers *or* fins. Fur and forest suits me fine."

"I can't speak for you," Runacar said, and heard the wistfulness in his own voice, "but I could wish for wings."

Suddenly Keloit's head came up. "Come on," he said, lumbering to his feet. "They've made their decision."

Pelere met them as they headed down the beach to where the bulk of the army was gathered.

"Rune!" she cried joyfully. "We're going to fight! I mean, at least we're going to burn the forest, but that means we have to evacuate it first, and, well, we might as well be doing something, so—"

Runacar caught up to her and hugged her. "That's no way to give a report, Cadet!" he said. "Who's decided, and who is with them?" *And do the Woodwose intend to sacrifice me for luck in battle?*

"Everyone!" the Centauress said, prancing in glee. "After all, if the witches are just going to keep attacking no matter what, the first thing we have to do is make sure they can't!"

❧

The mood of the Otherfolk was not as sanguine as Pelere had implied, but at least they were willing to listen to him now. Runacar carefully gave no orders—or at least, he phrased them as suggestions and indirect observations—but he had been considering what to do next ever since he'd come up with the idea of burning the Flower Forest. As each part of the plan was agreed upon, the elements of the army needed for that aspect departed to begin their work. A few candlemarks later the only people left on the beach were Runacar and a few tailles of Otherfolk, most of them the members of Runacar's original war band.

"You move very fast," Riann said. The Ascension leader would be leaving at dawn to speak to the other Ascensions. Radafa and four others would remain with the northern army to keep communications open.

"I was playing games like these while I was in the nursery," Runacar said before he could stop himself.

"But now you know this is no game," Riann said gently. "I am glad."

Runacar turned away, unwilling to let her see his face.

The flashes of purple light coming from the north—brighter now that the light was dimming—proved that the Hippogriffs were continuing to do their part, even though that part would necessarily end with the light. "The true test will come when we go against Areve," he said briefly. "And that depends on what we do here."

⊰⊱

The night passed without any attack.

⊰⊱

The following day, Runacar was in the south again. Word had come from Randin that they were ready to dam the Angarussa and put out the fire, and Runacar needed to convey new orders to the fire teams. Once again, Radafa volunteered to act as his steed; Runacar was beginning to think Radafa enjoyed showing him what it was like to fly. The Gryphon had suggested watching from the eastern bank of the Angarussa; it would have the advantage of being far enough away to not be caught up in whatever the Stonekin had planned.

*If only the Hippogriffs were willing to carry riders—and if only the Woodwose could ride. If and if and if . . . "Should" and "would" and "ought" are three great armies who always fight on the enemy side, so Toncienor Swordmaster once wrote. I think I would add "if" to that tally . . .*

Radafa crossed Delfierarathadan above the burn line, swinging wide across Cirandeiron before turning back toward the Angarussa to land. Runacar was glad he did, for this far south, the western bank of the river was an inferno. Most of the fire teams were already on the eastern bank waiting tensely to see if this gamble would work. The air smelled of smoke, and there were small burned patches on the eastern bank where sparks had been blown across the river, but everything was wet enough from the constant downpour that no fires had jumped the river.

It was still raining.

Nothing had really prepared Runacar for the sight of the burning forest, not even his previous visits. Even with the breadth of the Angarussa between them and the fire, the baking heat radiating off the burning forest made the air shimmer, and it felt to Runacar as if he was standing on the hearth in a Great Hall. The sound of the burning was as loud as if he were standing equally close to a very large waterfall; so loud there was no possibility of speaking, even at a shout.

The light from the flames made the turbulent surface of the Angarussa glitter redly. On the western bank, there was nothing but fire and scorched earth, though the width of the river had kept the Cirandeiron side from kindling into flame. The fire didn't have neat edges; it raced ahead, gorging itself on underbrush, and lingered behind in the blackened areas, where the hearts of dead trees were filled with smoldering embers. Leaves were seared from the trees, and even where the fire had not yet touched, its baking heat had withered leaves and turned grass and moss to dust and tinder that glittered with sparks. Even with the river between him and the fire, Runacar had the uneasy feeling he was too close.

*And you mean to do this not to one part of Delfier-arathadan, but to the whole of it at the same time . . .*

He consoled himself with the knowledge that the plan had been made to save lives—Brightfolk, Otherfolk, perhaps even *alfaljodthi*. If the Otherfolk army could not stop the Lightborn, the Western Shore array would cut them to pieces. And if the War Princes won . . . how long would Daroldan and Amrolion be content to sit and watch as an Otherfolk *king-domain* established itself beyond their borders?

Suddenly there was a sudden loud resonant booming, audible even over the roaring of the fire. A clap of thunder, a sudden strike to a war-drum; there was no sound Runacar had ever heard that matched it precisely. And then . . .

The level of the river before him dropped sharply, and began to flow backward, much as Runacar had seen when he had forded the river. He watched, fascinated, as the entire river drained into the hole in its bed. Where was the water going? He wondered momentarily where the Angarussa ended, and if anyone would miss it.

Upriver, water continued to pour into the hole. Downriver the water level continued to drop, exposing mud, stones, riverweed, and flopping, gasping fish. The draining had already gone on for much longer than before; he supposed the Stonekin had dismantled the counterweight in addition to everything else they'd done. "Isn't it supposed to come out somewhere?" Runacar asked, forgetting that no one could hear him. The moment stretched . . .

And then, suddenly, from the midst of the inferno, came a high, whistling scream and a sound like a thunderclap. A dense fog, red-tinted by the flames, billowed swiftly out over the river.

*Steam. It must be,* he thought. But this was not the scalding heat of steam from a kettle. This was cool, damp, and utterly impenetrable. In moments, Runacar could not even see his own hand before his face. *If there were some way to reproduce this effect, to use it on the battlefield . . . we would not even need Lightborn to utterly blind the enemy . . .*

The roar of the fire and the thunder of the river became distant, muffled by the steam-fog. Above the muted roar of fire and water came a strident hissing. It was oddly familiar, but it took Runacar a moment to identify it. *It is the sound red-hot metal makes when the smith quenches it.*

Then the billows parted and he could see.

The forest floor had become a shining, silver lake. Here and there, jets of water bubbled up from below, making it look almost as if the lake was boiling. As Runacar stared in fascination, there was a glooping sound. Bubbles rose to the surface and the burnt skeletons of trees toppled over with slow grace as the forest floor fell away. Only the tops of the trees were burning now, and the fire had nowhere to go.

A ragged cheer went up from the defenders. As it swelled and grew, Runacar looked around at the fire teams—Centaurs, Minotaurs, Fauns, Gryphons, Woodwose, other Folk whose kind he did not know—and found himself unable to see them as anything but *people*.

People whom he must convince to set ablaze the same forest they had spent a moonturn trying to save.

❖

". . . and that didn't work, either."

The War Room of Daroldan Great Keep was the highest chamber in the castel. Light entered through long barred shafts lined with angled mirrors—on all the Shore, there was no window large enough for a child of five to pass through. Where the War Princes of other domains might reserve such a space for a private audience chamber or even a withdrawing room, the business of Daroldan was war, and war did not wait for War Season.

Palinoriel Warlord sighed, gazing down at the sand-table before him. It showed Amrolion and Daroldan's territories, but more than that, it showed which parts of them the *alfaljodthi* could move through safely, which parts they had never seen, and which parts they knew nothing about—because no one who had entered them had returned alive. Daroldan and Amrolion were beautiful, and rich, and cursed by the Silver Hooves to be a forcing-ground for battle.

"I am sorry, cousin. I could not think of what else to try."

"It's not your fault." Damulothir placed a hand on Palinoriel's shoulder; a brief absolution. "Any season but this, it would have worked."

"It's the Elves," Ladyholder Ereneine sighed. "Hard to imagine any of our blood making common cause with those animals, but who am I to argue with facts?"

"Vile as it is, in one way it would have made my work easier," Swordmaster Martenil said. "Except for the fact that every soul of the two tailles of spies I've sent to infiltrate that mob all vanished without trace. I might as well be drowning them in my bath for all the use that's been."

"And Daroldan's spells of Farseeing and Scrying are unequaled—and still useless," Rondithiel Lightbrother said. "Nor can any of the Warhunt approach them, no matter what illusions and stratagems we employ."

Belfrimrond Lightbrother bowed in acknowledgment, his mouth twitching in rueful agreement. "The Beastlings guard themselves well. I have no way, even, to know whether those Elves who march with them are captives, or cooperate freely. And before you ask, Prince Leopheine, it is as impossible to Farspeak either the High King or the Sanctuary of the Star as it has ever been, and—"

His words were cut off by a bright flash of violet light from outside accompanied by a gonging thud.

"And we are packed in here as tightly as fish in a net, while those darkspawn monsters drop rocks on us," Damulothir finished wearily.

"At least you killed the Aesalion," his wife said. "All praise to Belfrimrond."

"Send and Fetch are not yet beyond my poor powers, my lady," the Chief Lightborn said, bowing. "And we can hold Shield over Daroldan Keep for . . . quite some time yet."

"So we are trapped—alone—and embattled—alone," Leopheine said. "That's nothing new. Only . . . I do not think this battle will have a happy outcome."

The lords and ladies gathered here fell silent. Since the Beastling attacks had begun, every gambit they had tried had failed. They had lost more than half their Lords Komen at Amrolion Keep. The smaller assays were more successful only if you counted "success" as the survival of some of the attackers. A sennight ago, they had sent Rangers and Warhunt Mages out together, hoping to strike off the head of the army, or at least its wings. All that had accomplished was to make the army vanish. But not—apparently—to retreat.

"My Rangers await only your command to set forth in search of them," Tiralda, Chief of Rangers, said. "There is no place in Delfierarathadan we will not seek."

"We will not ask that of you, Tiralda—not yet," Damulothir said.

"And I'm sure we'll see the creatures again soon," his lady added acidly. "Whether you've found them or not."

Abruptly, Rondithiel turned toward the door. "Fresh news," he said, just as the door opened.

Isilla Lightsister stepped through the door and moved quickly to the nearest chair. Her shoulders were slumped in weariness, and her face was pale with the strain of recent effort. Like nearly all the Lightborn, she had adopted Shore customs when she came here, wearing the same dappled camouflage that the Rangers wore. But today she was dressed as formally as any Lightborn in a Prince's court: the long robe in Lightborn green, with its wide sash of the same material and color, and low soft leather boots dyed to match.

"The news is not good," Damulothir commented, gesturing for a page to bring Isilla a cup of wine. She downed it thirstily before she spoke.

"No, my lord, it is not," Isilla answered. "As you

know, with all other methods of gaining information denied to us, Lord Palinoriel suggested the hawks. As Overshadow is my Keystone Gift, I made the first trial. The only good news I have for you is that it worked, and I was able to bring the hawk back to its mews. It saw no sign of the army beneath the trees, and I do not need to tell you what is in the ocean, for you can see it yourself. But in the south . . ."

She took a deep breath, and in halting phrases told of what she'd seen through the hawk's eyes. The raging fire, quenched. The Angarussa, turned from its bed.

"I think it will remain in its new course," she said. "Much of the forest floor collapsed when it diverted. It will run to the sea."

"Well, that's one good thing about Cirandeiron having lifted up her skirts and fled," Ladyholder Ereneine said brightly. "Girelrian won't be there to complain of our misrule when those sea monsters take their new road into the heart of the West."

"There is more," Isilla said in a low voice. Belfrimiod and Rondithiel stood beside her now, offering what comfort they could. "The Beastlings stood by to watch it happen. There were Elves with them. One rode a Gryphon. I . . . I recognized his face."

"Well, don't keep us in suspense!" Ladyholder Arhondiniel of Amrolion said, breaking the silence at last. "Who was it? Not Hamphuliadiel. That would be too much to hope for."

"No, my lady," Isilla said wearily. "It was not Hamphuliadiel Astromancer. It was Lord Runacarendalur Caerthalien, brother to the Oathbreaker."

※

A sennight later there was a different—and far more private—meeting. Leopheine and Damulothir stood on the battlements of Daroldan Great Keep beneath the shimmering veil of Shield. The two War

Princes were the only ones on the tower. There was no need to watch for attack from above with the keep protected by Shield. Two or three times each candle-mark a stone would fall from the sky, dropped by fly-ing things too high to see. The Shield would flare more brightly, the missile would either shatter or rebound, and the wait would begin for the next one. By now, the land around Daroldan Great Keep was littered with fallen stones.

"If we don't leave before we have to, we'll never leave at all," Leopheine announced.

"Cryptic as ever, old friend. Clearly the south gave you a taste for riddles," Damulothir said gently.

"Not riddles," Leopheine said. "Just common sense. Caerthalien joining forces with the Beastlings . . . Well, that changes everything, doesn't it?"

"Too much, and not enough," Damulothir said grimly. "But we do not face Caerthalien, thank Sword and Star. Before Farspeech became impossible, we heard it was erased, just as Farcarinon was erased. The whole of its royal line died, to the last soul."

"Except for one," Leopheine said grimly. "And whether he is prince of nothing, or lord of a hundred thousand swords, it does not change the facts. How many komen of our combined meisne remain?"

Damulothir sighed, shaking his head. They both knew the answer to that: too few.

"And we do not know where Lord Caerthalien's forces are—only where they are not," Leopheine went on. "All we know is that they have not vanished for-ever."

"Clearly we are both quite knowledgeable," Dam-ulothir said acidly. "And you wish to say that we should flee."

"Daroldan will fall," Leopheine said quietly. "To star-vation, if to nothing else. And you are right to wish to hold it as long as you can. I pledge myself to this undertaking. But . . . our farmers, our herders, our lands-folk . . . they have no part in our last battle."

"You would have me send them east," Damulothir said. He shifted slightly, turning his gaze from the open land between forest and shore to the forest itself. "Through that."

"No," Leopheine said. "Send them north. Delfier-arathadan stops in the foothills of the Medharthas—you know that as well as anyone. It will be hard going, but safer than if they stay."

"If they go with an escort that can defend them," Damulothir said flatly. Since the moment their last gambit had failed, he had known this moment would come—the day every War Prince of the Western Shore dreaded. The day the Shore would fall at last. "Let it be done. I send my people east, to the Sanctuary of the Star. What say you, brother?"

"I as well," Leopheine said. "Your Rangers, my ko-men . . . let us pray that the Silver Hooves will take their sacrifice from those who remain, and not from those who go."

"Be thankful that our ancestors did not live to see this day," Damulothir said starkly.

⸙

They're moving." Bralros's statement roused Runa-car out of a fitful doze. He couldn't remember the last time he'd had a full night's sleep. Or hot tea. Or dry clothes. Evacuating the Flower Forest was harder than either scouring the Western Reach or attacking the Western Shore. There were water spirits, pond spirits, the forever-insufficiently-to-be-damned Dryads (apple, oak, ash, and several other kinds, none of which cooperated with each other), something called a Least Drake and something else called a Greater Serpent (Runacar couldn't tell them apart), and dozens more—not to mention the non-magical creatures such as deer, squirrels, and shore-apes. All of which had to be convinced to leave Delfierarathadan so that Runacar could burn it down in peace—a matter which every single one of them, seen and unseen, apparently wanted to *discuss*.

And the Otherfolk, of course, wanted to fight a war without losses.

It had been a very long four sennights.

"Who are moving? What? Did you finally get those damned Dryads to see reason?" He shoved his hair out of his eyes, thinking that if it weren't for the politics of the situation, he would have been delighted to set fire to that oak grove of viper-tongued harpies himself. The last time he'd said anything like that aloud, Keloit had reminded him that Harpies were actually rather mild-mannered. Unlike oak Dryads. Runacar was just as glad that he couldn't see them, or most of the folk they'd spent last moonturn trying to evacuate from the Flower Forest.

Bralros gave a dry cough of amusement. "The ladies continue to be obdurate. Leutric is sending an emissary who should be able to persuade them. Melisha should be here in a few days."

Leutric's call for aid to those who would help if they did not have to fight had been astonishingly successful. Audalo was pleased at this sign of cooperation with the King-Emperor, while Runacar wondered if the new recruits were more trouble than they were worth.

"Melisha isn't one of those invisible cats, is she?" he asked warily.

The Palugh resembled the small wild cat of the northern forests—if such creatures had been striped in a vivid orange and black, had the power to become invisible at will, and could talk—assuming you could answer the riddles they posed, which you *had* to solve if you wanted to actually manage to have a conversation with them.

Bralros smiled. "No, Rune, not an invisible cat, I promise. But why distress yourself over tomorrow when I have good news today? Just as you swore—the Houseborn are fleeing."

"They've left the Keep?" The news brought Runacar completely awake. "Which way are they going?"

"North," Bralros said. "Just as you swore they would."

"Is anyone following them?" Runacar asked.

"Not on the ground," Bralros answered. "Not yet, anyway. We wanted to ask your advice, first."

Runacar looked up through the forest canopy. The sky was still a dark steel-blue. "It's Drotha, isn't it? Drotha's the one who is following them."

Bralros sighed. "He volunteered. The Hippogriffs did not and the Gryphons are asleep."

"Of course he did," Runacar said wearily. "I just hope he remembers that they're supposed to *escape*."

It was time to call a council of war.

⊰⊱

"We finally have them moving in the direction we need them to," Runacar said, peering at the map that lay unscrolled across his knee. "They're doing as I'd do in their place—going north along the old Northern Road. According to reports, their force consists primarily of noncombatants—Craftworkers, fishers, farmers—along with the whole of their mounted forces."

"But you said they're still defending the castel," Keloit said, puzzled. "Why would they send their fighters away?"

"Because cavalry is very little use in a castel under siege," Runacar said patiently, "and destriers eat a lot of grain. What they've kept at the castel—or, at least, what I would have kept there in their place—will be the majority of their Rangers and at least half their

Lightborn—I'd keep as many as I could, but since the High King told them they're all the equal of princes, Damulothir and Leopheine probably don't have enough control over them to enforce that."

"You said that when they ran, we'd won," Tanet said suspiciously. "But now you say we have to keep fighting. Make up your mind, Houseborn."

"We've won when *all* of them are gone from the Shore," Runacar answered. "If we don't take—and smash—Daroldan Great Keep, the War Princes will call their folk back to it the moment they can. Once they've reinvested it, then they'll want to be sure we're gone. That means Rangers and Lightborn sweeping the forest—and if they get any idea of how many of us are here, they'll set another fire. And we're not ready for the fire yet."

"You *think*," Tanet said dubiously.

"Yes," Runacar said levelly. "I *think*. I think as they do. I was trained as they were. And I am telling you what they will do if we do not press our advantage. So what we must— The strategy I *suggest* is this: send an element of our force to chase the refugees and keep them moving east. So long as they see us following, they'll keep running. Once they've gone around the northern edge of the forest, they should continue on a southeastern salient until they reach the Trade Road. We want them to follow that, so we need to send messengers ahead to make certain there are no Otherfolk anywhere near their route—we don't want them to veer off in another direction. Meanwhile, as soon as the forest is ready to burn, the rest of us will attack Daroldan Great Keep. It's well within reach of the Ocean's Own, which works in our favor. Our goal is to get the defenders to abandon it if we can, and to kill them all if we can't—the refugees already in flight will be enough to undermine Hamphuliadiel's control over Areve."

It all sounded very fine, Runacar thought, but if he

had presented such a plan in his cadet days, both Lengiathion Warlord and Elrinonion Swordmaster would have asked the same single question: *How* were they going to besiege Daroldan Great Keep?

And Runacar had absolutely no idea.

It was at least a sennight before he had to worry about that, however: there was much to do beforehand, and most of it fell to him. He suggested the dispositions of the available forces and got his commanders to agree—with Audalo acting both as leader of the Minotaurs and as the voice of the King-Emperor. He sent the Folk of the Air—those who were not dropping rocks on the Keep, acting as messengers, or trying to coax the Brightfolk to relocate—to harry the refugees and to clear the path ahead of them. Runacar's sympathy for King Leutric increased every time he was brought up against the unwarlike nature of the Otherfolk.

*Unwarlike and disorganized, both. But I suppose it is like trying to use Landbonds as armsmen: except that not only are the Otherfolk not trained for it, most of them have never even seen an armsman.*

He could not spare any landbound combatants to follow those who fled Daroldan, but fortunately, one of the races who had answered Leutric's call for aid were the Wulvers, and unlike the Palugh, they were actually willing to be useful. Wulvers bore a faint resemblance to a hunting hound—just as Keloit did to a bear, or Pelere to a horse—and they could walk upright, though they preferred not to. They had no objections to harrying the Daroldan refugees, so long as that did not involve attacking them. Runacar was fairly sure the sight of a bustle of Wulvers would be enough to keep the Shorefolk fleeing until they reached the Mystrals

The evacuation of Delfierarathadan was nearly complete and the rest of the Folk were set to burn the Flower Forest. They had been provided with firepots filled with oil and scattered across the whole of Delfierarathadan forest in small groups: in the oil was a substance supplied by the Bearward Spellmothers that would begin to burn unquenchably the moment it was exposed to air or water. Once Runacar knew they were all in position—by which time those damned Dryads and everything else with a heartbeat should have moved east—he could set Delfierarathadan ablaze.

And as all the elements of the final battle moved into place, Runacar gathered up his army and began to march north once again.

⊰⊱

The sky was brilliantly blue, and far above, a lone hawk soared. Runacar rode Hialgo, and his armor gleamed brilliantly. *Mark the day,* Lord Bolecthindial would have said. *You don't know for certain you will ever see another.* In a few sunturns it would be Sword Moon, the traditional beginning of War Season. Runacar wondered if he was the last one who remembered the old calendar and the old festivals. He wondered what the High King's Court was like. He remembered, when he was a small boy—six? seven?—being set to work to help his father's Arming Page clean his armor. He'd been so filled with importance at the grandeur of the task that he'd been quite insufferable, and his elder brother Thorogalas had threatened to throw him from the watchtower of Caerthalien Keep.

Now Thorogalas and all the rest of his kin were dead, and so much of that history, that world, was gone and lost. Runacar had burned a fair portion of it himself, too. He wished he could still truly believe in the glory of war, but he suspected he'd lost that on the Plains of Ifjalasairaet, where Ivrulion had brought eternal shame to Caerthalien. He shook his head at his own foolishness: Caerthalien had been erased beyond shame or honor.

Daroldan Great Keep was visible in the distance, its shape undimmed by Shield, for the Folk of the Air had stopped their bombardment three sunturns ago. The Keep, for whatever mad reasons of its War Prince's ancestors, was built on a cliff directly overlooking the sea, and the Ocean's Own would move into formation at the foot of the cliffs at the same time the landbound army took up their positions on the landward side. The army was arranged as much for its effect on the defenders as it was for use, and the sea force moved parallel to them. Runacar knew with certainty that the combined force of the Otherfolk outnumbered the castel's defenders, and showing Daroldan the Otherfolk's superior numbers was a part of his strategy.

Everyone was on edge, even though it wasn't very likely that the War Princes knew what was about to happen. And even if they did, they'd committed to a tactical position that required them to hold Daroldan Keep, not make attacks on its besiegers.

So much was guesswork. Runacar would have given a great deal to have at his command the tools he knew: Warlord, Swordmaster, Lightborn. Those were weapons—people—he knew how to use in the grand game of war. The Otherfolk ...

The Otherfolk had no interest in becoming weapons.

❧❧

When Gunyel brought word that the last of the Hippogriff Flight had reported back—meaning the forest was ready to burn—Runacar called a halt even though it was only midday. They would make camp here. Setting Delfierarathadan ablaze would be far more dramatic at night, and he wanted the enemy to get the full benefit of the display.

The army fragmented into its usual groups to cook and gamble and gossip. Only Gunyel, Drotha, Keloit, and a handful of others remained beside Runacar.

Waiting. Tonight there were to be more sentries and night guards than ever before, for fire was not a thing you could order to perform at your whim, and the army needed to be wary of it. The Ocean's Own had promised to evacuate them seaward at need, but there were still almost ten thousand persons in this camp and Runacar did not relish the prospect of trying to outrun a wildfire.

It was a candlemark before sunfall when Runacar at last gave the order.

"Set it alight," he said quietly, and as soon as Gunyel took off, the whole Flight of Hippogriffs rushed into the sky with a booming thunder of wings. They wheeled once over the shore, gaining altitude, then flew eastward, scattering north and south as they flew. The fires would be set from east to west. Only the eastern line of teams needed to be commanded to begin: as they set their fires and headed westward, their arrival at each site would be the signal for that group to set its own blazes.

Nothing else happened.

"Anticlimactic," Drotha said after a moment or two.

"It will take time," Runacar said. "But the final effect will be worth it."

⊰⊱

Night came, but aside from a certain watchfulness among the folk, it was a very ordinary night. There was singing and dancing—not harp or flute or any instrument Runacar had known in his life *Before,* but they made an exotic and beautiful noise. He caught a few scraps of "The Rout of Caerthalien," and took a moment to wish he'd never given in to Radafa's desire to learn the songs of his enemies.

*"Caerthalien ran and left behind / Bread and meat and silk and wine / Horses, hawks, and huntsmen bold / Chains of silver and chains of gold / Swords of price*

*and armor bright / Left behind there in the night / Caer-
thalien ran and left behind . . ."*

He found himself singing along under his breath and
forced himself to stop. The tune was mesmerizing, but
the battle itself held too many terrible memories. They
should have seen the truth even then. They should have
known what Vieliessar was. But greed and ambition
and willful blindness had been like fetters of gold and
lead. And no one had.

He collected a skin of beer—Bralros had told him
once that there was no point in doing anything at all if
you didn't have beer to drink while you did it—and
found a comfortable rock to sit on. He put his back to
the sea and stared in the direction of the forest. It was
still dark.

He tipped a little of the beer onto the sand. "Lord of
the Starry Hunt," he said, his voice a bare whisper, "forgive that this sacrifice is not blood. Forgive that it is
not made for your people, but for these others. Only
grant us victory here, and . . ." He could think of nothing to add. A promise of proper sacrifices? There was a
Shrine somewhere in Delfierarathadan, but he was
about to burn the forest over it. A promise of war? The
Otherfolk wanted battles without casualties. "Only
grant us victory," he repeated awkwardly. "Please."

If They heard, They did not answer in any way he
could hear.

❦

By the time the moon rose—a fingernail crescent in
the sky—Runacar could see a faint ruddy glow in
the distance: the light of the fire reflecting off the
smoke of the burning. *They can see it now, if they look.
But do they understand that by morning the whole forest will be burning?* There was little scent of smoke,
and anyone at Daroldan who did smell smoke would
probably think it came from the army's cook-fires.

It was the largest act of destruction Runacar had ever been personally responsible for and he could not keep himself from thinking of the Ghostwood. That Flower Forest had been even larger than this one. The manner of destruction was different, but the result would be the same.

*"I name this place Ishtilaikh! Ruin!"*

When he finished the skin of ale, Runacar wandered along the camp's perimeter, checking in with the watches and trying to gauge the progress of the fire. In theory, those not on watch should be sleeping, but nearly everyone was still awake. He knew he was not entirely welcome among them, even now, so before it became an issue, he returned to the edge of the shore to pace there. The wet sand was firmer, anyway.

*They started the burning before sunfall and it's nearly the wolf hour now. What's taking so long?*

"It won't burn either faster or slower for you staring at it," Pelere said, coming up to him. She held out a steaming leather tankard. "Drink, if you won't sleep."

Runacar drank thirstily. The mulled ale took some of the chill from the night. "So much could go wrong," he said aloud.

"And yet, you said this was the safest way to win, and everyone knows Leutric wants to win."

"So do we," another voice said.

Runacar turned toward the ocean. It was one of the Ocean's Own who had spoken: small as a Faun, it somewhat resembled one, save for the fact it was covered in shining scales. It was impossible to tell their true color by moonlight. Blue? Green?

"If the killers are gone, we will have the sand for dancing again," the sea-Faun said, blinking its large pale eyes. "We will have the rivers for swimming. No longer will we have to hide beneath the waves, waiting for dark moon nights to sneak ashore. No longer will our nests be destroyed, our eggs broken. You have given us the great river to walk upon and now you burn the nests of the killers. This is a good thing."

Having said what it came to say, the sea-Faun turned and dived into the wave, vanishing from sight.

Runacar sighed. "And I suppose the forest will grow back, someday," he said. "And the fire won't overrun all of us before it burns itself out."

"You're gloomy tonight," Pelere said. "I'll be glad when Andhel gets back to cheer you up."

"She won't approve, you know," Runacar said. "She complains about everything I do, and how I do it, and— probably—about the fact I'm still breathing."

Pelere gave him an opaque look, switching her tail meditatively. "And have you ever wondered why that is?"

Runacar shrugged. "Not really," he said.

Pelere shook her head. "And yet your kind became the masters of the world. I give you good night, Runacar. Some of us intend to sleep."

"Sleep well," Runacar said automatically. "And without dreams."

*I wish I might never dream again,* he thought.

⊰⊱

Dawn came, and in the far distance smoke was a dark veil in the air. By midday, Hippogriffs and Gryphons had begun bringing out the fire-teams that had been running across the forest since yesterday's sunfall. Despite the fact that many of them had been working desperately to stop the forest from burning only a moonturn before, there was a Festival Fair atmosphere to the day, with cheering and boasting and lurid recountings of wild feats of pyromania. It was both too familiar and too alien for Runacar to take any comfort in it—so much like the revelry following a sunturn of battle, and at the same time so different.

By sunfall, the last of the fire-teams had left the forest

and the fire was bright enough to cast shadows even on the shore.

*They'll see the smoke on the other side of the Mystrals,* Runacar thought, knowing it to be a fanciful notion. But the nagging question at the back of his mind never quite went away: *Where are they? Where is she? Why doesn't she come back?*

He found Keloit and asked him to pass the word that they would march in the morning, then curled up in his stormcloak to sleep.

## CHAPTER SEVENTEEN

# SWORD MOON:
# SMOKE AND VEILS

*As the Light is the heartbeat of the world, so the Lightborn are its guardians. They pledge to no faction, for their greatest allegiance must always be to Creation itself, not to any of the forms in which Creation manifests.*

— Mosirinde Astromancer, *The Covenant of the Light*

Herdwatch was one of the pleasanter tasks that a Lightborn might find themselves doing. It fell only to the older and more experienced Lightborn, for if their help were needed, it would be needed instantly, without self-doubt or hesitation. Today, Harwing was assigned this duty, and so he rose at First Bell and, in company with his brethren, quickly washed and dressed. But while they proceeded to the Refectory, Harwing did not. Today he and the other Lightborn sharing his duty would take their meals with the herders.

The chosen Lightborn walked in sleepy silence from the Sanctuary toward the Western Gate. Some Harwing knew well, like Ulvearth Lightsister and Irchel Lightbrother, and others less so—those who had trained at the Sanctuary outside of his Postulant years. The Candidates now came entirely from Areve, but Light be praised that they still came, for there was nowhere else for them to come from. The village had grown until its walls enclosed more space than a Great Keep. Stone houses and dormitories lined wide streets in orderly array—by unspoken agreement from the earliest days, living space expanded northward while storage and workrooms expanded westward.

*Which still doesn't keep the tanners and soap-boilers far enough away from everyone's noses,* Harwing thought irrepressibly. *How wise Hamphuliadiel was to find the komen who came to us so many tasks, for it would not do the people good to see them idle, yet they are truly not good for much but fighting . . .*

As always since his awakening, his thoughts ran in two rivers, and the uppermost one contained only the most loyal and innocent of thoughts. No matter where he was, or who he was with, Harwing guarded himself closely. The final task he had set himself was one too important to fail.

The drovers and their dogs were gathering their charges from goat pen, sheepfold, and barn, and the village gates had been opened by the komen. Harwing waved farewell to Irchel, who was (as always) sent with the horses, while he and Ulvearth joined Herder Ongil with the goats. The moment the beasts were unpenned they went racing through the gates, with the herd-dogs galloping after.

"Where shall we feast today, Master Herder?" Harwing teased lightly.

Ongil awarded him a small smile. "We go west to clear the nettles and thorn bushes, so the sheep may graze there after. T'will make good farmland next planting season, unless we leave it fallow another year," he said, turning to walk after his charges.

Harwing gestured for Ulvearth to precede him, and the two Lightborn followed the herdsman. Harwing had known Ulvearth from his Sanctuary days, and so he knew she was from the Western Shore—

*He knew she had come from Daroldan to beg the Sanctuary for help and had never been heard from again.*

—and so it would be reasonable of him to wonder how she had come here. But he never did. Nor did he think of what he knew anywhere anyone might hear his thoughts.

Even her.

They walked side by side through the grass in silence as the sun rose and brought color to the world. The dawn birds fell silent, and the birds of day took their place. The wind blew from the west, and the air was filled with the clang of herd-bells, the occasional barking of the dogs, and the muttered complaints of the herds as they dispersed to graze.

"Harwing," Ulvearth said, stopping and putting a hand on his arm. "Do you smell that? It's smoke."

"What? Where?" Fire was always a danger in a village or town. But the wind was blowing toward Areve, not away.

"There," Ulvearth said, pointing. "You can see it, too."

He followed her gesture with his gaze. There, on the far horizon, the sky was not blue, but grey. And not merely in one place, as a forest might burn from a careless fire or a lightning strike, but all along the horizon. The wind strengthened, and now he could smell it as she did. Smoke. A forest fire.

He quickly told over the map he carried in his mind. Ullilion lay west of here, but it had been burnt over a decade before. Beyond Ullilion lay Cirandeiron . . .

He looked at Ulvearth questioningly. Her face was pale and grim. "It is Delfierarathadan that burns," she said, as if to herself. "It can be nothing else."

⊰⊱

The messenger from Areve's watchtower had reached the Sanctuary just after the morning meal, but by the time he did the news he carried was already known. From the highest window of the Astromancer's tower, the veil of smoke could be clearly seen, and Hamphuli-adiel had seen it.

The Astromancer spent little time in the tower from which the stars were tracked in their courses, for to bring his acolytes here might raise thoughts in their minds of who was to be the next Astromancer, and that would be unfortunate. This abstinence was no hardship, for Hamphuliadiel took little interest in the paths of the stars at the best of times; the secrets he wished to know were written on the land, not in the sky. But this morning he had risen as early as any of his Lightborn and hurried to climb the long and winding stair to the tower's very top. His dreams had been unsettled—as they so often were these days—and he had . . .

The comforting lies his thoughts formed died away unfinished as he gazed out the western window of the tower. *You have come to prove to yourself that your dream was an empty and meaningless thing, Hamphu-liadiel of Haldil, while knowing it was not. No wind will blow away this black cloud . . .*

Hamphuliadiel's Keystone Gift was Farseeing, some-thing that had been of great use to him on many occa-sions. Today, it brought him horrors. The Angarussa gone, its bed dry and empty. The forest beyond, blaz-ing red-gold the whole of its length and breadth, the smoke of that great burning rising into the sky in just the way that blood would eddy through a bowl of clear water. The Flower Forest was burning. Delfieraratha-dan of the Shrine was burning.

Past that conflagration he could see nothing, for Far-seeing only permitted one to see things, not to see through them, but Hamphuliadiel did not need to see more than flames to know far more than he wished to. Amrolion and Daroldan were lost. The Beastlings had destroyed them.

Until this moment, Hamphuliadiel had been content to let the Beastlings bellow and rave through the wilderness until he had a use for the land they occupied. They had been useful in ridding him of challenges to his rule, and their raids against Areve had been easily rebuffed. At the bottom of his mind he had supposed that in a Wheelturn, or perhaps two, he would send an embassy to the Western Shore to humble those proud princes and bring them beneath his authority. They would swear fealty to the Sanctuary of the Star, and bring him their wealth and their armies, and that would set the capstone and seal upon his rulership.

And now he knew there were no longer any armies, any War Princes, any wealth. The Western Shore had fallen to the Beastlings.

Hamphuliadiel Astromancer, Sovereign Lord of Areve and the Sanctuary of the Star, was . . . concerned.

❧

"They will not come here," Momioniarch said. "They are afraid of us."

Hamphuliadiel had gathered his Lightborn advisors to him in his inner chamber. Galathornthadan had already set the whispers circulating: the Western Shore burned, but it was merely the just vengeance of the Silver Hooves on those who had pledged to the traitor and usurper, Vieliessar Lightsister. Those whispers would be enough . . . so long as the Beastlings stayed on the Western Shore.

"They do not seem to have been particularly afraid of Daroldan and Amrolion," Sunalanthaid said. "And those domains had many Lightborn aiding them."

"Unless they fled," Momioniarch replied. "Or refused to fight."

"Even to save their own lives?" Sunalanthaid asked.

"Silence." Hamphuliadiel had not raised his voice. He did not need to. His four acolytes fell instantly silent, looking to him to speak. "Many have suggested that the Beastlings have found a leader. These are only unlearned guesses, but even a fool may guess rightly on the Midwinter cake. What have you learned?"

"Little, Lord Astromancer," Momioniarch admitted. "Birds will not fly through the smoke, nor deer approach the flames, so Overshadow can see nothing. Nor can the weather be worked to bring rain to douse the blaze."

"My sister in the Light tells no more than the truth." Orchalianiel spoke for the first time. "The west reeks of Beastling sorcery. Nothing of the Light can pierce that veil."

"And yet," Hamphuliadiel said with heavy irony, "I have heard tell that among the Lightborn there are some whose Keystone Gift is Fire. Perhaps such a one might be of some small use."

"Tangisen Lightbrother was the strongest in that Gift who ever served here," Momioniarch said reluctantly. "But he was among those who went west with the traitor Rondithiel. And even Tangisen himself could not work Fire over such an area as we see burning."

"I do not wish to make this small matter seem great to tale-bearers by sending an array to investigate it," Hamphuliadiel said briskly. *Whether they were slaughtered and vanished without a trace, or returned bearing a river of gossip I could not staunch, the risk would be too great.* "But . . . perhaps a small party. Three or four at most. If there are any survivors of the Western Shore Domains, we must of course open our walls to them in mercy and charity, no matter our past quarrels. But those whom we send must be . . . adaptable. And loyal."

There was a moment of silence, then Momioniarch spoke.

"Why, I think you must already know what I would say if I were asked, Lord Astromancer," she said blandly. "Who shall we send but Harwing and Ulvearth? They will suit this purpose well."

Hamphuliadiel smiled. "Just such names as were already in my thoughts, Lightsister. They shall go upon this mission of mercy as soon as the moon is full once more."

⊰⊱

The Great Keep of Daroldan was a block of stone skirted by a vast open space of short grass and sandy soil, built at the very edge of a sheer cliff. The outermost castel wall extended past the edge of the cliff, making the structure impossible to surround, and there was no concealment to be found between Daroldan's walls and the verge of Delfierarathadan. The outermost edge of the Flower Forest lay four leagues away, and the land sloped slowly upward for the entire distance between there and the castel, so that any attack upon Daroldan's Great Keep must be made across a rising grade. The open ground near the castel was hard-packed from centuries of use as a mustering and drilling ground, and was now covered to the distance of a bowshot with the stones the Folk of the Air had dropped upon the tower, rendering the footing even more treacherous.

When the Otherfolk army was within a dozen furlongs of its walls, it began moving up to encircle the great dark tower on its landward side—as none of Daroldan's remaining defenders was lunatic enough to hazard a descent into the ocean and what waited there for them, a semi-encirclement would be enough. It would take the attacking force most of the sunturn to take their chosen positions—Runacar had not bothered with any specific orders, other than that they stay out of bowshot range and not fall off the cliff.

After sennights of aerial bombardment, Daroldan Keep no longer possessed any of its wooden watchtowers, but the Otherfolk army would be visible from any landward window—as would the Flower Forest. By now smoke poured from Delfierarathadan as from a smelter's chimney—the fire had not yet reached the near edge of the forest, but it was probably visible from the higher windows of the Keep.

Even at twelve leagues' distance, the Otherfolk army would be at risk from the fire once the fire reached the forest's western edge. The larger it grew, the faster it moved; his scouts kept an eye on its progress, but even they could not say when the flames would reach the western edge. Even before they did, the heat would be enormous, and because of the updrafts, the Folk of the Air would have to withdraw seaward early on. The fire would also make an eastward retreat impossible, and even so deep a battlefield was a small area in which to maneuver so many thousands of troops. Runacar was counting on the sight of the two Otherfolk armies— land and sea—and the sight of the Flower Forest unquenchably ablaze to convince Daroldan's defenders to commit to a hasty attack that might give the Otherfolk the chance to storm the castel. He had chosen his own position in the vanguard to put him directly opposite the entrance to the keep. There was no moat—why bother, when so many of your attackers could fly?—but the outer gates of the fortress were an interlocking series of bronze gridirons that ran the whole thickness of the outer wall. They glittered in the bright sunlight.

They glittered even more as they began to move.

Runacar stared for a moment, at first thinking it was the fire glittering off the metal that gave an illusion of movement. He instantly dismissed that notion as the cloudwittedness it was, but was left staring at the gates in disbelief. No besieged force opened its gates to the enemy in the first sunturn of a siege.

"What are they doing?" Keloit asked. "Are they coming out?"

"Maybe," Runacar said. "Stay back. Tell everyone to be ready." *Though for what, I cannot imagine.*

As Keloit bounded off to pass the word, Runacar let

Hialgo pace forward a few more steps, and then stopped, automatically raising his hand in the signal "halt column." He could almost feel the ripple of stillness pass through the Otherfolk behind him. If Daroldan had more komen than he'd thought, the mounted knights would be able to cut a column into shreds.

The gates took a very long time to open.

Frause came up on his tuathal side, and another Spellmother, Helfgand, to his deosil. The two Bearwards flanked him in silent—and wary—support. Runacar didn't know if their magic could protect him from the enemy's Lightborn, but he supposed he'd have to find out sometime.

Then Drotha landed with a thump just in front of Frause, causing Runacar to startle and Hialgo, responding to the unintentional command, to rear. Drotha turned toward Runacar, grinning widely. "They're coming out to fight? Excellent!"

"'Stupid,' you mean, you great fool," Helfgand said, wrinkling her muzzle disdainfully. "Why come out if they can sit and starve in peace?"

"I see something," Frause said quietly.

Runacar looked. A single mounted figure was coming through the gate—a Lightborn in the traditional green robe of office, riding a white palfrey mare. The Lightborn carried a banner: it was white, without blazon, and its carrying pole was wreathed in greenneedle boughs.

"By the hooves and teeth of the Starry Hunt," Runacar said incredulously. "They want to *parley*?" His mind reeled. It was the very last thing he could have imagined. *Are they that dismayed by Delfierarathadan's burning? If so, I could have set it alight moonturns ago and saved all of us this bother.*

The Lightborn was followed by two other figures, also on white palfreys, also carrying greenneedle-wreathed banners, and both dressed entirely in white.

But only the pennons of their banners were white: one carried the grey and gold banner of Daroldan, its gilded waves and flowers glinting brightly, and the other the three silver fishes against the blue of Amrolion.

"Sword and Star," Runacar whispered to himself. "That's Leopheine and Damulothir—under a truce flag."

The three figures rode through the scattered stones until they had covered perhaps a third of the distance between Daroldan's walls and the Otherfolk army. There they stopped. And waited.

"Do we kill them now?" Drotha asked brightly. The Aesalion's colors were brilliant in the sun, and his black wings held all the iridescent blues and purples of a raven's feathers.

"No," Runacar said. "Somebody find me a greenneedle tree."

Frause's head whipped toward him incredulously. "You aren't actually planning to play their stupid Elf-games, are you?" she demanded.

"Yes," Runacar said evenly. "I am. No one parleys this early if they intend to fight. If nobody fights, we win."

"And if you die?" Frause asked.

"Then you follow the plans I've already made. Kill them, and drive the others through the Dragon's Gate."

"Those are stupid plans," Drotha said, raising his barbed tail over his back.

Runacar merely shrugged.

⊰⊱

The party from Daroldan Keep did not move once in the candlemark it took Runacar's side to make its preparations. Frause insisted on going with him, in case magic was used; Drotha swore he wanted to see "Real Elves" up close, and as always, there was no way to make an Aesalion do anything it didn't want to. Runacar supposed that attending a parley with an Aesalion and a Bearward would at least make his position clear. He had participated in more parleys than he could number when he was Heir-Prince of Caerthalien. This was the first one he wasn't sure he'd survive.

"Do not, for the love of all, speak a word, either of you," Runacar said. "Even if they parley in good faith, the parley-truce may not extend to either of you."

Frause snorted dismissively and Drotha laughed.

The three of them moved forward. Runacar held his banner aloft; they'd tied the crown of a greenneedle tree to it, indicating he had agreed to the parley and would abide by its rules, but he had not removed his armor. He brought Hialgo to a stop at the prescribed distance and lifted the visor of his helmet.

"I am Runacar, Warlord to Leutric, King-Emperor. I accept your truce, abiding by the Covenants of War agreed to and upheld by the Hundred Houses, and will hear your words."

The Lightsister holding the truce-banner looked back at the two War Princes. Her face was white with terror.

"Allow us to dismiss our envoy, now that she is no longer needed," Prince Damulothir said.

"She may withdraw, but she may not leave the parley field," Runacar answered. "You shock me, Damulothir Daroldan. Surely Nimphaeros taught you better than that." Ladyholder Nimphaeros of Daroldan— Damulothir's mother—had also been its Warlord.

"By the Starry Hunt—it *is* him!" Leopheine said. "Runacarendalur Caerthalien, War Prince of Caerthalien-that-was . . . how come you to this evil day?"

"You called me here to ask me that?" Runacar asked in return, trying very hard not to show how hard the

inadvertent blow had struck. *"Caerthalien-that-was"*—
the whole of his House had been erased. *Just as Farcarinon was. Vieliessar and I are now equals in that at
least.*

Damulothir gestured to the Lightsister. She backed
her horse between theirs, retreating until she was at the
very limit of the distance that could still be considered
a part of the parley field. The two War Princes conferred, speaking too low for Runacar to hear.

"Will you approach, Lord Runacarendalur?" Damulothir asked. "Alone?"

Runacar looked toward Frause. "If they are honoring the truce this far, they are within their rights to ask
to speak to me alone. If you remain where you are, that
will be an acceptable distance. Should you move—either
of you," he said, looking meaningfully at Drotha, "the
truce is void and they will be within their rights to kill
all three of us."

"They can *try*," Drotha purred, twitching the tip of
his poisonous tail.

"What do they care what talking animals do?" Frause
asked bitterly.

"They don't," Runacar said. "But a parley truce has
rules, and they can't just toss out the ones they don't
like. Now hold this, and don't drop it—if you drop it,
the truce is over instantly," he said, passing her his
bough-adorned banner. He looked back at the two War
Princes. "My companions are protected under the laws
of truce. They are not to be harmed or influenced. Do
you agree?"

There was another pause as Damulothir and Leopheine conferred.

"We agree, with the condition that neither are they
to harm or influence any of our party," Leopheine said.
"Do you agree to this condition?"

"Do not cause me to forswear myself," Runacar said
softly to Drotha. Then, louder: "We accept this condi-

tion." He sent Hialgo forward at a slow walk. The distance to the two War Princes seemed interminable. "Well?" he said when he got there.

"Be grateful that your father did not live to see this day," Damulothir said in low furious tones. "At least he is spared that shame."

"If what my brother did could not kill him outright—and I was there: it didn't—you can't imagine this would have," Runacar said. "You did not call this parley to criticize my life choices. Tell me what you want."

"We want you to take your pack of monsters and your traitorous *alfaljodthi* and go away!" Leopheine said. "You—You have set fire to Delfierarathadan!"

For a moment Runacar stared at him incredulously, and then—he couldn't help it—he began to laugh. The insanity of all this was too much, coming as it did on top of sennights and moonturns of tension and unfamiliar fear. He laughed until his armor groaned in protest, until clutching at the pommel of his saddle was the only thing that kept him in it.

"You— You— *You did it first!*" he gasped between spasms of mirth. It was the essence of every childhood excuse: *He started it, Master—not I!*

At last he managed to compose himself. "Yes," he said gravely. "We did indeed set fire to Delfierarathadan. We evacuated it first, which is more than you bothered to do. If you have called this parley to lodge a complaint about our activity upon the battlefield, I must point out that you yourselves are also in great violation of Arilcarion's Code for rendering Amrolion Keep a trap, as the Code plainly says that commonly-held places of refuge must be maintained without trap or restriction. Though I am not sure where we would find a tribunal to judge the matter these days," he added.

Both War Princes were staring at him as if he had suddenly turned into an Aesalion. Runacar sternly controlled his hilarity at the thought. The sense of unreality he'd felt when Daroldan had opened its gates was even stronger now. It gave him the sensation of having downed an entire tankard of brandy on an empty stomach.

"He's mad," Leopheine said to Damulothir, loud enough for Runacar to hear.

"Mad or sane, he is the leader of this . . . rabble," Damulothir said.

"My lords," Runacar interrupted. "Did you mistake me? I am this *army's* Warlord only. Its generals remain with its troops, and we fight at the command of King-Emperor Leutric. Now. Why am I here?"

There was a pause, the only sound the crying of seagulls and the surf breaking on the rocks at the foot of the cliff.

"So that you may tell us your terms," Damulothir said levelly. "With Delfierarathadan burning, our Light-born are already powerless. We knew you were among those monsters, and originally I had thought to rescue you with this parley. But now I see you are worse than Ivrulion Banebringer ever was."

There was a moment of silence, and Runacar realized Damulothir would say nothing more.

"Our terms are these," Runacar said, and to his ears his own voice seemed to come from a very long way away. "Leave. Take with you whatever you wish—save any living thing you hold enslaved—and leave this place. Should you agree to these terms, we will give you a fortnight's truce, during which we will not pursue you. But when the moon is full once more, that truce is over."

"How can we possibly trust you?" Leopheine demanded. "You consort with those . . . things."

"As you have so kindly pointed out, my own brother was a greater monster than any you now call by that name—and his blood was notably pure. Whether you trust me or not is hardly my concern, my lord Prince.

You asked for our terms. I have given them to you. You may have three sunturns to consider them under truce. After that time, we will presume you reject our terms. Is this acceptable?" He knew perfectly well it wasn't, but the forms of the parley truce required him to ask the question and receive its answer.

"It is acceptable," Damulothir said, and Leopheine, still glaring furiously, echoed his words.

"Then we shall await your word, my lord Princes," Runacar said. "Eagerly."

After that there was nothing but a long nerve-wracking wait as the two War Princes backed their palfreys to where the Lightsister waited. As the three of them turned their horses' heads toward the gates of the keep, Runacar was finally free to return to where Frause and Drotha waited. He let out a sigh of relief he hadn't known he was holding: Drotha had stayed put.

"I don't suppose I can chase them *now*?" the Aesalion asked in pitiful tones.

"Not for three sunturns," Runacar said. "And a fortnight more if they agree to our terms."

Upon returning to the others, Runacar had immediately briefed Riann on the essence of the parley, and asked her to send her Gryphons to both the Otherfolk following the Elven refugees and to King-Emperor Leutric to let him and them know what had happened. Then he settled in to tell it all again, and in more detail, to the leaders of the various elements of the army, both of land and sea. This necessitated the war council taking place at the shore, which meant backtracking to a beach beyond the cliffs. He was glad of the interruption, for it allowed him to organize his thoughts, and to settle in his mind the answers he could give to the questions he would probably be asked.

"Do you think they'll do it?" Tanet asked.

"I have no idea," Runacar said. He looked around for Andhel and did not see her. Well, that was one less dissenting voice to deal with just now. "Damulothir said their original notion was to rescue me from you—from the Otherfolk, at least, as they still think you Woodwose are *alfaljodthi*. I can only assume that some of the Lightborn we fought must have recognized me; who they think *you* are, or where they imagine you have come from, only the Hunt knows. But my rescue couldn't have been their entire plan even if it was a part of it—I assure you, were I Damulothir's dearest child, he would not risk the lives of all under his command to save just me."

"So . . . they wanted to talk to you, and they knew that if they paraded their Houseborn nonsense, you'd come," Tanet said. "And you did. What do they gain?"

"Time," Runacar said instantly. "If all parties honor the agreement, that's three sunturns they have in which we aren't attacking them."

"That isn't long," Amrunor said. The sea-horse knelt in the wet sand, his elongated body stretching back into deeper water where he twitched his flukes irritably. "What can they do in three days?"

"Reinforcements?" Pelere asked. "When you know help is on the way . . ."

". . . you stall for time," Runacar said, finishing the Centauress's thought. "But help *isn't* on the way. They sent off their noncombatants and their livestock almost a sennight ago, and sent their komen to protect them. Our sentries have seen no sign of them turning back. Daroldan doesn't *have* the resources to make an attack."

"Maybe they just want some time to beg their gods to intercede," Amrunor said.

Runacar laughed shortly. "If a warrior doesn't die in battle, they don't go to join the Starry Hunt no matter how much they pray, nor will the Hunt aid them. But

they have to have *something* in mind . . ." He frowned.
Back when it had still been possible to spy on Vielies-
sar's army—before the False Parley, before the flight
through the Dragon's Gate—the Alliance had learned
that Vieliessar had gained the fealty and pledge of both
Amrolion and Daroldan with a single simple promise:
she would not ask them to leave the Shore undefended.
With that promise, she had bought their loyalty. That
Runacar and the Otherfolk could break their will and
their hope and force them to flee—that was possible.
But what was not possible was that Damulothir and
Leopheine would just surrender.

"This is a trap," he said slowly, "but I can't figure it
out. Are you *sure* there's no possible ally anywhere near
Daroldan Great Keep?"

"The only Elves outside of the Keep—and west of
Areve—are the ones who are running away," Bralros
said. "We had that report just this morning. You were
there."

"And they're still heading toward the Sanctuary,"
Runacar said with a sigh. "Even if they doubled back,
we'd have word of it sunturns before they got here, and
Daroldan's Warlord must know that. I suppose we'll
just have to wait Damulothir and Leopheine out." *I
know I'm missing something, but what?*

⊰⊱

B y now the whole sky was black with smoke, and if
the wind hadn't been steadily off the water, the air
would have been unbreatheable. The forest continued
to burn, and neither the Otherfolk magicians nor the
scouts reported any attempt to douse it. As the army
waited, Runacar made plans for afterward, since even
if the army took Daroldan Keep, there was a possibility the fire would cut off their retreat along the southern flanks of the Medhartha Range. The Ocean's Own

seemed confident that an evacuation by sea could easily be accomplished, even during the final battle, if necessary.

The fact that settling this necessitated his spending a great deal of time down at the water's edge—where the air was cool and fresh—nearly made up for the frustration of holding a conversation with any of the Ocean's Own.

"And how would you keep them from cutting us to pieces while we ran?" Runacar asked, striving to keep the exasperation out of his voice.

"Our folk can shake the earth—and better than any Earthdancer of the Minotaurs," Amrunor said smugly. "The difficulty, Runacar, is that it is not . . . precise. It is done by sorcery, true, but a sorcery that pulls the flaws in the rock apart. After that, it is the rock's choice what it will do."

"So it would shake us—and possibly toss us into Great Sea Ocean—along with them," Runacar said.

"And their tower would probably fall on top of you when it did," Meraude added. "Still . . . it can be done."

*And you've never thought of doing it in all the centuries we've occupied the Shore?* With an effort, he kept himself from saying the words out loud, but . . . *I know I will never truly understand the Otherfolk, the Ocean's Own most of all. Certainly while my people cruelly oppressed the Folk of the Land—and the Folk of the Air when we could—the Ocean's Own have always been able to swim away from that which displeased them. And Great Sea Ocean is a land a thousand times vaster than the whole of Jer-a-kalaliel. That they are willing, now, to work so closely with the Folk of the Land . . .*

. . . was a tribute both to King Leutric's diplomacy and to their fear—a fear the *alfaljodthi* had never managed to raise in them.

*They believe "the Darkness" is coming, and soon, and what they are willing to do makes me wonder if*

*they know anything more than that. Sword and Star
know that Vieliessar was wonderfully vague about the
great peril that meant she needed to become High King.
Perhaps if I see her again in this life I should ask her
for more details.*

But despite more meetings and councils than could
occupy a dozen Harvest Courts, no one could truly
make plans until they knew what Daroldan and Amrolion meant to do. And no matter what decision the
War Princes came to, they were unlikely to announce it
before the end of the parley truce.

*Even if Daroldan managed to get a spellbird to the
High King, they cannot hope she will lift the siege in
time to save them; I know she isn't on this side of the
Mystrals, because the Gryphons and the Hippogriffs
would send word. And it's a moonturn and a half—even
at the speed she moves—from the Dragon's Gate to the
Shore . . .*

And still Runacar had the frustrating sense he was
missing something.

⊰⊱

Today the War Princes would come when the sun
was at midheaven to give their answer, so Runacar spent the morning polishing his armor and Hialgo's
tack until they gleamed. It was simple mindless work
that left him ample time to worry about what was to
come. Over and over, he summoned the events of the
parley to his mind: the Lightsister with her white banner and greenneedle garland—poor creature, she'd
looked terrified. And so very young. She must have
been among the last of the Lightborn to leave the Sanctuary before the war . . .

She was young.

She was young and . . .

"*Sword and Star!*" Runacar gasped. He sprang to his
feet. "Pelere!" he shouted. "Radafa! *Frause!*"

※

I t was in front of us all along. A senior Lightborn, Chief Lightborn of one or the other domains, that's who should have been there for the parley. I don't know them by sight, but whoever it was, it wasn't her. She was only a child! Radafa—how many Lightborn went with the refugees?"

"Oh," said Andhel, "here's where the masterful Houseborn proves the Houseborn know things others can merely guess at."

Runacar gave her a poisonous look.

"None," the Gryphon answered, puzzled. "At least, none wearing their robes. I suppose they all might have been Lightborn. Or none of them."

"And that's what we—*I!*—assumed: that none of the Lightborn, or very few, had gone—because if Damulothir truly meant to hold Daroldan, he would have to use Lightborn to do it," Runacar said.

"But how do we know whether the Green Robes are here or there?" Pelere asked. "There's no way to tell by looking."

"Unless you're an Aesalion," Andhel put in.

Runacar rounded on her again. "If you have something to say, say it outright," he said in a dangerous voice.

"You already know you can't use magic on an Aesalion," she said in long-suffering tones. "And even you must have realized by now that they can't see it being used, either. Clever Houseborn—you managed to figure out how to kill Juniche anyway."

The only magic used against Juniche had been to Fetch the decidedly non-magical net into place. Suddenly Runacar remembered the night the Rangers had attacked them. Andhel was right: Drotha hadn't realized the Lightborn were using invisibility spells because they didn't affect him. But he'd kept Drotha back from overflying the refugees because he wanted them to escape, and Drotha saw most of the world as fat mice and himself as the kitchen cat.

"Where's Drotha?" Runacar demanded. "*Find him.*"

❖

Do we get to attack them now?" Drotha asked, even while he was landing in front of Runacar. The Gryphons who'd brought him wheeled once overhead before separating, one soaring away, the other— Radafa—coming in for a more sedate landing than the Aesalion had made. "You look upset," Drotha added mildly. "I could fix that, you know."

"No," Runacar said. "But I thank you for your concern." He was never sure how much of Drotha's behavior was a part of the Aesalion's skewed sense of humor, and how much was the way he really saw the world, but the last thing Runacar needed right now was to have his emotions scrambled. "Right now there's something I need you to do for me."

"Bite someone?" Drotha asked hopefully, stretching and preening. "Or sting them?"

"It may come to that," Runacar said. "I need you to overfly the refugees, come back, and tell me what you see. And take someone with you. I want to know what you don't see, too."

"Ooooh!" the Aesalion said. "Riddles!"

"I'll go," Radafa said quietly. "I think I know what you're looking for."

"I only hope I'm wrong," Runacar said quietly, as the two winged Otherfolk bounded once more into the air.

❖

The sun inched closer to midheaven. Runacar could tell his army to take up their battle positions—and he did—but they had not been trained in the discipline of waiting for an attack. They wouldn't just wander off, true, but they would become bored and inattentive. Something an Elven enemy would easily and instantly exploit—if one was coming.

If his wild guess about where most of the Western Shore Lightborn were was accurate.

In one sense, the threat of attack did not matter. When the sun reached midheaven, he was supposed to take his position on the parley field to hear Daroldan's words, though he supposed he could live with being foresworn and simply not showing up. But the fact remained that playing for time was almost as much in his interest as in theirs. The Otherfolk had little chance of breaching the walls of the Keep in direct assault, and if Runacar understood correctly, the earth-shaking magic Amrunor had offered was a last resort, since it would be as likely to kill Otherfolk as *alfaljodthi*. So whatever trap the false refugees from the Western Shore were preparing, what would follow the rejection of the terms Runacar had offered would still be a waiting game.

He glanced at the sky. It was nearly time. Where were Drotha and Radafa?

He saw the gates of Daroldan Keep begin their long slow opening.

He couldn't wait any longer.

He put his foot in Hialgo's stirrup and prepared to mount.

Suddenly two thunderbolts—one bright gold and azure, one black and silver and scarlet red—plummeted out of the sky. "You were right!" Radafa said, landing in a boom of wings and a spray of sand. "We've been following an illusion—six people at most. Or there *were*," he added, with a sidelong look at Drotha that Runacar had no difficulty decoding. "The main body cloaked themselves in invisibility and doubled back days ago. They're a candlemark away—if that."

"*All* of them?" Runacar couldn't imagine how castel servants, and farmers, and fishermen could be of any help in a fight, let alone a siege. Maybe they'd never left at all, and the War Princes had sent their army in disguise, all the while planning to attack from the rear when the Otherfolk began their siege. There was no way to know. Elven scouts would have been able to tell whether the refugees were servants or fighters, but the Otherfolk couldn't.

*Wasting time fretting about what you don't have loses as many battles as not having them.* Elrinonion Swordmaster had certainly beaten that lesson into him.

"The gates are opening," Pelere said, trotting over to the three of them.

"And I must go see what the War Princes have to say," Runacar said grimly. "But pass the word as quickly and quietly as you can. Someone go tell Meraude and Amrunor. We'll have to fight—and very soon."

⚔

As he set Hialgo pacing decorously onto the parley field, Runacar wondered why he was bothering. Even if he were still Lord Runacarendalur, there was no need for him to attend upon these enemies. Though the parley truce wasn't broken yet, he knew it was about to be, and etiquette allowed a War Prince (or his representative) to void the parley under those circumstances.

*I'm playing for time. Just as they are. Delfierarathadan isn't ash yet, and the Lightborn with the party doubling back on us are still using magic—from what source I cannot imagine. Every moment before the truce is broken is another moment for the Otherfolk to prepare and for Delfierarathadan to burn.*

He wondered whether the War Princes truly meant to follow the Code of War to the very word and letter—in which case he'd be safe until he left the parley field— or whether they'd decided to treat him as one of the Otherfolk—in which case, they were luring him in to kill him.

"It's questions like these that keep life from getting dull," Runacar said to his mount. Hialgo's ears twitched slightly.

Then he saw two mounted figures appear in the darkness behind the gates. When they rode out into the sunlight, Runacar could see that Damulothir and Leopheine were not in stainless white this time, and no Lightborn accompanied them. They wore full armor—save for their helmets—and rode warhorses. Leopheine's was a big burly chestnut stallion, while Damulothir rode a mare the color of burnished gold. The mare, Runacar noted distantly, was the better animal.

This would not ordinarily signify anything at all in terms of acceptance or rejection of terms of surrender, but considering that a good half of the population of two domains was riding hard to ambush his army from behind, Runacar did not take it as any good omen. Still, the travesty must be played out. He remembered how furious Vieliessar had always been with the niceties of the Code of Battle. For the first time, he could see her point.

"Well met, cousins," he said, as they reached his position. "I trust you have taken the opportunity to consider our terms?"

"We have indeed, Runacarendalur Caerthalien." It was Leopheine who spoke, with soft words and a smile of murderous rage. "But before we give you our answer, there is one thing I think you do not know. I would be remiss did I not repair your ignorance."

"And that would be?" Runacar did his best to project an attitude of bored indifference. That wasn't Elrinonion's teaching, but Bolecthindial's.

"No one on the Western Shore is a non-combatant," Leopheine said, leaning forward as if to confide a great secret. At the same time, his hand moved toward the pommel of his sword.

Runacar reached out and grabbed his wrist. "A secret for a secret then," he said. *"I am not War Prince Runacarendalur Caerthalien anymore."*

He shifted his weight and Hialgo reared, the motion pulling Leopheine from his saddle. As Leopheine fell, his destrier lunged at Hialgo, teeth bared, moving to drive off the attacker and protect his fallen master.

In the distance, Runacar heard a sudden uprush of sound, as if everyone had suddenly started cheering—the attack had begun. Then abruptly all was silent as he and the two War Princes were enclosed by a violet bubble of Shield.

"I take it this means you don't wish to surrender?" Runacar asked mockingly. He drew his sword as Hialgo danced backward out of the bay's reach. Two against one, and these were not High Table generals, but masters of combat itself.

"It would be rude not to dance when one has been invited to the Festival," Damulothir said with a death's-head smile.

"Then allow me to have the honor of being your first partner," Runacar snarled, and spurred Hialgo forward. Lengiathion Warlord's voice echoed in memory: *"In battle, a komen's weapons are three: his sword, his destrier, and himself."*

Hialgo was a stallion any domain's Horsemaster would have refused to train for war, for the destrier was far too excitable, and could never have been used as part of a meisne or even a taille. But unlike the destriers that faced him, Hialgo had spent his entire life being trained to exacting perfection by one hand alone. Now, horse and rider moved as if they were one body. As Runacar sought for both advantage and defense, his two attackers crowded him closely, forcing him against the spell-wall, their destriers slamming into Hialgo with punishing force. Leopheine's mount was the weak link: a stallion past his prime, with many good years of work still in him, but no longer up to the feats of endurance required in battle. Hialgo automatically directed the majority of his attack against Leopheine's bay, and Runacar could see the bay was flagging.

But at the same time, the dome of Shield was shrinking. Did the Lightborn who had cast it mean to seal the three of them inside a space too small for movement? Or—more likely—did they mean to trap him here alone somehow? The thought of the poisoned net that had ended Juniche's life flashed through his mind, and Runacar shuddered. But then, almost as if the thought had summoned him, Drotha landed on the parley ground as if Shield wasn't even there.

"No fair starting without me!" the Aesalion cried, lunging toward Leopheine. Leopheine's bay warhorse shied and spun, rolling eyes showing white, and Drotha's outspread claws missed their strike. But the lunge had only been a feint. Drotha lashed out with his tail, striking the destrier on the flank with its poison barb.

The flesh around the wound instantly swelled and blackened. The poisoned animal went mad. It ran into the Shield barrier and attacked it as if it were a living enemy, battering itself and Leopheine against Shield over and over until the Lightborn watcher unmade the spell in an attempt to save the War Prince—but too late. The dying stallion flung Leopheine from the saddle and trampled him to death before collapsing. Sound and scent rushed in as Shield fell: smoke, the sharp tang of lightning, the indefinable *something* that meant Lightborn spells were being cast, and the roar of the battlefield as it shifted inexorably toward this open space.

"I will see you buried in the ground like the refuse you are!" Damulothir shouted. His renewed attack was frenzied, as if Runacar faced a dozen warriors, and Drotha— either out of generosity or sudden distraction—had left Runacar to face him alone.

*I bargained in good faith. We would have let you go.*

Ghosts seemed to stand with him as he fought Damulothir. Lengiathion Warlord: *"The terrain of your battleground is an opportunity for the enemy to make mistakes. Be sure that he does. Study your ground. And use it."*

Elrinonion Swordmaster: *"You don't fight against a sword, but a komen. Learn your enemy, and you will inevitably defeat him."*

Thorogalas, his eldest brother, who brought him his first toy sword when he had barely learned to walk. *"Here is your inheritance, little brother. It is all you will ever need, in this life and the next."*

Bolecthindial, kneeling before him (the first and only time) to buckle the spurs of knighthood to his boots. *"Now I give your life in keeping to the Starry Hunt."*

And slowly, slowly, Runacar backed Damulothir's mount in the direction of the fallen destrier. It was too much to hope for that the mare would not notice the obstruction, but what he needed was the moment of inattention from her rider.

The combat was punishing. Runacar had lost his helmet's crest, his left pauldron, and his right upper shield to Damulothir's blade; his armor's enamel was chipped and its metal dented. He'd sheared away Damulothir's left polleyn—an illegal blow, not that such things mattered now—and the vambrace on the same side. Damulothir's surcoat hung in rags over his scratched and dented breastplate, and Runacar knew his blows had struck true. But Damulothir played a long game, bringing his attacks back to Runacar's now compromised right arm again and again. Soon enough the armor would fail, or the bone beneath it would break, and then Runacar would be dead.

Or his own long game would bear fruit.

Damulothir's mare felt something brush against her hock. Since she could not move forward, she turned to see what it was, and when she did, her hindquarters swung left. And there it was: that single blessed moment when Damulothir's adamantine concentration broke.

In that instant Runacar kicked free of his stirrups. Hialgo slammed into the mare's shoulder. And Runacar booted Damulothir in the stomach with all his strength.

With the unexpected blow, Damulothir lost his seat and fell to the ground, tumbling over the sprawled corpse of the bay stallion. The mare, her saddle empty, turned to attack Runacar.

That was how it was done, in the blood-soaked games the Hundred Houses had once played. Every trainer of destriers trained the same forms and figures and attacks into every one of their charges. When the rider was unseated, the destrier drove off their attacker and then guarded their fallen rider. It was dishonorable to attack a riderless animal. For such an act, a komen might lose their spurs and even be outlawed. But Runacar met the mare's rush with his sword. She wore only crinet and shanfron; her throat and chest were unarmored. Blood sprayed, and she made a terrible whistling noise as she tried to scream: his blow had severed her windpipe.

But even dying, drowning in her own blood, she tried to do her duty, staggering toward her master's side. She fell before she reached him, sides heaving desperately as she fought to fill her lungs one last time.

Damulothir struggled to his feet. He was covered in blood, and his sword lay on the ground behind him. *"The space between collet and gorget is only lightly armored. If it were not, young lord, a knight's head and torso would always have to move as one, and that would make such a one clumsy . . ."* Runacar struck that place with all his strength. Metal sheared and bent, blood spurted, and the War Prince of Daroldan fell to his knees, dying.

Runacar looked up: the castel gates were still open, but he could see the violet glimmer of Shield deep in the shadows; the defenders must be hoping that their relief force could make its way through the Otherfolk to the safety of the castel.

*But if they meant this ambush all along, they will have kept back komen to aid in it . . .*

He did not dare to linger to see if he was right, for the castel Lightborn would attack again as soon as the new War Prince gave them the order. Runacar turned and spurred Hialgo in the direction of the fighting.

⊰⊱

There were perhaps five thousand Otherfolk on the field. That should have put the numbers in their favor: after the Battle of the Kraken, the Western Shore had perhaps a grand-taille of komen, no more, an unknown number of Rangers, and an unknown number of Lightborn. Runacar stood in his stirrups, trying to see. Neither side wore livery, and it was impossible to tell Woodwose from *alfaljodthi*. His army knew how to kill komen, and the Rangers were much less effective without the camouflage and cover denied to them by the burning forest. As for the Lightborn . . .

The intolerable silver flare of Thunderbolt struck down out of the sky, momentarily blinding him. When Runacar could see once more, there was a large black circle burned into the ground where it had struck. The burned space glittered like glass. Like Ifjalasairaet in the dawn light, after Ivrulion Banebringer was struck down. A moment later, Runacar saw another strike. Each Thunderbolt killed dozens and left more maimed and burned, but the more the two forces intermixed, the less effective Thunderbolt could be, for the Lightborn would not risk killing their own people.

The earth shook as a troop of Centaurs raced northward to engage the enemy. The bright midday sun gleamed on their swords and their armor. Pelere galloped in the vanguard, tail flagged, her gleaming hide turned to polished gold in the sunlight.

Behind them came Minotaurs in an open column, moving more slowly but with a terrible inevitability, and chanting as they ran. At each third beat they struck at the enemy with their warhammers, the sound of the blows a punctuation to their chant. They left wounded and dying in their wake, and the Fauns swarmed over the fallen like charnel house rats, their small knives flashing, finding every chink and gap in enemy armor and leaving nothing alive behind them.

Hippogriffs swooped low over the field, plucking riders from their horses. Some veered west to drop their captives into the sea; others turned east, dropping their burdens into the flames and using the updraft from the burning to power their next assault on the battlefield. Some merely released their victims as soon as they'd seized them, letting them fall with as great an impact as if they had been flung from the back of a destrier at the ravall.

By setting fire to Delfierarathadan, the Otherfolk had denied the enemy any access to the battlefield but one: no matter how they had left Daroldan, they had to return by the so-called Northern Road, a route that was little more than a goat-track. Once they were west of the burning, they could enter the forest—and the Otherfolk no longer had eyes there, since it had been evacuated—and take the field at any point they chose, but there were no roads through Delfierarathadan, and if they miscalculated the speed of the fire's advance, it would kill them as certainly as the enemy would.

*I think they will have sent their komen as the vanguard, with that force following the Northern Road, and left their Rangers and Lightborn to find their way through the forest. It is what I would do. They lure our army north, while the komen at the Keep, and the enemy infantry, cut our force in half.*

*And there is no one I can tell of this, and no orders I can give to adapt our tactics. And I do not know what good it would do us if I could.*

There was no discipline, no order—it did not look like a battlefield at all, save for the dead. There was—he realized with a sudden flash of insight—no goal here, on either side, nothing to be gained beyond each army murdering the other. The Elves knew they could not rebuild their domain with the Flower Forest gone, and the Otherfolk could only claim the victory—and gain safety—if all the Elves were dead.

There was nothing either side could do except kill as many of the enemy as they could.

⊰⊱

In Sword Moon of the Wheelturn Vieliessar became High King, the Warhunt reached the Western Shore. They had crossed a Western Reach in turmoil, rulerless and anarchic, and—far worse—learned that the Sanctuary of the Star could not be relied upon to do anything but advance Hamphuliadiel's personal ambitions, for Harwing Lightbrother had gone to discover the Astromancer's intentions and had vanished as if he had never been.

The great-taille of Lightborn led by Rondithiel Lightbrother had gained Daroldan Great Keep with no further losses, and there they had awaited news that the High King's army marched west.

She did not come, and after Harvest Moon, there was no way to ask her why she did not, for the full moon at Harvest brought the beginning of what the Lightborn of the Shore named The Great Silence. Before they had left Tildorangelor, the Warhunt knew that the Sanctuary of the Star did not answer their attempts at

Farspeech, but after Harvest Court, it was no longer possible to use Farspeech anywhere, even within the Western Shore, for attempts to do so brought only disorientation and nausea.

And so they abandoned such attempts, for there was sufficient work before them. Amrolion and Daroldan were both embattled by Beastling raiders bolder and more numerous than ever before in living memory. All the Warhunt Lightborn could do was add their strength to that of their brethren. And wait. And hope.

As the Wheelturns passed, Scrying and Farseeing brought news of a Western Reach slowly coming to order, but it did not make good hearing, for it was an order imposed by the Beastlings. The Shore's defenders spent a decade of Wheelturns preparing for the inevitable day of their invasion, as, with inexorable ferocity, the Beastlings scoured the West of the folk left behind by the Grand Alliance, until Amrolion and Daroldan—and perhaps the Sanctuary of the Star—stood as the only remaining strongholds of Elvenkind in all of the West.

From the moment Amrolion fell to an unlooked-for alliance between the Sea-Beastlings and those of the land, the destruction of the Domains of the Western Shore had seemed inevitable, but the defenders had not despaired. Even when they discovered that the nightmare army was led by the brother of Ivrulion Banebringer and that *alfaljodthi* fought in its ranks, the combined domains of Amrolion and Daroldan fought on indomitably, for their Warlords agreed they might still gain the victory.

As the enemy force drew close, the Warhunt, along with eight-twelfths of the army, left Daroldan Great Keep. They took with them the flocks and herds of the Shore in order to make it look to the enemy as if Daroldan prepared herself for siege by sending away all of its Fisherfolk and Farmfolk and Craftworkers. But those who fled did so only to return.

At the end of a sennight's march, a handful of Lightborn were chosen by lot to continue westward with the livestock, and the rest gathered up Delfierarathadan's Light to cast two illusions: one, to feign that this tiny group was the whole of the supposed refugees, and two, to Cloak those who retraced their march in impenetrable invisibility. The Lightborn left behind at Daroldan kept in touch with them by spellbird, so that they would not show themselves until the trap was ready to spring, but no one expected the Beastlings to set the entire Flower Forest ablaze.

If the Warhunt had not disenchanted every Border Stone it found during its journey from the Mystrals to the Shore, the hope of victory would have been lost in that moment, for the conflagration meant a detour that added sunturns to their march. But even with Delfierarathadan burning there was Light to draw upon, and the defenders did all they could to delay the final attack, even pretending to make parley with the Beastlings and their treasonous commander.

There was no thought among the Cloaked army of stopping to make camp, or to catch more than a few candlemarks of rest, for if Daroldan fell, its Beastling attackers would not stop until every *alfaljodthi* in the West was dead. As soon as Delfierarathadan would let them, the Lightborn and the Rangers turned south, leaving six great-tailles of komen to make all possible speed along the Northern Road.

And when they reached the battlefield, they attacked.

⚔︎

Runacar galloped onto the battlefield, doing all that he could to rally his fighters, but he had lost control of the field before the battle began. In the maelstrom of battle, the Otherfolk were returning to their traditional modes of attack—small groups, gathered by race and clan, each reacting only to the immediate threat. Even when their captains rallied them, there was no enemy strongpoint to send them against. When the reserve demi-taille rode from Daroldan onto the field, the Bearward berserkers rushed it in a body, but their numbers were too few to drive the komen back, and the destriers were too maddened by the scent of blood to be affected by spellcraft. In desperation, the Gryphons began bombarding the Keep with stones once more, but the Lightborn simply cast Shield over it again. Shield made it impossible for archers to use the Keep as a platform from which to loose arrows upon the battlefield, but it also made it impossible for the Otherfolk to storm the castel.

The komen were outnumbered five to one—*and they were still winning.* The Otherfolk fought well and valiantly, but despite their willingness, their bravery, and their skill; despite the disadvantages the enemy labored under . . . the conclusion of the battle wasn't really in doubt. Skill and training had no chance against a Thunderbolt, any more than a komen's skill counted against a Ranger's walking bow. The two armies might as well have retreated to opposite sides of the battlefield and simply killed a hundred of their own people every quartermark.

Runacar told himself he'd been in larger battles, and more vicious ones. The Battle of the Shieldwall Plain had involved nearly every komen in all the Fortunate Lands—and a number of fighters who were not komen. The Code of War had been only sporadically observed there, for many of Vieliessar's combatants were mercenaries, outlaws, and Landbond. The two armies had fought through the night like beasts, with no goal save that of personal survival.

Just like this.

❧

Runacar shook blood from his sword and wheeled Hialgo in search of a fresh target. He was desperately thirsty, and he knew Hialgo was suffering as well. The battle had begun at midday, and now the sun was westering. There was no possibility that the fighting would cease at nightfall: it would go on by firelight and Silverlight, and there was no place for either army to retreat to. The fact that their own forces were intermixed with the enemy was the only thing keeping the Lightborn from deploying even more devastating spells.

*We are losing.*

That realization tasted of blood and metal, horrible beyond grief or fear. His people were dying, and there was nothing he could do to save them. The beautiful mask of Code and custom had been stripped from the face of War, and all Runacar knew was that he never wanted to see that face again.

*We are losing.*

Runacar yanked Hialgo's head around and dug spurs into the destrier's sides. Hialgo danced for a moment and began to run, carrying Runacar away from the fighting.

*We are losing this battle.*

❧

Few of the Western Shore Lightborn had ever seen a war, much less taken the field in one. The Shore was a place of constant skirmishes, raids involving a few hundred enemies at most. Not like this. Not like today.

Rondithiel Lightbrother had marked the reigns of seven Astromancers before he first fought on a battlefield, but he had ridden to war a thousand times in those Wheelturns, for no War Prince had ever ridden to battle without Lightborn to Heal them at the end of the day's fighting. Rondithiel had been hardened to the waste and pain of war long before Vieliessar was born, and he joined her in hope of something better. It was a black joke such as only the Silver Hooves could relish that he would surely end his life on the field of a war that was not a war, never knowing the fate of she for whom he had renounced so much.

He had gathered at his side those who would only be liabilities on the field itself. They guarded their position with Shield as they loosed every spell that might gain victory for their comrades. Transmutation, to turn earth to water and then to stone. Fetch, to fling a sword or a dagger through a Beastling body. Thunderbolt, to kill a hundred at a time.

Silverlight, to illuminate the field so the killing could go on.

Each time the wind shifted, smoke from the burning forest rolled over the battlefield like a noxious fogbank. The air was filled with the screams of injured horses, dying Beastmen, and the boom and crackle of spells. Even when the air was clear of smoke, it stank of blood. Shield flickered intermittently between Rondithiel's position and the field itself. The Beastlings knew where they were and were doing their best to overrun them, and a wasteland of black glass marked where the Lightborn had Called Thunderbolt to drive them off. It glittered in the evening light and steamed where fresh blood fell on it.

A komen, afoot and half uncased, flung herself frantically across the glazed earth toward the Lightborn gathered around Rondithiel. In her arms she carried a Ranger, his body feathered with Beastling arrows, his flesh blackening with poison.

"Save him—Lightborn," she gasped. Her words were inaudible in the bedlam, but it did not matter, for her meaning was clear. She felt to her knees in the sea-grass where Rondithiel and his fellows knelt, clutching her dying comrade to her chest.

Rondithiel placed his hands upon the boy, summoning the power to Heal even as the death-song of Delfierarathadan keened in his bones. If Isilla and the others could save a fragment of the Flower Forest . . .

He shook his head, banishing the thought. There was no time to hope for what the future might bring. He would save who and what he could for so long as breath remained in him.

Perhaps his people could save Daroldan as well.

⊰❊⊱

The Shore Road ran south from Daroldan Great Keep, skirting the sea-cliffs and leading past the remains of Fisherfolk huts and half-burned piles of drying nets until it vanished in the sand of the shore itself. To the west, the sea was churned to a red froth by the Ocean's Own, and those of Daroldan's defenders who came within their reach died in heartbeats. The tide line swarmed with nixies, their high voices like the calling of gulls, cheering on the slaughter as they waited hopefully for some unwary komen to come close enough to kill. In the deep water below the castel cliff, Meraude and her court attacked the Shielded Great Keep, watching eagerly for a moment's inattention from the Lightborn above.

When Shore Road became seashore, Runacar galloped Hialgo into the water, heedless of who he trampled to get there. "Aejus!" he shouted at the top of his lungs. "Amrunor! Meraude!"

One of the sea-horses turned toward him and he shouted again, every name he knew. One of the Nisse at the edge of the group saw him coming; she turned and spoke to another. He drove Hialgo onward until the stallion was swimming. For a moment Runacar thought he and Hialgo would drown here—madness to ride into deep water in full armor—but then Amrunor and Meraude appeared at the edge of the press of bodies and swam strongly toward him.

"Runacar!" Meraude said, looking surprised but unworried. "The battle has begun," she added, as if he might be unaware of that fact.

Amrunor slid his tail beneath Hialgo's barrel and lifted the destrier out of the water. The stallion panted, near exhaustion, legs still churning reflexively.

"Yes," Runacar answered, as calmly as he could. "And we are losing. Daroldan did not send refugees eastward—he sent his *army*. They hid themselves with Magery and returned to fight."

"But their warriors are few, and yours are many," Meraude said, clearly puzzled. "And their witches have no power now that you have set the forest alight."

"Burning Delfierarathadan didn't work," Runacar said. "The Lightborn have another source of power. I don't know what it is, but they are using it to slaughter us—and they will win." *And with the forest in flames, we have no place to retreat to. They will leave no survivors. I could not have arranged matters better for Daroldan and Amrolion were I their ablest Warlord.*

Meraude said nothing.

"Amrunor, you told me once that you had a sorcery that would give us victory," Runacar prompted. He heard the pleading note in his own voice, the desperate hope that these most magical of the Otherfolk could still save the day.

"At an unknown loss of life," Meraude pointed out coolly.

"It can be no greater than that which our enemies will inflict," Runacar said grimly. "They'll kill us all. No mercy, no quarter. The Code of War does not apply to . . . monsters." He felt a hot flush of shame—he had been supposed to teach the Otherfolk, to lead them, to give them the victory. All he'd done was turn the West-

ern Shore into a barren wasteland and lead Leutric's
army to the slaughter. He'd failed.

Again.

"Then go," Meraude said decisively. "We shall do our
part."

Without waiting for a reply, she swam away. Amrunor regarded Runacar steadily.

"Get as many of the Folk as you can down to the
shoreline. Go as far south as possible," the sea-horse
said. "And if you think your Gods will listen, Star's
Child—pray."

Amrunor withdrew his support from beneath Hialgo,
and Runacar turned the stallion silently landward. He
knew Hialgo was exhausted, but Runacar could not afford to let him rest. He took the most direct path back
to land, and when Hialgo staggered ashore, Runacar
headed him toward the edge of the burning forest.

❀

She had been Ladyholder of Daroldan when the sun
rose this morning, and now, by Caerthalien treachery, Ereneine of Daroldan was Ladyholder-Abeyant. She
prayed to the Silver Hooves that she might live long
enough to claim Lord Runacarendalur's life in payment.

By miracles of warcraft, Ereneine had kept the taille
of Daroldan komen she led alive and by her side through
the candlemarks of fighting. When they had first
planned this battle, Warlord Challaron had said that the
komen must do their best to force the Beastlings south
and away from the Keep. The Lightborn worked to
douse the burning forest to the north, but only there—if
the army could push the Beastlings south and regroup,
then it could drive them into the forest where they
would burn to death.

Her armor was battered and her surcoat was so
blood-sodden the grey and gold of its sea and flowers

could no longer be discerned. She had been unhorsed so many times she no longer knew the name of her mount. But Ereneine fought on. Tonight she would join Damulothir among the Starry Hunt or the Western Shore would be swept clean of vermin at last.

"My lady—look there!" Princess Valliane of Amrolion said. She pointed to where a troop of Centaurs had surrounded a group of unhorsed komen.

Ereneine raised her sword in the signal to charge.

"*Isterya Adzab! Isterya Adzab!*" she screamed, roweling her destrier's flanks with her spurs.

⊰⊱

R unacar knew he had no hope of being heard if he rode directly into the fighting, and the folk caught up in the heat of battle would not be able to heed him, even if they wished to. But if he could get those at the edge of the fighting to retreat . . .

Hialgo stepped mincingly over the body of a Faun riddled with arrows as Runacar looked for someone to whom he could deliver Amrunor's message.

"*Meraude says retreat! Get to the shore!*"

Time after time he forced Hialgo into a cluster of embattled Otherfolk to help them fight off the enemy and to shout out his message. If it had any effect, Runacar did not see it. Then—shockingly, suddenly—Hialgo went to his knees, dead before he fell, a Ranger's arrow quivering in his flesh. Runacar leaped free, looking automatically in the direction of the shot. He met the eyes of a Daroldan Ranger who tipped him a mocking salute before nocking another arrow. Runacar fled into the melee to escape, wondering why he still thought one death was better than another.

It was sunset now, and the light was as red as the fires to the east. The dimness of the dying day made it hard to see clearly, or even to distinguish friend from foe. Events took on a dreamlike, episodic quality; moments strung like pearls on a cord, each one self-contained, but all of much the same type. He found himself helmless, holding one of the long shields the Centaurs used. Carrying it made his arm ache, but it was an effective defense. He slashed and cut and kicked mindlessly: any being who wore his form and face was the enemy.

Moments.

A Ranger standing, his face sheared from his head, the red ruin fountaining blood, but still on his feet.

A Lightborn, only a green armband to proclaim what he was, sitting on the ground, his lap full of his own entrails.

A Minotaur, wielding an Elven leg as a club.

A Gryphon, its wings and beak sheared away, screaming in agony as hammer-wielding Elves battered it to death.

The flare of Thunderbolt, here, there, everywhere, somehow never striking him, a column of white fire that vaporized bodies where it struck and turned the blood-soaked earth to sizzling glass. The smoke of the burning forest and the smoke of burning flesh mingled in the air.

His sword shattered. Runacar found another. It had begun to rain, and he tilted his naked face up to the warm wetness for a moment of respite, then searched for a new target. Clouds of Silverlight began floating out above the battlefield like a malign shining fog.

⚔

Isilla Lightsister crouched at the edge of the trees, clutching a sword she had no idea how to use. The Light was a single constant note in a cacophony of alien spellworkings. She felt as if she could taste them in her throat, and feel them clinging to her skin.

Once more she summoned Thunderbolt, though the effort made her vision cloud. Her target was not the battlefield—she could not see it well enough to tell friend from foe—but the fire in the forest behind her. Each time she struck, Thunderbolt doused flames and left a charred space where the fire could not pass. *If we cannot retreat into the forest, we will not survive the night,* she thought grimly.

Around her, she knew other Lightborn were doing the same. It had been the last order Warlord Challaron had given before he had vanished into the fighting.

The Gryphons had stopped bombarding the Keep when the storm began. The defenders had dropped Shield. But the ocean was glowing all the way to the horizon, and the great tower of Daroldan was a black silhouette against it.

She wondered how many were left alive inside it.

⌖

The warnings Runacar screamed had become meaningless noise in his own ears. Exhaustion numbed him, so that he did not know whether he bore wounds or not. He could not remember the beginning of the fighting, and he could not imagine its end. Soon he would fall to the ground and be unable to rise, and that coming moment seemed so inevitable that it held no terror for him.

Then the ground beneath his feet began to dance.

At first Runacar thought it was a phantasm bred of exhaustion. Silverlight was everywhere, brightening the long twilight and making the colors of evening look false and unreal. He saw a crack appear in the outer wall of Daroldan Great Keep, and shook his head, trying to clear his vision of the illusion, but the crack only widened, and now the shuddering of the ground was too strong to ignore. It flung him to his knees, and for the first time, the screams of terror on the battlefield were louder than the howls of rage. He looked up and saw—above the fog of Silverlight—that the sky was filled with black clouds that glowed with lightning. People had fallen, people were clutching one another for support. Despite the storm, the winged fighters circled frantically just offshore, and the knights' destriers, at last ignoring their riders' commands, fled.

The earth shook like a winnowing sieve. It pulled itself apart, great jagged canyons racing across the ground like earthbound lightning, opening beneath bodies both dead and alive, tumbling them in, and then grinding closed again. People ran if they could. Some ran from one opening fissure only to have another open beneath their feet and swallow them. The sounds of the battlefield were overwhelmed by a roaring louder than storm or ocean or fire, a sound so loud and so relentless that the clamor of the tortured earth almost seemed like silence.

The burning forest fell, torn apart by the shaking, and the air was suddenly filled with smoke and embers. Great trees, still burning, hurtled from the forest as if they were arrows loosed from some monstrous bow, bouncing and tumbling across the battlefield. The great tall column of the castel cracked and tilted and bulged as Daroldan Great Keep began to crumble like wet sand.

The shaking stopped, and Runacar lurched to his feet. Eastward, Delfierarathadan—or what was left of it—was hidden in a cloud of smoke and dust reddened by flames. On the battlefield, the survivors stood dazedly, or ran, their motion oddly aimless, as if it did not matter what direction they chose. Some ran toward the disintegrating Keep. Some ran toward the fire. Some ran northward. Many of the chasms in the ground remained open, gulfs few dared to cross, blocking escape.

The castel was still crumbling, and now the cliff was crumbling, too.

Runacar took a deep breath.

"To me!" he cried, in a voice that had been trained

to carry across battlefields. "Otherfolk—*to me!* Leaf and Star!" He swung his sword through the air, brandishing it for everyone to mark where he stood. *"Leaf and Star!"*

The air had become very still. Slowly the fighters—many so covered with muck and gore that their species could not be identified, much less their allegiance—began to stand, to gather together, to come toward him. It was an endless-seeming time before the first of the survivors reached him—a Minotaur, three Fauns, and a Bearward—and in that time, the ground shook again several times, but only in small tremors. Once again Runacar repeated Amrunor's message, and sent them southward. But he remained where he was. It was all he could do for the remains of the army he had led.

Otherfolk drained away from the battlefield as though they were water flowing from a cracked cup, leaving behind them a slaughterhouse that the land itself had seemingly tried to erase. Gryphons and Hippogriffs dove among the survivors, rising up carrying away whomever they could reach, flying them to safety, returning over and over. Scattered groups of Otherfolk quickly became a steady stream, and Runacar dared to hope that some of the people he'd led into battle might still be saved. Incredibly, many stayed behind to fight on, pointless as that was now.

The rumbling had stopped, and his ears rang with the silence. Battle cries and the clang of metal on metal were sporadic, muted and distant. Soon Runacar's eyes burned and he was coughing constantly, as the smoke boiled down from the forest to fill the air. He was desperately thirsty, and thought longingly of the Angarussa, of submerging himself in its sweet fresh water. The Otherfolk moved past him in a wide slow column, wounded supporting wounded, Centaurs carrying Woodwose and Fauns and even Wulvers on their backs. Perhaps some of Daroldan's defenders had slipped in among the Woodwose. What did it matter now? In a cracked, hoarse voice Runacar urged those who passed him to move faster, faster, get to the sea . . .

And still he stayed where he was. He knew he should go with them—Amrunor's message had been passed, his obligation met—but he could not bring himself to do so.

A flash of movement caught his eye. A swoop of black wings, and suddenly Drotha was perched upon the top of the still-crumbling castel, wings spread and howling with demented laughter.

"Get down from there." The words emerged as a harsh whisper, but Runacar doubted Drotha would have listened even if he'd been able to shout them in his face. Some of those still fighting stopped at the sound of the Aesalion's laughter and pointed toward him.

The ground began to shake again.

This was not one of the small tremblings that had followed the first great shaking. Runacar saw the ground ripple like Great Sea Ocean itself, saw the great fissures reopen as the smoke skirled away. The Otherfolk began to run, screaming as they fled, trampling their comrades in their panic. Runacar tried to stop them, or follow, but it didn't matter which he chose, he could not keep his balance as the land went mad beneath his body. All around him, Otherfolk were falling, floundering, trying desperately to stay on their feet, trying to *run* . . .

Someone grabbed him and set him on his feet—he did not see who. He managed to stagger after his benefactor across the traitorous ground, when—behind him, loud enough to cut through every other sound—he heard a cracking, a roaring, a thousand times louder than the sound the Angarussa had made when it was turned into its new bed. He stopped and turned back the way he had come. He had to see.

Daroldan Great Keep teetered and lurched as the cliff beneath it disintegrated. He saw its cellars and deep hiding places opened and exposed, saw the whole granite outcropping upon which the Great Keep was built begin to crumble into the ocean below as if the granite had become gravel. Cracks in the earth became wider, spiderwebbing madly in all directions, and more earth fell into them, until even the burning forest was falling into great gaps in the earth. He stared at the destruction in horror, transfixed.

*I should run,* he thought vaguely.

But it was too late.

## CHAPTER EIGHTEEN

# SWORD MOON
# TO THUNDER MOON:
# THE END OF THE WEST

*From the death of the High King will come unending
war. And when a new High King is raised, then war
beyond imagining will come.*
— *The Laſt Song of Pelaſhia Celenthodiel*

The early-morning fog lay heavy on the ground,
reducing visibility to the length of one's arm, and
making the morning chill bite bone-deep. The
Northern Road was a narrow track, and rockslides had
destroyed much of it, but it was the only route to safety.
The Lightborn cleared what obstacles they could, but
the going was slow.

"We should go back," Isilla Lightsister said dully as
she walked. *The last time I was this tired we were on
the run from half the Hundred Houses, and weren't
even sure where we were* . . . She did not know how
long she'd been walking, or even who was with her.
"There must be some of our people still there."

"Alive?" Ranger Thorodos asked simply, and shook
his head. "Any who live, the Beastlings will have slain
by now. All who could escape are with us already."

They had marched to the battlefield expecting to conquer, and now all they had left was what they could
carry, and the bitter knowledge of their defeat.

Most of the survivors were Lightborn, for they had
been east and north of the fighting. With them were a

few Rangers and a handful of Sword Pages. Of the
meisne that had survived the destruction of Amrolion,
of the array that Daroldan could once have placed upon
the field, not one of the Lords Komen had survived.

If Rondithiel had not been with them, these combatants might have perished as well, for everyone of noble
rank had been on the field, and there was no one to give
orders. But after the first shaking of the ground, Rondithiel had ridden onto the battleground on his palfrey,
ordering everyone who would listen to retreat to the
Northern Road. Some listened, some did not, and when
the second shaking of the ground came, all the few survivors could do was run.

They'd followed the Northern Road as the smoke-
darkened twilight gave way to true night, and on
through the night as well. They had not even dared to
make Silverlight, lest someone should see—their only
safety was in flight, both from the rage of the Beastlings
and from the anger of the earth itself.

Most of the injured they'd managed to rescue died
in the night.

The dawn winds, in an act of mechanical cruelty, had
swept the dust and the smoke from the air. Visibility
was good in all directions, but after a few glances, no
one looked southward, for to do so was to look across
a landscape utterly changed.

Far to the south, Delfierarathadan still burned. The
Shrine was in the part of the forest that was still aflame,
and that realization gave Isilla a pang of panicked
relief: she did not think she could have borne to look
upon the place where it had lain and seen it erased. But
nearer to hand, all that was to be seen was churned
earth and charred and splintered wood. Nothing remained of the Flower Forest that had once stood.

When the sun at last rose high enough to burn away
the morning mists, Rondithiel called a halt. The survi-

vors dropped to the earth wherever they stood, or walked a few steps more to group themselves near him.

"What do we do now?" Isilla asked numbly, expecting no answer. Dinias, who had walked beside her, took her hand silently in his.

"Wait for the Beastlings to come and slaughter us," Thorodos said bleakly. "I just wish I knew why."

That drew a ragged laugh from one of the other Rangers. "Do they need a reason?" Arathorn asked, passing his waterskin to Thorodos.

"You know as well as I do that the Gryphons rarely come this far west," Thorodos replied, rubbing his face wearily. He had his bow, but no arrows. None of the Rangers had any arrows left.

"Yet there they were," Isilla said, taking the waterskin he passed her and drinking before handing it on to Dinias. *The hills here are still covered in wildflowers, as if nothing happened. I don't know whether that's wonderful, or horrible.*

"Because Caerthalien called them," Pantaradet Lightsister—once of Caerthalien—said, with a combination of bitterness and shame.

"We can rest here for a candlemark or two. No longer," Rondithiel announced. "And we should eat and drink while we can. Kathan has summoned us up a spring of sweet water, and we do not lack for fire, so there will be tea at least. Isilla, I know you are weary, and I would not ask this of you if our situation were other than it is, but—"

"—but we must know what lies behind us." She finished his sentence for him, trying not to snarl. He was their leader, if they had one, not by virtue of being Lightborn, but by virtue of age: he was the oldest of them, and those who were more nobly born than he were too young to take up the task of command. It was not Rondithiel's fault that the Beastling army—*led by the War Prince of Caerthalien!*—had butchered their people. "All right. Let me see if there is anything within range of my Gift. I shall come and tell you what I find."

"I can ask no more," Rondithiel said gently.

Isilla closed her eyes and took a deep breath, reaching for the stillness that would allow her to cast Overshadow. But her mind would not quiet itself. *How have we come to this? How? We spent ten Wheelturns waiting for Vieliessar High King's return—waiting for word of her. She sent us as surety for her sworn pledge! And she did not come, and in a handful of sennights the Western Shore has been erased as surely as Farcarinon ever was . . .*

At last a lifetime of discipline and training asserted itself, and Isilla's world was reduced to an empty blankness through which her disembodied will sought for a target for her spell.

And suddenly it was there. Brightness and shape and sensation returned, and she looked out at the world from the eyes of a gull. *Lord Palinoriel always called them wind-rats, saying they were too lazy to hunt their dinners, and not even as useful as ravens at cleaning up a battlefield . . .* She blocked that thought from her mind at once, lest grief distemper her spell before she had seen all she needed to see. The gull and its fellows were feeding along the shoreline, for anything light enough to float had washed up there.

She turned the gull away from its flock and sent it aloft, soaring over a landscape starkly changed. Eastward lay the dry bed of what once had been the Angarussa. The vast forest that had once bordered the river was gone; all that remained of Delfierarathadan Flower Forest was stones and charred tree trunks mixed in with churned earth, the whole as level as a field readied for spring plowing. To the west, the cliffs upon which Daroldan had built its castel were gone; the land now crumbled down into the sea, as if something larger than a kraken had taken an enormous bite from the coastline. Bodies—Elven, animal, and Beastling—cluttered the churned ground, and a few great gaping fissures in the ground remained. Carrion birds picked their way delicately through the feast.

Of the great army and the Beastlings it had fought, there was no sign.

At last Isilla released the gull to its meal, and opened her eyes to find Dinias holding a cup beneath her nose.

"It's not much, but it goes further this way," he said apologetically. "There's tea, too."

She smiled, taking the cup from him. "Dare I ask who fled a rock storm with a kitchen in their pack?"

Dinias smiled, just a little. "With better than a kitchen," he said. "With a dozen blank scrolls or more." Vellum could be easily shaped into a number of useful forms, and then Transmuted for use.

"Praise the Light for Alasneh Lightsister and her eternal chronicling," Isilla said, taking a drink. It was a thin gruel, for only a few of them had been carrying food, but it was here and it was hot.

"And she may eventually forgive Tangisen for telling on her," Dinias said. He cocked his head, studying her critically. "You don't look as if you're going to tell us we need to flee for our lives."

"I'm not," she said, handing him back the empty cup. "Come on. Let's go find Rondithiel."

❦

While Isilla had been entranced, the refugees had redistributed themselves to settle naturally around the fire in a ring two and three bodies deep. A cookpot, its angular form bearing witness to its recent existence as part of a scroll, was balanced on a tripod of sticks over the fire pit. The fire pit was dug down into the ground and lined and edged with stones— Isilla recognized Ranger handiwork in that and blessed

Sword and Star that at least a few of the Western Shore Rangers were with them. They were as much like the Foresters of the domain in which she'd grown up as a destrier was like a goat, but their woodcraft would be vital if they were all to survive their journey.

But their journey to *where*?

Rondithiel was moving through the group, pausing here and there for a word. Isilla could almost feel the jangled nerves and high-strung emotions of her companions soothing themselves out, though he was not using any Light to calm them. Somehow he reminded her of Lord Vieliessar, who had managed to care for— and care about—every soul in her great army, from her War Princes and Lords Komen to the newest babe born to a family of Landbonds.

*And that care was no lie, for no one can force me to see what isn't there. And yet . . . if she cared, she would have come to us. And none of this would have happened.*

Then Rondithiel looked up and saw her. He kept his face schooled to neutrality, but she knew how desperately he must hope her news was good. She forced herself to smile, and picked her way through the folk sitting around the fire, Dinias following, until she reached his side.

"We are not pursued," she said quickly.

Then, in the hearing of all, she told what she had seen: the Western Shore devastated and deserted. Neither their own folk nor the Beastlings were anywhere to be seen.

"Not alive, anyway," she said, finishing.

"Are you sure you saw all there was to see, Lightsister?" Lady Aglahir asked, getting to her feet. It occurred abruptly to Isilla that the young Sword Page—she had flown her kite only a few moonturns ago—was probably now War Prince of Daroldan, for she was the greatchild of one of Damulothir's elder siblings. "I mean no disrespect," Aglahir finished anxiously.

"And none taken, my lady," Isilla said. "Such questions are welcome, for I know that not all here are Lightborn, and I must not take anyone's knowledge of Lightworking for granted. I borrowed the eyes and wings of a gull, and flew over the battlefield, the shoreline, and a good distance along the road we are on. I saw no one. And to cast an invisibility spell able to trick a beast's senses is a difficult matter."

"Thank you, Lightsister," Aglahir said gravely, seating herself again. "You are most patient."

"So it seems we are to be undisturbed," Rondithiel said, looking around to include everyone in that statement. "Yet you all know as well as I what awaits us in the west. There is no haven for us there."

"Save the Sanctuary of the Star," Alasneh Lightsister said. "It may yet stand. Surely they would not turn us away, knowing it meant our deaths?"

There was a murmur of agreement from the exhausted refugees. Even though they were all the High King's people—and Hamphuliadiel Astromancer most emphatically was not—Isilla knew it was difficult for them to believe Hamphuliadiel would not grant them refuge. *But Harwing has not come back to us, or sent us word, and I listened for him until I no longer could . . .*

"And *surely* Harwing Lightbrother went in to the Sanctuary and never came out," she said sharply. "And Ulvearth Lightsister before him. Do you wish to do the same?"

"What choice is there?" Thorodos asked, and his fellow Rangers to either side of him nodded. "We have little more than the clothes on our backs. Even if we wished to go to the High King, we cannot. Just to reach the Dragon's Gate would be a journey of moonturns through lands infested by Beastlings, and after that . . ." He shrugged. "How shall we find her, who has not come to us in all this time?"

"This is true as well," Rondithiel said. "I have known Hamphuliadiel longer than any of you, I think, and the High King was once my student, as all know. Hamphuliadiel has little love for the High King and her partisans, yet if the Sanctuary of the Star yet remains, I cannot believe he would turn us away from the only place of safety that remains in the West. And perhaps he will wish to hear what we know of the fate of Daroldan and Amrolion, and have fresh news of the lands we will travel over to reach him."

"Do you mean we must swear allegiance to him, Master Rondithiel?" Dinias asked cautiously.

"I say we should not anticipate the strike before the hawk is loosed," Rondithiel said gently. "I will not compel anyone to travel with me, and still less to break a sworn oath. But I think there is little safety to be found anywhere else."

"So we go to the Sanctuary of the Star," Isilla said heavily. *And pray we do not all wish ourselves back on the Shore once we have.*

❧❧

Even though there was still something left of what he once had been that thought and wondered, Runacar had the sense that he ought to be—might actually be—dead. His mind carried him back to a time long ago, when he had been the acknowledged leader of the castel children who would grow up to become his komen and vassals. As he drifted through the long-ago memory, it seemed to Runacar that he could feel the sun, warm upon his upturned face, and smell the raw green scents of late Spring. Sword Moon. The beginning of War Season. In those long golden days of childhood they had played games of knights and war and dying gloriously in battle. They had never quite dared to play at being the Huntsman and His Rade, but there had been much talk—often ending in

blows—of what sort of death would *count* as enough
to ensure their eternal membership in the Starry Hunt.

"*What if you died during a battle, but you weren't
on the battlefield at all and died of something else? But
you were near it?*"

"*What if you were out hunting outlaws and one of
them killed you? Would that be a death in battle?*" ("*Of
course it would!*" young Runacarendalur had answered
scornfully. "*You'd both be fighting with swords!*")

"*Or Beastlings? They don't have swords. What about
then?*"

"*What if you were, say, wounded in a battle, but you
didn't die until, maybe, a sennight later? Would it
count?*"

*Would it count? Would it count? Would it count?* The
eternal question, beating out its insistent rhythm beneath everything the *alfaljodthi* did and all they as-
pired to be. Wanting a glorious death as a gateway into
an even more glorious Eternity riding among the stars
beside the Riders to Whom they pledged every heroic
feat, to Whom they made sacrifice and of Whom they
begged favor. To ride forever with the Starry Hunt, the
hooves of Its immortal destriers chiming their silvery
music among the stars. A warrior's death and a warrior's paradise: eternal battle.

Only eternal battle was now the most terrible thing
Runacar could imagine.

He groaned in anguish.

*Hush,* someone said. He felt a touch, infinitely gentle,
on his cheek. *Go back to sleep, darling. You don't need
to wake yet.*

⊰⊱

He slept. He dreamed.
      In his dreams, Runacar was not merely one of
the Rade, but its leader. He rode a stallion formed of
storm and fire: tireless, eternal. All around him the stars

burned brightly, and the silver hooves of his stallion chimed as they met the surface of the Starry Road. *(He remembered the child he had been, the child who pointed upward at the Road in the night sky, asking his nurse if he would know when his father and his siblings rode upon it. Would they look down and see him? Would they care?)*

And slowly, in the way of dreams, it came to him. Not who he was, or where he was, but what his dream-self, the Starry Huntsman, was doing. The Rade was not riding to battle.

It was *running away*.

But the Rade did not run. The Rade was invincible. In its ranks rode every warrior who had ever lived. It could not be defeated. He tried to stop, to turn his stallion's head aside, and could not. The impossibility of it made dream-Runacar cry out. He raised himself in his stirrups and looked behind. The Starry Hunt spread out behind him in its thousands upon uncounted thousands. Their swords and armor of silver and starlight gleaming in the vast darkness that surrounded Them.

But Darkness followed.

With more than sight he saw the Riders in the fantail of the great array wink out one by one. Behind Them there was no longer a star-strewn path. It, too, had vanished, along with the stars around it. He could not tell whether the Darkness destroyed them, or if they simply faded away, but when he turned again to gaze at the road ahead, there was nothing but light before him. No stars, no road, only a light as bright and blazing as if it was all the Light there could ever be, gathered together—just as the Darkness behind him was all there was of Darkness. The Light would destroy the Starry Hunt as surely and as mercilessly as the Darkness devoured Them. There was only a choice of deaths.

*There is no choice,* a voice whispered in his ear. *There is only death.*

❖

This time Runacar came fully awake, shouting and struggling as he demanded horse, armor, sword . . .

He fell back with a groan, gasping not so much at the pain—any komen was used to pain—but at the *wrongness* he felt in his body, a thing of grinding weakness and barely-healed breakage and bone-deep ache. His staring eyes were dazzled by the brightness that was all that he could see, and he began again to fight, thinking he was still in the dream.

Hands pressed down hard on his shoulders, forcing him back to the mattress.

"Hold still, Houseborn. If you try to get up your guts will probably fall out again and I have no intention of cleaning up after you."

"Andhel." The relief he felt at hearing her voice was shocking. "You're . . . ?"

"Alive? Of course I am. I'd hate to think that you and I were destined to share an afterlife," she answered tartly. "Now hold still." He heard the familiar sound of a cloth being wrung out over a bowl of water, and then the soft wet cloth was applied (surprisingly gently) to his face. "You've been asleep for a long time," Andhel said. "And we put dream-honey in your eyes to heal them."

She took the cloth away. Runacar blinked rapidly. His sight was still blurry, but he could see.

It was day. A soft hot breeze blew over his skin. Summer wind, summer light. He lay on a bed in some sort of pavilion. The pavilion couldn't be meant as much of a protection, for the walls were of some gauzy material, and billowed like banners. Through the gaps he could see the horizon, and the endless ocean stretching out to greet it.

"Where . . . ?" he asked, struggling to sit up.

"One of the islands a little way off the coast. The nymphs use it sometimes. Now it's a hospital."

Andhel shoved him back down again with a certain amount of relish, unable to conceal a smirk as she sat down on the edge of his bed to hold him still. Her face was scrubbed clean of paint for the first time since he could remember. Her hair was chopped short, and she hadn't dyed it recently: there was about a finger's width of natural black showing at the roots. She wore a simple sand-colored tunic and leggings of very fine cloth, plain and unornamented, and her feet were bare. He wasn't sure what he'd done to merit the Woodwose as his nurse. Perhaps it was a punishment.

At least she was alive.

"Who—" he began, then suddenly became aware of how dry and parched his mouth and throat were. "Thirsty," he said.

Andhel reached for something on a nearby table, and put an arm behind his head to lift him so he could drink. The cup was a spouted invalid's cup, and the taste of its contents was unfamiliar, but Runacar was of no mind to complain. Whatever the cool liquid was, it was wonderfully refreshing.

"Better?" she asked, though as one who already knew the answer. Trust Andhel to seize the opportunity presented by his helplessness. He was probably lucky she hadn't just smothered him as he slept.

"Why didn't . . . someone . . . Heal me?" he asked haltingly. *I've been here for a long time. She said so.* Not that he wasn't grateful for as much care as he *had* received, but still. He knew the Ocean's Own were sorcerers with power to rival the Lightborn. And the Lightborn Healed. It was one of their most useful functions.

Andhel snorted rudely. "They *did*, Houseborn. After the ground stopped shaking, it took Drotha candle-marks to find you, and you were nearly dead when he did. He said he would've eaten you except for the fact you'd probably chew your way out of his stomach, so count yourself lucky. And it's not as if you were the only one who needed care, you know."

Runacar remembered what he'd seen of the battle and its aftermath and winced inwardly. "How many died?" he asked.

"All of them." Andhel's tone was gleeful. "Their big stone tower is gone—Meraude says she likes the new coastline much better—and all the Houseborn are dead."

"No," Runacar said. "How many . . . of us?"

Andhel's look of bloodthirsty delight vanished abruptly. He saw her bite her lip and look away, and knew that whatever she said next would be a lie.

"If you had not evacuated everyone from Delfier-arathadan, they would have died in the earth-shaking whether the forest burned or not. Your plan saved many lives, Runacar."

Even her unaccustomed use of his name couldn't distract him. He reached out and grabbed her wrist, ignoring the dizzying weakness even so small a movement brought. *"How many?"* he demanded, locking his gaze with hers.

*"Half!"* she cried furiously, pulling away and springing to her feet. "Half of us died! There! Is that what you wanted to hear? Are you happy now, Houseborn?"

Runacar turned his head away and closed his eyes.

*Half. Because I did not spot a simple trick I would have used myself. Because I failed at the only thing I'm any good at. Thousands are dead. Because of me.*

He could hear Andhel moving around near him for a little while, but she did not speak, and eventually she went away. He was left alone with his thoughts, and they were not pleasant ones. *No wonder she wanted to be your nursemaid. She wanted to be the one who told you.* Even as he thought it, he knew it was unfair: she'd tried to lie. To spare him, incredible as the notion was. But . . . half. Half of the army he'd led into battle, dead. The sheer utter *waste* of it was like a heavy stone laid over his heart. So many dead, when none of them had needed to die at all. Now, when it was too late, he saw all the things he could have, *should have,* done. Evacuated Delfierarathadan before he'd even begun the fighting. Spoke with the Ocean's Own—and with any who had dealings with them—until he had a full and complete understanding of what they were willing and able to do. Should and could and would have. And didn't. And hadn't.

He'd been a knight—or in training to be one—his entire life. He'd been a general, a commander of armies. He'd planned battles and led warriors into them. He didn't know why this failure was different from the other times his mistakes—or the cleverness of others—had cost Caerthalien the victory, but it was. He grieved over this loss as he had never taken the time to grieve for the death of his brothers, his father, his mother, his *House.* Somehow, this was worse than all of those.

Was it because the Otherfolk weren't used to fighting? No. They'd fought the Hundred Houses ceaselessly. They'd had no choice. Their style of combat—and their attitude toward it—was different from that of those who followed the Code of Battle and the Way of the Sword, but they knew about fighting. They had fought and died since before the founding of Caerthalien in a war eternally lost.

But he'd expected to change all that. To lift them out of their incessant round of failure, to triumph in battle over the only two domains that still existed; their most ancient enemy: Daroldan and Amrolion.

And he hadn't. Nothing he'd done had made a real difference. Leutric could have done as much without his help. Meraude, Aejus, Amrunor—they could have ended the fighting before the first clash. They'd agreed to support Leutric: that had changed everything. It had changed more things than he had bothered to know.

He'd been asked to advise them, but he hadn't. Not really. He'd spent the last ten Wheelturns trying to turn the Otherfolk into second-rate komen, and look where it had gotten them.

Maybe Andhel had been right from the very beginning. Maybe the Hundred Houses *did* destroy everything they touched.

## CHAPTER NINETEEN

# THUNDER MOON:
# THE UNICORN'S PROMISE

The bones of the earth shall be given flight, and who
dares to make no choice and speak no question / Shall
yoke the unchained unicorn once more . . .
— *The Laſt Song of Pelaſhia Celenthodiel*

Runacar didn't know how long he spent torment-
ing himself with might-have-beens before he became aware of a new presence in the pavilion.
Not Andhel. Probably one of the Healers, come to tell
him to be joyous because he'd survived. And he couldn't.
Not even knowing his death would kill Vieliessar could
make him happy to be alive. Nothing could.

"Well," the intruder said. "It's good to see you awake
at last. I do admit this is rather a surprise—oh, not that
you're awake and alive; that was only a matter of time,
with all the help you've gotten—but that you and I can
have this conversation. A welcome one, all things considered. We could use a few of those."

The voice was feminine. Warm and welcoming—as
if they two shared some unvoiced joke—but grave and
rueful as well. Despite his determination to block out
the whole of the living world, Runacar turned his head
in the direction of the voice . . . and saw what could
not be.

A unicorn.

He should be used to seeing impossible things by
now, he told himself, but everyone knew the unicorn

was only a symbol. *Lannarien's Book of Living Things* devoted entire chapters to listing such wholly-imaginary creatures, after all. Lannarien had written that the unicorn, being made up from parts of wholly incompatible beasts—deer and lion and goat and serpent—and crowned with a single horn of miraculous powers upon its brow, was the symbol of the High Kingship.

The unicorn standing beside his bed, regarding him with patient and sympathetic humor, was nothing like the depiction in that scroll. It—*she*—was roughly the size of a young deer (though she reminded him more, somehow, of one of the great cats). Her body was covered with short plush silvery-white fur unlike the coat of any creature Runacar had ever seen, and the mane that ran from poll to nape of her long slender neck was stiff and roached. She had a long tufted tail that she held upright and curled, as if she were some sort of giant housecat, and her narrow pale hooves were cloven. Her head was not precisely like that of deer or goat or horse, just vaguely similar, in the way a housecat resembled a snow-tiger, and her eyes were as dark and Elven as his own, surrounded by ice-pale lashes so long and thick he could barely see her eyes when she gazed through them. And all those things were cast into insignificance by the horn in the center of her forehead. It was long, not smooth but spiraled, utterly straight, and came to a point as impossibly delicate—and as sharp—as a rose thorn. Though here inside the pavilion she was in shadow, her horn glowed as luminously as a jewel kissed by the sun. It was every color and none. It was beautiful. *She* was beautiful.

Without thought, he reached for her. She took a step toward him, and he wanted to weep with gratitude, because he did not think he could have survived without being able to touch her. His fingers stroked down the side of her neck, and he found her coat was even softer than it looked.

"I love you," he blurted out, and then cursed himself for it. It might be true—but Drotha had played mind-games with him often enough when they'd first met for Runacar to be aware that some ideas might not be your own no matter how much they seemed to be, and Ivrulion had certainly taught him that the body and spirit could be placed in ethereal chains they could not break. Even while he believed these were his own true and unfettered thoughts, Runacar wondered if he could believe even his own mind.

But the unicorn seemed to smile, and suddenly Runacar realized how unworthy his fears had been. What need could a being like this have of secrets and trickery when she had merely to *be*?

"Thank you," she said gravely. "I love you, too. My name is Melisha, by the way. I've been one of the people helping you heal. I'm sorry that you could not receive better news when you awakened. I came as soon as I heard."

"Is this real?" he asked hoarsely. "How can . . . How can you *be*?"

Again he had the sense Melisha was smiling. "That's the very end of a very long story," she said. "I will tell it to you, but not today. For now, child, let me say that I am *very* grateful that one of you is pure enough for me to approach, for I have much to tell you. And I would rather not have to rely on intermediaries."

The idea of anyone thinking he was "pure" would have been enough to make Runacar laugh at any other time. Right now, he was too enchanted—in every sense of the word—by Melisha's presence. But she seemed to expect a response. "Pure?" he echoed.

"Everyone has their limitation. As a living symbol of purity—don't laugh; you'll find yourself glad of that in the days to come—I am unable to bear the presence of those who are not both chaste and celibate."

Even with Melisha still standing right here, his mood

darkened instantly. "If you'd known almost from birth that your destiny was to marry for the advantage of your domain—and if you knew that every woman's first thought was of the advantage she'd gain by having you for a lover . . . you wouldn't find chastity that difficult," Runacar said. He'd grown up hearing his siblings' complaints: while none of them was the Heir, they were the Heir's brothers and sisters. And any of them might become the next War Prince if enough misfortune befell Caerthalien . . . as it had, in the end, leaving him its only survivor.

Melisha tossed her head and laughed. It was a glorious sound, like silver bells chiming, and Runacar found himself smiling almost against his will. It already seemed as if he'd known Melisha forever—friend, boon companion, all the things Caerthalien's Heir so rarely had.

"Why am I important to you?" he asked suddenly. "Not because of my birth—Caerthalien has been erased. And not because of my self—the Western Shore Campaign has to have been enough to convince anyone I'm of no intrinsic worth." *Except as a hostage. If someone knew I hold the High King's life in my hands . . .*

Melisha bowed her head in sadness. "I wish you could see yourself as others see you, my dear. You won. You did all that you told poor Leutric you would. And you fought hardest not against your own people, but to save the lives of Otherfolk."

"They aren't my people. Not anymore," he said roughly.

Melisha snorted rudely, lashing her tail. "If you cut off your hand, does it stop being your hand, stubborn one? I know you grieve for your failures, and for all who died, but your successes are as vast. And Andhel spoke truth: if you had not cleared the Flower Forest of its inhabitants, they, too, would have died when the ground shook."

"I should have planned better. I should have made certain I knew all I needed to before I began. My mistakes cost lives."

Melisha regarded him steadily. "Yes. And what of it?" she said.

He had expected words of comfort. Her honesty stung. "People died," he said.

"That is the nature of war," Melisha said gently. "And you grieve for our deaths. Do you know how great a gift that is?"

"To see what my ancestors should have seen from the beginning?" he said bitterly.

"What they saw, and what you think they saw, are two different things," Melisha said firmly. "Now sit up," she added briskly. "I'll help."

Following her instructions, he put an arm around her slender neck and levered himself to a sitting position. He'd been afraid of hurting her, or at least pulling her off her feet, but she was far stronger than her delicate form implied. When he was finally seated on the edge of the bed, Runacar had to clutch at its frame for support, for earth and sky seemed to rotate dizzily around him. Again, he had the sense that he *ought* to be in pain, but wasn't.

"There," she said. "Much better."

"If you say so," Runacar muttered. He vastly preferred the Lightborn Healings: no matter what injury befell you, all it took was a good meal and a nap and it was as if you'd never been hurt.

"Yes," Melisha said, as if she could hear his thoughts. "Risking your body is far less appealing when you know you are the one who will have to pay the price of it."

Runacar winced slightly, even as he thought to himself that the Winter War had certainly given all of them a taste of that. The Flower Forests of the Uradabhur had been so drained the Lightborn couldn't even heat water, let alone Heal a case of snowbane or frostkiss. *But you weren't fighting then,* a small inner voice reminded him. *Only chasing Vieliessar and her army . . .*

"I don't think I ever want to see a battlefield again," he said honestly.

"That is unfortunate," Melisha said after a long pause. "Because the battles you must fight are only just beginning."

For one horrified moment Runacar thought she meant for him to become High King in Vieliessar's stead—but he could never bring the High King's army to the battlefield when the army he would bring to face it would be seen as nothing other than vermin to be slaughtered. "Is this why you came to me?" he asked slowly. "To make sure I would fight for you again? Who is there left to fight? Areve remains, yes, but . . ."

"We will speak of that soon enough," Melisha said. "Right now, let us test the extent of your recovery. Stand up."

He would much rather have gotten explanations of the mysterious hints Melisha kept dropping, but he was reluctant to disobey her. She was so beautiful, and she seemed so kind . . . *And did you never adopt a mask of kindness when it suited you, only to discard it as easily?* He didn't want to heed that inner voice, especially when every instinct told him to trust her. But while she might not be deceiving him for some evil purpose, she might well be withholding information "for his own good," something Runacar disliked nearly as much as being manipulated for selfish purposes. Still, he'd be able to put up a better fight against whatever she had planned for him once he was dressed—and perhaps fed. Or at least knew whether or not he could walk under his own power.

Standing took effort, and the world seemed to tip crazily about him again as he did. But it settled at last, and he released his death-grip on Melisha's mane rather shamefacedly. To conceal his embarrassment, he turned his gaze away from her, and got a good look around the mock-pavilion for the first time.

It looked very much like a war pavilion built by someone who had never seen one. The space was one open chamber, very large, and the walls were nothing more than billowing sheets of thin coarse-woven fabric in pale shades of green and blue and grey, attached only at the top edge to a framework of what looked like heavy reeds. The roof above was more firmly constructed, but the wind still billowed through it—there were vents cut into the fabric to permit that. Whatever ground lay beneath his feet was concealed by several overlapping mats of what looked like woven grass. The space contained several raised pallet-beds on wicker frames—clearly this was, as Andhel had said, a hospital—some storage baskets, a few stools and small tables, and little more. Nearly everything looked to be made of reeds or grass.

"This place looks as if it would blow away in a high wind," he said.

"The Ocean's Own do not build to last," Melisha agreed. "But here. There are clothes for you—and boots, which you will appreciate more once you venture outside." She walked over to one of the woven baskets and flicked its lid deftly off with her horn. Runacar was vaguely startled to see something of such unearthly beauty being used for so mundane a task, and told himself he must stop expecting these people to be limited by the range of his imagination. Easier said than done, especially when the people looked like things in a very good dream.

She looked at him expectantly, and Runacar walked cautiously across to the basket, still careful of his balance. His muscles trembled with the weakness of long disuse, and his nerves thrilled to the memory of intolerable pain, as if he had been Healed of a grave injury.

*Which is apparently the case, though I remember taking no wound upon the field. Perhaps the Keep fell on me. If it did, I wish it had fallen harder . . .*

He lifted a bundle of cloth from the basket—carefully, still testing his strength—and carried it back to the bed. When he unwrapped it, its contents looked familiar enough: tunic and leggings and vest and soft boots; fine soft cloth, brightly dyed in jewel colors. Centaur work, or perhaps it had come from one of the castels they'd taken while sweeping the remains of the Hundred Houses out of the Western Reach: the Ocean's Own wore adornments, not clothes, and all the army's baggage had been lost in the disaster.

He dressed slowly and carefully. Muscles protested their use, and though the fabrics were soft to his hands, they felt harsh against his skin. He wondered again in what state he had been brought from the battlefield, and decided he did not wish to know.

One of the items in the bundle was strange to him, and he regarded it curiously—a deep hood with long lappets. Though it bore a faint similarity to the sort of cowl that was worn in the Hundred Houses against the cold of winter, this hood was not lined with fur, and the thin pale fabric was stiffened with an interlay of horsehair so the hood would not simply collapse against the head, but could be pulled forward to shield the face. He looked at Melisha in puzzlement.

"The sun is strong here, and there are no trees," she said, giving the impression of a shrug. "With water on every side, sometimes the brightness is too bright."

"It must be like being in the middle of a snowfield in deep winter," he said slowly, trying to remember that once he'd thought that being cold and going hungry was great sport. Winter hunting was best of all, and one winter he had guested in Vondaimieriel during the Midwinter Truce, and the Prince-Heir had taken him up into the Mystrals to hunt. Those days were gone, along with the world they belonged to. He tried the hood on to see how it fit. The lappets wrapped beneath the chin and were thrown over the shoulders, though perhaps he could tie them if the wind was too strong. "I suppose I can use it as a disguise, if nothing else," he said, trying to make a joke of it.

"I suppose it is easier to be a hunted outlaw fleeing for his life than it is to be a leader upon whose judgment so many lives depend," Melisha said, as if the thought had just occurred to her.

Runacar turned away abruptly. That gibe had hurt. He was being realistic—the Otherfolk would never trust him again after the battle at Daroldan Keep—and she thought he was *sulking!* He wasn't. But if he had to demonstrate that unwelcome truth to Melisha, so be it.

He picked up the comb from the table beside the bed, and sat down to comb out his hair, still looking away from her. Someone had clearly done so before him, for it was not a mass of knots and tangles. When he was done, he plaited it into his usual simple six-strand braid; it would stay of itself until he found something to secure it with. Dressed, he felt much more like himself, and turned to face her again.

"Now go find your friends," Melisha said gently. "The path leads down and around to where they're waiting for you," she said, pointing with her horn.

They weren't his friends. If they had been, they weren't any longer.

"Why can't I stay here with you?" he blurted out. He hated himself for asking, but he didn't want to leave her side. In his experience, beautiful things were the most dangerous—but Melisha was somehow both beautiful and the most welcoming person he had ever seen.

"Because while I am many admirable things, I am not a cook," Melisha answered, amused. "And you need food. And to let Andhel see she has not managed to kill you."

"If she thinks that, she'll be turning handsprings for joy," Runacar said before he could stop himself.

"And if she does, she will surely fall into the ocean and be eaten," Melisha answered teasingly. "You must hurry to save her from that fate."

He could already see that when Melisha wanted something, she got it. He might as well get it over with as soon as possible. And he *was* hungry. "You'll still be here when I come back?" he asked. Even though it was perilously close to begging, and he despised himself for such weakness, he was unable to keep from uttering the words. Melisha was unlike anyone he had ever known. *And knowledge of her folk is only one of the things we lost to our endless wars. How many other things did we lose to them that I can't even imagine?*

"Perhaps," she said gently. "I have other matters to attend to here as well. But if I'm gone, I'll come back. I shall always come back to you. This much I can and will promise you. We have many things to talk about."

"Which we can't talk about now."

"It will go far better on a full stomach. Trust me."

Runacar sighed. It would have to be enough. *Sword and Star defend me, but I do trust you.* He forced himself to turn away from her and duck out under one of the blowing flaps.

The moment he stepped outside Runacar was grateful for the hood he wore. The sun beat down as insistently as the sea breezes blew, and he was paradoxically too warm and chilled at the same time. The road Melisha had mentioned was easily visible: a wide smooth track covered in white sand and edged with seashells, winding gently down the outcropping he stood on. He stood in place and turned slowly, orienting himself as he tested his strength.

The pavilion he'd just left was on the highest point of the island. The island was tiny, barely a dozen hectares in size, and here Runacar was about as far above the water as he would have been above the ground if he were standing on the battlements of Caerthalien Keep. There were two other pavilions flanking his own on the small bit of level ground. Through the billowing walls, he could see they were utterly empty of anything but the grass mats on the ground.

*"The Ocean's Own do not build to last."*

Far below, the sea crashed against half-submerged rocks. On his right—the north—the land ended in a sheer drop-off to the water. There were neither trees nor grass to be seen, only some sparse low-growing scrub. To his left was the bulk of the island. He could see a cluster of slightly more durable structures below—buildings whose walls were made of woven mats instead of gauze. One of them, the largest, seemed to have been built around a stone hearth, and a wisp of smoke came from its chimney. Behind the pavilions—eastward—the islet curved gently inward, and there was a crescent of sandy beach. Two small skiffs were beached there—he supposed they'd be a safe enough way to travel if one had the favor of the Ocean's Own.

There was no one in sight.

Steeling himself for what was to come, he raised his eyes to the eastern horizon. He had little idea where the islet was located, but any war-leader had to have a strong sense of both geography and location. He judged his location to be nearly due west of Daroldan Great Keep. Or . . . where it had once been.

The distance made detailed observation difficult, but—unfortunately for Runacar's peace of mind—not impossible. The forest that should have run nearly the length of the coast was gone, though here and there a small copse stood miraculously untouched. The granite cliff upon which Daroldan Great Keep had rested was gone. The sea there was frothy, throwing up spatters of foam in such a way as to tell Runacar the water was no longer deep. The edge of the land was pale with new exposure, crumbling away into the sea. With time and rain it would be washed down into the ocean, perhaps to form a new spit of land over granite rocks and sundered castel walls.

Daroldan was gone.

There was little more he could learn here, and Melisha—he checked quickly—was now nowhere in sight. Runacar couldn't imagine where she'd vanished to—since he was standing at the head of the only way down from here—but since he'd come to live among the Otherfolk, he'd seen so many strange things that he had nearly lost the ability to marvel at them. Perhaps she could fly. Or turn invisible. Since he hadn't known unicorns existed until a halfmark ago, he really couldn't say what they might be able to do.

As he turned away from his inspection of the coastline, a shadow passed over him. He looked up to see an Ascension of Gryphons soaring eastward in perfect formation. He wondered how many Ascensions of Gryphons—gentle scholars interested in poems and history—had died in that last battle. He wondered if Riann and Radafa had been among those who died.

It didn't matter whether or not they'd survived, he told himself. He wouldn't see them again. Anyone with any sense would fly far and fast from him—and wings would make that easier.

He turned away and started down the path.

❧❧

When he was barely halfway down the footpath, folk began coming out of the reed-mat houses. Though there were perhaps a dozen Otherfolk at most, and their presence made the island feel suddenly overcrowded. Runacar inspected the gathering, searching for faces he knew. He recognized Andhel, naturally, and Tanet and another Woodwose named Maruin were with her. Pendor, Bralros . . . Audalo was here. One great horn was sheared half away and its stub was counterweighted with a gleaming silver ball; his chest was covered with fresh scars, but he lived. Pelere was absent, as were Keloit and Helda and Frause. He made a vow not to ask after them. He could not bear the thought of being told they were dead.

Then the last of the group exited the house, and to Runacar's stunned amazement, he saw that Leutric was here. How? Why? Leutric was the closest thing the Otherfolk had to a leader, and for Leutric to be here meant he'd crossed from Cirandeiron to the Shore after the Battle of Daroldan Keep. Just to see him? To preside over his execution? Only Runacar didn't think—not really—that he was to be executed, and that was even more disturbing, since it meant that what was to come was utterly unknown. But he had made a new life of confronting the merely disturbing head-on and imperturbably. He did not slacken his pace toward the gathering.

Just before he reached the point where the path leveled out and ended, Andhel pushed herself away from Tanet and ran off. As Runacar stared after her in bafflement, Audalo stepped forward to swoop him up in an enthusiastic hug.

"You live! By Leaf and Star and the Great Bull Himself—I said you would conquer death just as you conquered the Shore!"

"Not for much longer if you don't let me go," Runacar said, pounding on Audalo's shoulder. With a last enthusiastic squeeze, the Minotaur released him. Runacar staggered a bit, gasping, but managed to keep his feet.

Leutric was frowning, but in a way more puzzled than angry. "When Andhel came down from your bedside, she did not give anyone much hope of your recovery. I believe she said you would be dead by dawn."

Runacar gave a sharp startled laugh. "She probably meant to ensure it," he said. "But I am well enough, all praise to your Healers."

"Andhel nursed you herself," Tanet said. "She has only small magics, true, as do any of us, but she could tend you with what others created."

"Then my thanks to her," Runacar said slowly, now confused himself. "But I did not look to see you here, King Leutric."

"And why shouldn't I be here?" Leutric said. "Thanks to you, we hold the West from Meadows of Aralhathumindrion to the Sea—and will soon hold all the land west of the Mystrals!"

The Meadows of Aralhathumindrion were in Farcarinon-that-was, and Runacar could not suppress a twinge of memory at the name. *And if Vieliessar comes to take the West back again, I am not sure Leutric can stop her.* "I did little," he said shortly. "And the victory came at a very high price."

"We have been paying such prices for a very long time," Leutric said, meeting Runacar's eyes steadily. "And received little enough in exchange. But now that will change!"

Runacar wasn't sure how to respond. He didn't want to be the hero of this song.

"You come in good time," Leutric went on. "We plan what is to happen now."

"And you look like you could use a solid meal," Bralros said. "Come along and fill your belly."

⊰◈⊱

The chamber to which Bralros led him held a table and bench-stools. Since this was a Centaur-made table, it was higher than Runacar found comfortable, but the stools around it were of varying sizes and widths, clearly designed for the comfort of a number of different races. He'd seen such an arrangement before, of course, but it never failed to please him with its . . . fitness. Odd, that the race that had no magic at all could produce such comfort, ease, and convenience without it. Runacar remembered the first time he'd seen a Centaur-made building. He'd thought of how *Elven* everything looked and thought himself magnanimous for praising the work so highly. Now he knew enough to wonder who had copied whom, but the fact remained: the Centaurs were master woodworkers. Even so, at this precise moment, Runacar was more interested in what might soon be placed on the table than in its ancestry.

Everyone sat—or stood—where they chose without any particular regard to rank, though Leutric did sit at one end of the table. By the time Runacar had selected a seat, Centaurs and Minotaurs had begun bringing food from the wicker house with the stone hearth. The dishes were as elaborate as the fare during the campaign had been plain, and when the last had been brought, the servers joined them around the table. There was silence while first hunger was satisfied—Leutric, King-Emperor of the Otherfolk, did not keep as much state as even a Less House War Prince—but when Audalo left the table to bring back two more pitchers of cider, Leutric began asking questions about how the campaign had gone. As much as Runacar tried to stay out of the conversation and let the others speak, they kept turning to him for confirmation or elaboration of what they said.

"I'm tempted to keep you here while I work out the details of what the Ocean's Own will pledge, Runacar," Leutric said. "After the work you have done, they will be willing to grant us more aid—and able to do so as well."

"The Angarussa is running well in its new bed," Audalo added. "It cuts deep and true, even after the earth-shaking. Some of the Selkie-clans have already gone upriver."

"I had . . . very little to do with that," Runacar protested. "Others did all the work."

"At your suggestion," Pendor said. "You were the one who thought of it."

*And I thought of many other things, too, and most of them were utter disasters,* Runacar thought. He did not speak his thought aloud. Informal as Leutric's court was, he was its ruler, and if his empire rested only on the most fragile network of treaties and promises given by uncounted numbers of Otherfolk clans and kinds, that made it very little different from Caerthalien-that-was and its ever-shifting alliances.

"The campaign did not go as well as I had hoped," he said deferentially. "I would have preferred to make the Elves of the Western Shore a burden upon Areve, to sow unrest there."

"Some yet flee toward it," Audalo said. "That is enough. As you have taught us, no campaign of battle ever goes entirely as we hope it will. But we have gained the victory."

"At a great cost." Runacar knew he should keep silent, accept the tacit praise, but he could not. "Andhel told me we lost half our people."

Tanet regarded him in astonishment. "She told you that?" he asked. "But . . . we are not certain . . ."

"The earthshaking caused a great deal of confusion," Leutric said mildly. "And bore away many of the combatants. It will be a long time before we can number the lost. Perhaps it will never be possible."

*But you can number the living,* Runacar thought angrily. *So do not tell me you do not know how many died!*

"No one was there that day who was not willing to

die," Tanet said, as if privy to Runacar's thoughts. "And all saw how you walked uncomplaining into the trap the Houseborn set for you, so that you could delay the battle."

Runacar said nothing, unable to find words with which to answer. Tanet's words were . . . both true and not true. He startled as Leutric reached out to put a hand on his arm.

"Many died in battle, killed by our great enemies," the King-Emperor said. "And many perished for no reason beyond ill luck. Do not make of yourself nothing more than a memorial to their deaths. Living flesh is not meant to be stone."

"Nor is this the last battle we must fight in the name of battles we hope to avoid," Bralros said cheerfully. "But come! Sad faces and mournful words do not belong at a feast! Let us toast to the Liberation of the West, and the freedom of our people!"

When every cup was full, Leutric got to his feet. He held up his cup.

"Against the Darkness!" he roared. "To Freedom!"

And Runacar drank as deeply as the rest.

❧❦❧

Talk ranged widely, both of familiar things—the recent battles; the flight of the defeated Elves; the resettlement of those evacuated from Delfierarathadan—and of matters Runacar had not known.

He knew, for example, that Leutric's goal was to drive all the Elves through the Dragon's Gate and into the Uradabhur, and so forestall the mysterious Darkness, but the Otherfolk—even those Runacar could call "friend"—had never really spoken freely before him. Those who *had* spoken of the Darkness had done so as if it were something so true and real that its existence need not be debated. Around this table, Runacar learned for the first time that the Otherfolk had prophecies that spoke of something they called the Red Harvest, and that the destruction of Janglanipaikharain and the reign of a new High King were omens that foretold its coming. And with dawning horror, Runacar realized that these prophecies and omens did not relate to some nebulous future event, to blow away like smoke once its date was reached, but something that was *happening right now*. Something that had been going on beyond the Mystrals for nearly as long as Runacar had been in the West. *This* was why Runacar had never been able to get any of the Folk of the Air to cross the Mystrals on a scouting mission.

But the Darkness, while of paramount concern to those who believed in it and hoped to survive it, was still nothing more than a footnote in the table talk of those for whom more homely matters were more immediate. Runacar discovered that he was one of the last casualties to rise from his sickbed; the isle was to be deserted by the Folk of the Land within the next few days. The temporary structures that had been built would be left to blow away in the autumn storms, or salvaged by those of the Ocean's Own who could walk upon the land. All that would remain here would be the table they ate at, and the stone hearth upon which the meal had been cooked.

Before he returned to the mainland, Leutric intended to speak with the leaders of the Ocean's Own, to see what help they would be willing and able to lend to what all hoped would be their last battle: the conquest of Areve and the Sanctuary.

"And once they are all gone, we shall close the Dragon's Gate forever," Leutric said with relish. "Let the masters of war make their wars upon the masters of death."

Runacar said nothing, and fortunately nobody asked him to add anything to the discussion, because his mind was too full of thoughts he really didn't want to share.

After the False Parley and the Winter War, he was very familiar with plans based on hope rather than reality, and it seemed to him that this plan of Leutric's was much the same. What guarantee did Leutric have that this "Darkness" would leave the Otherfolk alone once they had banished the *alfaljodthi* across the Mystrals? And even if their banishing were a component of a spell—for every race of Otherfolk save the Centaurs had magic, and Runacar knew very little of how any kind of Magery worked—would this spell make a distinction between Woodwose and *alfaljodthi*? Or for that matter, between Runacar Warlord and the High King's subjects?

No matter his confusion, there was one thing of which Runacar was quite certain: if banishing the last of the children of the Hundred Houses eastward was the only way to secure the west, he would go willingly.

⬥⬥⬥

Y ou do not ask after your friends, Runacar," Audalo said gently, when the conversation lulled.

"There are many dead," Runacar said briefly.

"And many who live," the Minotaur answered. "Keloit wished to stay until you awakened, but there is much work to be done east of the Angarussa, and so he left with Helda and Spellmother Frause as soon as he was healed. Radafa and Riann you will see today, if not tomorrow, for their Ascension watches over this place."

Runacar closed his eyes, not wanting Audalo to see his relief. "And Pelere?" he asked, after a moment.

"It is as Tanet says," Audalo answered quietly. "Many are still missing. The Great Bull grant that we may discover her alive."

⬥⬥⬥

After the meal was over, the dishes were returned to the kitchen, and more dishes were brought out, these wrapped and covered for presentation—for Leutric and Audalo, along with a few of the others, were going down to the small beach to present them to Aejus and Meraude, at least partly as a symbol of unity. This would not be a time of negotiation, however, so Runacar had no difficulty in politely excusing himself, saying he wished to stretch his legs a bit.

It was true as far as it went, but his main reason for seeking privacy was to look for Melisha. As forthcoming as Leutric had been at the meal, he hadn't mentioned Melisha—or the existence of unicorns—and while there'd been no particular reason to do so, it suddenly seemed like a glaring omission.

He didn't get very far toward the path back up to the hilltop pavilion before he spotted Andhel sitting curled up behind one of the smaller woven pavilions. Her knees were drawn up to her chin and her arms wrapped around them.

"You should have eaten with us," Runacar said, stopping.

Andhel turned her head pointedly away.

"Well, perhaps you weren't hungry," he said. What was wrong with her? Normally she leaped at any chance to tell him about his inadequacies. "The talk was . . . well, I wouldn't call it 'interesting,' but it was certainly informative. Tanet suggested that we could have no idea of who had died, but I suspect you're right about the numbers. Somehow nobody seems to care," he added.

"Oh, we care." Andhel apparently addressed this remark to a bush in the middle distance. "It's just that it's nothing new. Our kind fights yours, we die. You fight each other, and you're all raised up by magic so you can go back to killing us."

"That time is over forever," Runacar said. *Vieliessar*

*has seen to that.* He wasn't sure why he was attempting this conversation—talking with Andhel at the best of times was like walking into a thorn bush, and he really was tired.

"Just as you say," Andhel said.

"Actually it's Vieliessar High King and Leutric King-Emperor who say it," Runacar said, with a flash of anger. "So I suppose it might be true." And another thing that might be true was that Andhel and the rest of the Woodwose might well be a further sacrifice to Leutric's hopeful peace. At least Vieliessar would accept them into her ranks. She'd accepted Landbonds and outlaws, after all. *If she is still in power, for I can only know that she's alive, not whether she dwells in palace or dungeon.*

"Have I done something—recently—to offend you?" he continued. "They said I was unconscious for more than a fortnight, so I don't see how, but of course I'm held to be very clever. Perhaps I managed somehow."

"Do shut up," Andhel said wearily. She looked up at him for the first time and Runacar saw that her eyes were red and swollen with weeping.

"What's wrong?" Runacar said instantly, crouching down beside her. "Did you lose someone you love in the battle? Tanet was here, and I didn't think to ask . . ."

He reached out to touch her cheek, and Andhel jerked away. "Better not," she said, a trace of her usual sneer in her voice. "Melisha wouldn't like it, you know. She has plans for you."

"You've seen her?" Runacar said instantly. "Talked to her?"

"I *worked with her,*" Andhel snarled, goaded past irritation. "Unicorns *don't have hands.* It was hard, because she and I had to stay so far apart. But it was possible."

Runacar wondered, suddenly and irrelevantly, if that was the reason the Healing Tents had been perched on the top of that rock. Was it so Melisha could approach her patients?

"Then I suppose I should thank you for your care of me," Runacar said, straightening up again. Then he realized the rest of what Andhel was saying. Melisha said that she was only comfortable in the presence of the chaste and celibate. So now everyone knew. It hardly mattered.

"I tried so hard to hate you, Houseborn," Andhel went on. "I hoped the war was just a game for you, and you'd go back to your own kind as soon as it wasn't safe or fun any longer. But you didn't. You kept on staying, and in the end . . . It's a small thing to die for someone, Houseborn. It's easy and it doesn't mean much. But to cry for them because you couldn't save them . . . to cry for *us* . . ." She pushed herself to her feet, standing with her back to him. "No Houseborn has ever done that before."

"Then maybe someone should," Runacar answered. He didn't know if it was possible to reconcile Elvenkind and Otherfolk, but that hardly mattered—either Leutric was right or he was wrong: depending on which it was, the Elves and the Otherfolk would either be permanently separated, or permanently dead.

"So I thought things could be different now," Andhel went on, ignoring him. "But now you belong to *her*. And she's going to get you killed."

Runacar had not survived as long as he had by being either stupid or oblivious. He wondered how long everyone around them had been able to see this situation clearly while he'd taken everything at face value. Andhel loved him. She loved him despite herself. And now she thought that Melisha had stolen his choices from him.

Had she?

No.

Melisha was beautiful. She was dazzling. She was

wonderful. And with time, Runacar knew, he could become inured to those qualities, take them for granted, dismiss them in his mind, until she was no more spellbinding than, say, Meraude or Riann. Even if Melisha had the magic to do it, he did not think she would be able to force him to act against his will—not more than once, anyway. Andhel was wrong because there was something she didn't know. But he thought—now—she deserved to.

"She isn't the one who's going to get me killed, Andhel," he said quietly.

Andhel turned to look at him, meeting his eyes stoically.

"Do . . . Do your people—the Woodwose—do they ever experience the Soulbond?" Runacar asked.

There was a long moment of silence.

"You want to know if you're my destined Bondmate?" Andhel asked blankly. Confusion swept every other emotion from her face, if only for a moment.

Runacar quickly shook his head. "No. I wanted to know if you knew what it was. If you didn't, you wouldn't understand when I told you that . . . I'm Bonded. I have been since before I came back to the West." It was out now. The truth he'd tried so hard to disclose while his brother Ivrulion held him magically enchained. The single secret he'd kept from the Otherfolk.

Andhel gave him the look of someone who had no notion what expression was appropriate just now. "You aren't," she said. "You're lying. If you were, Melisha wouldn't come anywhere near you."

"Perhaps it's because I've never been closer to my destined Bondmate than half a battlefield away," Runacar said. "At least, not since she was eleven," he added meticulously. The conversation was becoming more surreal by the moment.

"Bonded," Andhel said, tasting the word. "Do you— You must— You know that if she dies, so do you."

"I know," Runacar said. He spread his hands in a baffled gesture. "So I know she's alive. I don't love her. I don't think I even know her. There's just . . ."

"The Bond," Andhel said. "If you're really Bonded," she added dubiously.

"We are," Runacar said grimly. "Say what you will about my brother's sanity and morals, Ivrulion Banebringer was a powerful Mage. He tried to influence the Bond—change it, use it to draw her in, I don't quite know. All he did was prove it was there." *And nearly kill me in the process.*

Andhel worried at her lower lip, thinking. "She must be an important Houseborn if she's an enemy of the Banebringer," she said at last. It was not a question. Runacar realized suddenly that Andhel had never asked him a direct question, not for as long as he'd known her—at least not of a personal nature. The closest she came was making outrageously false statements that he might contradict if he chose.

He never had.

Runacar laughed, a little jaggedly. "You might say so. She's the High King. That's who my Bondmate is. And someday we'll both die, probably without even seeing each other again. Soon, if everyone's right about the Darkness already being on the other side of the Mystrals."

"And Melisha . . ." Andhel was clearly trying to make all of this make *sense*. Runacar didn't think it could.

"—says I am to be of some use to her," Runacar said, finishing her sentence. "I don't know what kind, or even if it's me she really needs, or my dear Bonded. But . . . if our situation is as dire as Leutric says it is, I suppose I don't mind being used." *Again,* a traitorous inner voice added.

Andhel gazed at him, and all her heart was in that gaze. Runacar wondered how he could have been so blind. But he realized that since the candlemark Caerthalien had fallen, he'd thought he was no more than a collection of skills. Not someone anyone could want. Only a tool, and he'd been grateful beyond measure that Leutric had been willing to wield him. He'd believed, so deeply he'd never even questioned it, that if he was not Prince-Heir—War Prince—Runacarendalur Caerthalien of Caerthalien—he was nothing.

And he'd been wrong. Andhel had hated him as a person, and she loved him as a person. She'd never seen him as anything else.

"I'm sorry," he said gently. "I've been very stupid, and I've hurt you. I have actually never wanted to hurt you, but this . . ." He groped for a word to define it, and gave up. Perhaps there wasn't one. "This isn't Melisha's doing. She hasn't taken me away from . . . from anyone. I think, now, that I wish everything was different. There are so many things I never knew I wanted, because what I could actually have was . . . limited. And then everything changed. But what you want from me, I can't give you."

Suddenly his mind was filled with the memory of a sunturn long ago, a grey and rainy morning in early spring. He remembered walking along the line of mounted komen who were to escort the tithe-wagons and the Candidates to the Sanctuary, his thoughts full of the secret he had been told barely a sennight before. He had helped Varuthir onto her palfrey; she was silent and distant, and he was grateful for that because he thought it meant she did not know the truth. How much worse would it be for her, being imprisoned in the Sanctuary of the Star for the rest of her days, if she had known herself to be War Prince of Farcarinon?

But she *had* known, because his mother had told her.

Perhaps that was the moment that had laid the foundation for all the rest.

He shook his head, dismissing the memory. "I'm sorry," he repeated.

"Then what can I ever be to you?" Andhel asked in a low voice.

"What you have always been," Runacar said. "A good friend."

Her mouth quirked a little, and if her whole being did not blaze with joy, then wry acceptance was still better than angry despair. She closed the distance between them, enfolding him in a fierce—but very brief—hug.

"Friends, then," she said roughly. "Now go. Melisha's waiting for you."

⊰⊱

Runacar walked slowly up the path to the top of the hill. The sun was westering now, and everything around him was long-shadowed and brilliant with the long golden prelude to twilight. But though they were beautiful, Runacar paid very little attention to his surroundings. His thoughts were too full of that long-ago morning. Was that when the doom of the Hundred Houses began? If he could somehow step through a door to that day, could he prevent all that came after? If Vieliessar had never known her true name—if she'd died on the road—if he'd even had the wit to give her some slow-acting poison so that her death did not come until after she'd returned to the place where she was born, thus fulfilling the letter of the terms of Celelioniel's Peacebond . . . Perhaps the armies of Darkness would still have come, but if nothing else, the Hundred Houses knew how to fight. What would have happened then? Hard to decide when he knew nothing about the enemy but a name.

Only . . . the Hundred Houses would not have fought

that new enemy as allies. That much Runacar was sure of. Each would have accused the next of being responsible for the attacks; thought, perhaps, that the Darkness was merely a new Free Company . . .

So engrossed was he in trying to decide how *What Had Been* could have gone differently that he barely noticed Melisha was waiting for him in the pavilion.

"You don't look as if the banquet was very good," she commented, flicking an ear sideways.

"Oh." Recalled to himself, Runacar smiled dutifully. "It was very good. You should have come."

Melisha snorted, shaking her head in the way a horse would, neck stretched out and head cocked. The gesture looked odd coming from so one so obviously . . . not a horse. "Chaste and celibate, remember?" she said. "And trust me, most of your friends don't qualify."

"But I do," Runacar said. "And for the first time, I'm wondering why."

Melisha looked very much as if she was trying not to laugh. "You told me why," she pointed out. "The rest is between you and your life choices."

"I did tell you—what I *thought* was why," he agreed. "And I admit it's a very good reason. But I'm Bonded, and I wonder . . . if I always have been."

"Hard to say," Melisha answered. "That's Elven magic. Every race has its own mysteries."

"Even yours?" Runacar asked.

"Ours most of all, child," Melisha said. "I'd tell you the story, but you might throw yourself off the cliff."

"I doubt that," Runacar answered, with a genuine smile this time. "And you don't think so, either. Because I think you know who my Bondmate is."

Melisha blew out a long gusty sigh. "You're quick. And not stupid at all. That makes as many problems as it solves, you know. Yes, I know. Your Bondmate is the High King. And I hope you've come to terms with that, because you're going to see her again relatively soon."

Runacar had been in the process of sitting down on the bed, as none of the wicker hampers looked quite sturdy enough to serve as a chair, and the stools were too low. He shot to his feet again at her words.

"The High King is coming *here*?"

"Not precisely here," Melisha temporized blandly.

"Where is she? Has she crossed the Mystrals? No? How long will it take her to reach the Dragon's Gate?" He was fairly certain he didn't have an army left right now—or if he did, it wasn't one in any condition to fight. And an Otherfolk army was *slow*—he remembered with a sinking heart the lightning-fast way Vieliessar had moved the elements of her army, both in flight and in pursuit. Even with Gryphons and Wulvers for his vanguard—if he could convince them to fight or even just to *show up*—he'd never match her speed. "Why didn't you tell me earlier? I have to—"

"—sit down," Melisha said, finishing his sentence. "That's what you have to do right now. She's still on the far side of the Mystrals. And there's a lot I have to tell you before the two of you see each other again."

"So I was right," Runacar said crossly. "You didn't want me at all. You want *her*."

"Tsk," Melisha said. "You're jumping to conclusions again, my darling. To be perfectly precise, I want both of you. Or neither of you. It depends on how you look at it."

"I am not in a mood for riddles," Runacar said, in a tone he'd been sure he would never use to her.

But Melisha didn't seem offended. "I told you: it's a very long story. And I will tell it to you, I promise, but not right now. What matters is this: we have known the Darkness was going to return for a very long time. To be absolutely accurate, it—*they*—never left. Your folk just didn't see them. That was one of the things, I think, they were very careful about. The last time your kind *did* see them, you were horse-herders of the Golden-grass, followers of Aradhwain the Mare."

Runacar shook his head in baffled disbelief. "The . . . Aradhwain Bride of Battles?" he asked in confusion. The name was barely familiar; an old Power, almost forgotten.

"That was later," Melisha said kindly. "First, She was the Great Mare, and as such She is still honored. How much of your own history do you know?"

"Probably not much," Runacar admitted. "It never seemed very important. I know Amretheon was the first High King." The whole world knew that: after the Windsward Rebellion, every half-literate War Prince spent years haranguing their castel Lightborn to dis-cover every scrap of prophecy that could prove—or disprove—the various claimants' right to the Unicorn Throne.

"Amretheon was the last of a long line of them," Mel-isha corrected, "but close enough. To give you some idea of the span of time we're talking about, the last time any of your kind ever saw the Darkness, you had not yet built Celephriandullias-Tildorangelor, let alone fled it in fear of your lives. It was built after the Red Winnowing, for obvious reasons."

"Not obvious to me," Runacar muttered. But Meli-sha did not seem moved to explain the connection be-tween this "Red Winnowing" and the building of a city he still half-believed was myth. "So the Darkness has left us—the *alfaljodthi* at least—alone for a long time. And now it's back," Runacar said, grasping for some-thing he understood.

"Now it is back *in force*," Melisha corrected, still gently. "The Darkness worships *He Who Is*, the Formless Uncreated. To them, our existence—yours, mine, the fish in the sea, the birds in the air, random dandelions—is an abomination. They mean to correct it—once and for all, this time. This is the time of the Red Harvest. They mean it to be the last Winnowing there will ever be."

"You've known this all along?" Runacar demanded. "Why didn't you tell us?"

"We tried," Melisha said simply. And Runacar, understanding all she didn't say, hung his head in shame.

"Will Leutric's plan work?" he asked at last.

Melisha sighed. "No," she said. "The Darkness is delighted to begin with your people, but they won't stop with them. There's a slim chance for us—*all* of us—to survive, but . . . Well, there's a certain amount of opposition to it."

"From Leutric," Runacar guessed.

Melisha sighed in agreement. "From Leutric. Admittedly, he has the weight of history on his side."

"So what is this chance?" Runacar asked. "And why does Leutric refuse to take it?" He had a vague feeling this was still a fever dream, that none of this was real.

"There exists a way for us to have a chance of defeating the Darkness," Melisha said, choosing her words with care. "A. . . . Well, you might as well call it a weapon, though that isn't precisely what it is. It's very powerful, though. And only the Children of Stars can wield it." She stopped, and gazed pointedly at him, clearly expecting him to work out the details.

"And if you put a powerful weapon in Elven hands, the first thing we'd do with it is attack you," Runacar said.

"Possibly not the *first* thing," Melisha said. "But yes: things wouldn't go very well for the Otherfolk if the Elves gained that kind of power just now."

"But the Woodwose are Elves," Runacar said. "Give it to them. They'd fight for the Otherfolk." *And use this weapon to wipe out the Houseborn, of course, but I can't imagine any of the Otherfolk weeping over our destruction.* "They're Elves. It doesn't matter that they say they aren't—they are. Can't one of them . . . ?"

"Once the trout is in the pan, there's no point in putting it back in the river," Melisha said. "And once the Bones of the Earth are awakened, anyone might use them—and that's precisely what Leutric fears. Did I mention that Leutric is the only one who can provide this weapon?"

*Oh, of course he is. Why did I even have to wonder about that?* "So he won't," Runacar said. "Not even to the Woodwose." *I don't suppose I blame him. I suppose we're lucky the Otherfolk didn't just ally themselves to the Darkness in the first place . . .*

"He won't. And I can't convince him to," Melisha agreed. "I've tried—since before this last great war of yours, in fact—but for some reason, Leutric doesn't see much to choose between the Children of Stars in possession of the ultimate weapon and an attack by the legions of Darkness. He feels that even if he gave it to one of the Woodwose—even if a Woodwose were capable of using it, which is something no one knows— the Children of Stars would stop at nothing to gain it once they knew of it. He hopes, as you know, that this is another Winnowing, and not the Red Harvest, but the truth of the matter is that he would rather see all of us erased than see the Bones of the Earth used against us. Which is where you come in. And the Woodwose, of course, but mostly you."

"Me," Runacar said, now deeply suspicious.

"You," Melisha said. "All you have to do is convince the High King and her people to ally themselves with the Otherfolk and hold us as their equals until the stars grow cold and the last leaf falls, and Leutric will have no further objections to surrendering the Bones of the Earth to you."

Her deliberately casual words seemed to echo through the sound of the wind as the two of them sat

there, looking at one another. He knew which side he'd
fight on, but where did he belong? Which was he? Not
Woodwose. Not War Prince. What was left?

"'All,'" Runacar said at last.

"You'll get to see Vieliessar again."

"I have no interest in ever seeing her again. And besides, she'll kill me on sight."

"And that's why it is so very convenient that the two
of you share the Soulbond," Melisha said. "She probably won't."

"'Probably,'" Runacar echoed. *But I have one choice
you have not yet named. Slaughter every last one of my
own people—draw the dagger across my own throat—
and Leutric will give up his weapon to the Woodwose.
The Otherfolk will live.*

The silence stretched.

"So . . . what do we do?" he asked Melisha.

"We hope," she said simply.

# TOR

Voted

## #1 Science Fiction Publisher
## More Than 25 Years in a Row

by the *Locus* Readers' Poll

———•———

Please join us at the website below
for more information about this
author and other science fiction,
fantasy, and horror selections, and to
sign up for our monthly newsletter!

**TOR**